FAKING IT

Lydia Hart
A Blue Mountain Novel

ISBN:

978-1-960719-01-0 paperback (5.25x8 size)

978-1-960719-03-4 paperback (5.5x8.5 size)

978-1-960719-02-7 ebook

Trigger Warning List:

Due to strong language and mature, sexual content, this book is not intended for readers under the age of 18.

- **Explicit sexual content**

- **Loss of job & income**: shown act of being fired.

- **Childhood sibling rivalry**: discussed from character's past.

- **Divorce**: discussed briefly from character's past.

- **Bullying**: discussed briefly from character's past.

- **Learning & developmental disability**: discussed & shown throughout.

- **Anxiety**: shown throughout.

- **Coercion**: threats/manipulation to work with someone professionally. <u>No sexual or romantic relationship coercion.</u>

- **Language**: excessive swearing.

Chapter 1

December Fowl

M *mrrrr. Mrrrr. Mrrrr.*

I roll over in bed, pulling the blankets over my head. *Go away alarm clock! I'm on vacation!*

Mmrrr. Mrrr. Mrrrr.

I throw down the covers and reach for my phone. The white screen is blinding, forcing me to squint. A headshot of my client Sawyer Dawn blinks at me. I jerk back, my sleep-ridden brain not fully comprehending why she's on my screen. Then, with a jolt, I realize I'm not dreaming.

"Hello?" My voice is thick with sleep and I clear it before continuing, "Sawyer?"

"De...De...Decemburrrr," the singer manages between sobbing hiccups.

"What's wrong?" I wrestle with the blankets until I can wiggle myself free. The hardwood floor is cold against my bare feet, and I dance to the light switch. My bedroom lights up like the Griswold's house on Christmas. "Are you okay?"

"Na-na-nooooo."

My head instantly goes to the worst-case scenario: *Savage Song* has canceled her performance. As soon as the thought is out, I smack myself on the forehead. She could have been in an accident! Someone could be *dead* and I'm thinking about a stupid performance! I pace the room – walking from one side and back again, trying to get a word in.

I manage to catch a few things: Late. Dress. Ruined. Mom?

My mind races to arrange the words. She's late. Her dress is ruined? Her mom? I snap into a straight line: She's late. Her dress won't fit. Her career is ruined. She's going to be a mom.

I press myself to think of how many young mothers have been on the Billboard 100. I can only think of a handful: Deya Moon, who the public adores. I recall the twelve page spread *People* did for the birth of her second child. Not to mention the hundreds of other articles written by other gossip mags.

I even picked up a copy and the only babies I like are of the animal variety. Her publicist did a heroic job influencing the stories that sold. I could manage Sawyer's image like that; oversee the stories released, the photos they use. A baby wouldn't mean ruin...

Then I think of the others, like a member of Lady Magic who was criticized for coming back four months after giving birth. People accused her of not being loving or caring enough for her child. Then there's Michelle Drew. She had three Top 100 songs and the next year dropped off the radar to raise her twins. She never came back.

"Late?" I pry, taking advantage of her gasp for air. "What's late?

"My dress!" She shouts, her voice astonished I hadn't understood her.

My chest loosens. I squeeze my eyes shut and let out a tremor of relief, moving the phone away from my mouth. *Not. Pregnant.* Her dress is late. Not pregnant. A dress is something I can take care of.

"–shipped in from Milan. This was going to be *the* dress. The dress everyone was going to know me by, you know? Like Carrie Underwood has her thighs; Michelle Obama has her arms, and it was going to be me and that dress." She sighs dreamily.

Oh, I know *that* dress even though I don't *know* that dress. I own a few too many skin-tight jeans intended to win the hottie in college, but all they ever won me was a glance and a late credit card payment; I had the hair cut that was supposed to tell my ex-boyfriend (who I was *soo* totally over) *I'm not fine without you, I'm better without you*! But all it proved was my bone structure does not coordinate well with a pixie cut.

"I'm in New York," I begin, picturing the beautiful lace, bohemian dresses in the East Village. "I could –"

"Not just any dress will do, *December*," her voice is clipped, like I just don't get it.

At twenty-two Sawyer thinks of me as an older sister. A much older sister. As if a five-year difference means I have no idea what she's going through. Because only twenty-two-year-olds, who wear their hearts on their sleeves, can feel this way. I bite back my tongue.

"This is a bad sign. I don't think I should do the show."

I hear her words exploding through my brain.

"Sawyer, you don't want to be remembered for a dress! You're more than what you wear. You're more than how you look or what people think. Those are the principles you preach. I love those principles. Anyone can sing about lust or parties, but you write about reality and finding security in insecurity. You can't let Hollywood steal that from you!"

The line is silent.

"I have a friend." My mind retraces my steps these last few days. I go back to standing in a narrow hallway with my college roommate. She's talking about doing something new, starting her own fashion line. My mouth moves, "She's a designer. Very good. You wouldn't know any of her work – which is good. It's a good thing. You can both debut on the same night. The first person to wear a piece from Morgan Rernstein."

There's a sharp intake of breath and I know she's still there. I haven't lost her yet. Finding my groove, I move around the room. The blood pumping through my body helps me think. My free hand waves around like it's helping me bring forth ideas.

"You don't want a dress to make you. You want to make the dress. People are going to think '*I want a Rernstein dress because Sawyer Dawn wore it*'. Not, 'I like Sawyer Dawn *because* she wore this fancy Milan designer *everyone* else is wearing.' Which one feels more like you?"

On the other line, I catch the *creak* of a bedspring, rustling sheets as she tucks herself in. I claw my face. It would be nice if she'd say something, but this is how Sawyer is. She shuts down. Tucks herself into a ball and contemplates everything from who she is to the reason why sloths move so slow.

"Alright," I say, ripping my suitcase out from under the bed. "I'll be in LA in…" I glance down at my phone. 5:31 a.m…I toss my bag on the bed. "No less than twenty-four hours."

I end the call and sigh. Mom is going to be furious when I tell her she'll need to find another plus-one to the family shopping extravaganza. But I am my mother's daughter. The job always comes first. I pull open my planner app and make a list:

✔ Wake up
○ Get Morgan on board to design the dress
○ Book flight to L.A.
○ Drag Sawyer out of this funk before it takes hold
○ Live happily ever after

I'm wriggling into a window seat. Morgan's curvy figure squeezes in next to me. A thin older man sits on the outside and as soon as we're seated, he pulls out his e-reader and sighs like we've taken lifetimes instead of seconds. I roll my eyes, my mood taking a further nosedive.

In my hand, my phone vibrates. I glance at the screen half expecting Lionel King, President of DKS, the public relations agency I work for, to be calling. Instead, I have an email notification. I quickly pull it up before airplane mode is announced.

My jaw clenches as I read. *Xtreme Sports Monthly* has informed me my client Everett Abrams never joined their Zoom call for an interview. This is the fifth straight interview I've set up for him that he hasn't shown up for or responded.

I pull open my mobile OneNote and begin to make notes about his behavior in the profile I've created. I've been wanting to drop him as a client for the last six months now. This will just be more kindling.

"Ohmygod. I volunteer as tribute." Morgan leans into me for a better look.

On my screen is the man of my nightmares – Everett Abrams. I've never met him in person, but have studied his photographs. As his publicist, it's my job to share his best headshots with journalists. But I'd be lying if I said he didn't give my heart a start, or that I sometimes find myself flipping through his media kit for a good man-candy pick-me-up.

In this snapshot, he's captured walking through an airport, a bag slung over his shoulder, and a cart of luggage wheeling behind him. He's dressed in a white t-shirt, blue flannel shirt, and dark jeans. His hair is a mess but in a sexy, *did I mess this myself, or did someone else do it for me?* sort of way.

My eyes linger on the veins in his arms. They're prominent and he's just walking through an airport, not even taxing himself. The neck of his shirt is wide enough to reveal a sliver of his collar bone, and it makes me tingle. I stare at the lump in his throat, swallowing. There's something about him that makes me drool. Maybe it's his neck, or the scruff along his sculpted jaw; the freckles spattered in large spots and dusting his cheeks. It could be the way his dark, dark eyes seem to say: I'm intense.

"Get a good look while you can, friend. The man refuses to do interviews, meet-and-greets – anything!"

"He can have me forever in exchange for a few interviews." Morgan smiles wickedly as she rests back into her seat.

I laugh, her words reminding me why I accepted him as a client. I specialize in musicians and actors, not snowboarders. But, I glance again at his image, the man is gorgeous. He makes women think naughty thoughts – myself included.

Everett could be the next David Beckham if he'd let me channel his raw sex appeal into dollars.

But he refuses. And he's a dick for wasting my time.

I finish adding my notes to his profile and sit back to watch Morgan work as the plane lifts off.

Working from her tablet, she begins to sketch dress designs and potential color schemes. When Morgan declared she'd be coming with me, I thought my head might explode, but she insisted she meet Sawyer, or no deal. And if I turn up in L.A. with no designer and no alternative, I know Sawyer won't do the show.

And she *needs* to do the show. No performance, no career. For either of us.

Chapter 2

DECEMBER FOWL

"**M**r. King, you want me to be the new Public Relations Officer? I am so honored."

I practice my encounter with the CEO weaving in between traffic. I've always been told the power of visualization and positivity can shape reality. This morning, I'm going to test it.

I really want this fantasy to become reality. So badly it hurts. Over the weekend, I received a meeting invite with the CEO and President, himself, Lionel King. It can mean only one thing, news about the position I applied for and killed in the interview: DKS' Public Relations Officer. Now, the day is here and I'm channeling everything I have into getting this promotion.

My stomach turns as I pull into the towering iron giant that is 801 Grand. I park my car in the back and gaze up at the little sparkling windows at the very top. My hands grip the wheel. *I will have a corner office with a view. I will, I will, I will.*

I draw my bag over my shoulder and step out into the early morning light. The sun has yet to breach the skyline.

I catch my reflection in the glass pane of the building and new confidence spreads through me. My soft cashmere sweater in crème is tucked neatly into the red pencil skirt I bought myself in New York. My Dad's old pocket watch, now repurposed as a necklace, dangles against my chest. Earlier this morning, I pulled my long ashy brown hair into a taut ponytail. Dressing extra professional makes me feel extra powerful.

At my cubicle, I fire up my laptop and begin sifting through my emails and schedule for the day:

Monday, November 26th

- 9AM: Meeting with Todd. Discuss: SNL performance, upcoming press releases & hosting the children's banquet.

- 10AM: Meeting with Lionel King. Discuss: Possible interview #2??

- 12PM: Meeting with Sawyer. Discuss: Follow up with Savage Song & her dress. Make sure she's not sulking!

- 1-?: Available & on-call for clients. Work on updating media kits, press releases & further media training.

I take a breath and repeat in my head: *I choose to believe this meeting is about the Public Relations Officer position, not flying to L.A.* I begin to organize my notes, pulling up footage of Todd alongside Tom Hanks and quotes from reviewers. All the while repeating mantras in my mind: *it's better to ask forgiveness than permission. I made the right choice. My client needed me, and I stand by my decision. I am powerful. I am bold. I can do this. I can do this.*

"You're salaried, Fowl. Getting here early won't earn you anything." The male voice makes my skin crawl.

I swing around in my chair. Ryan Dawson leans his hip on my desk. He picks up my stress ball and tosses it between his hands. He's dressed in a gray suit, freckled with brown specks. His jacket is tweed, of course. I restrain myself from rolling my eyes. Tweed jackets are *so* 1900s.

"Do you mind?" I drawl, already bored with him.

He shrugs, "Not at all."

Glaring, I snatch the ball out of his hands. I squeeze it, imagining it's his head. His face quirks up, his eyes gleam. Ryan is the equivalent of Disney's Scar in human form. If given the chance, he'd let go instead of pulling me off a ledge.

He squints, "You look like you have something to say."

"I have lots to say, but nothing to you."

"You look nice," he says, eyes laughing at me in the way they do when he's not telling the truth.

I straighten, remembering my power, "I have a meeting with Mr. King this morning."

"What for?"

"That's none of your business."

He slaps his hands together and leans in, "Oh, I bet you're finally having a follow-up interview for the PRO position. I had mine before the holiday. So," he stands, adjusting his suit, "best of luck."

Before he completely exits, he turns and flashes me a magazine cover. His client Mimi Aldo is on the cover. In bright red letters the headline reads: I was the other woman.

"By the way, did you see this cover? This is how you spin an infidelity story, December. Unlike how you buried Todd's affair last year. Cheating is practically expected. Now I've just made my client relatable and redeemable. When I'm the PRO, I'll give you some pointers."

He winks and stalks away, and I shrink in my seat. Ryan had a second interview last week?

I shake my head, trying to get Ryan out of it. I know this is what he wants. Get in my head and under my skin to scare me so he can win. I busy myself with tidying my desk. Moving my pen jar here instead of there; restacking my pile of paperwork.

"Enough." I force my hands to stop moving. I walk from one side of my desk to the other and back again, lecturing myself. "Actionable. I must be actionable. I didn't get here by being scared. You can do this."

I swing my arms, roll my head from side to side like a boxer readies herself for a match. Because this is war. I zero in on my emails. I shoot one off to Sawyer to remind her of our meeting; another to the NBC Executive in my back pocket, thanking her for giving Todd a chance. I weed through the others, scribbling invites, events, publication dates beneficial to my clients.

With five clients, I have the fewest in the company – but they yield high. The devil is in the details, and I get the details just right. My strategy is to keep my client pool small. Personable. And it's worked. While Ryan Disgusting-Dawson and my other coworkers are managing twenty clients, juggling meetings and knotting schedules, I can communicate with my clients every day.

My mouse hovers over an email. I narrow my eyes at it, trying to figure out which client this could be referring to. I scan the little information I can gather without opening it:

`You're invited to the EMPIRE Gala!`

`Thank you for the response - We're sorry not to host you in Las Vegas`

A lightbulb switches in my brain. I click on the email and sure enough Everett has declined their offer to attend the Gala. I throw my head back and let out a monstrous growl.

"You don't know how many strings I had to pull!"

I pull up a fresh email. My fingers type feverishly on the keyboard. *Click-click-clickclickclick.*

"Or how many favors I owe just to get you an interview with *Sports Illustrated*," I rip the magazine out of my stack and flip open the pages. There's a photo spread of the three athletes and four pages of discussion. Thirty-five questions and he only peeps up for two. *Two!*

"*Ooo-oh*," I let out a dangerous laugh and the *clickclickclickclick*-ing commences, egging me on. "You will not ruin my reputation, Everett Abrams." I raise my finger in justified fury, about to slam SEND when my email dings. A notification flashes across my screen. I quickly grab the little blurb, not sure if I read it right, and my angry email shrinks.

`Calendar Notification: Todd Taylor has canceled your 9 a.m. meeting. Click to reschedule.`

Weird. I click to reschedule, and another message pops up:

`Scheduling Error: Cannot connect to contact. Please contact program administrator for more information.`

I make a face, "Scheduling error..." I shut down my email and open it again. "All you need is a little reboot." I click to reschedule and the error pops up for the second time.

Ding. Another notification flows in. Next week's meeting with Cheryl has been canceled. *Ding.* And Ricky's for three weeks away.

"What the hellll..." I squint at my screen.

Ding: Sawyer Dawn has canceled your 12 p.m. meeting. Click to reschedule.

Suddenly my computer is dinging like Nanna's doorbell on Christmas. My screen floods with canceled meetings, one sliding in right after another.

"Suz!" I shove my chair back and stomp towards the tech group, four cubicles down.

She looks up from her desk, "What's up roomie? I was thinking about making sloppy joes tonight – thoughts?"

I bulldoze on, "My computer has gone mad! Do you hear that?" I jab my finger back towards my desk.

She cranes her neck, putting her bagel down and wiping the corners of her mouth. I lead her back to my desk so she can take a look. She pauses a moment, taking in the sound of notifications as events continue to cancel.

"What sort of pervy site were you viewing?" Suz teases, moving into my chair.

"You're about to find out." I cross my arms and glare down at my misbehaving computer.

Chapter 3

EVERETT ABRAMS

L uc sits at the edge of the hotel bed. His knee jigs as we scroll through the presentation again.

We've run through this a thousand times. So many times, my dreams were in PowerPoint last night.

Sweat prickles at my brow and upper lip. My mouth moves as I recite my parts over and over in my head. I've had it memorized for days, and Luc is doing most of the presenting anyways. He's the people-person. I'm worried I'm going to walk into the room with sweat spots so huge they can spot them from space.

My eyes twitch to him now. His hand is cupped over his mouth, eyes staring at the screen as if there's a chance it'll tell him his future. I let out a shallow breath and he turns his head to me. I offer him a small smile, but it's more shaky than sure.

Luc slaps my shoulder, "Relax man. You do scarier shit than this every day."

I nod. It's true. Riding up a twelve foot vert at high speeds and twisting my body in all sorts of directions isn't safe, but it feels like it to me. Even when it's scary. When the spins make me dizzy, I know I can get through because I always have. This is totally new territory.

I rise and step to the desk to mess with the gloves we've brought as a demonstration. We brought two pairs of each: one we rode in yesterday and thoroughly soaked, the other dry to show the difference. We did the same with our mock pair. The difference between the dryness of our gloves and our closest competitor is striking and I'm hoping it will sell them.

I allow myself a moment to dream that the investors accept our proposal. We'll start with the gloves, then other outerwear, eventually to boards and boots. I'll still compete, but when I do retire from competitive riding, I'll have Elevate to fall back on. I'll ride every day; travel the world with our brand on showcase. I won't ever have to find a regular job. I won't ever have to be anyone but me.

We'll source environmentally friendly materials from fair trade suppliers. We'll produce it right here in the United States. It'll be more expensive than the average glove, but people won't have to buy five pairs just to keep their fingers warm.

And Elevate will only endorse riders who care more about riding than parties; riders who don't spread the poison of '*snowboarding's only for the young and wild.*' The way the culture is now, it excludes riders over the age of thirty. I rarely see riders even my age. It's like as soon as snowboarders reach a certain level of maturity, they no longer fit in. On the mountain there's plenty of retired folk spending their time skiing, but it's so rare to see snowboarders of that age.

Elevate won't be like that. We'll be there all life-long, not just for the young-sters trying to be cool and get mountain cred; not just for the adults trying to cut lose and escape from the every day. I want Elevate to be for more than one generation. Just like riding should be.

This could mean having a 'retirement' plan. This could mean Luc sending his sister to the best adult home instead of mediocre. This could mean having a lasting impact on snowboarding – even long after I retire.

No pressure or anything.

"Hey," Luc whistles from across the room. "Let's get going."

We pack the gloves up and double-check that our presentation is saved to the cloud. I tug my suit jacket on, spikes of nervousness ravaging my gut. My throat feels like it's closing. Especially in this suit and tie but Brett told us to dress nice, so here we are.

Brett Callenger was once my most ferocious competitor when I first joined the circuit, but after a bad fall and back surgery he retired. Now he's part of

Stanley Investors, one of the West Coast's largest venture capitalist firms. And our point of contact in this deal.

I run a hand through my hair, wishing more than anything I could be on the mountain, but I know this is a necessary pain to get someplace better. I just wish I could snap my fingers instead. But I know better than most, you can't get far without doing shit that scares you.

As we step to the elevator, I notice I have two new voicemails. One from a number I recognize as DKS, my publicist – I grit my teeth. I don't want to talk to December. Without listening to the message, I delete and move on to the second one from UnderLayer's Talent Agent:

Hi Everett, this is Laura Tolli, director of endorsement coordination with Un-derLayer. I just wanted to inform you that, unfortunately, we will not be renewing our contract with you. Good luck in your upcoming events. Happy Holidays!

I slip my phone back into my pocket and jam the button for the main floor. My head is reeling. I've lost another sponsor. The second in a month.

"What's up?" Luc nudges me.

"Nothing." I throw him a smile. "Nerves."

Internally my brain is screaming, *oh shit. Why is this happening to me?* I can't tell Luc, not now. He'll flip out and we need cool, confident Luc today. The money sharks can't know I'm unstable with endorsements. It's not a vote of confidence when long-time sponsors are pulling the plug – especially approaching a big Olympic year. I should be hot right now, but I'm selling even less than usual.

I swallow down the angry, sad lump in my throat and pretend everything is alright.

Chapter 4

December Fowl

"**S**houldn't you be preparing for your interview?" Ryan Dawson clicks his tongue, staring at the back of Suz's head as she works on my computer, and then glances at me.

"Shouldn't you be sniveling at Mr. King's feet?"

He laughs, "You're worried I had my interview before you, aren't you? You should be. He practically offered me the job then. But, you know, formalities and such."

"The only thing I'm worried about is who will hire you once you lose this job? No one else would deal with you like Mr. King does."

He snorts, "Coming from the woman who just *had* to embarrass our biggest investor in front of everyone? It's called decorum, December."

For a moment I stiffen. DKS executives Meredith Sally and Lionel King were the only other people from our office at the DKS Board Meeting in New York that night. Our biggest investor had been bloating key performance indicators all evening. I put up with it for a bit because he's a big investor, great for networking, and I thought he had just misspoke. But then he kept doing it. Misquoting some of our most important metrics like our client's share of voice and media coverage compared to our competitors. Something like that – without correction – could give the board completely the wrong impression.

But Ryan shouldn't know anything about that. On the flight home, King sat me down, red-faced, and told me while Mike Gibler had misquoted our figures repeatedly, I had no right to correct him in front of the entire board. I embarrassed Gibler and the agency tonight by speaking out of turn. King advised me to tell no one, or I'd find myself receiving a formal strike. Three strikes and I'm out. I, of course, told my best friend and roomie Suz, but not another soul.

Until this moment it's never resurfaced. Neither King or Sally have mentioned it and Mike Gibler has kept on partnering with us. But how – why – does Ryan know? Goosebumps prickle at the back of my neck but before I can retort the HR Director Mindy Marvel struts towards us.

"Ryan, Suz, get back to work. If I have to file another incident report I'm going to be pissed."

"I was just leaving," Ryan says and gives me a lazy look before slinking away.

"Suz is working on my computer. It's going wild," I explain and Mindy nods, moving on.

As soon as they're gone Suz spins around, "God, he is the fucking worst. When you get this promotion, please find a way to fire him."

I take a deep breath as Suz twists back around. I *am* going to get this promotion. Ryan may have the arrogance of the top performer, but he isn't. I am.

"I'm going to call my clients – be right back," I say, needing something, anything to do. I don't like feeling like things are out of my control.

Finding an empty meeting room, I scroll through my most recent calls. I don't have to scroll far. Todd and I are in constant contact. I press his number and wait for his answer. It rings three times and clips off straight to voicemail.

"Hi Todd, it's December. Give me a call back. It's urgent we discuss these press releases and the charity event tonight. And you were wonderful on SNL!"

I call Sawyer right after. Her line doesn't even ring and goes straight to voicemail.

"Hey, Sawyer. It was great to see you this weekend. I hope you're feeling much better and you like the dress Morgan is working on. She is ah-mazing! Anyways, my computer has gone haywire so just wanted to let you know our meeting is still on at noon. I'll give you a call then. Byeee."

I slide my phone into my pocket and head back to my cubicle. Todd and Sawyer are my only client meetings this morning. If the issues extend into the afternoon, then I'll call my other clients. But there's no need to bother them otherwise. It'll only annoy them.

I only manage a few paces before Mr. King's assistant brushes my arm.

"Miss Fowl, Mr. King will see you now."

I glance down at my phone. It's only 9:35 am. Our meeting isn't for another twenty-five minutes. I open my mouth to object and realize Mr. King must have learned about my computer issues and decided to use this for more interview time. Smart man. I give his assistant a smile and follow her to the elevator. She gestures for me to get in but doesn't follow me.

"Aren't you–" I begin as the door slides shut.

Oh, thank god. The man gets a new assistant each quarter. Terrible as it is, it's become easier to just refer to them as his assistant instead of learning their actual names. I take another deep breath. Rub my hands on my thighs and pull my shoulders up and back. Power pose. I am ready for this.

The doors slide open a moment later with a hiss and I step into the executive floor. My heels click on the marble flooring. Click-click-click. The sound gives me another boost of confidence. *And I could be walking here every day.* I clap my hands together gleefully. I straighten my skirt, smooth out my sweater, and strut for Mr. King's office. *You can do this December. You got this.*

The door to Mr. King's office is angled open. I step a toe inside and knock softly. He looks up curtly and down again, adjusting some paperwork on his desk.

"Come in Miss Fowl." I hesitate for a moment. Miss Fowl? He hasn't called me Miss Fowl since I was an intern. "And shut the door."

I do as he says and move towards his desk. With great restraint, I force myself to focus on Mr. King and not the expansive view of the city from his corner office. I take a seat in one of the giant leather chairs, probably costing more than my yearly salary, and elegantly cross my legs. Clarisse Renaldi from the *Princess Diaries* would be *very* proud.

Mr. King continues to review the document in front of him. My hands tighten together. My foot twitches across the floor. I try to keep it together –

keep my mind from running wild, my mouth from opening and rambling, my body from stirring, but the still and silence burns a hole through me.

"You may not have heard, but I'm having computer issues," I erupt. The strain in my body loosens. Mr. King gazes at me over his reading glasses.

"Suz is on it, of course, but all of my meetings for the next three months have been canceled. I've already called Todd and Sawyer and will follow-up with my other three clients after our meeting. I just thought you ought to know in case you hear anything through the grapevine." What I mean is, Ryan Fucking Dawson. He would totally twist the situation into sounding like I fucked up.

Mr. King crooks his head, "You don't think you should tell me about your girls' trip to LA?"

I suck in a breath. *That.* "Sawyer had an emergency. She was about to back out of *Savage Song*, and it's critical she performs. So, yes, Mr. King, I should have consulted you but if I hadn't gone in the moment, she would've lost it."

He nods, pulling a sheet of paper from his pile, "So you needed to purchase two, last minute seats on your company credit card? I may understand *you* going but why did you bring a friend?"

"She's not a friend – well, she is, but Sawyer was upset because her designer dress wouldn't arrive in time for the show. My friend is a designer. I brought her with to reassure Sawyer we had a plan."

"And you used the company card instead of your personal card, why?"

"It was company business, Mr. King. Sawyer *is* our top rising talent. If she doesn't perform on *Savage Song*, it would be detrimental to her career."

He harrumphs, sounding less than impressed.

This is not at all going like I wanted it to. So, I use a moment of silence as an opportunity to turn the tables in my favor, "Our company credit card policy is one area I'm interested in improving as the Public Relations Officer. Right now, it's strictly used for *planned* expenses, but what about emergencies? Working with celebrities, there are a lot. DKS always reimburses purchases anyways, why not allow specialists to use company credit? There are benefits for the company too: with each dollar spent we earn points for airfare, hotels, and rental cars. Which can be used for future business trips."

Mr. King leans back in his seat, and I sit straighter. I always find a way to turn a negative discussion into a positive one.

"Furthermore, I–"

"Miss Fowl we are not here to discuss the officer position."

I jerk. My hands grow sweaty. But I'm not about to let this opportunity slip by so easily. I've earned this company millions of dollars in the few short years I've been here. I spun Todd's affair as a whirl-wind true-love story. Colleen Hoover couldn't have written it better.

"I'll reach out to your assistant and see when we can set up a time to discuss the role." My voice is solid unlike the emotions spinning around my head.

"Miss Fowl, you've made a number of questionable decisions in the last few months. First, you embarrassed the company at our board meeting. You make a deal with NBC without consulting the client or their agent, and now you're taking your friends on a trip to L.A. on the company's dollar. Not to mention, your numbers are far, far below average and expectation."

My mind processes the words he's saying. Is he talking about *me*? He knows what happened at the board meeting. We talked about this on the flight home – even if Mike Gibler is our biggest investor, it doesn't give him the right to lie about our performance indicators, so he and the agency look better. But, because he *is* our biggest investor, we agreed (or rather, I was told) the agency wouldn't be ending our partnership or reprimanding him.

I can't stop myself, my anger has reached its boiling point, "With all due respect, Mike Gibler is a liar. If he doesn't want to be called out in front of the board, he needs to learn to disclose our performance indicators truthfully. I understand he's the agency's investor, but why are we continuing to associate with a repeat falsifier? And my numbers. Mr. King," I offer him a smile, taking a breath to compose myself, "my clients have generated half a million dollars so far this year. That's *double* what some of the other publicists are doing."

Mr. King's face reddens but he folds his hands and manages to hold himself back, "I've told you before, Miss Fowl, bring those issues to me. Privately. Don't spew it openly like you did to discredit a man. There was no need to make a scene. As far as dollars generated, you are correct, but gross revenue is not the only metric evaluated. Our business grows by recruiting clients. You've been here four years and you have five clients."

"Yes, four of which are hugely productive, profitable clients."

Mr. King is not deterred, "We are not happy with your performance. Delta, King, and Sally is thankful for your hard work and dedication, but we're going to let you go." He shuffles his papers like *that's that*. "The airfare will be deducted from your final paycheck."

"But – I..."

I am without words. My face burns. I just sit here staring at Mr. King as though he has more to say. Like he's about to start laughing, hand me a glass of whiskey, dry, and tell me the officer position is all mine. This was all a test.

Instead, he grabs his phone and dials security. Once he barks his order, he turns back to me, all cool confidence, "We've notified your clients. They've agreed to stay with the company. We're in the process of notifying Everett Abrams. He's been more difficult to contact but I assure you he'll stay as well. You're bright, December. I'm sure you'll land on your feet."

When security arrives, they lead me downstairs where a box of my personal items awaits. They strip me of my company phone and badge.

The guard all but pushes me out the door. I don't even remember walking to my car but I'm sliding into the cool leather seat. The door claps shut. I stare at my *former* office building, my hands gripping the wheel.

What the fuck just happened?

Chapter 5

Everett Abrams

L uc and I wait in the lobby flooded with warm afternoon light.

I have my headphones in but no music plays. Luc sits across from me, elbows on his knees. Legs jigging restlessly. He won't stop running his hands through his hair. I've told him twice already to chill. If the investors walk in and see us looking like nervous wrecks their doubts will grow.

They had so many questions – what will make Elevate's products different from those already on the market? How will we survive in a market that's already saturated? Where do we plan to find our sustainable materials? Have you considered the cost? Couldn't we use cheaper material and have the same product?

Luc and I handled them all in stride. These are all questions we'd considered ourselves. I left the room feeling confident, but the panel has been in discussion for three hours. And I can't get my most recent failure out of my head – UnderLayer was my first sponsor. To lose them feels like I'm losing everything.

Brett strides through the door and Luc and I both jump to our feet. I yank the headphones out and drape them around my neck.

Luc and I glance at one another. His face is pale, and he swallows roughly. I think he had a tougher time speaking to them than I did, which is uncharacteristic of life-of-the-party, Luc Orseno.

"So," Luc prods, waving his hand like he just wants this over with.

Brett rolls back on his heals, "You know your shit and they can tell. They all had great feedback about making the products with sustainable, fair trade practices in mind and giving back…"

"But?" My heart sinks. I can tell by the way he won't look me in the eye, he's prepping us for bad news.

"But…" He rubs the back of his neck, "They want you guys to have more skin in the game. This is a multimillion-dollar venture. Three hundred thousand between the two of you isn't enough. The investors would like you to come up to half a million."

Luc and I share a look as Brett continues, "Considering the whole venture will cost two million, they feel it's a fair percentage. They want a fourth of the venture funding to come from you guys."

I try to wrap my mind around all the figures, but the talk of percentages and money has me seeing only dizzying dollar signs and question marks.

"That's more than twenty percent," Luc thunders, knotting his hand in his hair.

I shake my head. We have to come up with an extra two hundred thousand? I've been averaging two hundred g's a *year* with endorsements and contest winnings. And with my sponsor dropping – I let out a ragged breath, not wanting to think about it. Luc's averaging about the same but he sends a lot of his green back home to his family in Colorado.

I let out another rough breath, running a hand through my hair. *Shit.* Two hundred thousand could take another four years. I hoped we'd have a line of gloves out by the beginning of the new year.

"They have a deadline, too. They'd like the funding requirement to be met by January 8th or they walk from the whole deal."

"What?" Luc steps forward. His eyes are burning coals. "November is nearly over. You know how tight things are with the industry right now. There's no way. No. Way. We can make this happen."

I'm with Luc. My mind reels. It would be different if we had at least one more year, but we barely have six weeks. six weeks jammed packed with contests, travel, and practice. Brett nods, his gray eyes sorrowful. I'm not about to let this go, though. We've worked too hard. I want this too much – and so does Luc.

"Tell them it's a deal. We'll raise two hundred thousand or the deal's off."

"What? Are you insane? Everett, that's never going to happen." Luc grips my shoulder and shakes.

"If we say no now, they're just going to walk."

Brett nods in agreement.

Luc's shoulders sag. He wanted this more than I did. To finally be able to give his sister, his parents something more stable to rely on. And his head has been going mad with ideas. Snowboarding has been his sole creative outlet since college. I haven't seen him so invested in something other than boarding before. Designing gloves, a website, logo. His hand hasn't stopped drawing.

As much as I want Elevate as my backup, I want it even more for Luc. Life has wrung him dry, but he always gets up with a smile on his face. He never lets it show, but I know him as well as I know myself. I see the tired beneath his smile.

Brett and I shake hands. We agree to talk again in five weeks. Luc follows me out to the truck.

He clears his throat, nods his head towards a BMW crawling into the parking lot, "I'll see you later."

"I'm not sure that's a good idea," I say, recognizing the striking brunette behind the wheel. The last time I saw her, he landed in jail with a DUI charge.

Luc spreads his arms out and backs towards the car like he's saying *what are you going to do about it?* I watch as he climbs in, and they disappear with a roar from the engine.

He's spiraling again. The first time since he and his on-again, off-again girl-friend, Torrance, officially ended things. Now when he thinks shit has already hit the fan. I shake my head and climb into my truck...

I have to find a way to make two hundred grand in five weeks. The only plausible idea includes selling my soul to the devil.

Chapter 6

DECEMBER FOWL

I sit on my bedroom floor, nursing a bottle of wine. My second bottle in eight hours.

Fired.

I was fired.

F. I. R. E. D.

I shake my head, squeeze my eyes shut, and peek through my lashes at my phone. DKS had sent me the formal termination notice an hour ago. It's staring up at me.

This cannot be happening. This is *not* happening. I power my phone off and stare at my vision board in front of me, trying to control my breathing.

My hands ball into fists, nails biting into my palms. Honestly, who's more qualified, more competent than I am? Six years I've spent at DKS. Two as an intern, and four now, full-time. I didn't go to grad school because they told me they needed me now. Meredith Sally promised they'd pay for further education once I'd been with the firm for five years.

I gave up dates. I gave up holidays. I gave up my weekends. Case in point: me heading off to LA to help a client in crisis days ago. I've worked hours upon hours of unpaid overtime. I've put stellar presentations together last minute for Sally and King. I have the most profitable clients. And yet, I'm fired?

I have the family history, the college GPA, the internships, and the numbers all behind me. And yet I'm still fired because of one ugly metric: my recruitment score. I stick my tongue out at the thought.

"So, what if I don't have ten clients? I have five *quality* ones." For a second, I consider the fifth, less quality client. Everett Abrams.

The image of him walking through the airport flashes across my brain: lips parted, wild hair, and dark, dark eyes looking for something to devour. His face sears into my mind like a brand. My stomach flutters and for a moment as my intrusive brain imagines he's walking home to me.

And as quickly as it enters my fuzzy mind, I reject it, gagging. I hold the wine bottle out in front of me. It made me do it.

I amend my previous statement, "I had four. Four perfect clients. And I am pouring you down the drain."

Moving to get up, my eyes catch on the photo from my birthday this spring. I'm wrapped in the arms of my father and sister Junie. The painted houses of the Amalfi Coast stand behind us. My lip shakes, and I suck in a breath to stop them. I will not cry again. I've been cried out.

They've never been fired, Dad and Junie. Neither has my mother.

"*Mom*," I groan, squeezing my eyes shut. How am I ever going to show my face again?

"I should have been a lawyer," I conclude.

My door creaks open and a gray cat rounds the corner of my bed, his tail carried high. *Mrrow.* He lifts his head towards mine.

"Hi, Frankie," I scratch him behind the ears the way I know he likes. "Yeah, you still love me. Dontcha Frankie."

He coos again and brushes against me. I stroke his silken body. There's something about petting a cat.

Across the apartment, there's a click and squeak as someone pushes the door open. Frankie stands at attention and then trots in the direction of the noise. Such a fearless kitty, going towards the unknown. Though, I suppose, he knows it's Suz. I glance at my phone. She's always home by five-thirty.

My door pushes open again and my roommate steps in. She holds Frankie tightly against her chest, who leaps out and circles a spot on my comforter. Suz sits on the edge of the bed, looking down at me. I roll my head away, pulling another drag from the bottle.

"Drink?" I lift the bottle in her direction. She takes it but doesn't drink. Doesn't hand it back either. "I suppose I've had enough."

"What the hell happened?"

I throw my hands up, "Fuck if I know!"

"People are saying you weren't meeting performance requirements?" She waits for me to confirm or deny.

I roll my head in her direction. The look I give her makes her sit up straight. I close my eyes and shake my head. It's not Suz's fault. I'm sure there's all kinds of shit they're saying. Really, it's the only way they can justify my firing. It's ludicrous and everyone knows it.

"Apparently, I wasn't meeting recruitment requirements. First time I've heard of it but what do I know."

She sits there a moment, staring. Then in true Suz fashion, she reaches down and pulls me to my feet. She's always there to pick me up. Even when I don't want to be.

She pulls me behind her to the kitchen, grabbing a dining room chair along the way. I'm not sure which makes more noise resisting, me or the chair. At the edge of the kitchen, she twists the chair around and forces me to sit. I slouch down into it, watching as she pulls out the wok, noodles, and veggies. Once they've been cut and she sets the noodles to soften, she lifts herself onto the counter beside me.

"What are you doing to do?" She asks matter-of-factly like I already have a plan. The December from this morning would have a plan – the December with a job. This December doesn't have a job or a clue.

"Hide in my room and let you and Frankie support me? The cat's got a following. He can probably make ten grand faster than I could right now."

Suz laughs and the sound makes me feel a little better about myself. This is what we do, sit, talk, and laugh at each other. Even now when one of us is a complete failure. At least some things never change.

She taps my hand, "Seriously. We need to figure something out."

I yank my hand away and jump up, "I don't have anything figured out. This wasn't part of my plan! I never thought I would ever be fired."

I pace along the cool hardwood floor of the kitchen, thumbnail between my teeth, "I don't even have savings for this. My credit card is practically maxed. Who's going to hire me now that I've been fired from the most prestigious PR agency in the country?"

Suz lets herself down from the counter and starts adding vegetables and oil to the wok. I follow her, still rambling, "All of my clients – all four of my five hundred thousand dollar clients stayed with DKS. Maybe I should go back to school and get my law degree."

Suz gives me a look, "You hated, *hated*, business law."

"Well, what do you suggest?" I toss my hands up and wait for her brilliant plan.

"Tell your Mom?" Suz drags out like it's obvious. "She has her own PR agency in New York. You know she's been trying to get you to join her but because you love – *loved*," she amends, "DKS so much she didn't bug you about it. This would be the perfect time. Maybe it's fate."

"I'm not telling my mother. She's the last person I want to know."

She gives me a perplexed look and shakes her head, turning back to the wok.

I sigh and fill her in on the details of Thanksgiving. How my mother thinks I've already been offered the Public Relations Officer promotion. I detail how her eyes filled when she told me how proud she was, "She's been telling everyone I'm DKS's newest Officer."

"Did you say, Mom, no I did not get the promotion yet?"

I sag, leaning against the counter, "I thought I pretty much had it anyways. I didn't think it would hurt anything not to correct her..."

"December! More reason you should tell her what happened." My mouth falls open and she rushes on. "Can you imagine how livid she'll be when she finds out you let her *continue* to tell everyone you're an officer just because you were afraid to tell her what really happened?"

"It's not my fault she assumed I had the job! She needs to practice active listening." I snap, wrapping my arms around myself. I know she's right, but I can't do it. Not right now. What will she think of me? I don't even know how I think of me.

Suz gives me another burning look as she makes me a bowl of stir-fry. We make our way into the living room with our food. I stretch out across the couch playing with dinner more than eating. We're four episodes deep in *The Great British Bake-Off* when Suz has had enough. She flicks off the TV.

"I was watching that," I say dryly, now staring at the dark screen.

"You have to figure this out, December."

I cover my face with my blanket and roll away, "I don't wanna figure anything out." The couch cushions tilt as she sits down beside me. Slowly, she rolls me over and pulls the blanket down. My eyes are burning and wet. I take a shaky breath, "I'm scared and sad. I don't want to think about anything."

She clicks her tongue gently, "You can be all those things, but nothing is going to make it better until you figure out a plan."

I hiccup, feeling exponentially alone and tired, "Can I have tonight?"

"Fine." She taps me on the nose. "We'll just sit here and watch baking shows. Then tomorrow start planning your world domination."

"You don't have to stay here. Please don't."

She hesitates, tempted. I know she has plans for the night. She always has plans.

"If you don't mind," I press. "I'd really like to be alone." To cry and have angry fits, which I want no witnesses for.

She nods and turns the TV back on as she walks to her bedroom. Twenty minutes later, her heels are clicking against the floor. She struts in front of me, wearing a little red dress and open-toed heels.

"You little hottie," I coo as she strikes a pose. A moment later the doorbell rings. "Don't do anything I wouldn't."

Suz laughs, rolling her eyes, because if that were the case, she'd never get laid. At least not in the year – except if you count that three minute, barely-a-bang fling at Suz's cousin's summer wedding. I certainly don't.

As soon as she's gone, I lay pitifully on the couch for another hour. Mostly, I stare zombielike at the TV, but a few thoughts filter through.

I still may have one client to work with. My regulars are staying with the company. I try not to feel betrayed but I am. After everything I've done for them, and they ditch me the second DKS asks them to?

But Everett Abrams – even though he's a disaster – may still be within my grasp.

"*Sshh, December's sleeping.*" Suz giggles as she and her guest slip not-so-stealthily into the apartment.

Floorboards creak as they make their way towards Suz's bedroom. I glance at my phone on my way back to the closet. 2:21 a.m. I pillage through my clothes, not certain what I'm looking for but knowing there's something else I'll want to bring. If I don't wear it, at least I may be able to sell it. And lord knows I could use some spare cash.

"What are you doing?" Suz hisses, voice still a whisper.

I jolt and yank a hanger so hard it springs back at me. I recover, carrying an armful of clothing to what used to be my bed, now just a heap of cotton, zippers, and buttons.

Suz blinks, a booze induced fog making it hard to comprehend what clothing monster has taken over my bed. I reach out and pull her into my chest. Slowly, she wraps her arms around me.

"I figured it out," I say into her black, jasmine scented head. My heart thumps a little faster. "I have a plan and I'm going to do it."

"Whhaa–" She pushes back and looks at me hard like she's trying to read my thoughts.

I wiggle out of her hold and move back to my suitcase. It's overflowing with clothes. I push the contents down hard so I can get the zipper around. They'll be like a jack-in-the-box as soon as I unzip it, but it fits. I clap my hands together. Everything is going so well right now.

I pull the bag off the bed, and it bangs on the floor. Good thing it has wheels. I grab my winter jacket, ten years out of style, and wave the airline app in front of Suz's face. She grabs my wrist to hold me steady, so she can take a good look. She draws back a moment and then leans in like she can't quite believe her eyes.

"No," She shakes her head, her rich mahogany eyes meeting mine, the clearest I've seen them since she's arrived back home.

"Yes." I move around her. My suitcase rumbles behind me. Frankie trots enthusiastically next to me, meowing.

"You'll take care of Frankie, won't you?" I say just so he knows I'm thinking about him. Suz babies the little furball just as much as I do.

"No. You're not going anywhere." She reaches down and grabs my suitcase, attempting to lift it and carry it back to my room. But the thing probably weighs more than she does.

I laugh just as someone peeks his head around the corner. I recognize him immediately. Anthony from accounting who's been shamelessly sleeping around the office since his fiancée ended things. His shoulders are bare, and he holds the rest of his body against the wall, out of sight, "What's going on?"

"Nothing," I give a Suz a crooked look.

She shrugs.

"Suz, I'll be *waiting*," he wags his brows as if she could miss the suggestive dip in his voice.

"What are you doing?" I hiss.

"Me? You're the one about to run off to a client you don't even know, who doesn't like you, in a state where you've never been!" She hisses back, glancing over her shoulder but Anthony's disappeared.

"I'm not going to sleep with him!"

"So, what, you don't have a sex life, so I can't either?"

I roll my eyes and say gently, "No. But *him*? He's clearly fucking his heart-break away."

Suz grins wickedly, "So? He's sexy and I'm horny."

I sigh.

She stomps. "So what if I have meaningless sex? I'm okay with it, you should be, too. Now tell me what you're doing."

I reach for the door. My flight leaves in three hours and the Atlanta airport is busy any hour of the day, "Everett is going to pick me."

"Pick you? What are you talking about?"

"DKS still wants him. But I'm going to get there first."

Chapter 7

EVERETT ABRAMS

"What do you mean you don't know where he is?" Haylee demands, pouncing on me as soon as I'm out of the shower.

I ruffle my damp hair and pad down the stairs, my feet sinking into the carpet as I head for the kitchen. I'm beginning to regret telling her Luc didn't come back with me from Boise. He's on one of his trips. Haylee hasn't known him long enough to understand this is something he does: he gets set off, disappears for a few weeks, and shows up like he didn't miss a day.

Three years ago, he and his longtime on-and-off-again girlfriend, Torrance, ended things for good. He was gone for more than two weeks without contacting me. He spent a month in the Pacific surfing, binge drinking, and sleeping with any eager, beautiful woman.

He's still not over Torrance. But it got the edge off.

The last time I saw him with the beautiful BMW-driving brunette, Cleo, he called me from a California jail. He spent two days locked up for driving under the influence. I've yet to find out what exactly happened and why, but this time, I know what set him off.

Two hundred thousand dollars.

"Hey," Haylee snaps her fingers. "We were having a conversation?"

I grin at her sass. Ten years younger than me, she's what I imagine having a younger sister would be like. Annoying and demanding, but I can't help feeling proud and completely, platonically in love with her.

I snatch up an apple, "Hays, he does this. He'll be back. This year is too important to skip town for waves and babes. He knows that."

"But why did he leave at all?" She makes a face, sad and reflective, and I wonder if this affects her more than me. Her parents died before she turned double digits. "He was supposed to help me with my double cork tomorrow."

"I'll help you."

"Yeah right. Your cork is the worst."

"And yet I still manage to win every weekend."

She rolls her eyes and huffs, marching to her things scattered by the dining room table. She gathers them all into her backpack and I follow her to the entryway.

"See you bright and early tomorrow. We'll work on your double cork and cab 360. See if you'll be going back to Luc after what I teach you."

Haylee rolls her eyes, her smile spreading wider as she opens the door, "Whatever, old man. Just tell Luc to get his ass back here."

"Hi! Is Everett here?" A voice from outside gusts in with the cold air.

"Right over there," Haylee jerks her head in my direction and then calls at me, "See ya tomorrow."

My attention is lost on the other woman. She's bundled in a velvety blue dress overcoat and white hat – the kind the wind blows right through. Behind her leans a luggage bag. For a moment I wonder if she meant to ask for Luc instead of Everett, but there's something oddly familiar about her face. Rounded jaw, pert red nose, glowing green eyes, and a bottom lip I'd like to take a bite of.

I swallow. She's gorgeous. Her eyes are direct, certain, and sharp. Her mouth looks the same way.

"Everett?" She says again and suddenly I realize she's been talking this entire time. She holds her arms tightly against herself and shivers.

I clear my throat, but it still sounds thick, "I don't know when Luc will be home."

Her nose scrunches up a little, "Luc? I'm here to see you."

"Me?" I point to myself like she couldn't possibly mean *me*. Women aren't usually showing up at my doorstop looking for me. If she were an Amazon box, definitely.

The woman reaches out her hand, "I'm December Fowl. Your publicist."

Chapter 8

December Fowl

E verett's jaw goes slack. His eyes roam up and down my body like he's trying to make sense of my introduction. A spike of worry flutters through my chest. Has DKS already gotten him?

He repeats, "December Fowl."

I offer him a smile, "In the flesh." He stiffens further. It's almost like I can see his drawbridge rising up, closing him off. "You look like you've seen a ghost."

"Sorta feels like it," His eyes drag over me again. His face is blank. "You are not who I was expecting you to be."

I'm both defensive and amused, "A welcome surprise?"

He looks away, jaw tensing, "Not really."

Insecurity and rage roar up inside me: *I'm not good enough for anyone.* And, *the asshole doesn't even know me!* I take a breath and tuck the voices into the dark recesses of my mind. I'll bring them out when I'm alone with a bottle of wine and see which wins. My money's on the rage.

After a moment of silence, Everett's dark eyes shift to me, "I never expected to meet you."

"We can both agree on that, but I have a proposal for you, if," I gesture towards his house and shiver, "I can come in?"

He looks down at himself and I take the moment to look him over. Afterall, he's just spent forever looking me up and down. Fair is fair. But I'm dressed in my best winter clothes. Everett is bare chested, wearing thin athletic shorts. I swear I can see the bulge of his dick against the fabric. I don't allow my eyes to linger. The man is cut – each ab perfectly defined. He sighs, turns, and I catch sight of his ridged obliques. I never knew obliques could make a girl's legs weak, but his do.

Everett turns, but not before pushing the door open for me, and continues up to the second floor. He mumbles words under his breath I can't hear. As he disappears, I hurry inside, rolling my eyes and stick my tongue out at the back of his head. Asshole, like I'm asking a *whole* lot from you.

I shut the door behind me and take off my jacket. When he doesn't return a moment later, I use it as an invitation to check out his house, moving deeper inside. Beyond the entryway and hall, I meet the kitchen with modern appliances and rich blue cabinets. The kitchen opens up into a combined dining and living room. Arranged in a semicircle around, is a large sectional gray couch. To the right is a long table but no chairs. There's a stone fireplace, and a giant TV hanging above it, in the center wall. The wall tapers off to floor to ceiling windows on either side of the fireplace.

The entire space looks out across the mountains. I have an itch to step outside onto the wrapped deck and inhale the cold mountain air.

I turn back to the kitchen. A stack of mail rests on his counter. My eyes latch onto an orange envelope. DKS' signature light color. Before I can even think, I'm there, pulling the letter from the pile. I don't breathe. Mr. King's words float around in my head: *we haven't been able to reach him yet.* It's their letter to inform him I've been fired.

The stairs creak as Everett bounds down. My mind goes fast and slow at the same time. He doesn't know but he doesn't like me already. If he finds out I've been fired, he's not going to give me a chance. I only need one chance to prove to him I can help him, then I'll come clean.

I hear his feet on the floor, stalking closer. Panicked, I swing open one of the blue cabinet doors and toss the letter inside. A moment later Everett rounds the corner. He eyes me suspiciously and I wonder if he heard the swing of the cabinet door, but he doesn't say anything. Only, pulls out two chairs from the breakfast bar across from me without a word.

His voice is dry, "Let's get this over with."

My stomach tightens. His dark hair is messy like he's just raked through it. He's thrown on a tattered black NIN t-shirt that matches his eyes. Brown freckles sprinkle his cheeks and forehead. He's gorgeous in photographs, but in the flesh he's...I suck in a breath.

He's looking at me all businesslike, his lips pressed together. His eyes like a tiger. Full attention on me. I blink slowly, trying to bring my mind into the moment.

"December." He says again, his voice deep and cut with impatience. "You had something to say?"

It's good he's so mind-bogglingly attractive. It will make this so much easier, "I want to make you snowboarding's hottest bad boy."

"You what?" Everett leans forward, blinking. His features are torn between surprise and fury. The first real emotion I've seen from him since I introduced myself.

I don't repeat myself, "You're the number one snowboarder in the world, but at the bottom of the pay scale. Hendrik Legrand isn't even ranked and is in the top five for highest paid. Ever. You need to be on top – and I think we should emulate his success."

He goes rigid again, his eyes grow more deadly, "I'm not going to be Hendrik Legrand, or anything like him."

"I'm not saying you need to be him. But we can use his tactics."

His voice is cutting, "Like what, get piss drunk and do stupid shit for publicity?"

"Like show up where your fans are." I cut back at him. "*Yes,* at parties, but also on social media and meet-and-greets. Right now, you're nowhere."

"Exactly where I like to be."

Everett rises from his seat and lumbers the few steps into the living room. He launches himself over the back of the couch and pretends I'm not here.

My stomach gnarls with anger. *Jerk, jerk, jerk.* I stomp into the living room and stand in front of the couch he's lounging in. He's washed himself clean of the angry expression he wore a moment ago. He stares at me lazily. Like he's bored I'm still here.

"You want to keep losing sponsors then?" A flash a lot like hurt cuts across his face. "Good tactic. Just let your career shrivel up and die."

"You don't know what you're talking about," His voice is cold, controlled.

I can't stop myself. *This is my job.* I move back into the kitchen and pull out my *Everything Everett* binder and wave it at him.

He'll never know the number of hours I've spent compiling it. The strings I pulled to land him every single invite and interview he's ever been asked to do, and he just throws them away. I've been taken for granted by every single client I've had. I won't let Everett walk all over me, too.

"I know last year you lost your sponsorship with Rocket Mobile, this summer Ready Energy, and now UnderLayer. If it weren't for prize money, you'd be at the very bottom of earnings."

"Well then, I guess this is your fault, isn't it? You're a shit publicist if I'm losing all my endorsements."

There's roaring in my ears. I glower at him. *You're a shit publicist.* Those exact words have been tumbling through my own head since Lionel fired me. But when he says them, not just an echo in my head, I know it's bullshit.

I say calmer than I feel, "I want to make sure you know where you are."

"I'm *very* aware without you throwing it in my face."

Guilt pinches my chest. Then I hear those words again, '*Well then, I guess this is your fault.*' I tilt my head at him, "Maybe if you had taken even a few of the invites and interviews I got you, you wouldn't be here."

"No," he says, shaking his head, dark eyes burning coals, "I don't know what's in that binder of yours but if you knew anything about me or this industry you would know the suggestions you made were trash."

I take a breath and force myself to simmer down. I pace between the windows and the couch until my blood is no longer pumping solely into my ego.

There are other publicists Everett could hire; his agent Corey could get off his ass and find him some new sponsors, but I know I'm the best at focused, personalized representation. Right now, Everett desperately needs me. And I need him.

I concede, squeezing my eyes shut. "Help me understand then. I want to make your career as big as it can be."

"You're still here?" Everett's eyes haven't cooled a degree.

I swallow the urge to continue to tell him off. We've both poked the hornet's nest. I took my pitch in the wrong direction as soon I threw his losses in his face. Like I can't be the only failure here.

"I'm sorry. This isn't how I wanted today to go. Let's take a break, but I know I can help you. I can be here tomorrow morning-"

His voice is iron, "I ride in the morning. This is exactly why I don't want to work with you. You don't know about me. You haven't even tried. You just want to mold me into someone I'm not."

"And how many times have you answered my emails or my phone calls? You said I don't know and haven't even tried, but I have. You've refused to work with me and look where you are now."

My words settle in the air between us. He turns away, jaw flexing, and he lifts the TV remote to turn up the volume, effectively dismissing me.

Defeated, I stuff my binder back into my bag, "I'll be here at 7 p.m. We're going to discuss goals. Get to know each other."

Everett closes his eyes and shakes his head, "Just leave already."

Chapter 9

December Fowl

"Wow,"

Before me, snow covered, towering trees; the roof of Blue Mountain Lodge is made of snow; the ground, white cotton candy. This is where Hansel and Gretel met the witch, I'm sure of it. It's far too magical to be real. I turn slowly around, enchanted.

My jaw hits the ground. In front of me stands a monstrous mountain. I tilt my head back to see its peak. Dozens of tiny specks weave down the mountainside like ants trying to pick the safest path. Fairytale-like cabins line the foot of the mountain along a boardwalk. Packed outdoor seating areas made possible by blazing woodfires and metal poles that lick with flames.

"Holy sh–"

Thunk-Thunk. *Slam.*

I turn my attention back to the car. The driver has pulled my things out of the trunk and rests them against the vehicle.

"Twenty-five dollars," he says, stretching his hand out.

"I don't have cash." I pull out my card and flash it at him.

The driver throws his arms up in frustration, "I told you, cash only!"

"I'll find an ATM," I point towards the lodge behind him.

He nods and kicks at the snow, muttering as I scurry away. I step inside and am welcomed with a blanket of warmth and delightful aromas. But I don't have time to savor it. Money first, basking later! I trot to the ATM, furiously pushing at the buttons when prompted.

On the bench near the machine sits four teenage boys. They're still in their snow gear, "I hope we meet Hendrik!"

"My friend said he saw him here once but never got a picture. If I see someone famous, I'm *definitely* getting a picture."

"I've heard Blue Saloon is a hot spot. We'll have to ask if we can go there tonight."

The machine *wrrrs* as it spits out my cash. Blue Saloon, interesting. I push the name into my memory bank in case this doesn't work out with Everett, which is most likely, and I need to find myself a new client.

Money in hand, I hustle back towards the cab. The doors slide open just as a cold wind blows down from the mountain. I hesitate a moment, frozen. Wrapping, my jacket tighter around me, I hand the cash to the driver. He doesn't offer to help me lug my things to the lodge before he pulls away. And that's what I get for not listening.

Picking up my things, I drag them into the lodge. I head straight for the reception desk and to a tidy, stunning blonde woman. I pull my wallet out and lay it on the counter with a sigh. I'm finally here! I'm so ready for a soak in the tub and food and *wine*. I want to forget about my meeting with Everett, but at the same time think of a way to fix this.

The woman smiles, "Can I help you, Miss?"

"Yes," I smile back. "I'd like to book a room."

"Ooh. I'm sorry, we're all booked up." She says and offers me a beaming smile instead.

I blink. My brain taking a moment to catch up, "Booked up?"

"Mmhmm." She nods and again with her bright smile.

"Soo...you have nothing available?"

Her smile faulters a fraction, "All sold out. No vacancy."

"Do you know if any place has room?"

She shakes her shiny blonde head, "I'm sorry, no. Blue Sky books up months in advance."

I nod and clutch my bag, stepping away from the desk. Sure, I spent hours cyberstalking a client but didn't think about booking a room in the middle of freaking high season! *This is what happens when you get tunnel vision.* I chide myself.

"Excuse me." I look up as a woman with flowing, black wavy hair and amber eyes approaches.

"Oh, sorry, am I in your way?" I shuffle to the side of the desk.

She shakes her head, her smile jerking up one side of her face, "No. I was just dropping off some flyers and heard you were looking for a place to stay."

"Oh." I take a step back. *Stranger danger* blinks through my mind.

"Like she said," the woman tilts her head towards the receptionist, "this area is all booked up. I rent my villa out most of the season, and someone just canceled. I have room if you'd like."

"Really? That would be great!" I burst and then mentally yank myself back. I can't stay just anywhere. Even if she is a woman. "Do you have a website or are you on any rental sites?"

A few minutes later I have her place pulled up on my Solo Travelers app. She has over two hundred five-star reviews and it's only fifty dollars a night.

I release a breath, placing a hand on my chest, "This week has gone so wrong. You have no idea how much it means to finally have something going right! I'm December, by the way."

"What brings you to Blue Sky?" Torrance says once we've packed my things in her gray SUV and are pulling away from the lodge.

"I'm confused. The receptionist said Blue Sky, too. I thought this was Blue Mountain?"

"Blue Sky is the town. Blue Mountain is—"

"The mountain," we say together. I lean forward and gaze out of her windshield at the looming giant. "Good to know."

Torrance clicks on the radio. The volume is low but it's unmistakably a Latin station. Caught up in the surrounding beauty and the pace of the song, I catch none of the words.

Before the great divorce, my father used to take me and my sister Junie to the mountains. Mostly as part of a business meeting but Junie and I would have free roam of whatever mountain resort we were at. He'd pay top dollar for the best ski instructors to babysit us, and we zoomed down the slopes faster than we knew better. Eventually, after the divorce, Daddy only had time for Junie, and Mother was pulling me away to one of her functions. I lost my connection with the snow and sky. Here, there is no barrier between the two.

"Last minute visit, huh?" She glances at me, her face drawn up in a smile.

"An emergency visit," I huff out a laugh even though it's not at all funny. "Do or let my career die."

She laughs and shakes her head, but a look passes across her face like she's all too familiar with such a thing. I look at her closer now. She's my age, maybe a few years older. Her skin is flawless and glowing, a rich tan one can't simply earn from sitting in the sun. Her hair is black and silken, reflecting the light of the snow. Much like Suz's hair. I run a hand over mine. It never shines like that.

"Welcome to the A."

The SUV jerks to a stop. Torrance climbs out and I follow her lead, slamming the doors behind us. I tighten my jacket around myself but can't take my eyes off the A-frame cabin. It glows from within. A snow-covered deck wraps around the front. A path cuts through the snow leading to a red front door, lamp illuminating it with a soft, welcoming warmth.

"Sorry for the mess," she gestures at the piles of snow leading up to the house. "I didn't have a chance to shovel this morning. Follow in my footsteps."

Torrance turns and marches forward. The snow she strides through is mid-calf. I glance down at my business flats and favorite pair of dress slacks. Biting down on my lip, I swing my carry-on over my shoulder and heft my large suitcase as high I can, and I follow her. She reaches the door and she throws it open, waving at me to come in.

As soon as I step inside, I'm hit with the crisp scent of my childhood holidays: fresh evergreen laced with cinnamon, and the faint scent of burning wood. The entryway consists of a bench nestled just under the window, pushed against the wall. A pair of slippers and tennis shoes are pushed underneath. On the opposite wall hangs a coat rack.

I shrug mine off and hang it by its hood. Stepping out of the way, I cross the doorway and find myself beside a stack of firewood.

"Stay right here," Torrance says, slipping out of her jacket and boots, and sliding into the pair of slippers. "I'll be right back."

I watch her as she disappears down the hallway, deeper into the house. A moment later she returns with a pair of pink fuzzy slippers.

"These are for you."

I glance down at them suspiciously, "I think I'll be okay."

As if reading my thoughts, she laughs and shakes her head, "They're brand new, I promise. I keep a few extra for special guests."

"I'm a special guest?" I say, accepting the slippers.

She shrugs, "Honestly, you just look like you could use a hot shower, some warm slippers, and a hearty meal. I've got two of the three: a shower and slippers."

I smile, slip off my soggy flats and slide into the fuzzy slippers.

"I'll show you to your room."

We walk down a short hallway, past the kitchen into an open area with two leather couches facing yet another deck and wide windows. An unlit fireplace is nestled in the corner. We turn and head up the narrow stairs. On the second floor, there's one bedroom, a bathroom straight across from it, and a little corner at the end of the hall with two chairs. A little reading nook. A lamp separates the plush seats. There's another set of stairs in the back and we spiral up and to a door. Torrance pushes it open and steps inside.

I grunt, yanking my suitcase over the last step. The whole floor is one loft room. There's a bed against the wall, a love seat and chair in the corner over-looking the window, and a beautiful view of the backyard and deck.

"Bathrooms are on the first and second floors. Help yourself to either one."

"Thanks," I mumble, gazing around the room again, eyeing the luxurious looking bed.

"Are you hungry? I was going to order something?"

I wave her off, "No, no. You've done enough. I'm really not hungry but I am exhausted. I've been all over time zones the last few days – New York to LA to Atlanta to...here." *Not to mention the firing and hideous fight I just had with my only existing client.*

Admiration flashes across her face, "You are a busy woman."

"Not on purpose." I turn my head away, thinking about all the times I would rather have stayed nuzzled in my bed with Frankie than running off to the airport for one of my clients.

"Sleep well. If you need anything, I'm just downstairs. Or text me." She gestures for my phone. I unlock it for her to add her number. "See you in the morning."

The second the door shuts, I fall face-first into the soft bedding. I hardly make it under the covers before sleep has me.

The sun spills through the window, both warming and blinding me. Groaning, I roll over and I glance at my phone – ten minutes to two p.m. I jump up and rifle through my things for my shower bag and make my way down to the first floor. I spot Torrance through the large bay windows, hunched over a shovel. A tinge of guilt feathers through me. I step towards the sliding door but stop, catching my reflection in the glass.

Tired, puffy eyes and greasy, tangled hair. The sight catches my breath. I should be in Atlanta right now. Setting up my corner office. But instead, I'm here, looking more haggard than a seasick skunk. The guilt nibbling a second ago shifts into a burning determination.

I will show Ryan and the agency what I'm worth. And it starts with convincing Everett to work with me. But first – I need to clean myself up.

After a shower, I blow out my hair and style it the best I can without any product. I fix myself a cup of coffee just as Torrance steps inside with a cold burst of air.

"Good *morning*," Torrance teases when she spots me.

She pulls off her gloves and joins me in the living room with a cup of her own coffee. We sit in silence for a moment. I gaze out the window at all the snow. New York is known for snow, too, but not pure, white snow like this. New York City snow is black and full of trash.

"Business today?" She nods towards my outfit.

"My meeting did not go well yesterday." I don't know where the admission came from. The last thing I want is more than one person knowing what a disaster last night was. I press my lips together to stop myself from saying more.

"Who's your client? I might be able to help. I know almost everyone worth knowing around here."

I shake my head, blowing on the steaming black liquid, "I'd rather not say. At least not until he agrees to work with me. It's kind of this...new superstition I have. Don't announce it until it's sealed." Never again will I tell anyone about an opportunity until I have it.

"Do you need a ride?" She asks as I stand up.

"No, I think I'd like a walk. I haven't been in the snow in years."

She tilts her head, giving me a funny look, "At least take my boots. I have more than a few pairs to spare."

I thank her, set my cup in the sink, and head to the entryway. I pull on the cutest pair, purple with a quilted pattern. I *so* owe her. And I so need to get out of here. I pull on my jacket, slinging my bag over my shoulder and head outside.

My mind needs me to stretch my legs and cycle my thoughts in the right direction. Once I was stuck on a final project in college, all it took was a walk around campus to get my creative juices flowing. I need all the creativity I can muster. I'm already asking for a miracle.

Chapter 10

EVERETT ABRAMS

Sometime around 7:30 p.m. the doorbell goes off. And when I say off, I mean *off*.

Dingdingdingdingdingdingdingding.

I throw the door open and there she is – my nightmare – poking her finger into the button like a woodpecker hammering into a tree. Her back is turned to me as she gazes around, soaking in the neighborhood.

My hand wraps around her fingers and pulls them away from the bell. She jerks around to face me, evergreen eyes wide. *God, why do her eyes have to be the color of the forest?* – dark, deep green with flecks of brown.

She glances at her hand, mine gripped around her two fingers. I shake them.

"I heard you the first five times." I let her go and she follows me inside.

When the hour turned, and she wasn't here, I was hoping she decided last night was such a disaster she didn't want to try again. Instead, here she is, waving a notebook around. *Goals* written in gold on the cover.

She's the last person I want to discuss my goals with. My heart sinks at the conversation we had yesterday. I am far from where I want to be and it's embarrassing someone else knows, too.

"I was hoping last night taught you what a terrible idea this is." I say as I watch her kick her boots off and unzip her jacket, undeterred.

She waltzes the rest of the way into the house – down the hall until she reaches the breakfast bar. Pulling out a chair, she arranges her things: two notebooks, pens, highlighters. Just making herself at home as though last night didn't happen.

I'm slightly relieved. I said some things I'm not proud of, but mostly I'm annoyed she thinks she can ignore the tension in the room.

"Well, I guess you're staying then." I mutter and she looks up, her green eyes zapping with mine. I ignore the residual electricity as it pulses down my body and saunter into the kitchen.

I didn't like her before we met and now I really don't. Inviting me to a gala right before a contest, setting me up for a meet-and-greet three hours away? Now showing up at my doorstep saying she wants to turn me into the hottest bad boy? I mean, come *on*. The woman knows nothing about me or what I want, and yet she pretends like she does. Or, worse, she doesn't care.

"I'd like to apologize," My soon-to-be-ex publicist begins.

I stop myself from turning and showing her what I think of her 'apology.' I don't want one. I'd rather she left and leave me be. Instead, I clench my jaw, use the spatula to mix the stir-fry, and pretend her words have no effect on me.

"I'm sorry for the way I acted last night. How I *said* the things I did."

I roll my eyes and stifle a growl, she's sorry for *how* she said them instead of what she said. Sounds like a *great* apology.

She takes a breath before continuing and annoyance rattles through my head – if she's pausing to allow me time to apologize, it's not happening.

"I'm going through something personally I never...expected I would." My stirring slows. I tilt my head a little to hear her better. "It's been difficult to wrap my head around, and I took it out on you. It won't happen again. I betrayed my promise to be professional and respectful. I'm sorry."

In her silence, I hesitate. My mouth opens and closes as I try to find the right words; organize my thoughts so it comes out how I want it. To buy more time, I turn down the heat and face her, leaning against the counter.

Her brows shoot up. She winces, ready for me to fire back.

"You ex-ex," I pause to collect myself, "exposed something I didn't want anyone to know. Worse, you used it against me." Her face twists. "So, thanks for the apology but I don't want to work with you." *I don't want you exposing any other secrets about me.*

Her eyes go wide, she reaches her hand out to slow me down, "I don't sugarcoat things. It doesn't do anyone any favors. I think it's important we both acknowledge where you are before we make the necessary steps to take you where you want to be."

I turn her words over in my head, working my jaw as I watch her. No one has wanted to acknowledge how far behind the industry standards I am – not me, not my agent Corey, not Luc. The only ones who have been, are the sponsors who drop me.

Behind me, the food sizzles. I pivot and stir, glancing over my shoulder at December. She's softer than she was yesterday. She lifts her brows at me again and I wonder what she meant when she said she's going through something. She's so hard-pressed to keep me as a client, even after having a taste of what a difficult mess I am. What is she going through to make her think *I'm* a good idea?

"I'm a great publicist. I know it hasn't been…" I'm too familiar with the mix of panic and confusion that crosses her face when words lodge in her throat. "Evident in our past arrangements, but I can do better. I know I can help you. I just need to get to know you."

I must have made a face because she hurries on, "Professionally, I mean. What your goals are. Things I missed last time."

I glance down at her hands. They're in fists at her side and I press down a grin. Not easy for her to say. December Fowl, dressed in a pressed white blouse and high-waisted jeans, hair pulled back in a neat bun, makeup exact, is not the type of person to admit fault. And yet she did.

"So," her lips pinch, her patience running out, "what do you say?"

I click the heat off, grab two plates and pairs of silverware, and carry the stir-fry to the counter. She glances down at the concoction of brown rice, chicken, and vegetables and then up at me, shaking her head, asking *what now?*

I reach for one of her notebooks, "I don't want to be snowboarding's hottest bad boy. First, I'm a man, not a boy, which I'm sure you're aware of." I watch her swallow as her eyes roam down my throat, over my shoulders. "And second, I'm already pretty hot."

She laughs, meeting my gaze, "Tell me what you do want, and I'll get started," She hands me a pen as I hand her a bowl – our silent agreement. "I'll write my goals down, too, so you're not the only one sharing."

Twenty minutes later, the stir-fry is all gone. December taps the butt of her pen against her notebook. I shoot her a glare but continue brainstorming. I have a list of three goals without telling too much. I'm keeping Elevate to myself, so I've written around it.

"Okay," I slide my notebook in her direction. She does the same and then dives right into my list. Her head twists sharply as she reads, her mouth making funny shapes.

She leans into the sheet, then away. In again. My gut tightens. I hope I haven't written something wrong, spelled something so completely off she can't understand it.

Her jaw drops, and she looks at me incredulously, "You want to earn two hundred thousand dollars in five weeks?"

At her reaction, I consider adjusting it to one hundred grand. *Maybe it really is impossible?* But then I think about the mock website Luc designed; the gloves and material we worked tirelessly to get just right. I want Elevate to become a reality just as much as I want to win. I'll do just about anything I can to get there. Even work with this woman.

"Yes."

"This is...how do you...I'm not a wizard! I didn't go to Hogwarts!" She presses her fingers into her temples. "That's impossible."

"Not with the star publicist from DKS. Wasn't there an article from the PR magazine with you saying: '*nothing is impossible if you keep an open mind*?' My mind is wide open." I flick my fingers by my head, demonstrating my mind blown open.

Her face melts into dread. She slouches in her seat, to my satisfaction.

"You're not the only one who can do a little research. To be the best, I have the best. I don't make bad deals for cash. I don't hire people without a solid track record." *She hasn't lived up to hers yet.*

"I'm not...I'm no longer–" She looks down, away, anywhere but at me.

I lower my head, so I can catch her eye, "What? You no longer...?"

December stands, walking around the dining room, "Two hundred thousand dollars. By January." She shakes her hands out, cracks her neck, "This is going to take some serious work from both of us. You know that?"

"No, no, no. You're the publicist. It's your work."

She grins primly, "I thought you said your mind was *wide open*?"

I shake my head, "You're the publicist. I'm the snowboarder. I do what I do. You do what you do. Whatever that is."

"Alright," She folds her arms over her chest, "I guess you won't be getting your two hundred thousand."

We stare at each other for a long moment, each waiting for the other to break. December just tilts her hips, waiting me out.

"Gah." I press my hands into my skull. "If we're going to work together, I will not do *anything* Hendrik Legrand does."

"Tell me more about your hatred for Legrand. The man is raking in the sponsors. Why don't you want to be like him?"

I let out an angry breath, running a hand through my hair, "I just – he's such..." I blanch, opening my mouth but nothing. My brain goes blank.

And all I can see is Hendrik barreling towards me. In my ears ring the crack and grinding crunch of our bodies and boards colliding. I clench. My knee sears with pain. I reach down to rub it and I catch December staring at me. She lifts a brow, expecting me to continue. My mind flashes to high school, third period history. I'm standing in front of the class mid-presentation. My mind blank but speeding out of control at one hundred miles a second – I'm saying as if on a broken loop, *"Paul Revere warned of the – warned of the – Paul Revere warned of the –"*

There's a warm hand on my arm and I jerk out of my memory.

"Are you alright?" Big green eyes – I almost get lost in them but jerk myself away from her.

"This," I say running my hands down my face, "is why I can't do this fucking PR bullshit."

December shakes her head, her forehead creases in confusion, "I'm not understanding, what is going on?"

My chest is tight, "I can't. It's too much."

December flinches, "I've rushed you again, haven't I. Shit. Let's take a break. Tomorrow we'll go over the details."

"Tomorrow?" I follow her towards the entryway.

She leans against the wall to pull on her winter boots. With a grunt she says, "You sprang this two hundred thousand dollar goal on me. My original idea isn't nearly drastic enough. I'll brainstorm tonight, and we'll go over the details tomorrow. And you just...remind yourself why you need two hundred thousand."

She's fully dressed in her outerwear now, pushes her hair away from her face and reaches for the door, her mouth split open in a pant.

"You have plans more drastic than making me the hottest bad boy around?"

With a secretive smile, she nods and slips out into the snow.

I thump my forehead against the door.

Fuck. This woman will ruin me.

Chapter 11

DECEMBER FOWL

I walk down a summer bike path, now snow covered, from Everett's to Torrance's A-frame. The trail is surrounded by white ash trees, bare but heavy with snow. A distance away, the soft rumble of tires on asphalt but here, the snow dulls all sound. Giving me a chance to think; to be silent. But tonight, my brain will not be quiet. Hot guilt is gnawing in the pit of my stomach.

"I lied." I say to the snow.

You didn't lie, you just didn't clarify, I imagine the snow answering back.

"As long as I get the job done, who cares." I shrug to myself as I meander down the slight incline to Torrance's porch. "Two hundred thousand. He's *ridiculous.*"

"Who's ridiculous?"

I jump at Torrance's voice. She's leaning against the porch railing, smiling down at me. "You talk to yourself sometimes, you know that?"

I sigh and huff up the stairs, "I think better when I talk out loud."

She nods, shifting to face me, "So, what about the job? Land yourself a ridiculous client, did you?"

"I don't know who's more ridiculous, him for setting his goals impossibly high, or me for agreeing to them."

"If your dreams don't scare you, they're not big enough, right?" She wraps her arm around my shoulder and gives me a squeeze.

Inside, we slip off our boots and I follow her into the hallway towards the living room.

Torrance shakes her head and utters something in Spanish, gesturing to the kitchen, littered with dirty dishes and leftover food, "The work never ends, does it?"

"Let me clean up," I offer.

She laughs, shaking her head, long hair falling into her face, "Oh no. As my guest, I could never allow you to clean up after me!"

Despite her rebuke, I head into the kitchen, "Back home, my roommate Suz always cooked, and I cleaned. We're like pieces to a puzzle; she hates cleaning and I hate cooking."

"Well, you're not home now. You're my guest." Torrance wrestles a plate from my grasp. "Please go take a bubble bath, work on the project for your client, and let me take care of everything."

"You don't understand," my voice cracks, pressure building behind my eyes, "I need this. I need cleaning. I need some normalcy."

She gazes at me for a moment. Her features soften, and she nods, handing the plate back. For a moment, I feel the weight of her eyes as she watches me stack dishes and package what I can for leftovers.

"Since you've got this, I'm going to change and run off to Blue Saloon. Try to catch up on some work. Come visit if you feel well enough and if you need anything, let me know."

"Where is Blue Saloon exactly? I heard some skiers talking about it yesterday."

Torrance beams, "That's wonderful! I own it!" She claps her hands together, a mystified look on her face like she's the luckiest woman in the world, "Best booze and food for miles."

I blink, "You own it?" My mind spinning up ways I can use it to my advantage. I could ask Torrance to recruit me new clients...

I shove the thought away as soon as I have it, shaking my head. What is wrong with me? Have I spent so much time in cut-throat public relations the first thought I have when I meet a new, successful friend, is how I can use her influence for my own gain? My stomach gnarls with the thought.

Torrance is talking, "Head to the main lodge and take the gondola to Blue Mountain. Your first drink is on me."

I stare at the cluttered counter. I can't meet her gaze. Not after she's been so kind and inviting – and the first I learn she's *somebody* I want to use her.

"I should get going," she says, and I mumble my goodbye.

Alone, with only the steady sound of the dishwasher, and a cloth against my palm, I think about home. Right now, Suz and I would be sitting down to watch some reality TV, Frankie curled between us, and a bowl of Suz's steaming pho in a bowl in my lap.

The thought of Suz alone in our apartment makes my stomach twist. I hope Frankie is keeping her company. And she remembers to put half the amount of soap in the dishwasher. The last time I left her alone she had to call maintenance to fix the overflowing machine.

Having finished cleaning, I trot up to my room and plop into bed. I had plans to call Suz, but there's so much for me to do. And, truthfully, I'm afraid the sound of her voice will send me to tears.

I let myself lie a moment in self-pity. Then a moment longer. And finally, I drag myself up and fetch my computer. I'm going to make a path. I'm going to trample the weeds until I see the sky.

Opening every resource I know, I dive deep into the world of snowboarding. Deeper than just Everett. Deeper than the last seven years. I go all the way back to the beginning. Devouring article after article of snowboarders being booted out of ski resorts; arrest records for the early pioneers who woke before dawn to scale mountains by foot and ride down at sunrise, only to be charged with trespassing and disturbing the peace on private property.

I read the interviews and watched the videos of these rebels trying to fight for their slice of snow. And then watched it evolve from true rebellion and progression into the wild boy's club. Today, Hendrik Legrand and several other snowboarders hail at the top of the sport. Not for their skill or winningness, but their popularity.

And how does one win a popularity contest? By the thousands of Twitter comments, YouTube views, and Instagram tags. Those who have the wildest social lives. Hendrik Legrand and the like have hijacked snowboarding's true roots of living free and bold as a noble excuse to drink and act like a hellion.

And the industry loves it. Premium brands pour millions of dollars into the industry. Those who act the part cash in; those who don't are given a bone and told to chew.

I sit back against the wall and take a breath, gazing out through the windows.

I know Everett doesn't want to be a part of Hendrik's world and, as I glance down at a video of a snowboarder sitting in a hot tub taking turns making out with a woman under each arm, I respect him for it. But it's clear – being seen and social, interacting with fellow snowboarders and fans, pays. My job is to prove to Everett acting the part, even a little, will reap huge returns.

I dive back into research about him. What is his issue with Hendrik? I get he's the symbol of the part of the industry he despises, but it seems to be more than that. Scrolling through Hendrick's video channel, I pause at one listing Everett's name. It's a video from a contest last year called Mammoth.

I click on the link and the video plays of an event called Combo. It starts at a scene labeled Round One. After Round One, I get the gist of the event. Paired together, Everett and Hendrik are to ride down a pattern full of rails and jumps. Round One and Two they both move as though this is an individual event. The commentators remark while their combo is still earning them adequate points for the final round, as they're not attempting to work together, they are not likely to land on the podium.

The third round starts. Everything is going smoothly like the first two rounds until Everett takes a rail and instead of moving on to a jump further down the line, Hendrik cuts to the jump adjacent to Everett. The camera pulls back, giving a wider view of the track. The railing ends just after the jump, and at this intersection, the trail narrows to make the area more technical.

My heart begins to beat faster. There's not a lot of room for both Hendrik and Everett to land there. Usually, Hendrik takes the jump further down the slope, so Everett can land cleanly. But he didn't this round. Hendrik's moving fast. He soars off the end of the jump, twisting in the air. Gravity begins to pull him back down just as Everett drops off the rail. I gasp.

Everett lands cleanly, but Hendrik is already there, coming down on him. Hendrik flails his arms as Everett attempts to twist away. But it's too late. Hendrik's board crashes into Everett's legs.

One of Everett's boots snap out of his binding. The other leg caught in his snowboard and Hendrik's equipment. Their momentum twists them further down the slope. I clap my hand over my mouth as Everett's free leg turns at an awkward angle at the knee.

I snap my laptop shut.

My stomach turns as the image flashes through my mind again. I shiver, gagging at the way his knee twisted.

This explains so much. I just wish I didn't have to find out so graphically.

Shaking my head, I mutter to myself, "Time to see this for myself."

I do my best work after observation, and only one place comes to mind for celebrity snowboarders: Blue Saloon.

Chapter 12

December Fowl

I t's past eleven by the time I slip out of the Uber at Blue Sky.

Gazing up, the mountains are silhouettes against the starry sky. They remind me of teeth. Like I'm in the mouth of a giant. The lights over the slopes are long out, the last run of the day well over. I approach the Blue Mountain gondola and ride up alone.

In the middle of the gondola pod, it sways slightly as it ascends the great mountain. There's not much to see in the dark – like floating into darkness.

Several minutes later, the gondola grinds to a halt at a well-lit platform. The operator behind the control desk barely looks up as I step out. Hesitating, I head to the exit, hoping there's a sign to show me the way. As I exit the gate, I step onto a shoveled path etched out of snow thigh-high, leading to the lodge. Blue string lights glisten from above. Zigzagging between staggered wooden beams. *Quaint*, I think as I wrap my jacket tighter around me. The cold grips me just hard enough to force me into a trot.

I pull the glass door of Blue Saloon open. The bar is a mix of tall four-to-eight-person tables with stools and bench seating. The walls are lined with booths. Snowflake-like lighting hangs from the ceiling above the private booths. Their glow is soft, only bright enough to cast vague features.

Torrance waves at me from behind the bar as I meander around. Her hair glows black and glossy blue. I wave back and weave between the tables and patrons. She meets me at an empty seat near the bar wells as I climb onto the stool.

"Hi chicka," She grins. "What can I buy you?"

"Vodka sprite and a water, please." She nods and gets to work.

I gaze around the bar, shrugging off my jacket. There are plenty of people here but no one I recognize as a prominent boarder. I turn my attention back to the bar and recognize someone across from me.

He's in a few of Everett's photos at the house, and in nearly all the few YouTube videos I've found of him. His blonde hair is all over the place. He notices me staring, and gives me a two-finger wave as though we might know each other, but just as quickly turns his attention back to the group of guys he's sitting with.

His name finally clicks in my head: Luc Orseno. Everett's best friend, by my account. He's ranked in the top ten worldwide and can apparently pop a *sick* front 720 nose-dive, whatever that is, and the industry has affectionately called it the Orseno since he is one of two snowboarders who can land the maneuver. Everett is the only other one. Apparently, the boys share more than a roof.

Torrance returns with my drink, leaning against her elbows on the bar top. Behind her, Luc's eyes trail her.

"So, which hottie are you thinking about taking home tonight? I can point you in the right direction."

I nearly choke on my drink. Torrance hands me an extra napkin, laughing, "Oh come on! You can't go on vacation. *Alone*. Without getting a little action."

"Speaking of action..." I nod in the direction of Luc.

Torrance swivels around. When she does, Luc nods, nipping his bottom lip between his teeth. Holy dimples galore. My first wave of butterflies since middle school. Torrance waves back but turns around and rolls her eyes.

"What!" I slap her hand. "He's cute."

"Been there. Done that. He's a nice guy, if you're into that."

I lean in, "Into nice guys? Who isn't?"

She shrugs, suddenly very interested in shining the counter with her towel, "Athletes who travel and never have time for you. Flakey commitment-phobes."

"He looks like he wants time with you now," I offer.

Torrance slaps the counter like it's done her wrong, "Yeah, when it's convenient for him. *Whatever*. I'm over it." She steadies herself and walks away. Very much *not* over it.

For the next hour I take in the atmosphere, sipping on one Vodka Sprite after another and watching as the people roll in and out. For the only bar on the mountain, I'm surprised to see most of them greet one another and nurse only a beer before leaving again. I'd expected this place to be a party hotbed. But by a quarter to one, the bar is empty and Torrance excuses all her other employees.

"Let me help you," I say, reaching for the stack of glassware in her hands.

She shifts it out of my reach, "December you are a guest. And you've already cleaned up my house. I'm beginning to think you're suggesting I'm terrible at cleaning up after myself."

I laugh, waving her off, "I told you – cleaning helps calm my nerves. Please. I'm renting a room for not even a third of what the hotel is charging. *And* you've let me borrow your winter clothing. I'd like to return even a bit of your kindness."

"I like things done here a particular way," she explains.

"Show me."

Torrance lets out a sigh but smiles. She shows me how she likes the glassware displayed and how to wash and place the condiments just so on the tables. She begrudgingly leaves for her office after five minutes straight of me begging her to leave it up to me.

Alone, I shut my eyes and take a deep breath. I let myself get lost in the busy work. My insecurities about being fired fade, but do not disappear. They hide in the shadows. There but slightly out of mind. I carry dirty glasses to the wash and return to the bar to wipe it down. Next, I lose time stacking the warm and washed glasses into the display as Torrance showed me, and almost lose my grasp on the last glass when she speaks.

"I lost track of time. Let's get out of here before we're stuck."

I laugh, but she doesn't, "Wait – we could be stranded up here?"

Torrance nods at the clock, reading five minutes to two, "The lift closes at two."

Tossing the rag in the wash bin, I wrestle with my jacket, and I make my way to the lift behind Torrance. The gondola ride down is silent. We both watch the darkness pass by, lost in our own heads. The drive to her house is different. My eyelids and brain feel too heavy for conversation, but I come clean. I tell Torrance about losing my job and coming up here to try to resuscitate it. She doesn't ask me questions just tells me she understands.

Back at the A-frame, I sit in bed and reopen the email my mom sent nearly a week ago when I'd jetted off to L.A:

Good morning Prospers,

December will not be joining us for the shopping extravaganza this year. She's headed to LA for an emergency meeting with a very special client. I mean, could she be any more of a legacy? Following in my footsteps to become a PR professional and (soon to be announced) the youngest Public Relations Officer at Delta, King, & Sally!

I could not be prouder.

xoxo—P.S. Cynthia, please do not bring Daphne. I know she fits into your handbag but two years in a row she's tinkled in the dressing rooms.

I read it over again. And again. Until it's permanently etched into my eyeballs.

Mom is so proud of me. The entire Prosper family is. They all know about the promotion and think I have it. I'm lucky I didn't tell my father about the potential promotion, or he likely would have told his entire side of the family, too. Maybe if I handle Everett's situation perfectly, they'll hire me back. Give me the promotion.

I pull open a web browser and the DKS website. It's like pushing on a bad bruise – it hurts to look, it hurts to think about, but I can't help myself. Their website flashes up. Orange and black, the potent brand color. There's a photo of all the Officers. There's Joseph Delta, Lionel King, and Meredith Sally. I imagine myself standing proudly next to Meredith as the Public Relations Officer. It's in my mind's eye for a second and then flickers out.

It won't ever happen.

Hot anger and shame rush through me. I snap my laptop shut. I will not let Lionel King win. I'll show Ryan fucking Dawson and King what I'm capable of; I'll make them regret firing me.

I feel so desperate, so lost, I grab my phone and pull up my contact list. My thumb hovers over the screen, ready to press my mother's smiling face. My stomach twists. I can't. I can't admit what happened. Where I am right now. What an utter failure I am. Prospers and Fowls do not fail. We exceed. The shame of failing my parents claws at my heart like a feral animal.

If I call either of my parents, I'll have to tell them. Dread gnaws at my gut. I can't. And another agency or a talent scout is out of the question – not after being fired from the best PR firm in the country. No one will hire me. Even if they considered it, I'd have to explain what happened, and I can't face the truth right now. I'm too ashamed. There's no way I'd survive discussing my firing in an interview. Not without breaking down in tears.

Swallowing the lump in my throat, I scroll to Suz's number.

"Oh my GOD!" She shouts, "I was about to send a search and rescue party."

I fall back into bed laughing, chest loosening a knot, "Suz, we've been texting practically all day."

"So? You're like five thousand miles away. *Alone*. And there could be bears, mountain lions, or mountain men. *Oh*, are there any hunky mountain men?"

"I'm not alone," I say mostly to convince myself as I look around this bare bedroom that is not my own. "There's my host Torrance. You would love her."

"Don't go becoming best friends and forget about me down here." There's a laugh in her voice, but I still catch a hint of fear.

"Suzie," I coo, "you'll always be my best friend. And I'm not sure about the hunky men. I haven't really been hunting for them."

"You're hunting for athletes, so they're probably all hunky."

I laugh, rolling my eyes. "How are things?" I ask and selfishly mean, how is DKS without me?

"Ahh...same as usual. It's lonely here without you. And Ryangottthepromotion. *SO*, when do you think you'll be coming home? Soon?"

My mouth goes dry, "Ryan is the new Officer?"

I can hear her wince, "I was hoping you didn't hear that. It's conditional. I don't know..." Suz continues but my brain is caught on Ryan Dawson having my promotion. I knew it would happen; I did. Once I was gone there was no one standing in his way. "December?"

"Mm? I'm still here." My voice sounds thick. I wipe at my wet cheeks, taking in a shuttering breath.

She's quiet for a moment, "I'm sorry. You don't deserve this."

I take a deep breath, my voice harder, "No, I wasn't performing to standards. I won't let it happen again."

"December–"

"I'm tired. Can you put Frankie on for night kisses?"

She sighs. There's a moment of silence and then, "He's here."

"Hi Frankie. Love you bunches! Make sure Auntie Suz is behaving. I miss you." I make kissy noises.

"Hey! Not fair! I always behave."

"Yeah right," I huff. "Goodnight, Suzie. Love you!"

She mutters 'I love you' back before I end the call and toss the phone to the other side of the bed. I crawl under the covers and stare at the dark ceiling. It's time to stop feeling like a victim. I wasn't performing, and they fired me. As hard of a pill it is to swallow, it's true. Like I told Suz, I won't let it happen again.

Just as I'm about to fall asleep there's a knock at my door. I crawl out of bed and open it to a grinning Torrance.

"I know how I can help you."

Chapter 13

Everett Abrams

Evil Publicist

> Meet me at Blue Saloon no later than 10:30 tonight.
> EP

> 10:30?! That's too late.

> I'm beginning to think you don't actually want $200,000.
> EP

> What does having a solid sleep schedule have to do with that?!

> Hello?? Fuck. You're going to ruin me.

Blue Saloon.

That's where I'm heading after a full day of riding and a grueling training session in the gym. I wish I could fall into bed and hibernate. December texted me this afternoon to meet her at the Blue Saloon, and ignored all the retaliation messages I sent. So, I go alone since Luc is still off dealing with his newest set of demons tonight.

I lean back in the seat of the gondola and close my eyes. The sway of the pod is enough to lull me to sleep. I force my eyes open and sit up, looking down at my phone. 10:30 on a Thursday night. I groan. It's nearly time for me to crash in bed and fall asleep to the tune of Netflix.

Thursday night is well night. And the worst night to visit the bar.

As I suspected, the place is swarming with people. I look around the crowd, making my way around the perimeter and then into the mouth of hell. *She better be worth this.*

I'm making my way to the bar when someone starts shouting my name. I don't recognize the voice, but I turn towards the call anyways. As I do, someone rams into me, chest to chest. Beer splashes down my back. I grit my teeth. *This* is why I hate this place at night.

"Everett!" The dude sings, taking a step back. His breath reeks of beer and his eyes are half-hooded. The parts I can see are red and dilated. The guy's toasted.

"Man, I was just telling my friends I hoped to see you here! You're never out, man." He waves his arm out, sloshing more beer on the floor and his shoes. He gazes down at the mess for a moment and then pushes me forward with his other arm, directing me to a table with his buddies.

"Yo! Dudes! Look who I ran into." He chuckles and slaps me on the back.

"Hey," I slap his back in return, maybe a little overly aggressive, but he doesn't seem to notice, and lifts a hand at his friends. They stare slack-jawed at me. "Good to meet you guys."

Finally, they seem to collect themselves. At least enough to start elbowing each other, giggling, and uttering 'dude' to one another.

"You guys here cruising the mountains?" I say to feel less like a *thing* people gawk at.

"Yeah, yeah, man. We've been here four days. Our last night. Some of the best runs in the world."

Now he's talking my language. Mountains and riding I can do. Being gawked at, not so much. I never know what to do with my hands. Or if they're looking at me like this because I walked out of my house with my face half-shaved. I run my hand along my jaw now, just to check.

"Did you guys go down Vixen?"

They laugh, clapping their hands together, "Yes! Yes! My favorite run. I think I did that one like all day." Says one guy from the middle of the table.

"Awesome! Mine too. That and Blue Moose." Their mouths drop open. I shrug, "Yeah it's an easy run but for half the trail you can see right down the valley. I never get used to it."

They nod, glancing at each other. Obviously, they didn't take the trail, but from the looks on their faces, they wish they had.

"Well, it was good to meet you guys. Hope you come back." I throw them a hang loose sign with my hand and continue through the crowd to the bar.

Jemina is handling drinks and cash like she has eight hands. She smiles at me when I approach, and signs for me to wait before she moves to the other side of the bar to help some guy waving a fifty dollar bill. I leapfrog onto a stool and drum my knuckles against the counter, glancing around the bar.

No steely green eyes anywhere in sight. December may be my only chance – no matter how far-fetched – at getting the required cash and she's nowhere in sight. I turn my attention back to the bar, noticing for the first time Jemina isn't alone.

I appraise the new girl, having a great view of her behind. Her hair is held in a high ponytail, strong shoulders sloping into an hourglass shape. And, I think as I draw my bottom lip between my teeth, her ass makes me want to rethink my no-women-during-the-season policy. How do women get their asses so big and round? As if my thought stirs her, she turns, and my eyes meet evergreen.

What the hell? I jerk back, making a face. What is December doing behind the bar? I run a hand down my face. And I was just caught shamelessly checking her out.

"Everett," Jemina hisses as she and December step towards me, whacking me with a dry hand towel. She glances at December and then back at me. "Were you just checking her out?"

I could murder her right now. Instead, I say dryly, "Never. You couldn't pay me to."

My eyes cut to December. She folds her arms over her chest, giving me a look, and Jemina swats me with the towel again. I don't know how I'm only now realizing how hot December is. Maybe because she's the devil in disguise.

Annoyed with myself I say, "Why did you want to meet here tonight? Is bartending part of your typical job?"

Jemina backs away slowly like she doesn't want to get caught in the crossfire.

"I am working, asshole."

"How exactly? And last time I checked, calling your client an asshole isn't very professional."

She rolls her eyes, letting out a huff, "I'm mingling. Getting to know your peers and the fans. You know, immersing myself since you told me I know nothing. And," December gives me the just-a-second finger and scoots out from behind the bar to stand next to me, "You're about to be tested."

"Tested?" I lean back. My pulse jumps. I glance around the bar to see what I could possibly be tested on.

"Yes. I have to make sure you're willing to cooperate. Reaching your goal is going to take a lot of effort on my part, and I need to make sure we're both in this one hundred percent."

Why is she always second guessing me? "I'm here, aren't I?"

"Which is a great sign. I'm happy you are, but I need to make sure you're truly willing to get out of your comfort zone."

"Slow down, speedy McQueen, I have a few non-negotiables for getting 'out of my comfort zone.'" She just looks at me with her deadly green eyes, waiting for me to continue. "Copper Mountain is next week. Drinking is on hiatus. As I said before, I'm not going to become a raging partier like Legrand."

She looks around the bar. Her eyes purposefully land on the several other professional snowboarders and skiers in the room. All with drinks in their hands.

I lean in and flick my fingers for her to come closer, "My secret to winning: no drinking."

December, still leaning in, points to the other side of the bar. "Over there, you'll find representatives from Watkins Liquor and Magic Energy. As an act of good faith that you're willing to be flexible, go over there and talk to them."

My stomach drops and I glance in the direction she's pointing. There are more people congregated over there than anywhere else in the bar, but through the crowd I spot boxes arranged to make a mock ice castle.

Worse, I spot Legrand in his token battered leather jacket followed by his regular posse of friends. My jaw clenches.

"If Legrand is working with them, I want nothing to do with it."

She gives me the same look she'd send an irrational toddler, "By that rationale you shouldn't even be snowboarding."

"I started first," I blurt, knowing I *am* using the rationale of a toddler, but my heart is racing. All I can think about is how much I don't want to go over there. The only way I know how to protect myself is to fight back.

"Everett," December pushes her hand into my shoulder, and I'm forced to meet her gaze. "I'll go with you. We're in this together, okay? I just want you to trust me."

"Trust you," I let out a laugh. "You have a funny way of showing it–I mean, putting me up to a te-test? What kind of fucked up reverse psychology is this December?"

My heart is in my throat. I brush prickling sweat from my upper lip. Glancing back over at the ice castle, my eyes search for the leather-wearing shithead, but Legrand seems to have disappeared. Even that is little comfort. The thought of going over to complete strangers and introducing myself–trying to sell myself? At the bottom of my stomach, lunch is starting to cause a scene, gurgling.

December squeezes my shoulder, ripping my attention away from my panic, "I'll introduce you. You just be a ray of sunshine."

"I've never been a ray of sunshine in my life," I grumble.

"Fake it 'til you make it, baby."

I huff and roll my eyes, but follow closely behind her. My frame towers above hers as we shift through the crowd, "Is your whole plan to run me through all the clichés until one sticks? I won't turn into one."

She twists around to look back at me, the corner of her mouth turned up, "I have big plans for you."

With the teasing tilt of her lips, *I have big plans for you* echoes through my brain.

An image flashes in my mind: me pressed over her, her legs draped over my shoulders, mouth opening into an O. The thought takes me by surprise and blood surges to my groin. My eyes drop to her lips and then back up to her eyes. She lifts a brow and I get the feeling she's asking me what I'm thinking.

God, what is wrong with me?

I look away, running a hand over my face. For the first time I'm annoyed by my own rules: no sex during the season. I was so distracted by the sheer amount of women approaching me my first season as a professional, it cost me. But here I am, imagining fucking this devil of a woman because I haven't allowed myself to touch or think about someone in a month.

December considers me for a moment longer before turning her attention to the ice castle as we approach.

"Scarlett," she calls out. A woman spins around. She's dressed in skin-tight jeans, and an oversized sweater tucked in at the front. Her hair is cut short – and immediately I am reminded of Taylor from *Point Break*. Red painted pouty lips. Full hips to cling to.

Oh my god, she's fucking gorgeous. The thought of December evaporates from my mind.

"December!" Scarlett pulls my publicist in for a hug, "I'm so happy we are in Blue Sky at the same time! That Legrand – he is a *charmer*." She laughs.

Fuck. I grit my teeth. Of course, Hen-fuck is sinking his teeth into her already.

"Well, I think you'll like my client Everett even more," December turns and places a hand on my shoulder, forcing me into the spotlight.

Scarlett's face lights up and, for the first time since December suggested we approach the talent scouts, my stomach does something other than want to explode – it flutters. A rope falls from the sky, and I take it.

"Hey," I lift a finger. "I'm Everett."

"Everett," she reaches out and grips my hand. "It's so nice to meet you. I would love for you to try our new black cherry flavored gin."

"I don't actually drink during the season."

"Oooh," she says, her eyes flash to December. And then dart around the room.

December jabs her elbow into my back.

I grit my teeth and glare at her, resisting the urge to growl. I want to say: *this is why I don't put myself out there.*

"I think what Everett *means*," December cuts in, "is that he doesn't *typically* drink alcohol during the season. You know, drinking responsibly."

"Oh. Oooh," Scarlett says again, this time tilting her head and looking me up and down. "You know, we are partnering with Magic Energy for a campaign about responsible drinking."

December lets out a little tut, but I roll my eyes. As if she didn't already know. She's got schemes on schemes.

"Everett would be perfect! He's all about setting a good example and being responsible."

"Great! I'll be right back with a couple of samples of Magic and then we'll chat."

Scarlett slips away and I take the opportunity to give December a look, "I'm all about setting a good example and being responsible?"

She turns to face me head-on, sighing, "If you're unhappy with my summarization, please clarify your personal brand. Because I'm pretty sure I'm spot on."

This time I do growl at her. She returns a smug grin. December's not wrong. Being a good example and responsible is exactly what I'm about. But the way she said it made me feel so...unsexy. Like I'm dull and a drag.

"Did you have to say it like that though?"

She narrows her eyes, shaking her head, "Like what?"

December tilts her head and stares at me. Her mouth says she's amused but her eyes tell a different story. The bar's colored bulbs cast her in a blue hue. In the light of day, she's a green-eyed lynx with her rosy cheeks and red lips. Ready to pounce the second she senses weakness. Here, she's muted. Giving the illusion I can speak – and really look at her – without the risk of being mauled.

"You said it like being those things are..." I lick my bottom lip, my brain spinning for a moment searching for the right word. "Beastly."

She throws a face, crossing her arms over her chest, "Beastly?"

I get a sinking feeling I used the wrong word. The way she narrows her eyes. Turns her head to the side to look at me in a way that'll make it make sense.

"I'm not sure you understand the definition of the word." My blood chills. My chest tightens. And it's like I'm being sucked back through time to middle school.

Then she says, "Beastly would be *that*."

She points over my shoulder, and I shift to take a look. Hendrik, a few tables away, licks tequila from a chick's navel. The bar roars with laughter and cheers. I make a face and turn away.

"Whatever. I meant unsexy."

I look away, but her eyes linger on me. I shift from foot to foot, trying to catch a glimpse of Scarlett to distract December's attention. *What does she see?*

A moment passes and her gaze hasn't left me. My eyes dart to hers. She narrows them and I narrow mine back. She crosses her arms, and I follow with mine. Her mouth opens to speak when Scarlett appears.

"So, here is the Black Cherry flavor," Scarlett hands a small glass to December, filled with a dark liquid laced with red. "And my favorite – strawberry banana." She hands this one to me, smiling.

I raise it to my lips and sip, coaching myself not to gag. Sweet strawberry with an aftertaste of banana. "Hmm," I say pulling the glass away and glancing at it.

Scarlett's smiling "Good huh?"

"Better than I thought."

"The black cherry is amazing!" December says before knocking back the rest of her glass.

"I though you looked like a cherry lover," Scarlett laughs.

"I knew there was a reason I liked you. Now tell us about this new campaign you're working on."

Scarlett dives into it, December nodding along, and I try to pay attention. But my mind wanders. I wonder how they know each other. Was it college? Or is this one of those strange frenemies situations I've seen on TV?

I take another sip of the strawberry banana. I wish more energy drinks tasted this way. I wonder if we could make sports drinks for Elevate? I'd want it to taste like this, but also be good for you.

December places her hand over her heart and my brain takes it as my cue to zone back in.

"–Lett, this is inspiring. Everett would bring so much to the project."

They turn to me. Scarlett's eyes glowing like talking to December was kerosene to her spark. My eyes dart to December. She has the same excited, glow-from-within radiance. And they're looking at me like they're expecting me to stoke the fire. But I don't even know where the woodpile is.

"Uh," I shift my weight from foot to foot. My eyes dart from my publicist to Scarlett's. Down into my empty glass, "Do you think we could make healthy sports drinks out of this?"

Their heads snap to face each other again.

"He's perfect." Scarlett says matter-of-factly.

My shoulders release and with them a breath.

December tilts her head and looks me up and down, "He's a work in progress."

"Men. Aren't they all?"

The air splits with their laughter. I look away, rolling my eyes, and spot a trash can. Stepping away, I toss my glass, needing a second to myself. I roll my shoulder blades back and around, breaking the place I've always held tension. If it wasn't already so late, I'd want to go home and do some yoga to work out all these tension kinks, but all I have time to do tonight is climb into bed.

When I turn around, December is stepping my way, an echo of a smile still on her lips. I glance over her shoulder and find Scarlett deep in conversation with someone else.

I toss my head back, "Thank god." Shoulders slouching, "It's over."

"All right, Total Drama, good job. You can go home now."

"I bet this is how the genie felt when Aladdin finally released him."

She cracks a smile, shaking her head, "I'll see you tomorrow. We have lots to do."

I sigh, running a hand through my hair, "This feels much too much like schoolwork. Hard, uncomfortable, unwelcome, and never-ending."

She looks at me sideways as we make our way out of the packed bar, but thankfully doesn't say anything. Pushing open the door, the cold air bites at my lungs as a puff of white breath escapes my mouth. Even without the wind, this late, Blue Mountain's frigid air nearly sucks my soul out.

December wraps her arms around herself and trots down the path to the gondola. I glance at my phone as I meander my way there. Nearly midnight.

The gondola lift buzzes and creaks, the thick metal wires vibrating hard from the cold as they pull the floating cubbies up the mountainside. Lucky for us, a pod just swings around the loop and rests at the landing pad, swaying slightly.

Following December, I take a seat in the heated booth. I blow out a breath, eyes on the floor. I am so ready to be in my bed. I want to ask her what this test was about. If I passed. What work we have to do tomorrow, but I'm too tired. Tonight, I'd rather throw myself into a piranha tank then spend another second listening to her strategy.

I look up. Her eyes are on me. I stare back for a beat then break away. Her gaze is too focused, too assessing to hold.

The way she's looking at me has my stomach knotting – like she's hell-bent on ripping off my mask and revealing all of me.

Chapter 14

December Fowl

I stand shivering at Everett's front door at 6:30 the next morning. I hunch my shoulders up to my ears, dipping my head into the collar of my coat. I pull at my hat, but it's already pulled as far as it can. My teeth chatter and I stomp my feet on the step, wiggling my body to keep warm. I shove my finger into the doorbell again.

"Come on. Come on."

At last, the door swings open. Everett stands in the doorway, his black hair tousled. He squints at me, dressed in a white t-shirt with a drawing of French fries. The shirt is hitched halfway up his side. My eyes instantly latch onto his bare skin – the V taper of his hips and the muscles cutting up his obliques. My mouth goes dry.

"If you want to stay outside, don't ring the doorbell like a maniac," He pulls at his shirt. It falls all the way down and I can think again.

Ignoring him, I step inside. He mumbles about it being too early, rubbing at the corners of his eyes as he turns into the kitchen and starts the coffee machine. Once he's finished, he leans against the counter, crossing his ankles and folding his arms across his chest so his biceps bulge, and glares at me. I pull my bag from my shoulder and set up camp at the breakfast nook.

"I'm trying to fit into your schedule. You said you ride in the morning, so I'm here before. And, I did tell you I'd see you in the morning."

"I didn't know you meant *this* early." His voice is thick and slow from sleep. If he wasn't so annoying, it might be a bit sexy. He stares me down from across the room.

"We have a lot of work to do." I say, sounding like a broken record.

He just swallows, and I'm drawn to the thick lines of his neck and the way it dips. I just want to wrap my hands around his neck and...

I shake the thought from my mind and power up my laptop, opening his client portfolio. After the bar last night, I spent the early morning compiling all the research I had. Everett was willing to meet one recruiter last night but, he's going to need to do a lot more if he's ever going to reach his full financial potential. I now have compelling evidence to convince him he can't continue to be a hermit.

I pull out two calendars, some pens, and highlighters from my bag. We're going to make a schedule and he's going to stick to it.

Everett wanders towards the counter. Reaching out, he turns the chair beside me around and straddles the back.

"This is going to be a quick-fire class. How to Sell Yourself 101: The Master-class."

Everett dips his head, meeting my gaze. The darkest eyes I've ever seen. Like black holes.

"Sell myself?"

"Yes. The fact that you still have any sponsors is a true testament of your riding ability."

"Thanks," He grins, straightening.

"That wasn't a compliment." His forehead scrunches and I explain, "You're the best snowboarder in the world but you have zero social media presence. Zero fan interaction. I mean, *literally*, your sponsors have signed you for your name alone. But that's not going to be enough. Three of your sponsors have dropped and we're coming into an Olympic year. That's not good."

"I'm aware."

"I don't mean to offend you–"

"Oh, you don't?" His dark eyes are cutting. "Didn't you just make a promise not to throw shit in my face?"

I take a breath, backpedaling. He's right. I can't seem to stop knocking him down a peg while at the same time trying to build trust. I'm working against myself. It's like I'm trying to show him he's not perfect. So, we can be on the same playing field.

Except, this isn't about me. It's about *Everett*. He wants to make a ton of money, quickly. That's my job. It's not fair to tear him to shreds so I feel better about myself. Destroying my client's confidence is the last thing I want to do. *So why do I keep doing it?*

"Okay," I take a breath and twist my chair around to face him, "Let's start fresh. You want two hundred thousand dollars. We can't get there with what you're doing now. Your brand needs a facelift."

He throws me a skeptical look as he moves to the flashing coffee maker for some brain juice. He pours me a cup, too, and walks it over to me, straddling his seat again. After I take a sip, purposely *not* staring at the fine dark hair of his muscly thighs, I pull my calendar front and center.

I mark a giant green X on today's date and flip to January 8th and mark it with a red X.

"Today, we start by setting up Instagram, YouTube, and TikTok. We'll branch to other platforms later if we need it, but this is where your fans are thirsty for content."

When I look up, Everett is staring. His intensity takes my breath away. Dammit why does he have to be so good looking and heated about everything? If he looked at me like this for any reason other than hating me, I'd probably combust with the amount of sexual *something* in my nether regions.

I squirm uncomfortably in my seat and continue, "I thought today we'd start with an Ask Me Anything on your Insta-story and then we'll spend tomorrow answering as many as we can. On YouTube and TikTok, we should go with fresh content. We could wait until after your AMA to see what people are interested in. Do you have anyone who can film you?"

Everett shakes his head, his jaw clenches. If I thought he had a dark look on before, it's nothing compared to the way he's staring at me now.

"What?" I burst, throwing my arms out.

A vein in his neck pops beneath his skin, "Posting every day? I don't have enough shit to say. People are going to get bored. And an Ask Me Anything? Luc did that and ten people responded. I'm not about to put myself out there and then be embarrassed when no one cares!"

He shoves his chair back and marches into the kitchen. I sit there a moment, processing. My chest squeezes with how...*honest* he was with his concerns. Everett Abrams can be vulnerable and self-conscious – *and* he's not afraid to share them with me? Who would have thought?

I gulp, *Lord have mercy*. I've never had a client be so forthcoming, let alone a man in any of my relationships – professional or personal. I have to be careful, or I'll start feeling guiltier for not being as truthful as he is.

Too late. I squeeze my eyes shut as guilt and shame gnaw at my stomach. I take a deep breath, pushing those feelings away, and follow Everett to the kitchen.

"Hey," I say pressing a hand on his shoulder. "Lots of people are going to respond to you. And if they don't, I'll ask a million questions, so it looks like a lot of people have." Everett's mouth twitches and my stomach zaps with something unlike guilt or shame. "No one's going to know the difference. No one needs to know. I've got you."

I pat his shoulder. Then squeeze it. Not at all relishing the ridges of his very hard, very muscly shoulder beneath his shirt. The small lift of his mouth shifts into something else. Something that says I'm feeling him up and he knows it.

I take a step back, wiping my hand on my jeans, "I won't expose anything you don't want me to."

I try, very hard, not to glance down at his athletic shorts when I say *expose*. Instead, Everett's eyes dart to my breasts and linger. A trill of hot surprise shoots through me. Usually, I'd toss a glass of champagne at a client for looking, but I'm delighted not to be the only one aware of each other.

"So," I flounce back to the breakfast bar. I stop when I notice myself doing it. "Do you think Luc could film you?"

"No," I can hear his head shaking, "but Haylee probably could."

Haylee. No doubt the beautiful smiley woman who was leaving just as I arrived the first day. The woman he was comfortably nearly naked with.

I can't help but feel a knot of *something* in my chest. The only other time I've felt jealous over a client was when Sawyer invited her agent Melinda to the Teen Choice Awards instead of me. I complain about doing too much for my clients, but the second I'm not their top choice, I'm upset.

Before I can stop myself, I'm talking, "I'll do it."

A grin splits across his face. It's like seeing the sun after days of darkness.

He lifts his brows, amused, "You snowboard?"

"No. I ski."

I haven't skied in years, but I'm sure it's like riding a bike. Once I'm buckled into the bindings, I'll remember exactly what to do.

"The shoe fits," he says, looking me up and down.

And I'm reminded of the loathsome rivalry between skiers and snowboarders. I don't want him to think about that and associate it with me. I'm not elitist. I don't, and wouldn't, look down on him.

"Copper Mountain is this weekend. If you're certain you can do it, let's get the video done this morning and then tonight we'll get Insta-whatever set up."

"So, you'll do it?" Excitement drums in my chest. "You're not going to fight me on this?"

Everett eyes me and then squints out the window at the mountains, "I'll trust you... For now."

Oooh. He trusts me? And I'm lying to him. I'm garbage. I don't deserve him as a client, and yet I know I can set this right by getting him what he wants – or as close to it as possible.

I shuffle my things into my bag. I wish I could bury this guilt deep down in there, too. But it keeps rising to the surface.

"Get your stuff and change. I'll meet you at the Thunderhead."

I look down at myself. *Get my stuff, change, meet at the Thunderhead?* "Isn't what I'm wearing good enough? I'll get boots and skis at the rental. I'd rather just go with you. I don't know what Thunderhead is."

Everett pauses. He backs up and gestures at me and my winter clothing at the door, "You'll need better gear then that. Didn't you say you ski?"

I glare at him. I guess my jacket is more business coat then snow coat, and my mittens only keep me warm if they're stuffed deep inside my pockets. But I don't have anything else, and I don't want to waste the money to buy any.

"I'll see if I can borrow Torrance's."

Everett blanches, "Torrance. Torrance Velasco?"

"Yeah. I'm renting out a room at her place. Why?"

"You know Torrance Velasco?"

I hesitate, studying his surprised, almost horrified expression. I get the feeling he'd have the same reaction if I told him I know the Boogeyman. Then I begin to piece it together: Luc is his best friend. Luc and Torrance obviously had a turbulent relationship, and an even worse breakup. Maybe Everett's taken sides and vowed not to associate with her?

The only question is: since Torrance and I have become friendly, will she expect the same loyalty from me?

Chapter 15

Everett Abrams

December is rooming with Luc's ex.

Which would be whatever, but we've been friends for the past six years. She knows just about everything about me. Including my plans for Elevate, and my...*challenges*.

My heart is in my throat. Breath coming on a little too fast.

Once I jumped into snowboarding full-time, it's like I jumped into a whole new life. No one knows I was in special education classes, had my tests read, or the reading ability of a ninth grader when I was a senior.

I started fresh as Everett Abrams, professional snowboarder. I've been called stoic, focused, great; instead of scatter-brained, disorganized, bad.

What if it's all going to be blown open again?

I don't want December to know, and yet she's staying with the person who could give her all the arsenal she would ever need. December wants to do something drastic, and there's nothing people love more than a rags to riches story, and that's exactly what mine would be.

I grip the steering wheel tightly as we roll to a stop at the foot of the hill. Instead of heading off to Torrance's, I pull to the left towards Blue Sky and Blue Mountain. I gave December a pair of snow pants in the house lost-and-found. It's really just a dumping ground for all the things Luc's girlfriends have forgotten.

"You sure you don't want to buy any clothes now? You can use my discount at the outfitters. I also have a discount for the lodge, if you're looking for your own place"

"They're all booked up. And probably would've been way too expensive anyways."

I chance a glance at her, "What do you mean? Isn't the agency paying for you to be here?"

She winces. Is this part of the personal problem she mentioned the other day? Maybe she's in debt over her head, but I glance at her Prada bag, and reconsider.

"I...there's..." she messes with her gloves, her bag, anything to avoid looking at me.

I sense there's more going on, but what could it be? I comb through my mind, recalling previous conversations. Nothing she's said before has thrown up a red flag.

I pull into a parking spot near the back of Blue Mountain Resort. The lot is nearly empty this early, but I like to walk. The view makes it more than worth it.

Beside me, December is quiet. Gaping at the mountain. She's like a kid staring up at something monstrous. I huff a laugh, shake my head as I climb out, and gather my things from the back of the truck. We walk to the lodge in silence, our feet crunching across the snow.

I show her to the rental station and point her to the Thunderhead. The ski lift that will carry us up the mountain. We agree to meet there and head up together. She doesn't ask me to wait for her and I'm glad. My first morning ride is always alone. It feels weird – not exactly wrong.

December is struggling to climb the small incline to the lift. She flails around like a puppy trying to run on ice – poles and skis all over the place. It's such a disaster, I can't look away. Finally, she unlocks her bindings and climbs to where I'm waiting.

"I thought you said you could ski?"

"Shut...It." She pants, buckling herself in again. She takes a breath and slides forward like I'm the delay, "Let's go."

I glide along beside her into line, inching forward each time a new chair swings around. Beside me, December takes a deep breath and then puffs it out. Deep breath, puff out. I slant my eyes in her direction. She's braced on her poles like Lyndsey Vonn about to jump down the mountain. *Or* a rusty skier about to have a panic attack.

"You don't have to do this. Haylee would be more than happy to help," I offer, staring ahead.

"Why? You don't think I can?"

"I think you *can*, I'm just not sure you *should*. When's the last time you were on a mountain?"

I peek down at her. She's staring up at me, open mouthed. My spare dark goggles and hat cover half of her face, but I'm sure she's burning a hole through my skull with her eyes.

"A while ago," December admits, glancing at the two people in front of us. They're all that separates us from traveling up the mountain to no return.

"Maybe you should practice on the bunny hill first," I nod towards a hill to the right.

She looks in that direction and scoffs. Only kids are going up and down.

"Come on," I nudge her with my elbow, feeling a little panicky myself as the chair arrives to pick up the people in front of us. "A broken ego is better than a broken neck."

"All right, fine!" She jerks herself out of line and slides towards the bunny run.

Rolling my eyes, I catch up with her. She fumbles to position her poles in one hand and holding the pull rope in the other. She can't seem to get comfortable and keeps gripping them in different places, switching hands. I notice her goggles are fogged up; she's breathing hard.

"December. Let's take a breath." I take the poles from her hands. She looks up at me, her lenses all clouded. I pull my goggles off and hand them to her.

"I'm really embarrassed."

Her admission makes me smile. I think it's the first thing she's said that hasn't been fully processed, vetted, and approved.

"Don't be," my mouth quirks, "the mountain air makes everyone breathe hard."

Sheepishly, she takes my goggles and hands me hers in exchange.

"Now get good, fast. Who else is going to film me before the weekend?"

"*Haylee.*" She says with a bitter twist to her words.

She twists in my direction just as the pull rope jerks forward. I cringe. For a second, she wobbles on her skis but manages to find her balance. I crackle with laughter and pull out my phone. This is too good to pass up.

There are kids under the age of ten everywhere and here comes December, twenty-something and shakier than all of them. Her first ski ride down, she's stiff. Her skis permanently in snowplow position. By the sixth time, she's more confident, sliding most of the way down with her blades straight. She's beaming by the time she drifts to a stop before me.

"Cute."

"What?" She jerks at my words. Smile faltering.

"It's adorable how quickly you've caught up with all the other third graders."

"Shut up," December reaches out to shove me.

She tilts a little too far, too fast. She gasps just as she begins to fall. Her shoulder drops into my sternum hard, knocking the wind out of me, so I can't catch her. We end up a pile in the snow. A knot of skis and poles. By the time I catch my breath, she's already trying to tug herself free.

Of course, being an amateur skier and panicked, she fumbles around, twisting my board and her skis further.

"Hold on. I'll just–"

The pole she has propped up to push herself gives way. She falls face first towards the snow. Her hand shoots out to catch herself and heels me in the groin. I see stars. Shocks of pain lightning through me. I fold into myself with a groan.

"Oh my god. Oh my god, Everett, I'm so sorry!"

I manage to wrench away. Rolling to my side where my hot, aching front can get some cool relief. December kicks her bindings lose and grips my coat. She repeats over and over how sorry she is.

A moment later, an eternity, I push myself onto my knees and push out a breath. By now a small crowd has gathered. *Great.* A few of them have their phones raised. Someone must have told someone, who told someone Everett Abrams was on the bunny hill.

"Everett, I'm so–"

"Sorry. I know."

Her cheeks are pink. She hands me my goggles looking away, not knowing what else to do. I dangle them around my arm. My board is a reach away. I grab it and get to my feet, trying not to pull a face for the crowd. December scrambles around to pick up her things. I reach down for one of her poles.

"I'll see you later," I offer as I pass her the tool.

I have to get away from her. She doesn't try to stop me or offer another apology as I step away.

This was not how I wanted to start the season or bring in my new 'presence' on social media. By the end of the day, this will be all over the internet.

Chapter 16

December Fowl

"What is with *you*?" Jemina smiles as I slump face-first into the bar.

Her smile is an unwelcome ray of light in my shit mood. All I want to do is crawl into my bed back in Atlanta and forget I exist. Today was okay. Until I let my weird competitive jealously get in the way.

I got this pinch in my chest the moment he suggested someone else would help him. Like I'm not good enough or incapable of doing it – which he wasn't saying at all. My firing has fucked with me in more than one way. I beat my hands into the bar. I have a bad case of Imposter Syndrome.

"Hey," Jemina holds my hands down until I look at her. "Don't take it out on the wood."

On the wood. I squeeze my eyes shut and cringe, "Like I took it out on Everett's wood this morning, and not even in a fun way."

"What?" Jemina's jaw drops. "You did *what* with Everett's wood?"

I pull my hand away, wishing I hadn't said anything. I don't want even one more person sharing in my embarrassment, "I went skiing with him and sort of...punched him."

She puts her hand up, "You punched him...in the goods?"

I nod slowly and she slaps her hand over her mouth, muffling a squeal. A couple people at the bar look in our direction.

"Wait," she says, her eyes narrowing as she pulls her hand away. "How do you know him?"

I fill her in on the details. Leaving out the part about being fired, and information about sponsors dropping Everett. I give her enough to make her feel informed, but without spilling everything. Like how he has eight very defined abdominal muscles and a smile that could melt polar ice caps.

I make a face when I've finished explaining. It's frightening how good I am at selectively leaving things out. I supposed I have been practicing the last four years with my clients. Half-truths and white lies are standard in the biz. Still, I like Jemina. I don't want to lie to her, but here I am.

"So, how big is his dick?"

"What? No!"

She leans in, lowering her voice, "A friend of a friend said it's *big*. Rocked her world, but then he never called again. Snowboarders. Everett's a really good guy, so it surprised me." She rolls her eyes.

"You know, *know* him?" Everyone around here knows of Everett, but the way she says it implies more than him being a local celebrity.

"Yeah. I grew up here. Stay long enough and you'll know everyone, too." She fetches a group another round of beers and continues when she returns. "Mostly, I hang out with Luc. Everett doesn't get out much."

"Torrance is okay with you being friendly with her ex?"

The grin returns to her face, "I'm not sucking his dick or anything. We're friends not 'friendly.' And Torrance is totally chill about it. But, it's about to get busy here. I'd find myself a booth to work in if that's what you're here for."

True to her word, in a matter of an hour the stools around the bar are filled. Parties take advantage of the tables and booths, flashing twenty-dollar bills for faster service. I watch as the tip jar, bolted onto the counter, fills. Dollar signs roll in my eyes, and for a heart-rushing second, I think about asking Torrance to let me bartend. But, I slump, gazing back down at my computer screen. Bartending would only be a temporary solution. A Band-Aid for a gaping wound. I have to focus all my energy on Everett if I want to claw my way out of this hole.

I stick an earbud in and click on a docuseries called *Boys of Winter* with over ten million views.

"Yeaah man anyone who's anyone is here," slurs a guy with no shirt, waving his arm behind him and Vanna White-ing the massive house party.

The camera man pans across the crowd and then transitions to a curvy woman outside behind a bar. She's dressed in a bikini top paired with snowpants and goggles on her forehead, but her blond curly hair makes her unmistakable. My eyes flash to Jemina and then back down to the screen.

"I wouldn't say alcohol companies sponsor the parties. But they show up and pay me and other bartenders a bonus to serve their drinks."

A voice from behind the camera says, "And you wouldn't call that sponsoring?"

Jemina laughs, "The parties are going to happen with or without their participation. Like I said, they just pay me a little extra if I push their products. There's a recruiter – you should talk to him."

The camera twists to catch a tall man in jeans and a Watkins Liquor t-shirt.

"You work for Watkins Liquor?"

He nods, taking in the camera, "That's right."

"And what do you do?"

"I'm a talent scout," the man glances around the snow-covered patio as if he's hunting right now before focusing on the camera again. "These events are good ways to meet people."

"And push your drink?"

He laughs, a rich, crisp sound, "No. Sure, if I vibe with someone I might ask them to try the product, but I'm definitely not pushing anything."

"Why do you scout for talent at parties? Wouldn't competition be better?"

He shrugs, "I do that, too. But in this setting, everyone's looser. On contest days, professionals are usually hyper-focused and not as open to in talking partnership. Plus, I can get a better understanding of their character here rather than contests. And the age-old marketing law: be where your customers are. This happens to be where part of our clients are."

I pause the video and rub my eyes.

If Everett wants to meet his goal, I need to get him to parties. And talking. The other night he was practically mute when we met with Scarlett. Silence is certainly not going to get him two hundred thousand.

Taking out my headphone, I glance outside. The dark has set in and the outdoor string lights glow like a faux sun. The crowd grows louder all of a sudden, and splits to allow a group through the masses. People whip their phones out, sharing excited expressions. The one leading the pack stops to take a selfie and over the camera, his eyes connect with mine.

I don't want it to, but my heart stutters as Hendrik Legrand steps towards my booth.

"Aye," He sings. A crooked smile splitting across his face. "You're the chick from the video."

I shake my head, "No. You've got the wrong person."

"Yeah, yeah." He nods enthusiastically, pulling out his phone, and a video on his screen.

As it begins to play, my stomach tightens – I relive the moment from this morning. I watch as I trip, tumble into Everett, and we both sprawl into the snow. I'm like an Octopus with eight appendages and no idea how to use them. A moment later my fist, into his groin. Everett folds into himself and rolls away.

My face burns, "Oh god. I'm gonna be sick."

Hendrik taps on another video. He chuckles, "This one's my favorite."

This one is worse.

Set on repeat with weird stickers and pop-up images, it's like a gif of me punching Everett repeatedly in the nuts.

Watching the video, I feel like I've just taken a toy permanently away from a puppy. It hurts. Hendrik and his entourage laugh, watching it again and again. This is what his peers are watching, and if they've seen it, fans have, too. Publicity is what I wanted for him. What he's paying me for. But not this kind.

I was supposed to be proving myself. I was supposed to be impressing him with my mad PR skills. Instead, I made him into a bad gif.

He hates me. He has to. In my mind, I see him hurrying away from me a moment after he handed me my ski pole. I just fist bumped his dick and he still helped me pick myself up. And these guys – maybe the whole fucking world – are just laughing at him.

"That's enough!" I throw myself towards Hendrik, nearly toppling my beer in the process, but manage to catch it and snatch his phone away.

Hendrik doesn't demand his phone back. Instead, he slides into the bench opposite me, "What's your deal with Everett?"

"I'm his publicist."

"He could use it, but I can't help but notice you also work out of a bar?" I know exactly what he's insinuating: either I'm not good at it, or Everett is a bad client.

I dangle his phone over my glass of beer, "Say something like that again and you'll be needing a new one of these."

Hendrik laughs. There's a line around his mouth, his eyes alight and, all of a sudden, I understand why everyone in this place is obsessed with him. He's uninhibited to Everett's crippling self-consciousness.

Unconcerned with his phone he says, "There's this party tonight. You should come. It's gonna be massive."

He motions for his phone, "Let me get your number."

I hesitate. I know Everett hates him and I'm not exactly his biggest fan right now either, but it's *Hendrik Legrand*. Can I really pass up connecting with the hottest star in snowboarding? Besides, after the punching incident Everett really needs some good things to happen. This could be it. An invite to Hendrik's party could start something.

I pass him his phone. A moment after I recite my phone number, a shadow falls across our booth. I meet Everett's hard, dark eyes. He glances at Hendrik and the muscles in his jaw strain.

"Yo!" Hendrik flicks his head in greeting like they're old friends. He waves his hand in front of his own lower, frontal area, "How's the groin? Hopefully you haven't lost too many potential children."

"I'm confident I still have more swimmers than you do brain cells. Now run along so the adults can have a conversation." Everett motions between him and I.

Hendrik's face falls. He turns back to me, "I'll see you later."

A dark look passes across Everett's face. I can see him straining not to bark at me. Finally, he says, "Let's talk."

I nod at the newly vacant seat across from me. Everett stares at the spot like he's wishing he could set it on fire. Instead, he motions for me to scoot over and I do, not wanting to push him further away. Everett slides in beside me. He's so close there seems to be a heat rolling off him. But yet so far away, it's cold heat. Like setting my hair dryer to chilled air.

His eyes fall to mine and I jump right in, "I promise this was not at all what I meant by getting you more publicity. My hand slipped. Total accident."

"Next time I'll be prepared and bring a helmet for my boys."

"I think Haylee should help you with that. Or Luc. I'm a little...traumatized."

"*You're* traumatized?" He throws his head back and laughs.

For a moment my heart catches – and I watch him as if time is in a vat of molasses. Slowed down and rich. This is not how I'd imagined Everett to laugh. In fact, I've never imagined him genuinely laughing. Have I seen him laughing madly as he fires me? In my mind, yes. Absolutely. Almost every day since I've arrived.

But not this. Not this free Everett where his throat is bouncy, his eyes but cat slivers, and lips turned up and wide as chortles escape from his chest. And there's a sudden longing in my own heart to take a picture of this. To remember this version of him when I feel like quitting on him. To remind myself behind this stoic, nonchalant wall is a man with big dreams and gooey insides. And I just want to share it with the world.

"Unless you have a hot date with Hendrik, we should get my accounts set up. Do that whole social media thing."

"You still want to do this?" With me?

He narrows his eyes, "Why are you so surprised? I love riding all day, every day. I'd like to continue doing that. Whatever it takes."

I grin, "Whatever it takes, huh?"

His mouth stays even, but he rolls his dark eyes, "Within reason."

Chapter 17

DECEMBER FOWL

Hendrik Legrand

Hey this is Hendrik!

Party @ 101 Neering Street, Blue Sky. BYOB: bring your own babe ;)

I stare up at the glowing three-story chalet as Torrance drives me up to the gated entrance. So, this is what being part of the inner circle of snowboarding looks like.

"Have fun," Torrance sings like a mother hen letting her first hatchling out into the wild.

I wave to her as I get out. I make my way up the paved, snow-cleared drive, trees lining the road. It's peaceful except for the thumping beat radiating out of the chalet.

I squeeze through the front door. People are everywhere. I thought it was loud outside but the bass is turned up so high the floor shakes. I crane my neck, trying to catch sight of Everett. He texted a few minutes ago that he was here but I don't see him anywhere.

"He better not have left," I mutter.

"Who?" Someone shouts right into my ear.

I scoot away, hunching my shoulder so they won't do it again. Hendrick Legrand – Mr. Playboy, worth about one million in sponsorship deals. And owner of this massive house. I'm happy he followed through with the invite but I was not expecting *this*.

"No one." I shout back.

He nods, not caring either way. He takes a sip of his drink, gazing over my head, and then, as if remembering his manners asks me if I'd like a drink. I shake my head and as he gets distracted by a girl in a bikini I slip away.

I step down into the living room area. There's a giant screen TV and U-shaped couch packed with people. They all scream as their game of Mario Cart comes to an end. I spot Everett.

He's leaning against the wall, hands in his pockets, eyes roaming the crowd. Something about him standing there alone and stoic, mouth pressed into a line, dark scruff along the edges of his face takes my breath away. Around him is chaos: shouting, thundering music, topless women and none of it has any effect on him. He could be waiting for the tram in New York City and he'd look no different.

I tear my eyes away. Jemina is in the room over, waving for me to join her. I do just to get my mind fixed on something else before approaching him. Jemina looks even more beautiful than she did at the bar: crimped curly hair, loose sweater and yoga pants that hug her in all the right places. Luc is here too, playing a game of beer pong with Jemina against two guys I don't know. He smiles and throws me the usual wave as I approach.

"Girl you're looking fresh!" Jemina coos, checking me out. I glance down at my dark Calvin Kline jeans and Torrance's borrowed snow boots feeling wildly overdressed compared to her. *And* the bikini-clad women sauntering around.

"I wish I would have dressed like you. You look so comfy."

Jemina waves me off and hangs on Luc's arm, "I never stay at these things long. My buddy here just needed some TLC after being rejected for–" Luc nudges her and she zips her lips as if remembering she's been sworn to secrecy. Luc hands her the pong ball and she steps toward the table for her shot.

"What's up with Everett?" I call.

Luc shrugs, "What's wrong with him?"

"Nothing it's just...He's not talking to anyone."

"That's just who he is. The tall and silent type." Luc says as if this oh-so common knowledge.

Jemina swooshes the ball into an island cup and Luc erupts, lifting her into a bearhug and twirling her around.

I retreat into the living room. Everett hasn't moved. Only his eyes. They're on the group playing Mario and then move lazily to me. I weave through the crowd towards him, his eyes on me always.

"Hey," I swing around so I'm leaning against the wall next to him.

"Hey."

I take a glance around the room; see what he sees, and I know why he took his place here. He has perfect sight of every room. The doorway I came in, the kitchen where Hendrick shouted into my ear; the living room and Mario Cart; to the right, the space where Luc and Jemina are playing, and another hallway that leads to the stairs. A couple trots by, giggling, and I watch as they run up the stairs, hand in hand.

"So, what's up?" I say, turning my attention to the man beside me.

He glances down at me for a second. Looking up he sighs, "I'm here, aren't I."

"You are. And you're alone."

He glances down at me again, looking not so happy, "Is that a problem?"

I try to be as kind as I can, "*Yes* when we're trying to get you to socialize with the fans, the locals. Anyone."

"I'm talking to you, aren't I?"

"Yes, but I'm your publicist." *Not your friend.*

He takes a breath and mumbles, "I'm not very good at socializing."

My breath catches in my throat. It feels strangely intimate to share such a truth in the middle of a crowded room. Like, even though the house is bursting with people, for a moment, it's only me and him. And then at the next shout, the party fills in. My stomach twists. He's being honest while I'm just lying so he doesn't fire me like DKS did. *If I get the job done, it won't matter. It won't matter.*

"You had no problem socializing with that pack of party hounds last night."

He looks down at me, inclining a black brow, "You saw that?"

I shrug, staring at the game of Mario on the big screen instead of his dark eyes, "A good businesswoman knows exactly where the big fish are."

He laughs and the sound makes my stomach flutter, "I thought I was the little fish in a big pond. Isn't that's why you're here?"

"You're the prize fish who doesn't like to be noticed. And I'm about to shine a light on you, so be prepared for big juicy lures to be tossed your way."

I turn back to him, grinning at myself. He's watching me, a thoughtful, surprised expression on his face. Like I've pulled back the curtains and exposed him in a way he never expected.

I lean in to him slightly and he matches my movement, "It's my job to know and share who you really are; people love authenticity and you've got plenty to go around."

"Right," Everett pulls away, his eyes gazing anywhere but at me. His jaw tightens, and I can see an invisible shield closing him off.

I have him and then I lose him.

Chapter 18

EVERETT ABRAMS

I can see it now: my deepest, darkest secrets being sold to the highest bidder.

People will have an exclusive of how Everett Abrams went from no one to someone. Every time I'm stopped for an interview, even on the mountain after a high-90 score, I'll be asked how I did it. My shortcomings will reign again. It won't matter where I am now, only who I once was.

This is why I hated the idea of hiring a publicist. They want to make *everything* public in the name of authenticity. If she pulls on one string, all of me is at risk of unraveling. I'll just be the only kid leaving class again – some people laughing, some looking at me with pity in their eyes.

I glance around the room, feeling more uncomfortable than I did when I was alone. I'd rather go unnoticed, but December has definitely noticed me.

I step in the direction of the door, "I think I'm–"

"There's an open spot."

December grabs my hand and jerks me in the opposite direction. Her skin is so cold against mine it makes me jolt; makes me easier to drag to the couch. She replaces her hand with a controller.

"You have played before, right?" She asks as the game counts down.

"Never played before in my life," I reply dryly and look down at the controller. "What is this thing anyways?"

December reaches for the device just as the game beeps. *Game on.* My thumb presses the toggle forward and around as my character zooms to take the lead.

"Hey!" She grabs her own controller and tries to catch up. Immediately she runs into the back of a bus. "That's your fault!"

"*Ooh.*" I glance at her. Her eyes narrow in concentration, tongue pressed to the corner of her mouth as she drives her character around obstacles and towards power-ups. "Maybe you should take lessons. I charge fifty dollars a race. You have my number."

She turns her head sharply, pulling her character off the course as I near the finish line. "You forgot one very important rule: Don't Drink and Drive. You have to finish a beer *before* you cross the line." She pulls a can into her lap and cracks the top. "Oops. Looks like you don't have a drink."

"Shit." I crash into the side of the course just before the finish line.

I look around me. December has the can tilted back, drinking in great gulps. In one fluid motion, I hop over the couch and dash for Luc in the other room. He spots me moving towards him, loosens a beer from the batch, and tosses it over heads. Once it's in my hands, I jump back to my spot. December has already finished her beer and is half a lap behind me. I plop back into my seat. She tilts towards me, the couch cushions shifting with my weight, and I get a whiff of spiced cider.

"HA! Tallboy!" December shouts, glancing at the drink in my grip. Her cheeks flush with excitement.

I glance down at the can. I hadn't even noticed, but there's no changing it now. Her character grows closer every second. I crack the top and foam bubbles over.

"Chug! Chug! Chug!" The house is shouting.

All I can think about is winning. Seeing the look on December's face when I defeat her. I guzzle and when it's empty, I raise it above my head and crush it in one squeeze, nudging my character over the checkered line just as December drives around the final corner. She drops her controller, looking flustered and amused at the same time.

The crowd cheers.

"You cheated." She says just to me, leaning in.

"Just because you didn't get what you want, doesn't make me a cheater."

She rolls her eyes and smiles, making my stomach *zing*. "You have some—"

She breaches the space between us. Her fingers sweep across the skin of my upper lip. My stomach spikes – the feel-good roll at the top of the roller coaster. Gooseflesh explodes down my arms, and an electric squeeze jolts in my groin.

"Hey guys! What's up?" Jemina calls as she and Luc make their way through the crowd.

December and I move in opposite directions. She leans forward and away; I relax into the couch. As soon as there's space between us, and her eyes no longer drag over my lips, my body returns to normal. No more electric trills. I chance a glance in her direction – *did she feel anything?* But I'm not even on her radar. She's laughing along with Jemina. Like it didn't even happen.

I take a staggered breath, something like relief washing over me. My eyes move off her and meet Luc's. He's staring down at me. What a way to see him for the first time in days.

"Abrams." For a second, I'm thankful for the interruption, but then Hendrik slings his arm over Luc's shoulders.

"Let's battle. Bitter rivals on the mountain and at the table." He nods towards the pong room. Red solo cups are already tightly aligned. The crowd watches, eagerly awaiting the response.

"I don't think–"

"We don't want to embarrass you at home." December swoops in, jostling my shoulder.

Hendrik grins, sloppy and lop-sided, directing his charm towards December. I roll my eyes and brush a hand through my hair. Just like Hendrik to show up now. He always shows up where he shouldn't. Like on top of me during the Team Combined event last year at Mammoth. My knee aches at the memory. Right now, he's baiting me into a fight. He can't generate enough buzz about himself on the pipe, so he tries to make up for it with public attention. His primary tactic: seducing women he shouldn't. And right now, his goal is my publicist.

I nudge her with the back of my hand, staring directly at Hendrik, "Let's get out of here."

Hendrik's gaze moves to mine. He sizes me up for a moment and then looks around. He takes a step closer, leaning down to clap my shoulder.

"I know you've worked with UnderLayer since you started riding. They just signed me. Care to share a few pointers?"

I search his face for a sign of sarcasm. For the mean look I used to see in the eyes of my classmates. Any sign he's making fun of me. He tilts his head, asking me to spill. The grin is still on his face, but he can't be serious – *is he?* I rub my chest, soothing a pinch that won't go away.

UnderLayer dropped me and in the same breath signed Hendrik? It's a knife to the heart. My glare shifts from Hendrik to my publicist – the person who's supposed to help me land deals like this. Instead, she leads me to parties to do nothing but drink beer, waste time, and kill brain cells. I turn back to Hendrik feeling nothing but a tight squeeze in my sternum.

"You're the hot shot now. Figure it out yourself." I push past him off the couch.

I make it off the porch before December pulls on my elbow and swings me around. The cold bites at my skin, at my lungs. It's a welcomed burn. Anything to feel something other than this hurt and disappointment.

UnderLayer was my first corporate sponsor. Signing with them made me realize I could do this. I was good. Now I've lost them. It feels like I've lost my future; an omen that everything else will come apart.

"What's wrong? Talk to me," she says. Her eyes are soft. I won't tell her. The less she knows, the better.

"Why did you drag me here?" I blurt instead.

"I–" she rears back, wrapping her arms around herself. "I was trying to help you get some traction."

"Oh really? Was that what that was? The flirting and the touching?" She looks away and I feel a pang of guilt, but I don't stop. She needs to hear this. I need to hear this. "The only people who noticed were Luc and Jemina. I'm not paying you to sleep with me. You're here to create some buzz for me, not get me buzzed."

"*Wow*." She blinks. An angry grin twists across her face. "You're an asshole. No wonder no one wants to work with you."

"Plenty of people want to work with me."

"Oh really? Because I see no line," she gestures around us. "My phone isn't ringing off the hook."

"Because. You're. Not. Doing. Your fucking job."

She laughs, "Your problems started way before you hired me."

"I'm beginning to wish I hadn't."

She lets out an angry puff of air. She's a dragon about to breathe fire. I should take a step back, but I don't, "Listen Grump Ass, go home and get some sleep. Hopefully you'll wake up on the right side of your bed and when you do, I'll have something lined up that'll blow your freaking little mind. Because that's what I do."

I shrug, Grump Ass sticks me like a thorn in my side, "I haven't seen it yet."

Her eyes narrow in the dim light. I can tell she's on the edge of unleashing her unbridled anger but she reins herself in, spins and stomps back into the house. The door slams leaving me outside, alone.

I make it halfway down the drive before I stop. Push both hands through my hair, tilt my head back to the stars. My fingertips dig into my scalp and I stare up at the twinkling lights. The cold settles in against my skin. I take one long, cold breath and let it out, "Fuuuuuuck."

Chapter 19

EVERETT ABRAMS

The next day, I'm not alone when I get home from riding.

My disappearing roommate has made his grand reappearance. He doesn't hear me when I cross the threshold, a hockey game blares over the sizzle of bacon.

The guy has the audacity to make bacon first thing after he's been hiding for days? My stomach rumbles and I inhale deeply. Smell is the closest to bacon I can get for the next four months. Picking up the remote, I flick the TV off. Luc swivels around, his face twisting until he sees me. When he does, he stands up straight, blinking.

"Hey," I say gruffly, throwing him his signature peace wave.

"Hey."

I continue around the counter and drop in a seat. I wince, my dick and friends still sore from the other day, not to mention my wounded pride. December doesn't look like much, but she can throw a punch. And not just with her fist. Luc cups himself, grimacing along with me. Secondhand nut pain. It's a real thing.

"So, you've seen the video." I situate myself more carefully. Aside from tossing me a beer, he carefully avoided me last night. I guess I did, too.

He sucks air through his teeth, "I think everyone's seen it. I didn't know you brawled with skier chicks? Next time call backup."

I huff. Great now everyone thinks it was a fight and I came out the loser. I take a breath and blow out all the bullshit. *I don't care what anyone thinks* I tell myself – but the anxiety begins to gnaw at my gut. I push it down further until I can't feel it anymore.

"Where have you been?"

Luc twists back around to face the bacon, shrugging, "Around."

I let out an exasperated laugh, "When are you going to stop doing this shit?"

He glares at me over his shoulder.

I toss down my gloves and dig in, "Getting told no fucking sucked but instead of running, you should have come back here and worked harder."

"It was four days!" His face blooms red and he jabs the greasy spatula in my direction. "Stop acting like you're so much better than me. You hide from your own bullshit all the time." He opens his mouth to continue when the doorbell rings.

I jolt to my feet, not wanting to listen to a recital of my own shortcomings. I repeat them enough in my head the way it is. I don't want to hear it from my best friend, even though I know I started it.

The sudden movement sends a zap of pain directly to my knee. I lean forward, clutching the counter for support. A fierce pain rips through me. I go still. Black dots explode in my vision. All the air is sucked from my lungs. For a moment, it's like the injury is happening all over again. I feel it in painstaking detail; my leg twists one way, my body twists the other. A *riiiip* at my knee as muscle unzips from bone.

Luc's anger dissolves. He steps towards me, but I jerk my head towards the door where the bell is being attacked. I hobble to the couch, putting as little weight on my leg as possible. The second I'm seated, my leg carefully propped up on the coffee table, December flounces in.

"Mm, bacon," she says, craning her neck to see into the kitchen.

The couch shifts as she takes a seat. There's a bite of pain as the cushions move. I want to bark, *be more careful*, but my teeth are clenched too tight. A moment later Luc is handing me a glass of water, two pain pills, and a bag of ice. I sink back into the couch. Luc and December share words but all I hear is white noise.

I take a breath and remind myself this isn't her fault. The dick punch was, but I've been riding hard since I was back on my feet in June, and especially hard the last three weeks. This is my body's fury for not slowing down.

"Let's get this over with," I grumble, glancing at December.

I do a doubletake. She's pulled the corner of her bottom lip between her teeth. Her eyes glisten as she stares at my icing knee. Is she about to *cry*? My mind reels back, dissecting everything I've said and done since Luc let her in. Which hasn't been...anything.

A mixture of irritation and guilt swirl. I was such a dick to her last night. She didn't deserve all of it.

"December," I say slowly, watching her for a reaction.

She blinks, releases her lip from her teeth, and takes a sharp breath. Quickly piecing herself back together. She looks up at me, a semblance of a smile on her face.

My eyes linger on her. I want to say...something. Anything. About last night. But I don't know how. Words, even thoughts, have always had a way of evading me. Especially when I need them the most. My throat tightens as I try to think the perfect words, the phrases, the thoughts into my brain. But, as ever when they're needed, my mind is as empty as the backcountry.

Clearing my throat, I shove away the thought of apologizing. And my mind springs to life again, "Let's get this done."

She nods and it's like the gesture activates a different part of her. She's all business now. No glistening eyes or apologies. It's both unsettling and fascinating how she loses her emotions so easily and slips into PR mode. I watch as she pulls out her laptop and brings up the first social media site. Next, she takes my phone and plugs it in to her computer. From there, she begins to build a platform from her laptop, signed into my profile.

"I'm taking off." Luc calls from the kitchen. I'd forgotten he was here. I tilt my head back to see him. He's standing upside down from this viewpoint, a crisp BLT in one hand.

Before he gets out of earshot I venture, "Where are you going?"

His posture turns rigid and he turns partially, saying over his shoulder, "Out. Is that okay with you, *father*?" He leaves before I can even begin to form a response.

Great. My best friend leaves me to fend for myself with December. And I was hoping to go over next steps with Elevate when she's gone. Just because we don't have funding yet doesn't mean we have to stop working on it. This is when we should be working even harder. Just like when we were young and trying to learn a double cork. We didn't give up when it didn't come together. We showed up at the mountain and worked our asses off until landing it was second nature.

Pulling me out of my thoughts, December asks my opinion on my profile picture. I pick one of me standing at the top of a podium, hands raised, euphoric smile on my face. She ignores my choice and selects a moment captured from a trip with Luc and my brother Kelly a few years ago.

"If you're not going to listen to my opinion, why ask?" I growl, feeling more than a little ignored.

She glances at me, one brow angled up, and then back at the computer, "Your opinion was noted. This one's better."

My irritation simmers. "Superpipe is what I do, winning is what I do. Why wouldn't I have an image to best represent me as my profile?"

December scoots back from the computer and looks at me, "Because you're more than someone who wins at Superpipe. We don't want to box you in. You're a person first, snowboarder second." She glances at the picture. "And you look really happy in this one."

"I do in the other one, too." I argue even though my anger has run out of steam. Her point hits me right in the gut. It rings true with what my mom has been trying to tell me. Maybe even a little what Luc is demonstrating in his irresponsible way: I'm more than what I do.

I know that, obviously, but so much of how I see myself is grounded in Superpipe. Before I was Everett Abrams, I was a kid with no potential. What will I be if I lose snowboarding now? I don't want to be a man with even less potential.

Leaning forward, December fiddles with something labeled 'Your Story.' She walks me through how to set up a 'story' and the different things I can do with it – add music, gifs, filters to photos, share websites. I'll tuck the information into the recesses of my mind so I can do the same for Elevate. Once Luc and I are finally able to get together and work on it.

So far, this has been like hitting two birds with one stone. She doesn't know, but with her help with my personal brand, I'll be using it with Elevate, too. A prickle of guilt sprouts in my mind. I squish it. She doesn't need to know everything about me.

I grudgingly let her take a photo of me for the Ask Me Anything story. When she snaps the picture, she holds back a smile.

"What?" I catch myself before I say, *'do I look weird?'*

She shakes her head, struggling further to hold back, "Nothing."

"Give me that." I reach out and grab my phone before she pulls away.

I glance up at her, confused. When my eyes meet hers, she glances away, her cheeks flooding with color. I stare down at the picture again. I don't get it. I'm just sitting on the couch in my gray sweater. There's a shadow along my jaw, my reminder to shave. I'm not even smiling. It's just a picture of me staring at the camera. What's so funny about that?

"We should do another." I narrow my eyes at the screen. "How do I delete this?"

"No!" She nearly jumps at me, but thankfully remembers not to disturb the couch too much as she glances at my icing knee. With me distracted, she snatches my phone back. "This is perfect." Her sly smile again.

"Perfect? You're laughing at it."

"I'm not," She shakes her head, but the smile still rises on her face.

I jab my finger at her, "Yes, you are. Even right now. We're not using a photo people are going to laugh at."

She tilts her head and I notice her PR-professional mask has slipped. More emotion written across her face. I think I like her better this way. She's not so much a serious, soulless machine, ready to sell me out.

Color creeps into her cheeks again. She clears her throat, finally picking out what she wants to say, "I'm not *laughing* at you. You look really good in this photo and I'm thinking it's going to hit the mark."

Realization hits me, and I almost can't believe it, "You think I'm sexy."

I'm haunted by the words I yelled at her yesterday. *I'm not paying you to sleep with me.* My stomach squeezes in exhilaration almost like it does when I land a tricky maneuver. My publicist thinks I'm hot and I'm just sitting here in my sweats. Something like delight sinks deeper in my gut, spreading into my blood. She. Thinks. I'm. Sexy. And I'm not even doing anything. Even after our blow up last night. I don't know why, and I'm definitely not going to examine it, but I like this so much.

December throws me a look, "I think you're attractive. Everyone does." She says like that's not exactly the same thing.

A smile plays across my face. I'm loving this, "Sexy."

"Noo," she turns away and posts the picture with a box for followers to ask questions.

"They're basically the same thing. If you think I'm attractive, you think I'm sexy."

Her head pops up, like I've caught her hand in the cookie jar, "I do not."

I shrug, baiting her, "That's fine. Just know the harder you deny it, the more I know you want me."

She crosses her arms and glares. I'm acutely aware of how it boosts her breasts. "Fine. You're inconveniently sexy." Her eyes widen for a second and she tries to amend, "Inconvenient like when it rains, and I don't have an umbrella."

"Inconveniently sexy, huh?" I list my head, ignoring her last comment. "What you're saying is, you've thought about me naked." I say slowly, my blood turning hotter and pumping to an organ it has no business flowing to. *Oh fuck.* But I don't stop teasing her. "At the most inconvenient times. Like when you're at the grocery store."

She shakes her head, "You're so full of it."

"If you haven't, you will now."

And I want her to do just that. Even though twenty-four hours ago, I accused her of trying to fuck me. Now I want to be living, rent free, naked in her mind.

Chapter 20

December Fowl

I glare down at his knee, wanting more than anything to change the subject.

I've never thought of Everett or any other client of mine like that. I've worked with plenty of beautiful people. And as I admitted, he is insanely good looking. He's about as unnoticeable as Timothée Chalamet on a busy city street. He just stands out without trying. Without wanting to.

He's exteriorly gorgeous, yet his features are only part of the reason he's captivating. But, I haven't figured out what exactly makes him so alluring. It's there in my mind, but just beyond reach.

I stare at his leg, ice pack covering his knee, and an idea pops into my mind.

Everett changes the channel from sports commentary to streaming. I recognize the show immediately when the blonde, curly haired male lead, and the detective with a pointy chin and flawless dark hair take over the screen. *The Mentalist.* One of my all-time favorite shows, but one Suz refuses to watch. I hold my breath, waiting for him to click to something else, but instead he sets the remote down and rests his head back.

Before I can talk myself out of it, I move closer on the couch for a better look at his injury. Everett's eyes flick to me for a moment and then drift back to the TV. Slowly, I lift a corner of the ice pack from his knee. He hisses and my hand jerks away.

He rests his hand over the ice pack, shielding it from me, "What are you doing?"

"I think I can help you. Massage is one of the best things for sore muscles."

He gives me a look, "Are you a physical therapist, too? If not, no touchy."

"Listen, my college boyfriend played rugby. He tore his ACL in a tournament and his friends in PT school taught me some massages to keep the scar tissue from building up. It really helped."

"No. Don't be ridiculous. Let's just get this social media thing done."

"Please. It's the least I can do after what happened yesterday." I wave my hand at his groin. He flinches and shoos my hand away.

"That's exactly why you're not touching my knee."

"Please. Everett."

He takes a breath and casts a tired look in my direction, "All right. Just so I don't have to see your terrible take on puppy dog eyes. But if I tell you to stop, you have to. No questions asked."

"Basic consent. I got it."

Carefully, he adjusts himself on the couch and I help him move his leg so the heel of his foot rests in my lap. I lean forward to reach his knee. Tenderly, I press my thumbs into the skin around his joint. I pretend not to notice the corded muscles of his thigh or his fine black hair, which is oddly, dare I say, sexy. As I touch him, his skin is warm to the touch, despite being iced. He jerks back, sucking in a pained breath.

I pull my hands back as he glares down at me, "I thought you said you were good at this."

"I am. It's not my fault you haven't been taking care of it," I say, gently smoothing my fingertips over his skin. The muscle in his thigh ticks and I look up, Everett's bristled further. "Shit. I'm sorry. Did your physical therapist send home pamphlets or some reading material on how to maintain recovery?"

"Fuck that. I didn't have time. I practiced the exercises we used in sessions until it healed."

"I'm going to try again, okay?" I say, holding his gaze. "Your scar tissue is angry. That's why you're hurting. You're supposed to massage the tissue, so it doesn't build up like this. Didn't your doctor schedule regular appointments?"

"For the first six months, then they released me."

Anger flares up in me again. Eric's doctor had scheduled appointments a *year* out, so issues like this wouldn't arise. And he was only a college athlete with no ambition or potential to play professionally after graduation. Healthy knees are important for even the non-athletes like me, and Everett's career relies on a strong body. How could his doctor be so careless?

Everett glowers at me, eyes filled with venom, "Spare me your judgement."

He looks away, jaw clenching, and I gape for a moment before realizing he thinks the acid look on my face is directed towards him, "No. You misunderstand me," I shake my head and he turns his cold, hard gaze to me. "I'm not judging you. Someone should've taken care of you."

"Taken care of me?" He laughs but there's no humor in it. "You don't think I can take care of myself?"

I'm digging myself into a bigger hole and I'm not sure why. With Everett, I say the wrong thing at the worst time. And when I do, instead of thinking of me as an idiot, he thinks I'm insinuating he is.

All those years coaching Todd through messy situation-ships, guarding Sawyer from becoming the pop star she so desperately didn't want to become. I managed to make them feel understood and safe with me. Why am I failing so badly with Everett?

"No, I just mean *someone*, your doctor or therapist, PT, should have put in the effort to make sure you were scheduling maintenance appointments, so this wouldn't happen. It's honestly negligent."

He sighs, "Who knows. They may have mentioned it or handed out 'reading material,' but it probably didn't make it through my thick head."

"I know snowboarding and your body are too important for you not to have paid attention."

He tilts his head as he gazes at me so attentively, I think he can see right through my cool, professional exterior. Straight into me. My stomach zings like a firecracker in July. I swallow, my mouth suddenly wet and dry at the same time. Holding my gaze, he nods for me to continue. My chest expands, and I let out a breath. I feel like we've crossed a bridge. For once, we're on the same side instead of screaming at each other from across a thirty foot ravine.

I turn away from his attention and focus on the TV. I don't want him to see too much. I don't think he'll like everything. I don't even like everything about me – the hiding things, the getting fired, the not being good enough. I'm not ready for him to know those parts of me. *I* don't want to know those parts of me.

"Jane is my favorite," I say, pressing my thumbs along his scar line as the tall, blond ex-psychic steps onto the screen. My thumbs are poised on either side of his scar, beneath the kneecap. I pull the skin tight on one side of the pink scar, release and pull the skin tight on the other side.

Everett stiffens, takes in a sharp breath but manages to say, "Jane? I'd peg you for a Rigsby girl for sure."

I work my thumbs up the entire length of his faint red mark, "A Rigsby girl?" I smile. "He is sweet and resourceful and...*sexy*, but Jane is all those things and more."

"Nah. He's always lying and doing things for his own agenda."

My stomach tightens. *Always lying, sound familiar, December?*

"But he's the best at what he does, and always there when they need him. Plus, he and Lisbon make a great team."

"He's there when he's *there*, but he's always running out on his own without telling anyone." I look up at him. "He may be the best, but I don't know if it's enough. I couldn't put up with someone who's misled me as many times as Jane has."

I concentrate hard on working my thumbs back down his scar and pretend I'm too focused to continue the conversation as I start a different technique. My heart is thudding against my chest. I almost can't catch my breath. Oh shit, I'm Patrick Jane. I've avoided and lied and avoided some more, and Everett isn't going to work with me when he finds out.

I should just come out with it already. I want to tell him. I'm just...I'm just...not ready to face what I've done. It's too embarrassing to admit I've been fired from the job I love. Especially admitting my mistakes to Everett. He's too good at what he does. He won't understand. He'll think there's something wrong with me and neither of us can afford losing each other right now.

"How does this feel?" I say, pushing down the conflicting emotions swirling inside me.

"Better," He muses, and I let my hands fall away, "You should keep going just to...work everything out. Copper's in two days, I have to be at my best."

"Maybe I should charge," my lips turn up into a grin.

"I'll leave a raving review for you on Google. Decent publicist, great massager. Everyone will be crawling to the agency for you."

I let out a forced laugh, glancing away, "I'm afraid it would bring in the wrong clientele." I fuss over his scar. It's still inflamed but by tomorrow it should be better.

"Who are your other clients?"

"I don't have any." I freeze, realizing my confession too late. Damn distracted mind. "I mean..." My eyes shoot to his.

Everett's face knots up, he shakes his head, "You don't have any other clients? I thought you were the agency's best?"

I open my mouth not yet knowing how to respond when my phone begins to vibrate in my back pocket. Pulling it out, Suz's smiling face flashes across the screen.

I jolt up, using it as my escape, "I have to take this. And I should probably go. Could be a long one," I shake the phone and answer, "Hey Suz, give me one second." I press my phone to my chest, "Your flight to Copper Mountain leaves at five tomorrow afternoon, so I'll be here in the morning. Bright and early."

"Wait," he pushes himself back like he's about to get up, shaking his head, his face still screwed up. "I'll drive you home."

"No, no. You should rest. Copper, remember?" Before he resists further, I trot around the couch and down the entryway hall to the door. I yank on my jacket and boots, stepping out before he has time to respond.

I'm panting up his sloped driveway, far out of earshot, before I resume the call with my best friend, "Suz, you have the best timing *ever*."

"I also have the worst news ever."

My heart thumps in my throat, "Is Frankie okay? You, your parents? What's going on?"

I've been such a bad friend, so absorbed in my own mess-making. It's like nothing else exists but me, Everett, and trying to survive this unexpected firing.

"We're fine, thank you." Her assurance makes me smile. She hesitates for a moment, "But DKS isn't fine."

I let out a howl of laughter, turning from Everett's driveway onto the main road of Blue View Drive, "Tanking already, is it?"

"*No*. Ryan really wants Everett."

"What? Why? He has all my other clients, and Everett was massively under-performing."

"I don't know, but he's coming up there. You'll have to think of something great, fast."

My jaw clenches and I growl out, "Oh, I'll get something."

Chapter 21

Everett Abrams

"A re you trying to turn me into an ice cube?" December hisses between chattering teeth as she dances in the cold at my doorstep again this morning.

I step aside, running a hand through my already messy hair, so I don't reach down and drag her inside. She walked here again, her cheeks burning pink. Her nose bright red. With the windchill, today's high temperature is five degrees.

"You're gonna lose your nose out there in this cold, Rudolph," I say as she brushes passed me. I snap the door shut behind her, the stone underneath my bare feet already freezing from the air.

When I turn around, she's already shucked off her coat and boots, "I come bearing good news."

She's so focused, she doesn't even notice sleeping beauty, leaning against the staircase, staring down at us.

"You look like shit." I say to Luc, and he does. Messy, greasy hair, dark circles under his eyes.

December's eyes darken, "I was up all night working my ass off to get you a killer deal, asshole."

"I was talking to him." I jerk my head towards the stairs where Luc is slowly making his way down. "You look..." My eyes roam over her and I shrug. I can't think of a way to describe her other than *warm* – even when she's minutes from frostbite.

Luc meanders into the kitchen behind us like a zombie. Pale face, dazed eyes, crazier hair than mine, and dressed in the same clothes he walked out in yesterday. He grunts a greeting and stumbles to the fridge. Someone's still a little drunk. I shake my head and I pour him a glass of water. Once he finishes it, I turn him around and direct him back towards the stairs.

"Back to bed for you, buddy." I pat his back, not so softly. If December wasn't here, I'd tear into him.

Luc's always been the wild boy between the two of us; the irresponsible one, the fun one. But Elevate can't afford Luc bombing the contest at Copper. The investors will be watching, and we have to show them we're capable of handling ourselves under pressure. There's always pressure, but even more so now with this business deal on the line.

"So, killer deal." December says behind me as I pull out a pan, crate of eggs, and a container of chopped veggies. I glance over my shoulder at her as I crack an egg. She continues, "Guess who has an interview with Dan Keegan the day of Copper Mountain, 6 a.m.?"

I stiffen and turn, spatula in hand. Dan Keegan. Holy fuck. Everyone knows who he is. He's the greatest sports journalist in the world. When I was a kid, I used to watch him interview my favorite boarders and now December's telling me I have an interview?

Holy fuck. This could be huge. A grin begins to grow across my face. My chest swelling. When I was a kid, I always dreamed about talking to him. But – *fuck* – in my dreams I was perfect. I didn't slur or stumble over words. But that's not the real me. The swelling in my chest turns to a suffocating weight. Why didn't she ask me first?

"Don't say me," I bite out. If I put the blame on her, I won't have to reconcile with this being my problem.

Her mouth drops open. The full spectrum of shock turning to rage exploding across her face. Whatever truce we had last night evaporates.

"What is wrong with you?" She blurts as I turn back to the stove and scoop one omelet onto a plate.

I laugh, "Too long of a list." I walk the plate over to her. She glances down at the steaming yellow omelet, sprinkled with chopped red and green peppers and a line of Tabasco sauce. I can tell she's fighting with herself to either accept the food or argue with me.

I head back to the stove and make one for myself. As it sizzles, I lean back on the counter and cross my arms, watching as December digs in.

Mouth still partially full she argues, "You want me to make you two hundred thousand dollars richer, in five weeks, and when I get you this opportunity it's not good enough?"

"I never said it's not good enough. You just didn't consider my schedule."

"Screw your schedule! You won't have a 'schedule' if you don't have any sponsors!"

And there it is – I'm reminded why she's here; to make me money, plain and simple. I thought she understood what I would and wouldn't – can't do. All she sees is dollar signs.

I turn away, scoop my omelet from the grill and cut it into pieces, trying to get my mind into a more neutral place. All I can think is: she'd sell me out for anything.

As I eat, she jumps up from her chair and moves around the living room, "I thought you said you'd do whatever it takes; do you want your schedule, or the money? Because right now you're telling me you want your schedule. You can't have both."

It's not so cut and dry. She acts like the differences are black and white. My voice rises, "My routine is what makes me this good. I stuck to my schedule when I started while other guys didn't. I'm still here and they're not. I'm not going to fall off now."

"No, Everett. No." She steps into the kitchen, her eyes softer. "It's not your schedule that makes you so good. It's you. One factor is not the only determinate."

I know it's not. I also work out and ride like hell, but I stick to my routine. I do things at a certain time, so they're done right.

"Listen," she takes a step closer to me. "You have to be flexible. I know you love your routines just like I loved mine at D–." She seems to catch herself like she was on the brink of saying something wrong. Like she did last night when she admitted she had no other clients. "I miss my routine in Atlanta, too. I miss cuddling Frankie, going on a coffee run with Suz. My own bed, but I'm here. I'm here to work with you. And this is more important than my routine. See, pivoting."

Frankie – who's Frankie? I keep my face neutral as my heart sputters. Does she have a boyfriend? For reasons I'm not about to explore now, the thought pisses me off.

"I ride early because the snow is hard, no one's touched it yet. If I wait, the sun makes it soft and there's tracks from all the other riders. I start on fresh snow."

She stares at me. Waiting for me to go on. Like I need a better explanation.

She doesn't know I have a better explanation: fear, guilt, shame.

I push myself off the counter, "I ride early. No exceptions. Not even for Dan Keegan."

"Oh my god." She presses her hands into her head. "You are impossible! You want two hundred thousand dollars. I get you an interview with the most watched sports anchor in the country and you don't want to do it because it doesn't fit into your perfect fucking schedule!" She steps towards me, hands like claws. For a moment I'm taken by how passionate she is about this. The girl has no chill, and I like it. "Just shuffle shit around. Ride earlier, ride later. Ride during the fucking thing, I don't care!"

She perks. I can see the lightbulb popping in her head. "Ride during the interview. I like the ring of that. Everett Abrams in his natural habitat."

Oh shit, this is worse. This is wrong. She can't be fucking...*pivoting* like this on me.

"Whoa, whoa, whoa." I hold my hands up before she gets carried away. "I am not doing an interview while I'm riding."

A wicked grin spreads across her face, her eyes caught in the distance like she's picturing the scene unfold before her eyes. "An all-exclusive while the King of Superpipe practices." She claps her hands together, "Holy shit I've done it."

"No. No." I grab her by the shoulders and shake. "I don't want to do the interview."

"This is so much better," She grins, her cheeks turning pink as she grips my shoulders back. Her hands roam my arms to grip my biceps.

The hold she has on me, travels up my arms, across my shoulders, and into my spine. Her hands on me are a comforting pull, and I'm caught in the current. December shifts, but I don't let go of her. She doesn't let go of me. Slowly, she lets out a long breath, her green eyes stuck on mine. I like the way this feels: my hands on her, hers on me. Fingertips pressing into my skin. It feels strangely safe but wild. She's my publicist. She's a money hound. Not someone I'm allowed to enjoy clinging to me.

As if coming to the same realization, December drops her arms and wraps herself in them, spinning away.

"What did you say?"

I shake my head, still caught, "I don't remember."

"No, you said you don't want to do the interview. I - I'm just trying to understand you." She looks lost, alone, holding herself instead of in my arms. "I feel like we're playing a game I don't know the rules to, and you keep changing them."

"December," I squeeze my eyes shut, guilt settles on my shoulders.

I let out a breath, meeting her gaze. She's looking at me with wonder and warmth in her eyes like I'm this living, breathing puzzle she wants to help put together. And I'm struck by a tingling in the pit of my stomach. A moment passes, December's still gazing at me with nothing but curiosity – no judgement, no anger, just wanting to know. And I recognize the tingling in my stomach as a string trying to tell me something.

I take a breath and say, at least in part, what is true, "I don't know how to do this."

"What?"

"Any of this! I've been doing this pro snowboarder thing for years and yet I don't know how I got here."

She moves to speak but I wave her off, "I mean, I know I worked hard and I'm talented. Yeah, I know why I'm as good as I am. Why I win. But the other stuff, the sponsors and things feel like they just fell into my lap. And now with them disappearing, I'm not sure how to get them back."

December steps towards me and touches my arm with a tenderness I more than feel, "This is what I'm here for."

"No," I choke out. "It's not – it's not. I don't know how to say things. I've never been...Words never come out how I want them to."

A slow, sweet smile spreads across her face, "Did you say that how you wanted to?"

I roll my eyes, huffing, "No. It's always so choppy."

"Everett," She slides her hand down to take mine. "What you said was great. I know what I can do now to help you ease into this."

I shake my head, frustration building in my chest. She doesn't get it. I didn't say the right thing so she could understand.

Her eyes implore me to listen, "We'll do some media training. Prepare you with some questions and answers, so you know how to respond."

"We can do that?"

December gives my shoulder a pat, "Of course. So many of my other clients have needed it."

My shoulders relax. Cool. Cool. Cool. I'm not the only one in the universe who's needed to learn how to talk to someone.

"I have a few other things lined up for you at Copper Mountain, too. You'll do the interview. It'll be your first contest and your first chance to show people you're doing things differently this year. After you win, I set up a meet-and-greet for a couple hours, followed by socializing at this great bar called Splice. Everyone is going to be there – fans, locals, fellow boarders."

My body tenses at the mention of a meet-and-greet. "What if no one shows up?" I blurt.

My mind races for the right words to explain this to her. I'm ashamed to admit I'm afraid no one will show up and I'll lose more. Then suddenly there will be no way for me to deny I'm not good enough. I'll have proof my career is on a downward slide to being over. And if I have no traction in the industry anymore the investors will walk, and I won't even have a backup plan. Riding and Elevate are it.

Her sharp green eyes widen, "People are going to show up."

There's so much swirling around in my head. "Do - how you do you know? You don't know for sure anyone will."

"I don't know anything *for sure,* but I know you've never done one. And you've been ranked number one in the world for the past four years. People will show up." She tilts her head, "And if you won't take my word for it, just look at your Instagram."

"What does that – how does Instagram help me again?"

Her mouth falls open, "You're sharing a look into your life, your thoughts. You write cool captions. You ask questions, you answer questions. You engage."

My stomach squeezes. None of this sounds like anything I want to do. It feels fake, "This doesn't seem like a good idea."

"Everett, I promise. Media training will work. People will show up. Trust me. This," she picks up my phone, "is what your competition is doing."

She shoves the phone under my nose. We're on Hendrik Legrand's page. He has over a million followers. Hendrik. Who first entered the scene only two years ago. She then pulls up Luc's page with over seven hundred thousand.

"Followers don't mean anything," I say, even though there's a grating in my stomach.

"And here's your following."

I shake my head, not believing the numbers. Over a five-hundred thousand. In less than twenty-four hours.

I grab for my phone, wanting to get a look at it for myself. Make sure it's real, but she turns away, sprinting into the living room, shielding the device with her body.

"I want to show you something else." She plays with it, distracted so she doesn't see me moving in after her.

I reach over her shoulder and my fingers graze the phone. She jolts and flings herself on the couch. I'm a cat chasing a mouse. I wrestle her for it, reaching between her arms to tug it away. She curls herself around my phone, laughing evilly. I flip her around so she's on her back, hands in a death grip around my phone. I get one hand around it, chuckling as victory is on the horizon, and my body shifts. My hips jolt against hers.

Holy shit.

The air leaves the room. We both go still.

December's knees are splayed open and thighs pressing into either side of my ribs. I'm propped up over her. One elbow by her head, the other gripping my phone. Her cheeks are flushed pink, green eyes wide and staring at me. Her free hand grips my shoulder.

My hips press into hers. There's a shocking heat between us. It zaps right down my spine into my groin. And *fuck* it takes every ounce of self-control not to rock up against her again. The thought sends arousal coursing through me. I'm so turned on by *brushing* her. Just being on top of her. I pull back before my dick can tell her just how much.

What the fuck is wrong with me? She's my evil publicist.

I move away and she lets go of my phone.

"Looks like your massage helped," I nod towards my knee, bent underneath me and now between the two of us, just to say something.

December sits up. She ruffles her hair over her shoulder, and I get a good whiff of some sort of exotic fruit. It smells good and I want to bury my face in her hair. *Evil publicist.*

"Good," she says, her voice thick. She clears it, not looking at me.

Good, good. Everything is good.

While I'm reminding myself not to like her, December pulls open her laptop and continues talking about interviews and meet-and-greets, building fan rapport. I hardly hear any of it. My brain is fogged with lust. *Damn* and they say videogames rot your brains. What's rotted mine is my publicist. Just touching December has got my brain into *need-her-now* mode. I can think of nothing else.

I look up at her, she's pointing at her laptop, breaking down an interview of Tom Brady. She's completely unaware of just how much I want to bend her over the armrest and fuck her until neither of us knows anything else.

Chapter 22

DECEMBER FOWL

"We're going to film all your Ask Me Anything responses."

"What?" His head shoots up.

I make a face. I don't think he's been listening to me at all, "Film your AMA's." I repeat slowly. "I mentioned this like five minutes ago."

"Sorry I was distracted," His eyes rake over me and my body reacts. He's thinking about the moment on the couch. I'll be thinking about that later, too. But right now, it's business time. We only have a few hours until he leaves for Copper Mountain. We have to get in as much media training as we can. This is crunch time.

He sighs, racking a hand through his jet-black hair, "When do we start the *real* media training?"

I scoff, shaking my head, "We already have. I just spent the last thirty minutes going over Tom Brady's Superbowl interview and the Ask Me Anything is part of it, too."

"This is what media training is?"

"There are different techniques, but from what I know about you, I think watching others execute their training well *and* actively practicing will be most impactful."

Everett tilts his head, considering. His eyes shift around the room, shoulders stiff.

My chest clenches. I wish he'd just trust me. But I am lying to him. Maybe on some level he can sense it, or I just give off liar vibes. But I'm not lying about this. I'm doing all of this – lies and all – with the best intentions.

"We'll try it and reevaluate. If it doesn't feel right, we'll try something else."

"Fine. Let's just get this over with," I watch as he gets up from the couch.

I am going to make you trust me, Everett Abrams. I will prove to you and myself that I'm doing the right thing. Just give me time.

I'm in Everett's room.

It's cleaner than I expected. There are no piles of dirty laundry. His bed is half made, the sheets gray and blue. Hanging from the walls are photographs. Stories of his journey riding here and all over the world. I notice he doesn't have a single one of him standing atop a podium. And yet he says Superpipe is all of him.

"Let's get going." His voice is sharp. He stands uncomfortably near his wall of snowboards. His hands are on his hips, features drawn in annoyance.

We'd just spent the last hour watching videos I'd archived ranging from athletes to Oscar-winning actresses. I'd pause the video to show him critical points in the interview. Like how some of them pause or take a drink to collect their thoughts before responding. How they answer a question with another question. We pivoted to the AMA when I noticed Everett was jigging his leg, looking off.

His hand jigs against the seam of his jeans now. Still jittery. I nod and ready the camera. When everything is set, I signal him.

Everett steps towards the array of snowboards in what once was a walk-in closet, now a showroom for his boards. They're displayed hanging from the walls, the overflow placed in standing racks.

"Some of you asked what my favorite snowboard is. It's an Ambassador Red X," He picks the red board out of the lineup. He flips it over to show the backside and there's a bare-naked woman draped across the surface. She's turned around, so only her ass and back are visible. She gazes over her shoulder at the viewer, holding her breasts.

"*Everett*," I hiss, stopping the recording, "You can't share that."

He looks down at the board. His mouth twitches. And I know the only reason he picked this particular board is to get under my skin. He hates this, I know, but I also know people like to feel as though they really know their favorite artist, actress, *athlete*.

"I know you're trying to be a pain, so I'll give up. But it's not going to happen."

"What's wrong with it?" He counters innocently enough. "I thought it was a little edgy. I thought you wanted me to play the bad boy?"

"No," I cross my arms over my chest and am acutely aware how it draws his eyes to my breasts; and how his attention makes my stomach flutter. "You said you didn't want to be like everyone else. So, let's not share the naked lady you get off to every night."

He laughs but listens, returning the board to its rack. I step back behind the camera before he catches the growing flame to my cheeks and ears – because for whatever reason *I* want to be the person he thinks of when he's lying alone in bed. Which is completely ridiculous, not to mention unprofessional. And so sudden, I'm not sure I understand it. I knew Everett was hot when I took him on as a client, but...

He deserves so much better than me. I shake the thought off and we start over. Everett picks up a more appropriate snowboard. It says Get Bit in white and red with black Goosebump-style lettering. There's an abominable snowman with red around its jaws at the far bottom.

"I'm sure most of you recognize this board." He smiles into the camera and my breath catches. *This.* This is why I wanted him to film his responses. He just lights up when he talks about snowboarding.

His features darken for a moment as his attention drops to the board, "It's my deck from last year's Mammoth run. Even though I tore my ACL, no fault of the board, it's still my favorite from my sponsor Envoy. I ride everything with it from power to park. It's a bit stiff but forgiving. They're still selling if you're looking for a great ride. Get it before the end of the year, or," he waves his hand across his neck.

I clap my hands together gleefully and dance around the camera, jumping towards him for a high-five, "That was perfect!"

"Was it really?" His face scrunches like he can't believe it.

"I don't get it."

"What?" Everett says, his eyes momentarily flashing to my lips.

"Why you're so unsure of yourself. You're basically the *god* of snowboarding. You love it. You look great on camera. Why did you think you couldn't do this?"

"Ah," he runs a hand through his hair, bashfully directing his gaze to the corner of the room. "I'm not always good at collecting my thoughts or saying the things I want to. I told you. I don't want to say anything stupid or fumble the words."

I nudge him, offering a smile, "You're not."

"Thanks." He says as his eyes meet mine. There's a spark in his dark eyes, and it makes my heart rattle.

"Do you look at everyone with so much intensity?" I say, because dear lord, when he looks at me like this – with openness and a steady, calm confidence that says: I see you. I want it to be just for me.

His shoulder lifts casually and he doesn't look away. But I do. I take a breath, move back behind the camera, and look down at the iPad in my hand, "On to the next question. *What was your first board and how did you get started snowboarding?*"

Everett looks away, the whites of his eyes growing wild. Why is he looking freaked out? It's a pretty standard question.

Swallowing, he picks a board off the wall. The bottom is faded and rough. I give him the signal to begin, "My brother Kelly started snowboarding and

I followed him like younger siblings usually do. I got this guy," he twists the plain board to the camera, "when I was twelve. The next year I joined El Dora Snowboard Club and the rest is history."

Good. Not great. "Why don't you talk about yourself a little more?"

"I don't want to talk about myself." His stone face is back.

"Oh, I've noticed. What's up with that?"

Everett walks towards me, bearing down, "This isn't a therapy session." Then he plucks the iPad out of my hands and reads the next question: "'*Sorry about your balls. Who was the chick that beat you up?*'"

I snatch the device back and am immediately brought back to the moment not even an hour ago. His body bumping into mine as we wrestled for his phone. The memory makes my lady parts tingle like they're saying *I'd like to do that again. Please do that again.*

"Looks like you'll have to join me for this one," He smiles, eyes teasing.

"Absolutely not. This is about you."

"Come on," Everett walks around the camera to set it on countdown. "Give the people what they want."

I shake my head, "I can't."

"You have to pivot, December. *Pivot.*"

I laugh, gazing up at him. He returns the smile. The lines around his eyes and mouth crinkle. It's honest, and sweet, and vulnerable in the way only real humor can be. I suck in a breath, my chest aching. He is honest and sweet and vulnerable in this moment – and I am not. How I wish I could be. Just thinking about telling him makes me freeze. And Ryan wants Everett as his client. I have no doubt he'll be prowling his social media account. He's going to see me and then blow up everything.

I do the unthinkable, dropping his gaze, and reaching for the camera: "Doing this live was a bad idea."

Everett reaches for my arm and turns me around, "Whoa, whoa. What's up? You were all excited about this a moment ago. Camera shy, too?" He smiles while

I hesitate. The smile fades. His hand moves up my arm. "Does this have anything to do with the personal issues you mentioned, or not having any clients?"

Like a cornered dog, I snap, "This has nothing to do with me. I don't need to be in it. I'm your publicist, not your friend."

"My publicist who palm-heeled my dick. You're already involved."

"Everett," I whine and pull against him as he takes my hand and tries to lead me before the camera.

"*December*." He reaches around my waist and pulls me in so quickly I crash into his chest. He begins his monologue before I can scramble away, "This is my publicist, December. She's very clumsy, as you witnessed earlier." He glances down. The intensity of his gaze is out of this world. "She hasn't skied since she was twelve, probably, but thought she could handle filming me. So, that's something to look forward to. I will eventually be sharing videos, but not filmed by December, the nutcracker."

My jaw falls open and I swat his chest as the red light on the front of the camera fades, "Nutcracker, really?"

He laughs, catching my hands, "It's very fitting."

Everett pulls away from the A-frame. I wave to him until he's out of sight and head towards Torrance's place. I glance down at my phone vibrates with an incoming text.

I slide my phone into my pocket and step into the A-frame. There are six hours before my flight to Denver. With all his worrying and the Dan Keegan interview, I decided it's best Everett's not left to face this alone. I'm going to use the time now to nap. And will absolutely not use the time to consider Suz's texts, or think about the way my body reacted when Everett pulled me into his.

"December," Torrance steps out of the kitchen as soon as the door clicks shut. She wraps her arms over her chest, lips pressed into a thin line. My stomach drops. I have a bad feeling about this.

"I see you're making some progress with Everett." Her brown eyes tell me we're about to have a tougher conversation. "Did you tell him you were fired?"

I want to squeeze my eyes shut and curse myself for doing that live feed. Suz saw it, Torrance, and more than likely Ryan did, too. Why, why, why do I do these things? Despite everything about to fall on my head, it was the right move for my client.

My shoulders fold forward, "No."

Torrance looks away and lets out a long breath. When she looks back at me, she's more earnest than angry, "You need to tell him. He's a good guy. He doesn't deserve to be lied to. Tell him now before you get in too deep." She tilts her head, giving me a meaningful look, "Personally or professionally. He's going to take it very poorly if your relationship grows and you're still misleading him."

"Relationship. There's no relationship. Did he say something to you?" My brain is a light, hopeful maybe there could be something between us, but I remind myself. "I'm his publicist."

"December. Tell him. He doesn't like to be fooled. None of us do, but he *really* doesn't like to be."

"What do you mean? Has someone..." My heart rips and I struggle to say the words: *has something like this happened before?*

"Everett is very private. I'm not going to tell you something he hasn't told you himself. You never should have let him believe you still worked at that agency. The firing he could take but...the *intentional* misleading is not going to fly. Best to rip the Band-Aid off. Now."

Chapter 23

DECEMBER FOWL

My knuckles gently rap against hotel door 439.

Everett has yet to respond to my earlier text. I glance back down at my phone – 5 a.m. My mind swarms with the warning Torrance gave me last night.

I've decided I'm going to do it now. Just like she said. Rip the Band-Aid off. Right now.

"Don't tell me you've left," I mumble, knocking louder.

The door swings open, and Everett stands in the doorway. He doesn't look nearly as annoyed to see me as he did the first few times I barged into his house. My eyes quickly assess him. Messy hair: check, sleepy eyes: check, wrinkled old t-shirt: check (the kind of t-shirt that looks so soft, I would like to crawl into and build my nest), panda boxers: oh fuck.

My eyes dart up and then back down. I've seen him in basketball shorts but never *boxers*. His legs are lean yet brawny and covered in dark hair. Everett doesn't seem to notice his lack of pants or my staring. He just swings around to retreat into his room. I step inside and deadbolt it. I don't want him running off on me in the middle of my confession.

Everett doesn't just have a room. He has a suite. He is royalty here.

There's a kitchenette with a breakfast bar overlooking the bedroom with a massive king bed. He sits there, leaning forward on the corner of the mattress, skipping through the channels with his remote.

The TV reflects bright colors across his face, until he lands on the weather. His gear bags lay stacked neatly beside his bed. They're so big I could fit every piece of clothing I own inside one bag and still have room. But you know professional athletes. They can't just pack *one* waxing bar.

"How's the knee?" I ask, glancing at his legs again. I'll ease into this, I reason. Then tell him.

He takes his eyes off the TV for a moment, glances at his leg. He shrugs, turning his attention to the weather again, "It's better."

"I called this sports therapist I know. She suggested stretching your knee in the morning before your contest."

"Hmm," Everett grunts, running a sleepy hand through his hair. "I'll be fine. There's not enough time between my morning practice, this interview, and then preliminaries."

"I could do it." I offer, stepping quickly towards him.

He leans back, an arrogant smile creeps across his face, "You just can't wait to touch me again, can you?"

I roll my eyes, hoping the TV's light catches the movement, "No. You're my *only* client and you haven't made me any money yet. I have to keep you healthy until you do."

Before he can say anything, I push him down onto the bed. His eyes grow wide and then they roam slowly down my body like he's memorizing me. I suck in a breath. Everett and me alone in his dark hotel suite. Anything could happen. We could have another body bop but this time with our clothes off.

But nothing will happen. With steadier hands than I feel I have, I press my thumbs gently into the muscles around his knee and work out the scar tissue. He grimaces, now propped up on the bed with his elbows. I sneak a few glances at his boxers. I can't help it. I'm a sick woman. I'm curious to see if I'm having any effect on *other* parts of him. But nothing sticks out or bulges.

Heart sinking, I focus my attention back to his muscles. What's wrong with me? He's my client. My *only* client. The one I'm about to confess to. Any moment. Any moment now, December. But the words stick to my tongue.

"Are you alright?" Everett chuckles. "You look like you're waging war with yourself."

Yes, I am trying to convince myself to tell you the truth. "I think you're okay." I take a step back. A big step back. I stare at his bed, the floor.

Tell him. Tell him now! I open my mouth. Close it again. Open it. Nothing comes out.

"Hey," Everett says softly. He moves his head and then his body so he's in my line of sight. "Are you sure you're okay? You're acting...stranger than usual."

I want to shout at him for being so perceptive. *You're not supposed to be like this, Everett!* He's supposed to be someone who doesn't care about me, or anything, but snowboarding and getting laid. This was supposed to be easy. I wasn't supposed to feel so guilty about this. I was going to do us both a favor. I keep finding it harder to come clean and he keeps adding layers. Like being a decent person. Like noticing me.

"I..." Diverting my eyes, I run a hand through my hair and cover my chest with my arms. Shielding myself. "I think it's the elevation."

Who am I kidding? I can't tell him now. It's his first big competition. I don't want to throw off his game and be blamed for that, too. Lying is bad enough.

He cracks a smile. The lines around his mouth and eyes showing. *Why are you so gorgeous?!* My heart drums faster.

"Blue Mountain has higher elevation, and your brain seems perfectly operational there."

"What are you, a mountain wizard?"

Still, his smile widens. Jesus Christ. "Copper Mountain has been a staple on the world tour since 1997. Everyone who's anyone knows the elevation. Plus, I grew up around here."

"Oh," I say, "Was this where super-snowboarder Everett learned to ride?"

"No," He's gazing at me and I can't look away. "It was about two hours northeast of here. Little place called Fort Collins. You may have heard of it."

"Everyone knows Fort Collins. It's like Everest."

He shrugs, a crooked smile creeping over his features again, "I don't know. You didn't know the mountain's elevation."

"Shut up," I quip. My stomach doing barrel rolls. Or maybe a million butterflies have been set loose.

"Did you grow up in Atlanta then?"

"Connecticut actually, Hartford. Until I was fifteen, then the Big Apple." He's watching me, and it makes my stomach flip even more. "You know all about elevation but nothing about your publicist. How shameful."

He smiles, looking down, "I haven't picked up *December Fowl 101* yet. I'm learning it could be a good read."

He's staring at me. His eyes dark. They're always dark. The TV screen flashing across half his face, the other half cast in shadow. He looks so perfect sitting there.

"It's a little boring at times, but good. I could get you a copy if you're nice."

He nods slowly, swallows hard and my eyes are right there at his neck. I want to do something other than strangle him. I want to run my hands along the back of his neck and into his hair. Breathe near his ear and find out how he reacts; run my teeth along the lines of his throat. See the different ways I can make him groan.

"Maybe a first edition." His voice is gruffer than a moment ago.

We're talking about nothing, but it feels like something.

I gravitate towards him like he has a string wrapped around my waist and whenever he speaks, whenever he looks at me with those dark, deep eyes he draws me nearer until I'm standing between his thighs. My hands drop onto his firm shoulders.

His fingertips roam up the back of my thighs. Up and down they move. From the back of my knees to the curve of my butt. I take a breath. Close my eyes. His hands grow greedier as they venture over my round ass, up my waist and all the way down again. He presses his head into my stomach and the hot, pulsing need between my thighs grows wilder.

"December," He breathes.

I open my eyes and meet his gaze staring up at me. I raise my hand and trace the curve of his jaw with my fingertips. His head tilts into my touch. His cheeks both soft and bristled. His hands rest at the back of my waist, gripping both my hips and butt. There, his palms feel infinitely large and firm and safe.

My eyes flash to his lips. The most artful things I've ever seen. I feel myself being pulled towards them.

His eyes flutter to mine. And we're slowly leaning in.

The theme song of *Friends* blares. I jerk back. Digging through my purse as I step further away, bumping into the TV stand. What the hell am I thinking? The theme song starts over again as I find my phone. I dare a look Everett's way as I answer.

"What the hell December!" Suz's voice blares. Shit, it's on speaker. I frantically try to take it off before she says something that would tell him I'm not DKS' star employee anymore. That I never was.

I press the phone to my chest, so Everett can't hear, "I have to take this," I escape before he has a chance to say anything.

"December. December. *December* are you there?" My god it's like she's trying to wake the whole hotel!

I hurry down the hall and around the corner before I stop. I lean against the wall, resting my head back, "I'm here. Something weird just happened."

"Oh my gosh, are you okay? You sound breathless. Should I call someone?" Her voice instantly loses the angry edge.

"No," I rub my forehead and take a deep breath. "Nothing like that. Everett and I just..."

"Just what?" Her voice pitches higher. "Did you guys hook up?"

There's a pause like she's allowing me to collect my thoughts. All I can think about are his hands roaming over the back of my thighs, my ass, my back. Gosh, I can feel them, the electric ghosts of his fingertips. I shudder, clenching my thighs together.

"Ryan is coming."

I freeze. The ghosts of his hands evaporate, "Where?"

"Wherever you are! Liz, his new assistant, told me. He's going to be there tomorrow."

My stomach sinks like a brick in the ocean. Ryan's on his way here. And then there's Everett. And me. And I haven't told him I don't work at DKS. And the way we were touching each other...

"Everyone's been talking about your Insta-story. And then the news of Dan Keegan interviewing him. I could hear the crash of his printer from my desk after the news broke."

My mind catches on the little pieces of gossip, "He still hasn't moved up to the Executive Suite?"

"Nope," Suz oozes. I can tell she's grinning evilly on the other line. "He has a sixty day trial run."

My stomach twists, "Which explains why he's coming here. He's such a poacher. Steals when all the groundwork has been laid."

"Mm-hmm," Suz agrees, knowing all too well. "Be careful out there girlie. I have to run. I have a meeting with the guys from web design."

"Thanks for telling me. I miss you." I say and my chest hurts. I miss everything about Atlanta: my old job, Suz, Frankie, my stupid, squeaky computer chair.

I shove my phone into my pocket and fall into the chair at the little enclave. My legs are noodles. Both from Everett's touching and the news.

Now, I have to see Everett after whatever almost happened. And face Ryan. Wonderful.

Chapter 24

Everett Abrams

I t's only the first week of December but Copper Mountain is freezing.

Now I can't think of the month without thinking of her. Rose cheeks, pink lips, eyes the color of winter trees. I still feel the warmth of her body beneath my hands. I so wanted to kiss her and more. I don't know why. The desire came out of nowhere. I guess not *nowhere*. I've wanted to touch her since my dick pressed against her body a night or two ago. Fuck. I can't even get the days straight, or the feeling out of my mind. And we were both fully clothed. I can't even imagine where my brain would be if I ever got to feel her soft skin, raw, against mine.

I shake my head and try to focus on the task at hand.

For the third time, I pull loose the laces of my boots and tighten them again. They have to be just right. Not too loose, not too tight. Satisfied, I pull my snow pants over them and stand to stretch. The sun is nestled below the horizon, but orange fingers begin to sprout behind peaks and tree lines.

The mountain is silent. Just the breath of cool wind and the creak of snow beneath my board. The lights above the monstrous superpipe leave no shadow uncovered. The tech guy leans against one of the posts, ready for a front-row show. He waves when he sees me. I wave back and crouch down to tighten my bindings. My breath comes faster. My stomach squeezes. It feels like this, like I'm coming home, and like I'm about to jump off a cliff.

I straighten and hop from foot to foot, taking a deep breath. I adjust my mask over my mouth, so the air doesn't burn my lungs as brutally. Slowly, I let myself slide down the incline leading with my right foot.

Tucking myself lower, I drop into the pipe. My stomach dips. All the air leaves my lungs. It's like flying – only so much better. I grin as my board joins the snow again. *Home.*

I cut across to the next wall, right near the tech guy and grab the front of my board, pulling it in front of me. Time stops. I float in mid-air. In this moment, gravity is denied. I spot my landing and a moment later I'm there, crossing the pipe to the other side. I curve sharply before I make it to the lip. Snow sprays in an arc following my board's deep cut.

With my momentum lost, I weave back and forth between the walls, climbing only a few feet. I imagine my routine. Play it out perfectly in my mind. My body reacts the same way it would if I were actually performing the moves – heart in my throat, stomach at my feet. At the end of the pipe, I flip myself around, dig my toe-edge into the snow, and gaze at the beauty. As I slide to a final stop, I let myself drop to my knees and sink back into my heels, hands in my lap.

I stare at the pipe walls. Now having a feel for the snow, I begin to build out my routine. I put different combos together in my mind. Shuffle them around in case I don't execute perfectly on one wall. I always have several options just in case.

I'm not sure how many minutes pass. At the top of the mountain appears another rider dressed in a purple jacket and orange pants.

"Yew, yew, yewwww." Luc howls from the top, waving his arms.

Digging my toe-edge into the snow, I push myself off the ground, and call back to him. I slide further down the slope to the barricades, and out of his way. Luc jumps down into the belly of the beast. Unlike me, he does a full routine: 1080s, double cork, alley-oop. He flies out of the chute heading straight for me. I twist away from the spray of snow I know is coming, but it still hits like a frozen tidal wave.

"How did you like?" He stands after flicking a boot loose.

"Double cork is a little sloppy, otherwise not half-bad."

He throws his arm around my neck and noogies my helmet, "Shut up."

I push him away, laughing, and he catches himself on his free foot. I *click-click* a binding loose and push myself with my back foot towards the ski-lift. Luc follows beside me.

"Looks like you have an audience." He nods towards the balcony above us.

December leans on the railing. She meets my gaze and moves towards the stairs. Instead of sliding towards the lift, I change course to meet her there.

"See ya at the top, Lover Boy," Luc says, his mouth curved up.

"Shut up," I mumble. He throws me a two-finger wave and continues toward the lift.

December leans against the bottom stair post. Her arms wrap around it like it gives her strength. Or some place to put her hands other than me. And suddenly I'm jealous of a post.

Her hair hangs around her shoulders, blowing in the wind. She shivers as a giant gust billows through, tossing and twisting snow. Her eyes are bright this morning – the snow makes everything brighter. I shove my goggles up onto my helmet, squinting at her.

"What's up?"

"I just wanted to remind you to behave this morning."

I smile lazily, "I thought you wanted me to behave badly."

Like maybe this morning? I didn't even get a chance to *really* misbehave. Not like I wanted to, anyways. My eyes rake over her and I feel as hot as I did when she stood between my thighs.

"Only in certain circumstances." She says pointedly. I want to ask her if this morning was one of those circumstances and if I'll get another chance. "You don't have a very good rapport with the media. Mostly because you don't speak with them. Or when you do, it's never more than a few words."

"I'm the strong, silent type."

"We should focus on what you're doing now. Anything you want to mention?"

I don't react. I know she doesn't know about Elevate. And a part of me twists with guilt. "Nope. I'm working with a publicist I'm certain wants to ruin me, though," I tease.

We both look up at the sound of approaching feet. There's a group pounding across the balcony deck. I recognize the man leading the pack as Dan Keegan.

December turns sharply to me, "Just remember–"

"I know, I know: sell myself. Yada, yada, yada."

She jumps off the last step and pulls on the lapels of my jacket, jerking me towards her. She doesn't seem to notice we're only inches apart. I could kiss her if she just tilted her head up. She pushes my hoodie down off the crown of my helmet. Adjusts my yellow neck warmer.

"I was going to say, be yourself," She says, looking up at me. "But sell yourself is better advice. Mention your sponsors if you can but casually. Don't discuss your distaste for Hendrik. People love him. Don't be too humble. You usually are."

I grin and lean in, uttering in a low voice, "You're bossy. Are you always?" I grow warmer. My dick hardens, presses painfully against my zipper even in the cold – would you tell me exactly how you want me to fuck you?

December steps back, swallowing, and pulls at the lapels of her own jacket, "Being directive is one of my strongest qualities."

I nod slowly, "I bet it makes you *very* popular."

She narrows her eyes just as Dan swings around the stairs. His hands fall squarely on December's shoulders. He squeezes.

"December!" He thunders and spins her around. He looks her up and down.

Now it's my turn to narrow my eyes. He's at least twenty-five years older than she is but ogles her. My jaw tightens. My hands ball into fists in my gloves. I swear if he agreed to this only for a chance to sleep with her...

"Dan," December throws her arms around his neck.

"Your mother told me about your promotion. I was so sorry to hear you were–"

"Let's catch up after. Everett's busy, busy, busy today." She dances away and turns towards me. She meets my gaze for a split second and then to my neck warmer, my boots.

"Everett, it's a pleasure," Dan extends his hand. "It'll be a moment while we get ready."

He steps away towards his crew. A few begin to assemble the lighting and sound tools while a handful begin to pad his face with makeup. December steps closer to me, silent.

"So, you two know each other?" I ask, nudging her with my elbow. My curiosity gets the best of me.

She nods, staring at the ground, "Yes. He's a family friend and I've worked with him in the past."

Silence again. The wind blows hard and cold, whistling as it cuts through the trees and village buildings. December hunkers down in her jacket. Her teeth chatter. Unbuckling my helmet, I pull it off along with my cap and loop it around my arm. I tug off my neck warmer, messing my flat helmet-head hair.

"Hey–" December starts as I yank off her hat – strands of her hair raise in the air after it. I smooth them down and hold my neck warmer open, so she can slip her head through. She hesitates.

"Come on. You're cold and only going to get colder."

She hesitates a second longer, then she obliges, fitting the warmer over her head and down her neck. She pulls her hair out from underneath it and looks at me. I can tell she's not sure what to say – thank me or apologize for taking my warmer. Before she can say anything, I push her hat back on, pulling it all the way down over her eyes.

"What do you think?" I ask when she's folded it back up, so she can see again. "Helmet or no helmet, which do you think the ladies will prefer?"

She tilts her head, narrowing her eyes as if she's really considering, "Either looks good."

"Because, I always look good?"

She huffs, wrapping her arms around herself, "Not what I said."

I shrug, putting my hat and helmet back on. It's too cold not to wear them especially since I gave away my warmer, "You didn't have to. I know what you meant."

She laughs, raising her head to the sky, "Where did this cockiness come from?"

"I guess you bring it out of me."

"All righty," Dan Keegan slaps his hands together, interrupting us. He waves his hand for me to step over. "You ready?"

I shrug and crouch to unbuckle my other binding.

"Everett..." December begins as I pick up my board. She looks like she's caught between a hard and a harder place. Her lips move but she doesn't go on.

"Good luck," she manages finally, tucking into herself again.

I nod and move towards Dan and the camera, readying myself for slaughter.

Chapter 25

December Fowl

I let out a rush of breath as Everett glides to the entrance of the Superpipe. He drops in, doing a little hop with a twist. He cuts across the snow, racing towards the wall.

Everett rises into the air and maneuvers into some flippity-loopy-loop and the crowd goes wild. I gasp. A second later he's across to the other side. Now a double flippity-twisty-loop. He moves so fast. Smooth. Easily. Like it's his natural state.

My legs clench together as a warm heat erupts in my stomach and spirals lower. His passion and practice, the way he just throws himself head and heart first...

I shiver as Everett slides to the edge of the gate, fist pumping the air. He has no idea what he's done to me.

He has no idea how many times I walked to his door last night only to turn around and run away. He texted this morning asking if I'd like a breakfast omelet. I didn't answer until I knew he'd left for practice, pretending I slept in late. I got here extra early so I could claim my spot on a prime balcony seat. Made complete with multiple cups of coffee and hot cider; a winter fire pole cracking behind me. And from here I watched. Every practice round waiting to see him.

He's dressed in the same light blue jacket he wore this morning. His snow-pants slouch lazily on his hips. I'll never look as cool as he does in winter gear. The lenses of his goggles are blue, flashing a catch of green when he moves his head just right. A yellow neck warmer, the one he let me borrow just yesterday, is pulled up underneath his goggles. He's not showing a trace of skin, until he yanks it down. He's smiling. I've never witnessed a smile like his before. Not on him. Not on anyone.

Everett has me clutching the railing. A mean wind blows in from the mountain. I nestle deeper into my jacket, remembering the touch of his hands in my hair and wishing I still had his warmer that's draped around his neck. My senses remember the smell of him: evergreen and sweat.

The judges announce the highest score of the day: 92.8.

"Yes!" I shout. I forget about the cold and the heat blossoming between my thighs, and clap with the rest of the crowd.

He hoists his board in the air as Luc and a few other riders launch themselves at him. I can't stop grinning as they pull him towards the podium. Everett stands in the middle, a gold medal draped around his neck. Someone hands the top three competitors a bottle of champagne. As soon as the posed photos are done, they shake the bottles vigorously and fight to have their bottle opened first.

"You didn't tell him, did you?" I freeze, glancing around. Ryan is supposed to be here today. Has he caught up with me?

But it's just Dan. He slides into the gap between the heating pole and the deck, staring at the celebration below.

"He mentioned it in the interview. He still thinks you work at DKS."

"What?" My jaw drops. *Shit.* "Dan, you have to edit that out."

He shakes his head, watching the riders below, "I have no control over the edits."

"What do you mean?" I say frantically. "You're the star. The talent. The executive producer."

Dan turns so his side presses into the railing, elbow propped up, "I have a say in who I interview, the questions I ask, but I am the video-journalist, not the editor or the network."

"What exactly did he say?"

He lifts his head, recalling the interview, "I asked if there was anything else he'd like to say and he thanked you, said you worked with DKS." He grins,

"Then plugged his meet-and-greet. You did a good job working with him. Years ago, an associate of mine tried to get an interview with him and it was a disaster."

"Shit," I murmur and take a breath. The air burns, and so will my mistakes. If – no, *when* Ryan gets wind of this, he'll eat me alive.

Dan shakes my shoulder, "Kid – you're young. We all do stupid things. Even if it gets out, you'll bounce back. But...if there's a chance. If he's *more* than just a client, you can't lie to him." He pauses and gently adds, "You know how that worked out for your parents."

I stare down at the ground, not wanting to face him, "I know."

Two messy divorces and ten years later my mother still hisses when she thinks about my father. I've resorted to hiding photographs of him whenever she visits. It's better than listening to her nasty comments.

"I'm a professional. I never get 'personal' with a client." My cheeks burn thinking about yesterday morning. All the thoughts I've had since. I hope he mistakes the blush as windburn.

Dan gives me a grin like he knows something my young mind can't, "Just tell him." He pats me on the hand and steps away, "Call me if you're ever back in New York."

He leaves me alone in a sea of strangers. I glance down at the podium. Everett and the other riders are nowhere in sight. I strum my fingers across the railing, getting the inkling I should text him. Instead, I pull out my phone and text Suz:

Suzzy Goozy

> Everett's interview airs in an hour. Please watch and tell me how bad it is.

Why would it be bad??

SG

> He mentioned DKS. And me. In the same sentence. As if I still work there.

Whhaaat?? You didn't tell him?

SG

> I'm terrible. I know. Please just watch it.

I slide my phone into my pocket and maneuver through the crowd. Everett's supposed to be doing a meet-and-greet in forty minutes at a snowboard shop a few blocks away. By the time I make it to the shop, there's a line of people streaming around the corner. I flash the security guard a badge the shop owner sent to my room this morning, and make my way up the stairs to a private backroom balcony.

The room erupts in screams. I laugh as a few girls screech with joy as Everett steps into the shop. He fumbles with his wet, black hair and takes a seat. I pull my phone out and snap a few photos from above. The crowd will do the rest.

Two days ago, when the snowboard shop (The Binding) and I announced the meet-and-greet, I challenged fans to use hashtags if they're in the audience. I open Instagram, then TikTok, and find several already posted. Twitter has over a hundred and people are checking into the location on Facebook. I stomp my feet giddily. Questions and fan stories are flooding in. Already my mind is full of new ideas of how Everett can connect with his fanbase.

Comments, pictures, and hashtags keep flying in throughout the entire meet-and-greet. Finally, two hours later, Everett has made it through everyone who stopped by. Every single person who was waiting outside and then crowded into the hot room got a picture, a signature, or both. My chest swells with pride as he shakes hands with the shop owners and continues a conversation with them as they all retreat to the back room. He did so well.

I pull up his page on Instagram. There are a hundred thousand new followers and more raining in. I click on his hashtag and scroll through the shared posts, pausing to read a few.

I linger on one with Everett and a little girl. The caption reads: *Tawni was so excited to meet her hero! We waited in line for hours, after Everett had already seen and visited with hundreds of other fans. As we approached, he recognized her! The weekend after Fall Harvest, Everett helped Tawni learn how to snowboard. It was the best day of her life. Here they are together. She is just beaming. The next photo is such a sweet note he gave her. Can't wait for my Tawni be up on that podium in ten years!*

In the photo, Everett is squatting down at her level. Black eyes staring into the camera and mouth curved into a warm grin. The girl Tawni is missing two teeth and she's smiling so hard her eyes are slits. My heart tugs. I swipe to the next photo and Everett has scribbled next to his photo: Tawni – see you on the podium in 10yrs!

I close the app and slide my phone into my back pocket, taking a steadying breath.

Chapter 26

Everett Abrams

I notice immediately when she slips into the bar. It's like I have Spidey senses just for her.

There are plenty of gorgeous women wandering around, but I recognize December just by catching the back of her head. I separate myself from the Envoy crew and make my way to the second floor railing for a better view. She's dressed in a hunter green sweater and dark jeans that make her ass look sprung and my body ache. Her hair is pulled back into a messy bun, her neck exposed as if inviting hands and lips to run along her skin.

I lean against the railing, waiting for her to look up and find me. She cranes her neck, eyes dart around the bar – eager and anxious. My stomach flutters, is she anxious about seeing me again or someone else? My eyes move around the room, too, trying to catch sight of something, someone who she might be looking for.

A man in a checkered suit jacket approaches her and she bristles. I don't like the way he smiles when she does, like her anxiety is something for him to enjoy. I move towards the stairs, my hackles raised.

"Hey!" Luc jumps in front of me when I've made my way to the bottom. His head obscures my view. I try to look around him but can't see further. He playfully punches me in the shoulder to bring my attention back to him.

He nods to the twin set of tables where a majority of people are huddled, "Let's play a round of pong. Win more than just that gold medal." He smiles lazily.

In college, about all I did well was party games: pong, flippy cup, card games. Name it and I've probably won it. Of course, that all stopped as soon as I went pro full-time. I didn't have the energy or desire to play like I did to pass the time in college. Now, I'm actually doing what I want. I don't want to spend all my time competing. It's just not the frame of mind I want to be in all the time.

I glance at the tables. Hendrik and Marty are the kings. And a part of me wants nothing more than to beat him twice in one day – especially at something he's known for dominating.

"Yeah. Find me when we're up."

Luc's face lights up. He slaps my arm and hops to the tables to call next game. With Luc out of the way, I have an unobscured view of December. Except now she's not there. I glance around, trying to catch sight of her dusty brown hair.

"Hey," A voice calls. "Looking for someone?"

My head follows the sound of her voice. She's occupying the same space I was only moments ago. Her mouth curves up and my stomach flips like it does when I've finally landed a new move. Nothing other than snowboarding has ever done that before.

Keeping my eyes on her, I retrace my steps upstairs. She leans her elbows on the railing and watches me, sexy smirk still on her face. As I reach the final step she slides over. She smells like summer – daffodils and rosemary. It's strange how each time I see her she smells slightly different.

"You look..." My eyes rake over her. The green sweater hugs her breasts and flows freely around her waist. I've never wanted to be a sweater before. In the same moment her breath hitches, her lips part. I'm not sure if she's anxious for me to finish my sentence or anxious for me having started it. Yesterday morning could have meant nothing to her.

I clear my throat and jerk my head towards the bar, "Want a drink?"

She only nods, not taking her eyes off me.

We move towards the bar. She's so close all I can sense is her. Her perfume clouds my mind. Our bodies are apart but so close the air between us sizzles. She orders a drink with several different kinds of rum. I pay, ordering myself another beer, and she thanks me, glancing away. Everything is moving fast and slow at the same time.

I wipe my hands on my jeans. I haven't been this nervous since I was forced to read Shakespeare out loud in High School English. *Why am I so nervous?*

"You miss Atlanta, huh?" I jerk my head towards her pink and blue drink. Beachy.

"*Yess.*" She says it like she's been waiting for someone to notice.

My heart sinks. Once we reach my goal she'll head back to the city. Things will slowly – or maybe not so slowly – return to the way they were. We'll have stilted email conversations; she'll forget who I am, and I'll forget she's not an evil witch behind a computer. Soon there won't be any emails and it will be like we never met.

"What do you miss the most?" I ask, trying to prove to myself it won't happen.

"My cat!" Her eyes pop. She pulls her phone out and presents me with a picture. I notice the long whiskers first. Two golden eyes and gray fur stare back. "This is Frankie."

I laugh because she says it like she's introducing the two of us. Like the furball is here in the *fur* instead of through a glass screen. And now I know the Frankie she mentioned earlier is a cat, not a man. I can't ignore the relief that rushes through me.

"What?" Her nose scrunches up.

"Nothing. You're cute. I mean, *your* cat's really cute."

She gazes down at the screen, "He is, but he's a little hellion. I'm sure my roommate is having so much fun with him." Her finger swipes through a few photos – all of Frankie – until she stops on a woman. Shiny black hair and broad smile. She's wearing burning red lipstick and a golden dress hugs her curves. "This is my roommate/best-friend/cat-sitter, Suz. She's the best."

The way she says '*she's the best*' has me glancing at her. I hadn't thought about how lonely it must be for her. To be up here by herself. New environment, new people, and one pain in the ass client. She came here because of me. She's stayed because of me, and I selfishly want her to stay longer.

December meets my gaze. Her eyes clear, voice without a shake, like I didn't just glimpse her vulnerability, "Suz and I make a really good team. She cooks. I clean. She's the fun one. I'm the serious one. She drags me out to all these wild parties and tries to include me in every social event."

"So, this all really has been for my benefit – this going out, drinking scheme of yours to make me a *bad* boy? It's not how you'd spend a Friday night?" I'm not blind to the way her eyes zoom to my mouth when I say bad. Does she want me to be bad with her? To turn this more *friendly* than professional?

She looks away, her eyes canvasing the room. Her nail taps on her glass, "I go out to network but not often for fun."

We're a perfect match. Two lost puzzle pieces fitting together.

"No man waiting around for you then?"

She grins sultry and all my blood pumps to my groin. Maybe her hand could find its way there again, but not so aggressively.

Her eyes scour the room again before responding, "Just Frankie."

I take a deep drink of beer, shifting. The cool, hoppy liquid does little to put out my desire, but I let it make me bolder, "Atlanta must have been pretty dull then. I would have been on you like snow on a mountain."

Her gaze singes with mine. Her mouth falls opens in surprise and then we both laugh. *On you like snow on a mountain* – not my finest line. I thought hitting on women would be so much easier once I was a cool, successful snowboarder. It's not.

"So," she tucks a wild strand of hair behind her ear, "how do you feel after your first interview and meet-and-greet?"

She so smoothly shifts the conversation from casual to professional, and it's like a punch to the gut. Still much better than a punch to the dick, though.

"Surprisingly good. Over-over whelming at first...beginning..." I choke on my words, but she just gazes at me with her dazzling, steady green eyes. Not a flick of judgement crosses her face, "but then I remembered what you said. They're all here for me and if I want a good model for snowboarding, I'll just have to be it." I shove my shoulder into hers, "All because of you."

"The credit is yours. I just set them up and you knocked them all out."

I shrug, taking another drink, "I mentioned you. With any luck, I won't be the only one making bank out of this deal."

She gives me a tight smile, "I just wish you hadn't."

"Why?" I narrow my eyes, trying to figure her out. "I thought I was helping you? I'm your only client. Some of the guys have been asking about you..." She's looking off across the bar. My throat tightens. I look over her head to see what she could possibly be looking for. Maybe the guy in the suit from before. "Are you waiting for someone?"

"No, no." She snaps around. "No."

The way she oversells it sends needles into my gut. I'm an idiot. I'm here lousily hitting on her like someone way out of practice, growing more into her by the second, and she's waiting for someone else.

Running a hand through my hair, I finish my beer and rise, "I'm meeting Luc for a game."

The second I'm on my feet December's on hers. She presses her hands into my chest, pushing me back into my seat.

"What?"

December leans in, hand pressing into my chest. Her lips brush against mine. Her mouth, soft and warm. The kiss so sudden and brief, I wonder if it happened at all. But then her lips press against mine again. Careful. Measured. Unsure.

I drag her into me and between my legs like she was the other morning. Her hands wrap around my neck as mine settle on her hips. Her breasts press against my chest, and I want her closer. I run my tongue along her lower lip. She tastes like peach lemonade and Malibu rum.

She lets out the faintest of noises and I feel it in my groin. My dick is hard in a second. I pull her closer and shift, pressing my hips into hers. God, I want her.

I want her so bad. Her hands grip my shoulders as she lets out another needy noise.

"Yo." Luc's voice echoes behind us.

December jerks back and I release her, the two of us staring at each other. Her mouth is red, breath rushing out, and green eyes dark. My chest rises and falls faster than it should. She takes another step back, brushing strands of loose hair behind her ear.

"What's up?" I swivel around. *Casual. Casual. Act casual,* beats in my brain at the pace of my racing heart.

Luc wags a finger between us, "You do know you're in a bar."

I nod though honestly a second ago, it had all dropped away.

"What you two were doing is frowned upon in public places."

I make a face, shaking my head, "I don't know what you're talking about."

"*Yeah,*" Luc laughs. "I wouldn't have stopped you, but our game is up."

"Little busy here," I gesture between December and me.

Luc turns his attention to her, eyes alight, croaked shit-eating grin on his face, "Everett's going to play beer pong with me – for important PR purposes. Though," his eyes dart to mine and he smiles broader, "I think the two of you making out may draw more attention."

I ruffle my hair and glance around. Shit. A few eyes are on us. More than I'd like. This isn't exactly the example I meant to be making.

"Great!" Beside me December is nodding. "We were just–"

"Oh, I got what you were doing" Luc winks, laughing.

I groan, throwing my head back. He's never going to let me live this down. And a tide of unease rolls through me. What the fuck is happening? I feel like I've just crossed the bridge of no return.

"I'll be waiting." Luc sings as he backs away, but I'm already hardly paying him any attention.

"What was that?" I rise, giving her a sideways look and readjusting the front of my jeans.

She grabs her drink and chugs it, staring at the uncomfortable notch in my pants before dragging her eyes up to mine, "I have no idea."

And she giggles, wiping her mouth, "I have no idea. I never do anything like that – I just...did it!"

"Okay," I say, still not sure what to think. My chest pinches. I like having rules and guidelines. Schedules and routine. I like knowing exactly what is expected of me. And, while, I've wanted to kiss her and touch her since the morning in that hotel room – I just never thought it would make me feel like this. A little lost and uncertain, more confused than I was with all my hidden wantings.

Before this very moment we were client and publicist. We were defined. Now the boundaries have been blown over like snow in a blizzard. And it...terrifies me.

December continues as if she doesn't see how this has changed everything, "My flight leaves early tomorrow morning, so I'll see you back at Blue Sky."

She steps away from the bar and I grab her hand, my chest squeezing so hard it's hard to breathe. She looks over her shoulder at me.

"Are you sure? Maybe we should..." I shrug

"I have some work to do, anyways," she says, missing my meaning.

But I'm frozen. My mind moving in slow motion. Her hand slips from mine. She offers me a smile and then slides into the crowd. And she's gone by the time my mind has formulated the words for my thoughts.

Chapter 27

EVERETT ABRAMS

The first hour to Denver from Copper Mountain is a blur of shadows, road signs, and headlights.

Luc snores from across the cab, his mouth hanging open, sunglasses on despite the dark. I pull off at a gas station at the edge of town, so small if I blink, I'd miss it. The cold air bites as I get out to fuel up. While the pump is working, I hop back into the rental and flip through my emails. My thumb hovers over one sent from December's agency, DKS.

I lick my lips as if I could taste the Malibu on her lips again. I open the attachments, written in the signature orange and black letterhead of DKS. It's a new set of contracts. There's a gnawing at my gut and I hesitate. Why didn't she mention she'd sent over contracts?

Since Copper and the kiss, we've hardly connected. Four days have passed, and I've found myself looking more and more at my phone. Hoping to see a text, call, email. Anything from her. And when she has texted with updates about our my socials and potential sponsors, I'm hanging by every word. It's been nothing but professional. Yet my heart has raced every time I see a notification from her. I have truly lost it.

Scrolling to the bottom, I apply my electronic signature and forward it along as the pump clicks off. Hopping outside, I finish up and return to the truck, rubbing the cold from my hands. A moment later we're back on the road. I glance over at Luc. He lets out a snore, jerking, and I laugh.

Envoy has been hosting Luc and I, plus the other snowboarders on a brand retreat. We've been staying in Aspen and Sundown, shredding up all the runs and backcountry when the weather's good. Envoy has us all out here to try out new gear, take shoots and video, and pamper us. Each night we've had an hour of massages, long steams in the sauna, and even hooked me up with a physical therapist. But today, we're off to Denver to meet my agent Corey. Then back to Blue Sky.

I glance at the clock, taking a breath. As soon as the dash clock flips to seven I'm dialing Olivia.

After I'd gotten back to my room last night, my agent, Corey, called me. I squeeze the steering wheel, biting my bottom lip to stay silent. Even now just thinking about the news he broke, the great opportunity ahead, if Luc wasn't sleeping I'd probably let it out. Yell. Whoot. Anything to express this excitement.

A contract with a new sponsor!

We made arrangements to meet in Denver. Meet the executive team of Minotaur Auto, go over the contract details, and sign documents. He passed a copy of the contract to me, and I hastily sent it off it to my soon-to-be sister-in-law Olivia. My thumb had hovered over sending it to December, but I didn't. I'm not sure if contracts are something I'm supposed to send to my publicist.

I usually read the terms myself, but last night I was so burnt out, I passed out. Besides, I miss a lot of things when reading. Especially in the legal jargon. Olivia has been my buffer. She and Kelly started dating before I went pro. So, she's read every one of my contracts. As a paralegal and a critical reader, she catches the things I overlook and explains the parts I don't understand. Corey's great but it's better to have another pair of eyes. Someone I trust completely.

Olivia picks up on the third ring, "Oh my god Everett! This is fantastic! They want to give you their top tier sports vehicle, on top of the money!"

Her excitement stirs Luc. He jolts up and wipes his mouth. The papers against his chest rustle and he adjusts the seat to sitting position. I had printed a physical copy of the contract for him, but he's been too busy sleeping off the last party to read.

"And Magic Drinks? I've never heard of them, but they want you to make an exclusive drink? You're basically Michael Jordan right now," Olivia continues.

I nearly veer off the road, "What? There's two contracts in there? Corey only mentioned the one with the auto maker."

"Yeah. I guess he wanted to give you the best news or surprise you. Tell me about Magic Drinks, what's that about?"

"They're pretty new. I don't know so much. December introduced me to them a couple of weeks ago. Made me do this thing on Instagram with one of their drinks and it blew up," I explain, my eyes on the road.

"*Oooh* December. Who's this? Are you keeping a secret lover?"

"No. She's my publicist."

On the other side of the truck, Luc laughs and then whisper-shouts, "They made out at a bar!"

I shoot daggers at him but Olivia continues, "I think they're both really great offers. You should definitely accept and thank Corey and this December person for a job well done. Corey did great negotiating up to seventy-five thousand and even your royalties up to eight percent with Magic. You better give him a nice Christmas gift."

"What about the contract with the SUV? What does that look like?"

"Everett, you need to read these yourself."

"I know. I usually do but the last few days have been crazy. And Luc passed out, so I had to drive."

She laughs, "Okay, okay. You Abrams and your excuses. I swear Kelly keeps a list of them in his back pocket. So, the contract to Minotaur Auto is good. They offered ninety thousand paid over twelve months, plus the vehicle. Then it looks like after next year they want to reconsider the contract. Which is usually a good thing. Means if it goes well this year, they'll probably give you more money."

"All right," I mutter, not feeling nearly as confident as she is. They probably added the yearly renewal so they can backout if more sponsors continue to dump me. "Thanks Liv."

"Of course, what's a sister-in-law for?" There's murmuring in the background. "Your brother is up, and it's my turn to make breakfast. See you this weekend!"

"Burn his bacon!" I order. She lets out a bark of laughter before hanging up.

As soon as I'm off the phone, I turn up the volume on the radio. Music doesn't usually help slow my brain, but I need a little distraction from the news before it explodes. Two new contracts? In a matter of a week, I'm only a little short on what extra funding the investors want. This is unreal.

Beside me Luc shuffles through the contract. To the east, the sky begins to turn pink, bleeding into orange. Mountains cut into the darkness like jagged teeth.

"Holy shit, I can't believe we're so close already! We have three weeks left and only need thirty-five grand."

I hardly hear him, tapping my thumbs on the steering wheel, music ringing on. I'm anxious to meet with Corey and sign contracts. Make this official before anyone decides to back out.

"Thinking about your girlfriend?"

I glance sharply in Luc's direction. His sunglasses are pushed up on his forehead.

"What do you even know about her? Besides she's pretty and makes your dick hard."

"What the fuck," I say, letting out a half-laugh. "Would you stop."

"What, man? I haven't seen you kiss someone in public since college. It's great, but what is it?"

I take a breath. My knuckles turn white around the wheel. I release and stretch my fingers out, "I don't know. We haven't really talked since that night."

"Fuck, Everett," Luc punches my shoulder. "Do you even like her?"

I glare at him, "Do I even like her? Yeah."

I think about her massaging my knee, the focus written all over her face. My mind flashes to Hendrik's party. The two of us leaning against the wall, not saying anything at all. Then the look of rage and shock when she learned I wanted two hundred thousand dollars in five weeks; My mind shifts to the softness of her voice when she was in my hotel room at Copper. The way my neck warmer still smells of her. Her lips – soft and sweet against mine. I let out a breath. Calm settles over me.

"Yeah, I like her, but I don't want to sit here and talk to you about it. Let's go over things with Elevate."

Luc reaches behind the seat and grabs the laptop bag, pulling it out. The computer screen casts light across his face.

"Week two of five is nearly ending, so we have three weeks left to raise the additional money. Let's come up with some ideas," Luc directs.

My mind shifts back to Copper and seeing two riders under Pike Boards, "What about getting the names, figures, and maybe early signatures for snowboarders who want to join the brand? I'm sure it'll look good if we already have that lined up."

Luc's fingers clack against the keyboard as my mind races with ideas.

I open my mouth to speak but Luc interrupts, "Don't you dare say no Hendrik."

"Why would we want him? The guy's a dick and not even a great snowboarder."

Luc glares at me, "He's not as good as you or me, but he's good. And people love him. He could bring a lot of attention to our company."

I clench my jaw. Attention isn't what I want. I want Elevate to be successful, of course. I want to be able to retire my parents and Luc's; take care of his sister. I want to be able to retire. Only, I won't sell out my morals for it. But I don't argue with him. I won't talk to Hendrik and I doubt Luc will.

When we arrive in Denver an hour later, Luc and I have set up our plan of action. Luc's going to work on things at a breakfast spot down the street from the coffee house where I'm meeting Corey.

Luc grumbles about getting a table, stepping onto the cobblestone sidewalk, and heads towards the main doors. I move in the opposite direction, pulling out my phone. There are no messages from December and my heart plummets. I was hoping she'd at least text me after I signed her new contract.

I shove the device into my back pocket and yank the door open harder than I need to. As soon as I step inside, I'm bombarded with the strong smell of craft coffee and syrup. I'm not much of a craft coffee drinker, but I need it this morning.

Corey sits at a window booth in the corner. No one is sitting with him and a wave of relief washes over me. Looks like Minotaur Auto won't be joining us. I'm grateful. My battery is just about shot on social interaction. Corey waves when he notices me. I wave back and collect my drink from the barista.

Standing, he shakes my hand vigorously before unbuttoning his suit jacket and plopping down again. The two official contracts from Magic Drinks and Minotaur Auto sit right in front of me.

"Minotaur Auto sends their apologies. Unfortunately, they overbooked and needed to be in Anchorage today. But they're excited to personally deliver your new Minotaur SUV!"

Corey and I dig into the contract. He goes over all the nitty-gritty details, and what he expects next. By the time we've finished, three hours have passed and my brain feels like sludge.

"The first of many new contracts," I say, glancing up at Corey as I press the pen to paper.

A zap of excitement coils through me and I smile. It feels just like when I signed my first offer – but almost sweeter this time. I'm older and the recent losses I've had are reminders these offers aren't as easy to come by as they were when my career started; when the industry still saw so much potential in me.

Corey beams, "I told you December could work wonders. Too bad about her though."

My hand jerks across the paper, throwing off my signature, "What do you mean?"

"Oh, she hasn't told you?" He tries to suppress a smile. I know Corey. He loves to be the first person to share the news – good or bad. "She was up for a big promotion. *Big*, big. Her co-worker stole it right from under her, though. I've never worked with him, Dawson something, but I've heard he's a tricky little bastard. Stealing clients, skimming contracts, getting better publicists fired."

I stare past him for a moment. My mind pushes the pieces together. So, that's why she showed up at Blue Sky. He took her promotion and probably stole her clients, too. I don't know how someone could drop her just like that. She's done so much for me already – even though I was an ass at first.

I shake my head and flip through the pages, initialing, "She didn't mention it."

"Probably doesn't want to stir up trouble. You're a lucky guy to have her on your team."

Handing him the paperwork, he tidies it with a *thump-thump* on the table. I am lucky to have her, but at the same time, she's hard to pin down. Sometimes, it's like she can't wait to get away from me. And why didn't she tell me about losing her promotion? I sigh, I guess I haven't been the easiest person to talk to.

"It was great to see you, Everett. Hopefully I'll be seeing more of you soon," Corey stands and shakes my hand before leaving the coffee house.

I follow after him and make my way to Luc a door down.

He practically springs out of his seat and into the truck when he sees me.

"Let's get the fuck out of Denver. Blue Mountain is calling me home."

And maybe I'm excited to see December.

Chapter 28

December Fowl

B ack at Blue Mountain, the days have blended.

Everett has spent the last four days with the rest of the Envoy snowboard team prowling the mountains in Colorado. One day they were in Sundown, the next Aspen.

We haven't spoken – personally – since our encounter at the bar. I've made excuses to text him about social media, and our PR strategy. Since I left him to play beer pong with Luc my stomach has done nothing but somersault. I shouldn't have left him. *No*, I shouldn't have kissed him.

I blink at my computer screen, my vision going blurry. I scrub a hand down my face. So stupid. Ryan was there, but I was so wobble-legged and lust-minded I didn't even consider he could have cornered Everett as soon as I was gone. Or worse, witnessed our mini make out.

"*Okay.*" Torrance snatches my hands from my face. "That's enough of that. You're doing more harm than good."

I jolt at her words. How true are they? Am I going to hurt Everett more than help him? Learning I've lied to him will hurt him, but will I at least be able to offset that with sales? I haven't heard anything from his agent Corey since I sent him the Magic Energy contract, or Everett himself, but it's still early. Only Everett doesn't have months. He has *weeks*. And I'm still not sure why he even needs so much money quickly.

"*December.*"

Torrance snaps her fingers and I pop out of my thoughts. She opens her mouth to say something, but jerks her head towards the bar. A row of skiers just sat down, waiting to be served. She gives me a look but steps away.

"Decemburrr." Hendrik calls.

I pretend not to hear him.

He leans into my booth and says low, "I'll have whatever you were giving Everett the other night." I freeze, color rising to my cheeks. He laughs and waves his hand dismissively. "Just teasing."

"What do you want?" *Asshole.*

"Sorry, that was really in bad taste." He cringes.

I let myself take my frustration out on Hendrik, "You think? Here I heard you were this smooth-talking womanizer. I'd hate to hear the things you say to the women you actually manage to sleep with."

"Turns out," he shrugs, "I'm not very good at talking to women I'm not intending to sleep with."

I roll my eyes, snapping my laptop shut, "Even more unsettling is how you thought *that* confession would make it better." His brows rise in interest. "I'd be offended if you wanted to sleep with me. It's just sad the only women you talk to are the ones you sleep with."

I sigh. Thank god Everett is not – and does not – want to be anything like him. A surge of pride sprouts through me. I'm happy he was able to recognize he's better than this behavior. Sure, Hendrik makes loads of money but he's a dick.

Hendrick clears his throat, rubbing the back of his neck, "What I wanted to say is, I would like to work with you."

I sit up straighter, looking him up and down. Maybe he does have potential. And I want to roll my eyes at myself. I hate the part of me who's ready to forgive him as soon as he says the magic three works: *work with you.* I force myself to say anything other than yes.

"The first thing we'd have to do is rid you of that misogynistic attitude."

"Misogynist, really? I love women!"

I give him a look, "Didn't you just say you only talk to women you plan to seduce?"

"That's not what I meant."

"Okay, so tell me what you do mean. Why do you want to work with me? What are your goals?"

He blanches, "Isn't that part of your job?"

I narrow my eyes, "I may be a woman, but I am not your mother. I won't do everything for you. Come see me when you have some solid goals and motives in mind."

Hendrik stalks off without another word. A moment later Torrance pops her head into my booth.

"Did you tell him?"

She doesn't have to clarify who *him* is. I've only been working with Everett for over a week and yet he's everywhere, in every conversation, nearly ever thought.

"Nope." My throat tightens. This keeps getting messier and messier. Why did I kiss him?

Torrance dips her head to the door before stepping away, "Now's your chance."

I suck in a breath at the sight of Everett striding towards me dressed in his snow gear, eyes locked on me. Today he's outfitted in a dark purple patterned jacket and black snowpants. I love, love the purple. He looks...softer. More like himself, strangely. My heart races faster the closer he gets. I gulp down a lungful of air, suddenly finding it hard to breathe. I flip open my laptop again, needing my hands to do something.

My mind drifts from him for a moment as I pull up a document. As I turn back to him, he's unzipped his jacket, revealing an image of the same abominable snow monster from the deck of his snowboard. The hood pulled up over his head. His dark hair sticks out like licks of darkness. He pushes the hood down as he slides into the booth beside me. He allows the slightest hint of a smile.

I blink up at him. My panties are now soaked. *Soaked.*

At least he can't tell. His smile snakes into his eyes and he stares at me dangerously. *Or maybe he knows.*

He leans towards me, pressing his shoulder into mine "Did you miss me?"

"I..." my mouth opens and I blink, glitching out. My mind weighs both responses, yes, or no. Both are equally dangerous.

Lucky for me, Luc saunters over and smacks Everett on the back of the head, winking at me.

"Dude," Everett backhands Luc in the stomach. "What was that for?"

"I knew it. Your first stop would be to visit *her.*"

Warm fuzzies erupt in my stomach, heart racing. My eyes dart to Everett. The freckles on his cheeks. The softness of his lips. Fondness and desire equally tug at me, like I'm so full of feelings for him I could explode.

Everett gives Luc a cutting, shut-up-man look.

"December and Everett sitting in a tree..." Luc singsongs as he turns away.

Everett turns his attention to me and I feel like the sun – all planets orbit me, "What are you doing?"

"Working." I lean into him, tapping a key on my laptop to demonstrate.

"Well, as your one and only client, you should come over. I have news and we could work on stuff."

I cross my legs and squeeze them together in hopes of quieting the excited party going on down there, "Stuff?"

"PR stuff."

"Mhmm. Gotcha."

His eyes drop to my lips and his mouth crooks up as if remembering the kiss. My body heats as he repeats, "Stuff."

I'm nodding, "Stuff is good."

He laughs. His smile is gorgeous. *He* is gorgeous and it hurts. Those dark eyes full of light and laughter lines everywhere. I just want to, to – do something even crazier than kissing him.

"Come on then," He jerks his head towards the door.

I snap my laptop shut again and shove it into my bag. He slides out of the booth and stands, flipping his hood back over his head and zipping his jacket. I wrestle my way into my jacket, too flustered to do it smoothly.

I feel Torrance's eyes on me as we walk towards the door and I'm thankful I have this fluffy jacket to cower in.

Chapter 29

DECEMBER FOWL

Everett pushes into the house as the garage door groans into place. He smiles at me, and I smile back, a hum running through my body. Only two weeks ago I was shaking my fist at him, cursing his name in temperate Atlanta. A week ago, I was on his doorstep, still cursing his name. Now I eagerly walk into his home. My body is hopeful to be cursing his name in a different way.

It's a strange feeling to go from hating to tolerating and now *wanting* him in weeks. Even stranger, is how guilty I feel about it. I have no right to like him when I'm harboring secrets.

"I'm ordering a pizza." I declare as soon as we're inside. Pizza fixes everything.

"You are not ordering pizza." I shoot him a look and he goes on, "I can't eat it, so it wouldn't be fair."

"Sure, you can eat pizza." I spin around and walk backwards deeper into his house. "You're already in crazy good shape and I need nourishment."

"Why don't we make something we both agree on?"

My shoulders slouch, "But I'm hungry and lazy."

He drops his hands on my shoulders and gives me a sympathetic squeeze. I feel it ricochet through my entire body.

"I'm the cleaner. Not the cook," I continue.

"I'll teach you."

He turns into the kitchen and begins pulling out cookware.

"I don't think you're understanding quite how bad I am at this. I once burned mac and cheese. Mac and cheese, Everett!"

He turns his head and grins, "There won't be any burning while I'm around. Now get over here."

I sigh and leave the kitchen to deposit my bag and winter clothing beside the couch. When I turn, he's waiting for me. Leaned up against the counter. He spreads his arms wide.

"This is your playground. You can use anything you want."

I nip my bottom lip. I don't even know where to begin. The fridge seems like the best option. Maybe I'll get lucky and find leftovers. I pull the door open and peek my head in. The shelves are stocked with fresh greenery, colorful peppers, and my best friend, cheese. I pull out a bag of shredded Colby Jack and rest it on the counter, letting the fridge slap shut beside me.

"Cheese. All you're having is cheese?"

I puff out my chest, "No. All *we're* having is cheese."

He laughs and it's like I won the lottery. I rise up on my toes and start pulling open cabinets to distract myself from reaching for him.

Everett's right behind me. I feel his shirt brush against my back. His heavy presence only centimeters away. I shiver, goosebumps climbing my skin. I want to lean back and find out how it would feel with him pressed up against me. He doesn't touch me, and it makes me want him to even more. Instead, Everett pushes the cabinet shut. I open another. He shuts that one, too.

"Hey." I spin around. I'm eye-level with his throat. His delicious Adam's apple. I want to lean in and brush him there with my teeth. I tilt my head up to his dark eyes, "Why do you keep doing that? If you want me to cook, I need a cookbook!"

Swinging around again, I open yet another cabinet. As before, he shuts it. He drops his hands on my hips, and I swear to god I almost burst. This is how touch deprived I am. How much I want his hands there and everywhere.

He steers me to the refrigerator again. With one hand he pulls the door open. The other remains on my hip. My attention is there. The fridge could be empty for all I care.

His thumb slips under the hem of my shirt and I suck in a breath, leaning back into him.

"We'll make whatever looks good. No instructions needed," He takes his hands off me and digs through the appliance.

I step back, gripping the counter, and take a breath until my mind comes back. Everett has selected two chicken breasts, a bag of tomatoes, spinach, and basil leaves. His hands full, he indicates with his head to follow him over to the stove. He lays it all out on the counter.

"Stuffed breasts," He glances at mine. His brows shoot up a fraction when he meets my gaze.

"Seriously, so juvenile."

Everett just laughs and puts me to work.

He shows me how to cut four slits into the chicken just deep enough to stuff cheese, spinach, tomato, and more cheese into the pockets. We wash our hands and sprinkle basil leaves and other spices overtop.

Next, we prepare a combination of brown rice and quinoa. He makes me pick a seasoning to mix with it. Taking a sniff sample of each, I pick the lemon pepper. Now, we wait.

I sit on one side of the couch, legs crossed, and face him. He slouches back. His neck supported by the back cushions, socked feet propped up on the coffee table.

"Why no cookbooks?"

He glances at me out of the corner of his eye, "Did you not see me in there, woman? I don't need no cookbook."

"But what if you want to try something new?"

"Then I try something new."

"But–"

He sits up and laughs. "December, I don't use cookbooks. I don't like to read. If it's necessary, I will, or Luc will. But I've found I can do it without a guidebook."

My attention roams from him to the TV. *The Mentalist* is back on, Jane working with another psychic. I've seen every episode about a thousand times.

I can't sit still. I shift and reach down for my bag at the end of the couch. I pull out my laptop and power it up. There were a few things I wanted to discuss with him, and we did say I was visiting for PR reasons. I don't want him to think I'm just here to hang out with him...unless he wants me here just to hang out with me. But there's no way I'm asking him.

"So, you have another meet-and-greet Friday morning at Jake's Skate and Snow Shop. Don't worry," I raise my hand before he can refute it, "I made time for practice beforehand. Then, a meet-the-press event at the Grand Lodge at noon. Preliminaries to follow. After that, you're free to do whatever, but *please* make an effort to socialize."

I look up and he's watching me, "Didn't we say the last time that parties aren't really our scene?"

My chest flutters, caught on his words: *our scene.* Paired. Like chicken and rice. I glance down at my computer, pretending to be fascinated by something on my screen.

"I won't be going to the Dew Tour." I peek over my monitor.

"Oh." His eyes widen in surprise then narrow critically, "Why not?"

"Like you said, you're my only client and I've hardly earned us anything. But it will come."

"Wouldn't your agency cover it?"

"You know what's interesting?" I point my finger at him. "When I first met you, you had such facial control. You were like a brick wall and now you've opened up into this very expressive person."

"Expressive?" He balks.

"Yes! What's so wrong with that?"

He shifts, "It's sounds too close to *sensitive*."

"Well, it's true and I like emotionally available men – men who accept their sensitive side. Plus, it's a good indicator of your how our relationship has grown."

At the word *relationship*, Everett stills. His eyes slowly drift in my direction.

"Our professional relationship." I amend, heart skittering. "And, maybe, our personal relationship, too. We didn't have one before."

His eyes are steady and dark as ever.

Compelled to continue I say, "I've never had personal relationships with clients before. And you were the last person I would ever imagine having one with. I was so ready to throw in my resignation when you wouldn't go to the gala and then..." I swallow. "I came up here."

"I'm glad I didn't fire you for/because of that gala invite."

My mouth falls open, "You were going to fire me?"

My chest aches, bringing back the painful feelings of my meeting with Mr. King. And the guilt of being fired but keeping it from him.

Everett tilts his head and gives me a coaxing look, "You knew nothing about me or this industry when you sent me that invite. Don't worry, I've taught you well."

I throw the couch pillow at him as the oven timer goes off. I collect the plates and silverware as Everett pulls out the sizzling chicken. He checks the interior temperature as I survey the rice. Perfectly prepared.

We take our plates into the living room and eat in silence as *The Mentalist* plays on. This time the silence doesn't compel me to fill it. It's nice to be quiet together and I find my mind is too, for once.

Once we're finished, we carry our plates into the kitchen. I rinse while Everett places them in the dishwasher. Mess all cleaned, he lifts himself onto the counter, the muscles in his triceps and biceps working, and smiles like he has a secret.

"What?" I say looking at him sideways.

His eyes grow wide like a kid on Christmas morning, "Corey and I went over new offers yesterday."

"Everett, that's amazing!" I clap my hands together. Joy and pride spread from my chest – we've done it. Everett finally has another offer.

"Now can you go on the Dew Tour?"

Now I can get paid! With the realization, my excitement vanishes and dread sinks in. How can I ask him to pay me when he doesn't know I'm no longer with DKS? It would be like stealing from a friend.

Everett twitches. His eyes narrow a smidge, "What?"

I don't want to ruin this for him. He's the most moral person I know, almost annoyingly. What if he decides not to take the offer because it was nurtured out of lies? I can't do that to him, but I can't take his money either.

I clap my hands together again, forcing a happy smile, "Wow. This is great. You should be so proud. You've been so great."

He tilts his head, trying to figure out why my words are real, but my body language doesn't align.

"I have to go." I move back to the couch and snatch up my bag.

Everett hops down from the counter, and I move faster, hurrying to my jacket and bag at the floor. He follows me. He has that look on his face – like I'm a thousand-piece puzzle that won't fit together right.

"You don't want to finish the episode, or read the contract, or work on things together?"

I hesitate, heart squeezing. So, he did invite me over just to hang out. Without saying it. He could have easily texted the news, made his dinner alone, but he didn't. He wanted me here. My chest squeezes tight – so tight my next breath is a gasp. I blink back tears. I'm ruining this. I don't want to ruin this.

"Everett," I say with shaky lips, turning to look at him. "I need to tell you something."

Chapter 30

DECEMBER FOWL

Oh my god.

Oh my god. I'm telling him. I have to tell him. I'm telling him. I close my eyes and pray for strength.

His forehead crinkles.

When I first met him, he was a man of stone, a blank sheet of paper. A master of facial control. Now I know it wasn't true. I just wasn't letting him show me this side, but I am here for it now.

"I have to tell you something," I repeat. Tears well in my eyes and I pray he doesn't think they're my way out of this. "DKS, they-they–"

"Is this about that Ryan Dawson guy?" He steps closer, his hands reach for me.

I take a step back, my heart skittering to a stop. *Shit, shit, shit,* "What? How do you know?"

"I met Corey in Denver. He said this guy took your clients. Everything."

I look away, swallowing hard. Everett knowing even part of my secret hurts more than I thought it would. I don't want him to think less of me but it's impossible not to. I lost my job. I lied. I kept lying.

"How did your agency just let him do that to you? Why didn't you tell me?"

I look up and he's gazing at me with his dark eyes so tender it makes me want to cry. Not angry, not hateful. A soft curiosity. I take a breath, my lips shaking. I blink away the pressure in my eyes. I'm not going to cry. The last thing I want is for him to stay out of pity. I want to tell him the truth.

"That's only part of it. I'm sorry I didn't tell you. I was embarrassed. I was going to tell you so many times." His steady eyes are locked on mine. "I didn't intend to show up at Blue Mountain and lie to you. I was going to pitch my plan, so you'd see I'm the best publicist for you. But then I met you and you were so...*perfect*."

His eyes narrow, tilting his head. I raise my hand to stop whatever he's thinking.

"In the best way possible. You're so good at what you do, and you have these crazy expectations for yourself. How would they not apply to me? I didn't think you'd understand how I was..." I take a moment, colleting all the courage I have. "Fired."

"What?" His head jerks back. "When did they fire you?"

I take a breath, staring at the blue kitchen cabinet near his leg. The cabinet where I hid the letter. I step in front of him and open it. The letter is still safe in an assortment of pots, pans, lids. I pull it out and hand it to him.

"I haven't told anyone. Just me and the people at the agency know. My clients decided to stay with the agency, which was the biggest wound. I worked so hard for them. I didn't come here to lie to you. It just...happened."

"What?" He shakes his head. "What is this?" He rips open the envelope, pulls out DKS' letterhead. The paper shakes in his hand as his eyes scour over it, features twisted.

"Where did you? How did it?" Everett shakes his head like he's shaking a daze from his eyes. "Slow down. Where did you get this?"

I look away, "The first day we met, you went upstairs, and I was here having a look around. I saw the letter and I knew. I knew they were alerting you of my termination, so I put it in there."

"You hid this from me? You stuffed it into my cupboard?" He lets out a huff of a laugh but his face says this is anything but funny.

"I just acted. I saw it and I knew from your reaction at seeing me, you wouldn't listen to a thing I said if you knew I was fired. And I knew I could help you. And I did. You have new contracts–"

175

My eyes drift to his. His face is pulled tight as he searches for something in my eyes.

"What are you saying? I don't – I mean, when I first met you, I thought you were this ruthless publicist. And now I was thinking you might actually care. Like me. But," he spins around, knotting his hands in his hair. The letter crinkles and he shifts to face me again, "you were faking it. This was all to get what you wanted from me."

My chest aches. The way he's looking at me – his eyes once tender, now hard. Shifting, like he can't trust what's right in front of him: me.

"I'm sorry," I babble. "I knew right when I met you, you wouldn't give me a second chance. You wouldn't work with me if you knew. I had to–"

"So, this is my fault? It's my fault you lied to me and hid my shit." His jaw flexes. If eyes could light fire, his would. But there's more than anger written across his face. Doubt. Betrayal.

"No," I reach for his arm, but he pulls away. Ohmygod. How did this blow up? How did I let myself hope it wouldn't? I take a breath, "This is my fault. Not yours. I was fired. And then I came up here because you were the only client they hadn't taken yet. I wanted to tell you right away but then I met you and I couldn't."

Everett's hard gaze burn me. His jaw flexes in disbelief, and I see the trust he had in me falling away. I hurry on, hoping to piece this back together.

"I knew you wouldn't understand why I was fired. I don't even understand it. I didn't want you to get rid of me, too. We needed each other. I wanted to tell you every second after, I didn't. I just...didn't know how, and then it kept building."

"Did you really just say I wouldn't understand?"

I hesitate, "You have these expectations. You're so fucking good. You have the best of everything. If I told you I was fired for not producing, I wouldn't be the best. But I am. I'm the best publicist for you. Look what we've done. I mean, only thirty-five thousand left to go in two weeks! I've never worked so hard, and you wouldn't have been able to accomplish this with anyone else."

Everett blows out a hot breath, glaring at the ceiling and then turns his blazing gaze to me, "God, I'm such an idiot."

"You're not. You're not."

"I am!" He says, his voice charged with hurt. He stares at the ceiling again for a moment like it will bring him peace. "What's real with you and what's not? I'm having a tough time distinguishing. You say you wanted to tell me the whole time, but why did you wait this long?"

Before I can speak, "Were you trying to flirt with me to soften the blow? I mean, shit, I'm already heart over fucking head into you, come to find out you aren't you."

"I am me! You know me. This has all been me. You *know* me."

"I don't. I thought I did, but it's all been a lie. But I guess that's PR 101."

I blink. He just cut me. All those nasty things I've been saying about myself, he just confirmed them. The one person I wanted – *needed* – more than anyone to tell me I'm not as awful and fucked up as I think I am for being fired and then lying, just confirmed I am all of those things.

"I–" I choke, a knot in my throat. "I'm sorry. This is why I didn't tell you. If it's not perfect, if it's not precisely how you like it, you cut it. I am sorry. I am. I wish with every fiber in my being I could rewind time and tell you straight away, but I didn't, and I didn't, and I didn't. I fucked up. I did. And then I started to like you, but I knew Everett Abrams, King of the Mountain, doesn't lose. Doesn't do weakness and could not possibly like a fired loser like me."

Tears are in my eyes now, clouding my vision, "I lied and I would do anything, *anything,* to make it up to you because I know I hurt you. I didn't intend to, I promise. This is me, Everett. I fuck up. I do all the fucking time, but I'm a great publicist and an even better friend. I know you're mad and I'm not asking you not to be. I just...I want you to see me and accept me as I am, flaws and all."

Everett's mouth slips open. Then he clamps it shut, staring at something above my head. I'd shared this tip with him when we went over media training. A tactic used to stay focused and guarded. And it feels like a knife to my chest. He's boxing me out.

"You can't put this on me right now. I'll call a Lyft or Torrance to come get you."

"Everett, please. Can we talk about this? Let me explain."

His eyes drop to mine, "Oh, you have explained. You had me for a second. You did. I trusted you." Then his gaze slides away and he moves around me like I'm nothing.

I squeeze my eyes shut and listen to his footsteps move away, the creak of stairs, and finally the click of his door as he shuts me out. Covering my mouth, I cry into my hands, eyes blurring and burning as tears streak down my cheeks.

Chapter 31

December Fowl

My phone hums against the counter. I glance now and my mother's face flashes across the screen.

The third call she's made today.

I flip my phone over and guilt sinks into my stomach. I don't know how to face her. Or dad, or Junie. I told Everett and I thought it would be easier after I broke the news to him. But it's not. It's harder. Flashes of the scene at Everett's last night linger in my mind. I squeeze my eyes shut and try to take a deep breath.

I'm ignoring my mother. I miss Suz and Frankie. I could really use a cuddle session with the furball right now. I'm just trying to keep myself together, but the harder I try the more I tear myself apart.

How do I fix this? How do I fix this? The question tumbles around in my brain, exhausting me.

Huffing, I push myself off the couch. I have to get out of this house, out of my head. Dressing warmly, I sling my backpack over my shoulders, computer jostling inside. I'll go for a walk and maybe the fresh air will inspire me. Make me feel more like me.

The cold bites at my lungs as I make my way across Torrance's front porch and down the stairs. Overnight, the sky dumped another three inches of white fluff on the ground. I've only ever seen snow like this in pictures. New York snow is nothing like this. Snow at Blue Mountain is fluffy, pure white, and smells of pine.

I graze my hand along a pile of snow, like powdered sugar. I want to bottle some up and take it with me when I go back to Atlanta. I swallow. A sharp ache flashing through me – I don't want to think about going back.

I meander down the snow-covered bike trail to town. The snow is piled thigh-high on either side. The trees are draped in fresh snowfall, curtains of white. The *crunch-crunch* of my boots the only sound. Everything is muffled like a giant bubble has been dropped over the area, cutting down sound.

Even as I approach Blue Sky the quiet stays. I pull out my phone, compelled to capture the stillness. At least maybe later I can look back on the quiet beauty here and be put at ease. I snap a few of the covered trees, the trail marked with only my footprints, and the cabin fringes of Blue Sky as I approach.

Blue Sky consists of one main street, Ridge Way. I snap a picture of the snow-covered sign before turning onto the street. Ridge Way is lined with specialty shops, leading straight to the boulevard of villas, bars, and restaurants at the base of Blue Mountain. I walk slowly along, taking in the shops behind frosty windows, offering fancy chocolates and teas, handcrafted furniture, knick-knacks, and fair-trade clothing.

The light posts and buildings are garnished in green wreaths and garland, wrapped in blue string lights. At night, the whole town glows pale blue. I'm warm, even as the cold bites at my nose and cheeks. I love this place, I realize.

Despite the snow and cold, people sit outside on the boulevard, dressed in their snow pants, sweaters, and coats. Tall patio heaters are scattered around the restaurant area, licking with flame, and smelling faintly of gas.

With the town at my back, I lean on the railing, staring up at the mountain peaks. I feel immeasurably small, my problems insignificant, and relief rushes through me. There's something about standing before a thing so large and nearly eternal that puts everything in perspective.

This mountain has seen a lot and yet she still stands.

I take a breath – I can, too.

Torrance greets me at the door of Blue Saloon, "What are you doing here today?"

I throw my arms around her. She stiffens for a moment and then curls into me.

"How was I so lucky to have run into you my first day here?"

She pulls away, staring down at me. Her brows furrow, "What's going on? Are you leaving?"

I shake my head and she follows me to a booth near the bar.

"I was just walking through town." I rub a hand over my aching chest. "This place is wonderful. The people are wonderful. You have been so generous inviting me into your home."

Torrance slides into the booth. She gazes out the window and smiles dream-like.

"I fell in love with this place on my first visit, too." Her dark brown eyes return to me. "The first owner gave me a chance when I stumbled up this mountain. I promised myself I'd help the next lost stranger who ventures up to these parts. You are now," she looks up, thinking, "the third such stranger."

I jolt at her words. *Lost*? I never envisioned anyone would use *lost* to describe me. Successful, powerful, inspiring: that's who I want to be. I thought I'd be sitting in the Executive Suite, crown on my head, the youngest in DKS history. But here I am, sitting in a bar before noon without a real job, hundreds of miles from home. I'm not even sure where home is anymore. Hartford, New York, Atlanta. *Here.*

My eyes roam around Blue Saloon. There's a near equal mix of snowboarders and skiers as there are non-winter sport enthusiasts filling the bar stools and nearly all the tables and booths. A soft, folky song mingles with the voices of the guests.

"Last night when I picked you up, you told him, didn't you?"

I suck in a breath, the pain of last night a steady ache in my chest. I nod, unable to meet her gaze, "He took it about as well as you said he might."

My eyes jerk to hers as she folds her hand over mine. Her brown eyes are warm, "I hate it when I'm right."

We both laugh and it takes a little bite off the pain. Sometimes, I have this tendency to need to learn the lesson myself instead of heeding warnings. Maybe it's my toxic trait. One of them.

Torrance gives my hand a squeeze and slides hers away, "What's next?"

"I bring out the bigger guns," I pew-pew with my fingers.

We laugh and Torrance moves to slide out of the booth, "Holler if you need anything."

I sit back, a grin splitting across my face. I gaze around the bar. My eyes catch on things I hadn't noticed before. The pair of old skis crossing on the wall. A mismatched set. One old, one new.

Then there's the black and white photograph hanging above them. A gift from a photographer Torrance let stay in the loft above the restaurant. He's gone on to photograph for major publications, but every year he still sends Torrance a Christmas postcard from wherever he is in the world.

I blink, realizing for the first time, the subject in his photograph is Everett. I don't know how I never noticed before, but he's younger. His goggles are shoved up, resting on his forehead. He's laughing – the lines around his eyes and mouth crinkled. He looks so happy. Truly happy. Most of the photos I've seen of him riding are taken right before his halfpipe run, when his features are pensive and intense, if not hidden beneath his gear.

But this. This photo is him at his rawest. After or before he's about to ride for fun. Not for money or points. For pleasure. From this capture I can see exactly why he does it all. For the feeling captured here.

My heartstrings tug. I want to pull him out of the photo and hug him. Tell him I see him, I support him, and I want him to keep doing whatever makes him look this happy forever.

And I already know what does. With a sigh, I pull out my laptop and get to work. I wasn't joking when I said I'll bring out the bigger guns. I am December Fowl. I booked Sawyer Dawn to perform on *Savage Song,* the most popular acoustic performance show in the country, before she had a hit song. I successfully planned and executed Todd's redemption after he cheated on America's Sweetheart. I could launch Everett into the stratosphere if it's what he wanted – and honestly, it would be easier. But the man stands by his principals.

Opening the profile I've built on him, I begin reviewing his schedule for upcoming competition dates and potential slow periods. After I've established an updated calendar, I investigate sportscasters who cover the upcoming events and personalize media kits to their niche. I shoot all seven of them an email with a digital media kit and Everett's socials. We're bound to land three to four interviews. Generally, my percentage is higher but when cold emailing anchors and producers, the success rate is lower.

"I thought I might find you here."

The smile drops from my face. My heart races, breath catching.

Ryan Dawson slides into the seat once occupied by my friend.

"I didn't invite you to join me." I snap my laptop closed and move it closer to me.

He waves me off, glancing around the bar. My jaw clamps down. I want to jump across the table and strangle him, but I remain still. He smiles as his blue eyes roam back to me. He has beautiful blue eyes, so deceiving of what's inside.

"This place is adorable." He says like a southern woman would say 'oh sweetie.' I want to growl at him. He has no idea what this place means to so many people, me included. He's never known sentiment. The only thing he values are his pride and money.

I stare back at him, "Can I help you? Are you lost? I heard hell is that way." I jam my thumb in the direction of what I think is out of town. Since I've arrived, this place has left me completely turned around. In more than one way.

"You're a sneaky little thing, aren't you?" His Scar smile spreads across his face.

I blink, "Come again?" *Play it cool.*

"Don't play dumb. I know your little secret. You haven't told Everett."

For a second, I can't breathe. Like really can't breathe and the corners of my vision begin to darken. I push myself against the back of the booth and the pressure forces my mind back into my body.

"He knows. He knows I no longer work at DKS."

His smile widens. I feel like a fly being lured into a spider's trap, but I know this game.

"Don't worry." Ryan slides out of the booth and readjusts his jacket, gazing out the window. "Soon enough he'll be my client."

Without another parting word, he stalks away. My heart is pounding, climbing into my throat. The peace I had vanishes. Ryan is a money thirsty publicist. He'll sell and spin anything – even if it's not true. Controversy and half-truths are his tools of choice.

Fuck.

I fucked up when I didn't tell Everett the truth. He practically hates me now. And Ryan's already taken everything I thought was mine. What if Everett is next?

Chapter 32

EVERETT ABRAMS

I 'm standing at the top of the slope of the superpipe.

I smash my earbuds in, though there's nothing I listen to other than the sound of my board cutting through snow, the whoosh and silence as I hit air, and the crunch of landing. There's nothing more gratifying than to hear myself riding. Goosebumps travel up my skin as I think about it.

A quick breath and I pull my mask over my mouth and nose. My hands clap together as I slowly take pressure off my heel edge. I reach down and tap my bindings before popping the board around so I'm leading with my less dominant foot. I'm one of two riders who takes the right side first, but ever since my ACL tear it's safer to ride this way, and I do all right.

The lip of the pipe fast approaches. I dig my toe edge in and jump up, twisting myself around. I spot my landing just over the edge of the lip. I dip my toes into the snow with a *crrr* as I land and shoot off to the next wall.

I let myself go and everything stands out. Everything blends. I go faster, throw down harder. I'm just a boy and his snowboard: someone and no one. I'm a rush of adrenaline and movement.

It's not until I'm at the bottom of the pipe when the world fills in. My board crunches into the snow and the crowd erupts. I rip my headphones out and throw my fists in the air. It's not until the end, when it's over, that I want to acknowledge anyone else.

I spray the crowd with an arc of snow as I skid to a hot stop. The numbers are read before I even have my bindings off – 90.3. My chest swells. I shake my board over my head as Luc and Kelly come running towards me.

It doesn't matter how many times I win. It's the best damn feeling. Like being at the top of a mountain and looking down at all the things I overcame: my ACL tear, losing sponsors, being the kid no one believed in. It tastes sweeter now than it ever has.

Luc reaches me first and we hug it out. All the arguments we had leading up to this, the stress of Elevate, investors and, navigating new ground melts away. Kelly grabs me by the helmet and shakes my head. Mom's right behind him. Her eyes are glistening.

"I'm so proud of you," she rasps as I reach down to hug her.

My chest tightens. It feels like a gold star, or an ice bath after a difficult day. She's still happy for me, proud of me, even if she doesn't agree with my choices. Exactly what Moms are supposed to do. I pull her in tighter.

"Mrs. Abrams, what does it mean to see Everett compete?" A reporter rushes up as we pull away.

Mom squeezes me around the waist, gazing up at me with tear-brimmed eyes, "It terrifies me. I don't–" she chokes up and a lump forms in my own throat "–want to see him hurt again but it brings him so much joy. He's so good at it. I couldn't be happier."

She rises onto her toes and kisses me on the cheek, leaving a red mark. She laughs, wets her thumb like she would when I was a kid with jelly smeared all over my face, and rubs. I grin and lean in allowing her to continue even with a camera in my face.

"He's still that nine-year-old boy to me. Trying to figure it out. I'm so proud."

"I taught him that frontside 360," Kelly pops his head in front of the camera, and we all laugh.

After the award ceremony, I'm ushered to the main lodge. December booked me another meet-and-greet, this time with a press conference. I'm more anxious than I was the first time at Copper. And now with what she did on my mind. The anxiety compounds.

I can't stop flip-flopping between regretting and feeling empowered by keeping her on after the lying. I don't want to trust her and I'm trusting her with *everything* now. But another force in my heart, in my gut, in my entire being is telling me working with her is right.

Except right now. Right now, fear settles into my bones: what if no one shows up this time? It'll be me sitting alone with a room full of empty seats and camera guys to document it. What if I don't know what to say and they just sit there and stare at me.

I work my jaw, *why did I agree to this?*

"You'll go out in fifteen minutes." One of the event planners says, pointing at a space in the curtain where I'm supposed to enter.

There's a low rumbling from beyond the curtain. Who's out there now? Who will I have to follow up behind? I step forward and peek through the folds.

The show room is filled with rows of people. They're chattering excitedly but there's no one seated at the front table. My eyes catch on a sign. There's a photo of me, snowboard tucked under my arm, staring across the audience. *Everett Abrams – 7:30. Meet-and-Greet to follow.*

"Holy shit," I swallow, taking a step back. All these people are here for me. My chest squeezes.

I know two weekends ago they lined up outside the door, but two in a row? What the hell am I going to say that's going to interest them? I can't entertain a room full of people for an hour.

December. I pull out my phone and push on the phone icon by her picture.

"Hey. You did so great today!"

My racing heart starts to settle, and my mouth wants to smile at her praise, but I push it away. I remind myself she lied. And now she's put me in this mess with a room full of people, "You – why you? How do I–?"

Without hesitating, "Everett, I know this is still new and scary, but you've got this."

I'm moving around the room like I've seen her do many times before. It seems to help her chill out, but it does me no good. I knot a fist in my hair.

"So many people are here. It's in–" I break off and huff, unable to keep my breath even. "What do I say? What if I can't say anything? I don't know what they want from me." *What if they figure out I'm nobody special or interesting.*

"Everett," December's smooth voice cuts in, "everything is going to be okay. They're here for you just like people were there to see you the first weekend. They didn't pay to see Hendrik Legrand or anyone else. They came to see you so just...be yourself."

"Paid. They *paid* to see me?"

"Yes."

"Oh shit." I rake my hand through my hair and roughly down my face. "I'm even more of a fr-fraud now."

I thought hiring a PR lady was bad but charging people to see me? What the fuck! This is not what I wanted. Why is everything not how it's supposed to be?

"It came with their VIP package. Legrand has one. So do a few other guys. It's not unusual. You're not doing anything wrong. It actually helps the resort. The fans get box seats, a meet-and-greet with you, and a headshot for you to sign."

I stop pacing, the tension in my chest loosening, "It feels weird to charge someone to meet me. I'm...nobody."

"No, you're not Everett. You're special. You're someone's role model. Isn't that who you want to be? You're someone's favorite snowboarder. More than a few people want to be you when they grow up."

"Which makes me feel worse paying them." I freeze – shit, did she notice? I said the wrong thing, "I mean, charging them."

She takes a breath, and her voice feels like she's reaching out to me, running her hands up and down my arms, "Everett, they wouldn't allow us to hold the event without charging. Resort requirements. Everyone gets what they want: the resort earns some money, you earn some money, your sponsors earn some publicity, the fans get to meet you. Wins all across the board. Now get out there and give them what they want, okay?"

"I-I..."

"Hey. Everett. You're really panicking right now."

"Hey, no shit."

She laughs and it makes my shoulders rocket to my ears – is she laughing at me?

"I'm going to teach you something my therapist showed me when my parents were going through a divorce. You are in your flight-or-fight mode right now. I get in that zone, too. Just look around for the windows and doors. Do some stretching, show your body you're not stuck. You're safe."

I glance around. After confirming there are few witnesses, I roll my shoulders, shake out my arms as I look around the area, spotting the bright EXIT signs. And my breath comes easier, body softening. It's not an instant, complete fix, but she's right. I don't feel as trapped as I did a moment ago.

"You've been through therapy?"

The line is silent for a second, "Yeah. My parent's two divorces – from each other – was not easy on me. Plus, just generally existing in this world can be hard. Therapy helps."

"Wait, your parents divorced twice?"

"Unfortunately, yes, and that's not even the worst of it."

I do another squat and then walk it off, "And therapy actually helped you?"

"It did! I mean, I could clearly use some more." She tries and fails to say with a laugh. "Have you ever considered it?"

"Ah," there's a knot in my chest. Me? In therapy? I thought that was just a thing for people with real issues and needs. I've got my great fear of vulnerability, and once again being viewed and labeled like I was as a kid. But everyone's got something like that? Maybe? "I should go. Shows about to start and all."

"I've got you, Everett. You may not believe it right now, but I'll show you. And don't forget to talk about your partnership with Magic Energy. I think everyone will be really excited. You've got this."

My heart fires a mixture of excitement and fear as my head cycles her words: *I've got you.* And, *you've got this.*

Does she have my back? And do I have mine?

The line clicks and I stand there gaping at the black screen.

Beyond the curtain someone begins the introduction. My stomach pitches and I shelf those thoughts for a later time. I glance around frantically for someone to rescue me. Luc leans against the wall flirting with an event coordinator. I grab him by the arm and pull him away.

"What the hell Everett?" He shakes himself free.

"You're going out there with me." I point at the curtain and the space beyond.

Luc listens for a moment as the introduction continues. Soon they'll be calling me to the stage. He shrugs, a sly grin spreading across his face, "Fine."

He walks forward just as they call my name. The crowd bursts out in screams as the curtain parts and Luc steps through instead of me. The curtains fall back into place, blocking out my view.

"Hey everyone. I'm Luc Orseno, I'll be taking over for today."

There's a ripple of murmurs. I stand frozen for a moment, cold sweat prickles at my forehead. I begin to feel my body freezing, clamping. But December's voice echoes into my head: *look for the exits, move. You're safe. I've got you. You've got this.*

My head turns to the glowing red EXIT sign, and I realize I don't want to leave. I don't want to run. I want this. I want to be here. I want to do this. Shaking my hands out I take a breath and move, brushing the curtain aside with my hand.

There's a bright light shining down from the balcony. It takes a moment for my eyes to adjust. I move towards the table, walking behind Luc, and pull out a chair.

"Ignore him. He's just trying to get his share of the attention."

Luc shrugs shamelessly, not bothering to deny it as he drops into the seat beside me. Luckily, they had two sitting up here. I wonder if December asked them to include it just in case.

A reporter speaks up, "How do you keep such a great friendship being competitors? Do you find you're resentful towards each other for your different levels of success?"

Luc and I glance at each other and laugh.

"I'm just here to steal his tricks." Luc says lazily, drawing a laugh from the crowd.

"He can't think of any on his own," I bite back, feeling more like we're sitting on a lift bantering than at a press conference. I let the feeling ease through me and sit back. "No, we work well together. We grew up riding together and had the same dream of going big. It's pretty rare to transition from amateur to professional with the same person you grew up with. We both just love to ride."

"Except Everett does it with less tequila."

The crowd laughs again, and I jab him with my elbow, grinning.

Chapter 33

EVERETT ABRAMS

"Everett! I can't believe you're still here, man." Luc throws his arm around my neck. His eyes are glossy, and he smells like too much liquor. He points at Olivia and Kelly, "It's cause you guys are here. That's the only reason. If December were here, they'd probably be making out right in the middle of the bar."

I glare at him.

Olivia leans in, intrigued, "So you've met her. What's she like? Everett's being all secretive."

Luc shrugs, "She's attractive, I guess. But mostly, I like how she's nudging this guy out of his cave."

"My cave?"

He continues as if I'm not standing right here, "He's into her. I think he should just bang her and then see how he feels about her." I clench my jaw, my hands roll into fists.

"Isn't that your signature move?" Kelly teases.

Luc tilts his head back and laughs. But I see the way, when he's done, he takes a long pull from his beer, and his eyes show anything but humor. I move to talk to him – just the two of us.

"Luc," a leggy redhead grazes her hand along his shoulders, "good to see you. Wanna play?" She tilts her head to a newly empty pool table, and sashays away before he responds.

"Yeah, I'm gonna go." He says to the rest of us before bolting after her.

"How are you feeling?" Kelly asks his wife. His hand slides to the small of her back and she gazes back at him affectionately.

She twists and places her glass on the counter, moving to stand up, "Just have to find my jacket."

"I'll get it. You stay here."

Kelly winks at me as he walks away. I know what that means. Jealously cuts through me and I look away. I haven't had a steady girlfriend since I was a junior in college. It was for the best. I needed to focus on snowboarding. Girlfriends are distractions, but now...I do miss it. I miss having someone to talk about everything and nothing with. I've never had someone who understands who I am and where I want to go. I want what they have. To be so connected with someone, one glance says, *let's get out of here.*

I'm not an open book like Kelly or even Luc. There are pieces of me I've not been willing to share. I didn't want to risk it. Keeping myself safe has been more important, but it's come at a cost, too.

"What are you thinking about?" Olivia leans in and says conspiratorially, "Thinking about December?"

I hesitate, not sure even what I'm asking or how to say it. "How did you and Kelly...get together?"

"You know, we met in college."

"I know, I know but *how*? It's not like you just saw each other and synced up. How'd you know it was something worth doing?"

She narrows her eyes, "Why? You thinking about doing something with your publicist?"

I glance around us again. Neither Luc, nor Kelly are in sight, "She lied to me. I've just – I've had relationships in the past but nothing I really cut myself loose in. What do you – how do you do that?"

"Let yourself go?" She asks.

I nod. This wasn't a good idea. She's too spent to get what I'm asking and I'm not even sure what I am.

"Aw, Everett." She squeezes her hands over her chest, making a pouty face. "You're so cute."

"All right." I say, rolling my eyes. Not what I wanted to hear.

"How do you get up there and do what you just did tonight? Do all those spinning, flippy tricks? You trust and you train, and you go for it. Same thing goes for love. You put yourself out there, you do it scared, and you do the best you can."

I nod. She makes it sound so easy, so natural, but I don't know if I can do that.

She grabs my arm and forces me to look at her, "I know being vulnerable is scary. Letting someone see who you really are is scary. It was for me too, but it's worth it. Kelly and I don't have a perfect relationship – we fight, we do selfish things, but I want the best relationship I can have and so does he. And if you think December or someone could be the person for you, you need to take a chance."

I nod and Kelly returns a moment later. He helps Olivia into her jacket, and I follow them outside.

"Good luck," Olivia says, gazing at me meaningfully as we go our separate ways.

"He's an Abrams. We don't need luck." Kelly winks at me then pulls her in close and they slip around the corner.

I swing around, my boots crunching on the snow, and pull out my phone. My heart races when her text lights up my screen.

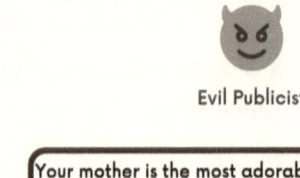

Evil Publicist

Your mother is the most adorable person I have ever seen. When she rubbed her lipstick off your cheek *swoon*

EP

I grin and press the phone icon by her name.

"Hello. Hello?"

"Not sure if you were crushing on me or my mom, so I thought I better call and find out."

I cringe at myself – caught between wanting to keep things professional and really not wanting to.

She laughs and a trill goes through me. I can't help but smile as I walk the empty street past closed window shops and thumping bars.

"What makes you so sure?" There's a smile in her voice.

"You couldn't kiss the way you did if you weren't a little bit into me."

"Maybe I was faking it."

"I don't think anyone can fake it like that."

"That good, huh?" She says breathlessly, making it harder for me to breathe.

I huff, walking through the sliding glass doors and into the glowing hotel lobby, "I can't stop thinking about it...or you. What are you doing?"

"Lying in bed."

An elevator door slides open as I approach. I lean back against the wall and can't get the image out of my head – December lying in her dark room, nestled in the blankets listening to my husky voice. I swallow. I wonder what she's wearing; what else she's doing.

I wait for the doors to slide shut, "Risky business talking to me while you're in bed."

She takes in a breath and my blood turns hot, "If only someone could be here to supervise, guarantee my safety."

My throat feels tighter, "If only. What I would do if I were there..."

Blood is pumping in the opposite direction of my brain. My dick presses uncomfortably against my jeans. I want her pressed up against me, her leg wrapped around my hip, her moans tingling my tongue like she was at Splice. The elevator door slides open, and I step out, readjusting myself. I make my way to my room, shove the keycard in, and shuck my coat as soon as I'm inside. I fall back onto the bed and stare up at the ceiling, wishing I wasn't states away.

I want to know what else I can do to hear her sounds. To drive her wild.

"I'm in bed now, too."

"Are you? What are you doing?"

My mouth slides into a grin, "Thinking about you."

"I think...before things go further, we should talk about what happened the last time we saw each other. I want to talk about the lying and firing, in person. I just want things to be clear between us."

I smile wider. My hand rests on my stomach. My cock is painfully hard, wanting her. I like that she wants to address it. To find out what I'm thinking since her confession and before anything evolves between us. It's a good idea and it makes me feel even better about continuing to work with her.

"Sleep tight. I'll see you tomorrow."

She hesitates, "Good night, Everett."

Chapter 34

EVERETT ABRAMS

The house is dark when I get home.

Luc hasn't been back since we left for the first leg of Dew Tour. I park the truck in front of the garage and pick my gear out of the backseat.

"Hey," A voice says behind me.

"*Shit.*" I jump even though I could recognize her voice anywhere. I turn around, my board in one hand. She stands a few paces away, her arms wrapped around herself. Even from here I can see her shivering. "Christ, December how long have you been out here?"

"I've been waiting for you to come home." Her teeth chatter.

I wrap my free arm around her waist and herd her to the front door. Inside, she just stands there shivering in her winter jacket as I unload my stuff. I drop what I'm doing and help her out of her jacket. I rub my hands up and down her arms.

"You're freezing."

"I'll be fine."

"It's below zero with the windchill."

"I wanted to see you."

She stares up at me with her green eyes, her cheeks bright pink, lips beginning to chap, and I shake my head. I direct her into the living room and wrap her in a heated blanket. Once she's seated and warm, I head into the kitchen to make her a cup of steaming tea.

December holds the cup with both hands when I pass it to her. I sit on the opposite side of the couch, stretched out, and watch her. Her eyes flick to mine and I point at the TV. She nods and I click it on. The device is still paused at the last episode of *The Mentalist* we watched.

The episode continues but I hardly pay any mind to it. My chest bubbles with frustration. I stare at her, gritting my teeth. Finally, I break.

"What were you thinking? You know, frostbite and hypothermia are real things. I know you don't have it in...in Atlanta, but out here it happens more often than you'd think."

"I wanted to see you." She repeats, looking at me directly. Her color is returning to normal, but her nose is still bright red.

"You could have texted, called." At called, I feel a tingle of shame, nerves. I called her last night and, as I expected, I feel weird about it now. I'm not sure where this leaves us. Or how I should handle her lying to me. A part of me feels like I need to punish her, but that doesn't feel right or fair either.

I rake a hand through my hair and say honestly, "I don't want to see you hurt. Ever."

She sets the coffee mug down on the ottoman and shifts to face me. Her hand falls to my ankle. I stiffen at her touch but the pressure and warmth is reassuring, and I find myself settling into it.

"I don't want to hurt you either."

"You did though."

Her hand gently squeezes my ankle, "I know. I'm sorry. It really wasn't about you. I just – losing my clients and the agency really fucked me up."

She finishes and I say nothing, watching her features for any clues. But her eyes are soft and steady, mouth drawn into a droop.

She continues, "I left Atlanta on a whim. When I showed up at your doorstep and you didn't like me, I wanted to prove to you, the agency, probably even myself, that I was good enough. Like killing it would be retribution for doubting me. I hid the letter from DKS and didn't tell you and pretended to still be part of the agency. It's fucked up. I knew that even when it was happening, but I just kept pretending. I'm not really sure why, but I think it was easier for me to pretend and lie than it was for me to admit to myself that I wasn't who I thought I was. I've always been this high achiever, and then suddenly I was fired, and doubted. I didn't like that you or the agency maybe saw something in me I didn't want to see in myself."

I nod, taking a moment to process. It sounds relatable. Maybe even familiar.

"They really just fired you for no reason?"

She looks down, "I don't know. It was the first time anyone had ever mentioned my recruiting marks, and I was way above everyone else in sales volume. I'm not sure why they fired me, but that's not what I care about right now." Her eyes flash up to mine. "All I care about is you. Do you think less of me? Do you think you can forgive me?"

The way she says it, just above a whisper, makes my heart crack. I know she's not fragile, but I still don't want to break her. I want to wrap her in my arms, take care of her. I pull at the fuzz on the couch, knowing I have to be honest with her, too. There are parts of me I haven't shared either. How big of a hypocrite would I be, if I'm mad at her for neglecting to share her shortcomings while I keep mine to myself?

I clear my throat. My eyes flick to hers and then away. I feel sick. My throat squeezes so tight it's like there's a hockey puck – a truth – lodged there.

"You know how I said I was nervous about doing a live feed? The meet-and-greets and interviews, too? There's a reason I was so worried I'd fuck up." My throat constricts tighter. There's a bear on my chest. I can't look at her. Oh god I haven't admitted this in so long. The last time I did, it was to Luc and we were thirteen.

None of my college girlfriends knew. No one in the industry knows. I've buried this part of me deep down. I've kept my past locked in a cage and threw away the key. I'm afraid what will happen when I let it out. I clear my throat again, still picking at the couch.

"I..." The couch suddenly feels lumpy and I adjust my shoulders. "The thing is." How do I say the right thing? I huff, growing frustrated with myself. I look up at her. She nods, gives my ankle another squeeze, and there I find my strength. I don't look away as I explain, "The thing about me is I don't know how to say the right thing. My brain gets all scrambled. Like right now."

"I think everyone's like that sometimes. I never know how to say the right thing until I'm saying it and sometimes it's the wrong thing."

"No. I..." I try again, slower, putting thought into each word. "It's not just speaking. It's reading. It's thinking. There's a disconnect somewhere in my brain." I rub my forehead. "It's like I'm thinking one thing and something completely different comes out. I'll look at a contract or an article and I'll know the words, but they don't make sense when they're strung together. It's like the words come in and somewhere in the process they get flipped and scrambled and they aren't what they were."

Our gazes hold for a moment then I look away, shrugging.

"What I'm trying to say is I know what it's like to be unhappy with where you are. I know what it's like to be ashamed and I don't ever want to make you feel like that." Our eyes lock. "You were right. I wouldn't have listened if you told me you no longer worked at DKS. I wanted to fire you anyway. It would have been the perfect excuse."

She looks away, staring at the TV. Her entire chin quakes. A tear and then another roll down her cheek. I sit up and move closer to her. Turn her chin to look at me.

"I hate that you lied to me." She opens her mouth and I shake my head. "But I'm glad you did. Fucked up as it is. I never would have made it this far without you. I never would have gotten to know you; or you me. And I think I would have kept being a self-righteous prick without you."

She shakes her head, "You still are a self-righteous prick."

"Hush."

I lean across the couch and press my lips into hers. It's a delicate kiss. I'm trying to tell her I'm sorry I hurt her. I don't want to, not ever again. She pushes me back with her fingertips.

"What you were trying to say, you're dyslexic? Like learning and reading, speaking even doesn't come easy?"

I sit back against the arm of the couch. A part of me wants to change the subject and not discuss this, but, like Olivia said, I do scary things all the time. I can try this too, "It's still a bit unclear. But school was a nightmare. My parents tried to take me to a specialist but that's expensive for a mechanic and an admin."

"I was a Teaching Assistant in college. Working with so many students, I noticed the huge variety of learners. For some students, the lectures and reading clicked right away; others needed visuals, examples, and actually doing the thing. You know there are actually multiple kinds of dyslexia? Sometimes it has a greater effect on written words, numbers, or speech – and sometimes it's all three. It's nothing to be ashamed of and I'm sorry if anyone made you feel like it was; or if your school didn't try to figure out the best way you learn."

My heart feels like it could burst.

Grinning at me, December stretches over me like a cat, her hands palming my shoulders. She lies down. Her arms fold over my chest, chin placed on her stacked hands. Her midsection presses into my groin and I whoosh out a breath, telling myself to behave. Think calm, non-sexual things.

She stares up at me, "Thank you for telling me. What was that like?"

I blow out a breath, staring at the TV instead. What was that like? No one's ever asked me before. I'm not sure I can even put the experience into words.

"Hey," December wraps her arms around me and presses the side of her head into my chest, listening for a heartbeat. "Tell me yours and I'll tell you mine."

I pass my hand over her silky-smooth hair. How does she get it so soft and smooth? She holds me tighter as I run my fingers into her hairline and massage her scalp.

"I didn't think anything was wrong at first. I thought it was normal. That everything was hard for everyone. Reading was hard. Math was hard. Sometimes I still didn't understand any of it. Then I was in fourth grade, and we had just taken our standardized tests. They called me and a few other kids out when it was time for the English lesson. After that, after roll call I left and had special instruction with another teacher and a few of my classmates.

"I still didn't think anything of it. Then we were in PE a few weeks later. We were playing kickball. I always used to be one of the first kids picked, then I was the last." December curls her hands into my t-shirt. I roam my hand up and down her back.

"I stopped being invited to the lunch table with all my friends. They'd get up and leave when I sat down. The birthday invites stopped coming in. Even the teachers treated me differently. My brother Kelly is...a rockstar at everything he does, so for me to follow him up was disappointing, I guess. I just kinda withdrew into my shell. It was safer than putting myself out there. My grades were horrible. I just tried to blend into the background, but it's hard when everyone thinks and treats you like you're–"

"Don't say it," December claps her hand over my mouth. "It's not true. And it's not fair to call yourself or anyone that."

My heart squeezes. It feels strange talking to her about this. I thought it would be scarier, but now it just feels...*good*.

"How did you get into snowboarding?"

"When my brother Kelly was seventeen, he took me to the mountains with him and his friends. It was like breathing new life into me. I thought I'd never be good at anything, but I was good at snowboarding. I didn't need to read. I didn't need to solve equations. All I had to work with was my body, a board, and the snow. It was like," I let out a laugh, "I was born for this."

December nuzzles into me closer, using her nose like a pig's snout. I grin down at her, trailing my fingers down her spine. My chest swells. I never thought telling someone all this would feel so good – so freeing.

I lean my head back. Stare at the ceiling. Take a breath.

"It's funny. I've been hiding this part of me for so long. Locking my past away, not letting people see my weaknesses like they're some kind of monster. But I don't want to hide from you."

Chapter 35

December Fowl

E verett Abrams is an angel. He just doesn't know it.

He's been told too many times he's not good enough, but I'm going to show him exactly what he's worth. My chest squeezes and expands so quickly with the thought I'm surprised I don't explode.

I prop my hands on his chest again and gaze up at him. Underneath my palms I feel his heart racing. Mine is in sync with his.

He gazes down at me. His lips slightly parted, his eyes full of wonder. Worry, I realize, too. He's never told anyone before and suddenly I feel like the luckiest girl in the world. Everett's exposed his deepest, darkest insecurity to me. And it's comfortable.

I reach up and tap his nose. Run my hand along his sculpted jaw, rough with man-fur. He doesn't move. Just gazes down at me. Allows me to trace his lines like he's art.

I make myself comfy on his chest again. I bridge my hands across his pecks and rest my chin on top, staring up at his neck, his chin. Lift my eyes a little more and there's his sinful lips. His hand passes through my hair, trailing down my spine. Petting me like his favorite cat.

"Tell me something," his raspy voice reverberates through his chest and into mine.

I consider for a moment.

"I'll give you the run down on my parents' divorces. The first one happened when I was ten. It was a nightmare. They split me and my sister in two. My father took Junie and Mom took me. They stayed in Connecticut. Kept the house I grew up in while Mom and I moved to New York. She made sure we had a nice place. Nothing scary but for the first few months she had to sell her clothes to make ends meet. And, if you knew my mother, it was like selling pieces of her soul. Then she finally landed with a good agency and her career took off – she's a publicist. I guess I followed in her footsteps like Junie did my father's.

"When I was fifteen, they married again. I hardly even remember when they started dating. It was like one night my father and Junie were moving in. I was so excited to be living with Junie again. I'd only spent holidays with my father and sister after the first divorce. We'd promised to stay close, and we did for a while, but then life got the better of us. Now we had a chance to start over. Be a family again. Except, my father was partner at a law firm in Connecticut, so I only saw him on weekends, and Junie had a boyfriend and was too busy prepping herself for college to pay attention to me.

"I think maybe they were happy together for a while." I let out a scorned laugh, "I'm not sure I even know what happy looks like. Even though they were together and *happy*, it always felt like they were competing. Pitting Junie and me against each other. I was a reflection of my mother. Junie, my father. She was in all these groups in high school. I had to keep up. I had to make my mom proud. I was in theater, debate, knowledge bowl, President of the Media Club."

A sad smile slips across my face, "I always felt like I was chasing her. Wherever I was, no matter how good, there was always a higher branch I needed to reach. My first year at NYU, they divorced. Again. Thank god I wasn't living at home. It was murder. They tore each other up." I trace lines into his t-shirt with my finger. "My father was dropped from partner at his firm. He and Junie *literally* packed up and moved across the country to get away. My mother's reputation was bolstered instead of damaged. Everyone wanted to be represented by someone who didn't take shit from anyone – even their cheating ex-husband.

"I'm most angry with my father. I know Mom wasn't innocent either, but he left me and took Junie with him. Again. Junie had been thriving as a corporate attorney, first year out of law school. The apple of my father's eye. And I'm just...the afterthought. I had to do something to make my mother proud; to make him regret not being a part of my journey. So, I dug my heels in. When I was fired...I didn't react like I should have. I saw another target. My redemption. My revenge, and I went for it."

I run my palm across his chest, relishing the way his muscles feel beneath my hand. My confession feels slightly less significant than his. I push the thought away. We both have different stories. Different doesn't mean less or more. We're puzzle pieces. Our oddities fit us together. Nice. And. Snug.

"So," I stretch my arm out, and run my thumb down the center of this throat. He swallows and his throat tightens. "That's my origin story."

I glance up at him staring down at me. The shadow of his lashes fan out against his skin. His eyes are soft, making my heart clench and melt at the same time.

"What about this Dawson guy and DKS?"

"I think Dawson hates me because I'm too...directive. For a woman. Like my last trip with DKS, they asked me to present projections. I commanded the room. Then an investor of ours, Mike Gibler, presented stats of how his initiatives were improving the agency." I press my hand against Everett's chest, savoring the feel of him below me. All hard, hot muscle. "Except he wasn't exactly being honest. So I called him out on his figures looking wrong. He fumbled through an explanation that they were updated numbers, but after that members of the board started questioning him further. The fucked up part is on our flight home, Mr. King talked to *me* about it. As if I did something wrong."

Everett rests his head back, letting out a growl, "Damn. Now your whole agency sounds sketch."

His hands travel down my body. Volts of electricity sizzle through me as his hands lower to my hips. He hesitates. I hold my breath. We lock eyes. His hands travel back up. *Dammit Everett! Touch me!*

"I like you bossy, December." His face slips up into a sexy, new grin. "Even though sometimes you are a pain in the ass. I wouldn't change anything about you."

My throat constricts. I grip his shoulders and sit down on him. My clit tingles. He feels so god-damn good beneath me. I stare down at him, "Ditto."

"Ditto?" He laughs and the sound echoes in my chest. "It's been a while since I've played that game. Let's see if I'm any good." He reaches for my hand and intertwines it with his. "You're sexy and smart and an awful skier."

My eyebrows jack up, "Ditto."

"Oh, you think I'm an awful skier? You haven't even seen me ski. They don't call me King of the Mountain for nothing. Let's see..." He nips at his upper lip, and he fixes me with a meaningful look. "You pace when you're nervous. Your favorite color is purple, and you secretly love it here." A grin splits across his face on the last one.

I squeeze his hand and lean closer, "I don't know how I'm supposed to follow that up with a ditto, but I see what you're doing. I can play, too."

He inclines his brows. His lips fall into an appeased line, waiting for me to surprise him.

"I think..." I tilt my head, considering everything he's just revealed to me and wondering how deep I should go, how hard I should hit.

Narrowing my eyes, "You think you're still marked as inferior. So, you have to perform better. You have to be number one on the podium and your morals are incorruptible. You think you have to be better than anyone to even be on an even playing field." Everett looks away, his jaw clamping. "Seriously, you could have earned two hundred thousand so easily. Sold yourself to the culture of wild, party boys. But you didn't. I'm so happy you didn't listen to me, but why did you need that much money anyways? Finally, your favorite color is blue because...blue cabinets, blue house, Blue Mountain. Did you pick Blue Sky to be your home because of the name alone?"

My hands trail along his body, feeling up his shoulders, his chest, his obliques. I never want to stop touching him.

Everett reaches for the remote on the coffee table and clicks off the TV. My stomach twists. He's going to walk me to the door. Send me on my way. Pretend this didn't happen. The thought sends a sharp pain splintering through my chest. I don't want to pretend this didn't happen.

He turns his head to meet my gaze. I move to climb off. But his hands are on my hips. *Oh. Ooh.* His hard cock presses against my inner thigh. I hover over him for a moment, my brain flooded with the flush of feel-good chemicals. It's like we've sucked all the air out of the room. There's only the throbbing need between my legs and the electric rush of touching him. I move again, brushing up against his erection. My clit throbs and I see fireworks in my brain. I bite down on my lip to stop from vocalizing as I grind myself against him. He tilts his head back, the lines in his neck straining.

"December."

"Ah-huh," I pant, flicking my hips. I'm sure I'll regret my shameless eagerness in the morning but right now all I want is this.

He joins me. His pelvis rocks off the couch in rhythm with my writhing. My breath grows heavier. So does his. My cheeks are hot and his glow pink right along with mine. We're like two teenagers getting their kicks for the first time; desperate but not sure how far to go.

"Can I touch you?" His voice is a rasp. He moves a hand from my hip, roaming over my stomach. His eyes are alight.

"God yes. If you don't, I will."

He grins, "Maybe that's a better idea."

"*Nooo.*" I sit down. "I've had enough of my own hands. I want yours."

"Hmm." His hand slips underneath my shirt. I jerk at the shock of his calloused palm against my skin. It's delicious. He savors my reaction, his tongue peeks out of the corner of his mouth. "Do you touch yourself a lot?"

"Only when I think about you."

Smoothly, he flips us over so I'm the one pinned down against the couch. A rush of heat and want floods through me. Everett presses into me and I love the weight of him. I fumble for the button on my jeans. I am desperate for him. I shove my jeans down my hips, and he helps pull them all the way off.

He sucks in a breath as he takes me in. Purple panties – not even the sexy, satin, or lacy kind. Gently he touches my knee, glancing up at me for permission.

I nod my head eagerly and pull my sweatshirt over my head. Leaving me in nothing but my underwear.

"Touch me," I writhe beneath him. I love the way his eyes devour me.

Everett leans down and kisses me. His hands move tortuously slow down my thighs. My hips rise off the couch and rock into his. I hate that he's still in jeans. I move my hands between us, reaching for the cool metal of his belt. He pulls back, pushing my shoulder down into the couch. He brushes my hands away.

"No."

My heart stutters for a moment. Suddenly I wonder if this is real. A man like Everett – gorgeous and sweet and sexy – wants me. How is it possible?

"Whatever you're thinking, don't."

"You can read thoughts now?"

"No," he presses his thumb into my forehead and smooths the lines out. "Your face."

Everett presses his mouth against mine. He takes his time. Exploring me with his tongue and lips and hands in ways I didn't know I wanted. Except, he doesn't touch the parts of me most wanting his attention. I know he's doing it on purpose. The moment our mouths let up for air, I let out an exasperated sigh.

His mouth crooks up, all red from mine, "Tell me what you want."

"You know what I want."

He shakes his head stubbornly, wanting me to say.

Instead of responding, I lie back down and gaze up at him. I slither my hands up his muscular arms, his shoulders, and back. My fingers bump over the hitches and divots of his toned physic.

"Touch me," I demand.

His eyes are black wells of fire. "Where – here?" He places his hand on my hip and slides it over my pelvis.

I nod and refrain from rocking off the couch. He's so close.

"Or here?" His hand slides lower. His fingers feather over my clit.

"God, yes," I tighten. I'm surprised his hand doesn't catch fire, he's red hot.

"You like that?" His voice is silk. His fingers stroke me over the fabric.

I can only nod. I'm breathless. My eyes flutter closed. The soft fabric between us creating tantalizing friction. I rock my hips into his hand. There's a knot tightening in my core. I want more. I *need* more.

"Everett," I open my eyes and he looks at me. I stop talking. His fingers are doing wicked things to me. Gaze holding mine, he slips his hand under my panties and cups me. "Oh god." I writhe against his hand.

He drags my underwear down and I kick them off.

"You're so wet," he pulls his hand away for the briefest moment and runs his fingers along my stomach, so I feel how slick I've made his fingers.

He strokes me at the same time he manages to maneuver us around, so he's positioned underneath me. He's a magician. I begin to protest but he strokes me so well I forget. I can't help it. I straddle him, my legs spread wide over his hips. If he wanted too, I'd be so ready to fuck right here, right now. I don't care if Luc comes home and catches us. In fact, the idea makes me want him more.

I lean down to reach his mouth. I arch into him with a gasp as one long finger slides into me. My hips rock into his hands. The heel of his palm brushes against my clit. Murmurs tumble from my lips. I hold onto his shoulders. *More, more. I want more.* As if reading my thoughts, he works a second finger in. I gasp at the stretching sensation, his fingers curling into me.

"Everett, I–" I can't help myself. I grip his shoulders tight, riding his fingers like I would his dick.

He strokes into me slow and deep, brushing me where I need him the most. I know he just started but I'm a volcano ready to erupt. He works his fingers so good. My eyes close and I focus on the sensation of him fucking into me, curling with each pass. My clit sings each time his palm brushes against it. I writhe against him, moaning.

"You're so fucking sexy," Everett rasps. My eyes flutter open.

The fire of his gaze hits me. His mouth is slightly parted. He clamps down on his bottom lip. I grind against him harder. It's so good. So, so good.

"I feel you tightening." He murmurs. He moves his other hand off my hip and massages his thumb into my clit.

I erupt, spasming around his fingers. He keeps driving into me and I ride against him wildly. I don't want this to end. As my orgasm begins to fade, I slowly stop writhing, and press my hand into his chest. I take a deep breath; having lost all the air I had left.

Everett slips his fingers out. My body sings with satisfaction. His eyes lock with mine. He pushes himself up. I hold on to his t-shirt. My legs fold up underneath me, surrendering around his hips. He leans forward and presses a kiss against my forehead.

"That was good."

I laugh. I wrap my hands around the back of his neck and squeeze. Understatement of the year. My clit and vagina are still zinging.

Chapter 36

December Fowl

"**S**o, you had sex?"

Suz gushes as I pin my phone between my shoulder and ear, scraping the spatula against the pan as I try to unstick the breakfast I'm attempting to make for Torrance and me.

"No, we didn't have sex! Just...in part."

Suz laughs, "My, my, my. Now you're sounding like me. Skip the main course and just get dessert!"

I hesitate, recalling the night before. A firework ripples through my stomach at the thought of his touch, and kiss, and voice.

"I hope you let him go down on you December. I know it freaks you out. I mean, it's literally the most vulnerable position you can be in, but it's just the beeest."

"Suz–"

"Sometimes you gotta ask for the non-listed items."

"The thing is, the orgasm wasn't just the best part. It was the connecting. He shared stories, I shared stories. I don't know, it was so special, the sexual stuff was just the cherry on top."

Suz lets out a wistful sigh, "God, you almost made me miss that. By the way, have you seen Ryan?"

I almost gag, "Don't you ever mix sex and Ryan again."

"Did you actually just gag?"

"You know the reaction my body has when he's around. And, unfortunately, he has made his appearance a couple of times."

"December! Why are you leaving out these crucial details?"

"I'm sorry! I've just been busy!"

"Yeah, with Everett," she sings and I roll my eyes, grinning.

"I saw him at Splice the night after the Dan Keegan interview. All he said was some bullshit banter not even worth repeating."

"Per usual."

I put the pan down and grab a potholder before lifting it off the burner again, "But then he showed up at Torrance's bar. Said he knew about my little secret and Everett would be his client soon. It's not like he knows about me lying to Everett about being fired, right? I mean, how could he know? And besides, what could he do with that information anyways?"

"I think that would be a great question to ask Junie. You know, your badass attorney sister. You know Dawson. I wouldn't be surprised if he somehow placed a secret camera in your contacts while you were sleeping."

I laugh, "I don't even wear contacts Suz."

"Like that would matter to him! I don't know, I'm not the evil villain here. I don't know how it all works, but Dawson would."

Finally, the omelet comes loose, and I toss it onto the plate alongside the other one. Both are darker than Everett's delicious, melt-in-your-mouth masterpiece. I frown but continue forward, dropping strips of bacon into the pan. *Tss!* the bacon sizzles, spitting grease onto my hand.

"Shit!" I drop the handle and the pan bangs onto the burner.

"Are you okay?" – "What's going on?" Suz and Torrance say at the same time.

"Just making breakfast." I give Torrance an apologetic smile as she rounds the corner. "Suz I have to go. Call you later."

My housemate steps into the kitchen, surveying the damage. She shrugs, not bothered by the dark brown and black flicks on the omelets. She stabs a fork repeatedly into the bacon strips and then flips them over.

"What did I hear about sex?" She turns brandishing the fork at me like it's a weapon.

I balk, my mouth flapping open, "No, no, Everett and I connected and talked things out."

"I swear if Everett is still being lied to-"

"No, no." I wipe my dry hands on the hanging hand towel. "He was mad at first, like I told you, but we talked about it last night when he got back. Only truths. And things are good between us."

I lift my plate for Torrance to drop the cooked bacon. We move over to the living room with our breakfast. Torrance curls up into a ball on the chair, her legs tucked up underneath her. I slice into my overcooked omelet.

Torrance sets her plate down, staring at me intently, "Things didn't go well for Luc and I, but Everett is a good person. I think you'd be good for him. You have been good for him, professionally, but I think he deserves someone like you."

"Thanks. That means a lot, Tor."

We sit in silence for a moment, me still barely eating my food. Torrance staring out the window, steaming coffee in hand. She turns her attention to me, tilting her head.

"Jemina has the night off for some rager tonight. You and Everett should go." I look up and she raises her brows, "Not as a PR thing, but just to be together. I'll forward you the details."

"Thanks," I murmur, as Torrance rises from her chair and heads back upstairs.

After I finish breakfast and cleaning up the mess, I send Everett a text:

Everett Abrams

There's a party you should be at tonight.

Are you ordering me as your client or...?

EA

See you there :)

You didn't answer my question...

EA

The snow falls in great white, silent sheets. The chalet is only a five minute walk from Torrance's A-frame but by the time I arrive my shoulders and hair are covered in flakes. I open the door to the house and hot air bursts out, turning me wet instead of snow dusted. I peel off my hat and stuff it into my jacket pocket. I only make it a few steps inside before I take the jacket off, too, or risk melting.

People are standing shoulder to shoulder. I turn myself sideways and squeeze between elbows and shoulders to make it through. Everyone is shouting to hear over the music. It reminds me of being twenty-one in New York City, pushing through the crowd with Suz to be in front of the stage.

I move through the crowd, my eyes focusing on the walls, straining to see someone tall, dark-eyed, and gorgeous. I don't spot him anywhere. A spark of hope flutters through me – has Everett progressed to mingling?

My chest swells when I find him. He stands to the side talking to a few guys I don't know, facing away from me. I could recognize those shoulders, his midnight hair from the moon. He runs a hand through it now, flicking the front farther up and back so it sticks out. My body tingles. I want to do that.

He looks back over his shoulder. His freckles. The shadow along his jaw. Pointed nose. The visible lump and lines in his throat. That mouth, parted. I lick mine now, remembering how he tastes. His dark eyes reach for me.

Lord. Have. Mercy.

For a moment, neither of us moves. We stare. We anticipate. *What happens now? Was earlier a fluke? What is he thinking?*

"December!" Jemina yells.

I see her jump up, hands in the air, but I can't take my eyes off Everett. His jaw tightens. Slowly he turns back to the guys. My heart skitters – does he regret kissing me? Has he decided he's mad at me for not being truthful? All my fears run circles around my head.

Jemina's right behind me, hooking her chin around my shoulder, "What are you thinking? You're looking at Everett."

"No, I'm not." I shake my head as I stare at him.

"Yes, you are." She grabs my hand and smiles wickedly, "Let's go say hi."

She drags me towards them. My eyes stay glued to the back of his head. Closer and closer we go. The party suddenly seems even hotter and louder than it did a moment ago. My throat constricts tight, mouth dry.

"Hey guys," Jemina smiles. She places me right beside him.

His eyes go wide. His hands shove into his hoodie pockets. I don't even know how he can wear that. I'm sweating just standing here in my t-shirt. I glance down at our feet. He's wearing white Jordan's and a pair of sweatpants tucked into his socks at the ankles. I'm dressed in a pair of Torrance's old snow boots and skinny jeans.

I want to hug him. I don't know what it is but seeing him here dressed so casually, but *here*, nonetheless, makes me want to explode. I am a bottomless well of affection for him.

Jemina begins chatting up the other two. I don't even know what she's saying. All I can focus on is not touching him. His hand moves in his pocket, and I sense it; he shifts his weight to his other foot, and I know it.

"How was your day?" I burst, not able to hold back any longer. *I want to know everything about you.*

His brow shoots up as he glances at me, "Not bad. Yours?" *You're giving me nothing Everett!*

I nod, pretending his short response means nothing to me, "Busy. I've been working on a project with Torrance and it's really starting to pick up. I spent half my day fielding calls with travel magazines and the other half building her social platform."

"Ah, moving on, are you?" There's a smile behind his cool demeanor.

"*Expanding.* I can't build an empire with one client, even as fantastic as he is." I glance at him from the corner of my eye. I try again, "So, how was your day?"

He shrugs and I feel his shoulder brush against mine. I hadn't noticed we moved closer. He says to the wall, "It was good, but the best part is being here with you."

I smile so wide and hard, my face tingles.

His eyes drop to his shoes, "Haylee landed her first 1080, so."

"You understate everything," I tease. Right now, it feels like my life has been leading up to this moment. The stars have all aligned. The clouds have dissipated. It's just me and Everett. Being honest.

"You want to play?" He nods at a game of pong about to end.

"Yes." Please.

I lead the way and call next game. We wait a moment while the game wraps up. He's standing so close I can feel him but we're not touching. I glance in his direction. His hands are in his pockets again. He stands with his legs wide like he does when he rides. His mouth is a straight line. There's a taut line in his jaw. My fingers want it to smooth it out. To feel the grittiness of his stubble. I hold my jacket tighter, so I don't.

It's our turn. I don't recognize the two we're playing against, but they share a few friendly words and nods with Everett. He throws first and sinks the ball in. I miss on my first shot.

"What are you doing this weekend?" I say instead of *tell me everything*.

"Probably just riding unless my *publicist* has other plans for me." The corners of his mouth tick up. He throws the ball and makes a cup still looking at me.

"Snowboarding and beer pong. How are you not a national treasure yet?" I throw and miss. Maybe if Everett wasn't throwing off my game so much, but I've never good at this game.

"I got good at this in college. About the only thing I did well."

"I'm sure that's not true."

He cracks a smile this time and it makes me tingle all over. His eyes flick over me quickly, "Yeah. You're right."

Oh. A heavy, hot coil of want zips to my core. I look away, watching the other guys throw. Suddenly, I want him so bad it hurts.

"Tell me about this Dawson guy. What's his deal? How did he get your job?"

I was hoping these questions would wait a little bit longer. I glance down at my feet and command myself to be brave. While he knows what happened, it's still hard for me to talk about. What if he changes his mind? What if I say something that convinces him I'm not worth it?

I squash the thought. I want him to know me. Everything. Including me at DKS.

"He's pretty friendly with the big boss Lionel King. I don't really know what happened." I swallow, looking at him. His brows are knit together. "I made a few decisions they didn't like and that was it. When I met with King, he blamed it on my recruiting numbers. I had five clients compared to everyone else having upwards of twenty, but my five were generating hundreds of thousands more than the other publicists. It was the first time he'd ever mentioned I wasn't performing.

"Then I took a red-eye from New York to LA on Black Friday. My client was having a moment. She didn't have the dress she wanted to wear for a performance, and she was convinced she shouldn't do it. I'd worked months on that deal. I couldn't let her back out over a dress. I used the company card and flew out there with a designer friend. I knew it was against company policy but the deal with *Savage Song* was huge. Not just for me but for the agency. Apparently, they felt differently."

I take a breath and meet his gaze. The way he's looking at me makes my heartbeat faster.

"I'm sorry," he says. I cock my head and I open my mouth to tell him it's not his fault. "For being a pain in the ass. I didn't make your job easy."

"You were an ass," I smile at him smugly. "But I didn't work hard enough to get to know you or the industry before, so I'm sorry, too."

His mouth tilts up. His eyes drop to my lips and linger. *Kiss me. Kiss me, please.* He leans in.

"Hey! Are you going to play or stare into each other's eyes?" One of the guys from across the table shouts.

Chapter 37

EVERETT ABRAMS

December's hair falls over her shoulders like water over a cliff. The heat of the party has made it frizzy. I want to brush my hands through it. Toss it over her shoulder. Anything just to touch her.

She smells like cold air and jasmine. I glance down at her as she looks around the party for Jemina. Her jeans fit her round ass perfectly, fitted into a pair of old boots I recognize as Torrance's. Did she not bring anything of her own here?

My heart sinks as another thought flashes through my mind – Why would she if she isn't planning on staying long.

"I can't find her. She must have left early." December turns and locks eyes with me.

We stare at each other for a moment. I want to reach out and pull her close. Drape my arm around her. Something to show everyone here she's mine. Something to show her that's what I want.

She pushes a strand of hair behind her ear, "Do you want to get out of here?"

I force myself to nod slowly so she doesn't know how relieved I am. I reach for her hand and thread us through the jostling crowd. We stop at the front door so she can pull on her jacket. When she's ready, she settles her hand back into mine. We share a look, grinning at each other.

Outside, the music thumps until we're at the end of the drive and turn onto the maintained biking path, then it's just the sound of our feet crunching on the snowpack. December swings our arms as we walk. There's a giddiness to her, an eager happiness. Her energy spills over into me and I smile, watching our hands swing.

"What are you smiling about over there?"

Her tease makes me smile broader, "Nothing. Just you."

"Me?" Her cackle splits the silence. "Why would you be smiling about little, old, annoying, bossy me?"

"You're not annoying. I never thought you were annoying."

"So, when I rang your doorbell obnoxiously you weren't annoyed? When I made you set up your social accounts, pushed you to do live feeds, and sent you all those bad ideas before I met you, you weren't annoyed?"

I laugh, "Okay, you got me. You were definitely annoying until I figured out you cared."

Our eyes catch and she swings into me. We're only inches apart. All I would have to do is tilt my head down and her lips would be on mine.

"Take me home with you."

Oh fuck. Heat rushes to my groin. I shake my head, wishing I knew the right words to explain where my heart and head are. Even in the dark I can see her face fall, but I say honestly, "Not now."

She turns away and walks a few feet in front of me, "I'm sorry. Was that weird? I just...never wanted someone as much as I want you. You're magnetic."

My brain scrambles, pulling in her words and tucking them away while trying to think how to explain, "I – you're. I don't..."

I don't know what to say. My brain is stuck. A gear spinning but with no traction. A moment ago she was in my arms. Now there's darkness and heavy silence between us.

"Would you please just say something? I think I've dug myself into a hole and I need to know I haven't ruined everything."

"You haven't." I want to say more. My chest is tight with all the things I want to say. There's too much. Too much to say. Too much feeling weighing on me. I'm frozen with it all.

Without a word December nods, taking my hand.

With a soft smile and her hand warming mine, we follow along the path. The lights from the mountain village begin to filter through the trees. Torrance's house is only minutes away. My throat constricts as I pressure myself to think of something, *anything*, to say.

"Have you moved off the bunny hill yet?"

Her teeth flash, "*Yes*. I've been practicing every day. I'll be Lyndsey Vonn in no time."

With a breath, "You should come ride with me tomorrow."

December stops and swivels to face me. We've reached the intersection, Torrance's A-frame is just down the hill. My house a few turns away.

"Your not afraid I'll dick punch you again?"

"Since you seem to have taken a vested interest in my dick, I don't think it should be a problem."

She bites down on her bottom lip to stop from smiling. Our boots thump on the pavement as we move down into the avenue of villas. I linger, not wanting to reach her stop just yet.

December pauses behind Torrance's SUV and waits for me to catch up. I make my way to her, hands shoved in my pockets, watching the way she glances at me and then looks anywhere but. My mouth tips up. It's like she thinks if she looks at me too long, she'll set me on fire.

"So, will I see you at the mountain or not?"

She sighs, glaring down at my kicks, "Fine. But only for a few hours. I have a lot to do."

I laugh, "Ten minutes ago, you wanted to go home with me and now you make it sound like spending a few hours with me is a chore. If you only want to fuck it's not going–"

"Everett!" She laughs, "You had nothing to say back there but now you're full of words."

"Sometimes that's just how my brain works." I pull at a strand of her hair and then look her in the eyes. "Thank you. For being patient with me. I know I'm not easy."

I glance down at her mouth. She's backed up against Torrance's vehicle. It would be so easy to give her what she wants. Instead, I lean in and press a kiss to her forehead and step away.

"It's not that. I'm just not certain we're not playing a game. Is this when you tell me you're not actually interested, and last night." She wraps herself in her arms, "Last night was some fluke?"

"You have no idea how badly I want you. But, you and I...It would be so much more than sex. Or what happened last night. You'll ruin me, but I'll ruin you, too. You'll be back in Atlanta with all the civilized men, and I'll be here. We'll be thousands of miles away. But nothing will feel as good as you and I did."

She swallows, voice thick, "Ruin me? You think?"

"There are a few things I do better than most."

Chapter 38

December Fowl

"**H**ow many girlfriends has Everett had?" I ask Torrance as she directs her SUV onto the main road.

"Ah," Torrance sticks her tongue out in concentration as she slowly maneuvers over a heap of snow. What I've learned in Blue Mountain is they don't clear roadways nearly as well as they do in New York. Four-wheel drive is a requirement unless you want to be stranded. "He had a couple in college, but none since I've known him. Why?"

"What about casual girlfriends? Hookups?"

Torrance laughs, I feel her eyes as she glances at me, "I don't know. Can't say we discuss his sexcapades. Ever."

"Have you ever heard stories? From other people about...you know?"

Her eyes narrow and she takes them off the road to look at me, "*No.* I don't know how big his...dick is or how well he uses it. Should I ask him to fill out a questionnaire the next time he comes by Blue Saloon?"

I tilt my head for a moment, considering.

Torrance laughs, tossing a friendly backhand to my chest "I think you two would be a really cute couple."

"*Yeaahh,*" I say slowly, feeling a knife wedge between my ribs and up into my heart.

"Or are you thinking more casual?"

"I don't know."

"I hate to be the momma bear, but you should probably get that figured out before you sleep together. Less messy, trust me."

"He said that, too. With more words." Torrance cracks up. I gaze out the window at the winter wonderland, the towering mountains. "I really like it here. I like the mountains and you and Jemina. I'm getting a lot of bites for clients, too, and even though snowboarders are wilder, they're easier to handle than my typical clientele."

The SUV slams to a stop. My seat belt presses into my chest, jerking me back into my seat. I press my hands into the dashboard for stability.

"What the fuck?" I search for a creature or a person or a roadblock that would have made her stop so fast.

"Sorry, sorry that was stupid. But oh my god, are you seriously considering staying here? Don't answer that. I'm going to show you this place. It would be perfect for you." She starts driving again. "Not that you have to move out, but I know you'd want your own place. Especially if you and Everett are going to be bowchickawowwowing."

Torrance pulls up right before the lodge. I scurry out and around to the back to retrieve my skis. The cold wind nips at my cheeks. I wave at Torrance before turning around and run awkwardly across the deck. My ski boots clomp against the boards in rhythm with the mantra repeating in my brain: *gotta hurry, gotta hurry, gotta hurry.*

Already I can hear the electric purr of the ski lift. I turn the corner and freeze. Everett is leaning against the railing at the bottom of the stairs. One foot still attached to his board, he slides it back and forth in the snow in front of him. A man stands beside him, a pair of skis hefted over his shoulder, and a jacket with fur around the hood.

My heart sinks. *Oh shit* – Ryan Dawson.

Not that it should matter. Everett already knows about DKS, but I don't like the idea of the two of them talking. Dawson is poison and Everett is a mountain spring.

My body tightens. I take a step back. A part of me wants to take another step and run. I don't want to face Ryan again. Taking in a deep breath, I move towards the pair of them. I take the stairs slowly, holding on to the railing and clunking down. Ryan looks up, his grin vanishing, but I don't care about him. I watch Everett as he swivels around. Slowly his mouth turns up. Heavenly angels go off in my head.

"Hey," I murmur, caught in his dark eyes – the snow making them pop.

"Hey," He reaches up to pull my hat over my eyes. I swat at his arm, but he squirms just out of the way. "No hitting. You don't want to ruin this perfect male specimen, do you?"

"Depends on what you mean by ruin." His eyes widen and I flick my attention to Ryan, who's leaning in to listen.

"See you around, man, my date's here." Everett dismisses him without taking his eyes off me. My legs turn to jelly, and I hold on to the railing tighter.

Ryan glares at me but stalks off. Breathing again, I drop my skis into the snow and step into them. My boots click into place.

"What was that about?"

"Think you can keep up?" Everett says and I look over my shoulder at him. He's watching me and it makes my stomach go fizzy. He can't stop looking at me.

Holding down my smile, I use my poles and I push myself towards the lift line. This time I make it all the way up without issue or punching him in the groin. Everett slides up next to me. His jacket brushes against mine, and it's like we're skin-to-skin, not separated by layers of clothing and heavy jackets. The line moves forward quickly and in no time we're next.

I look over my shoulder for the chair as it swings in and pushes against the back of my legs. I grab hold of the middle bar and sit down, holding my poles in my outside hand. The chair rocks and moves forward, my feet dangling in the air. I click my skis together, so the fluffy snow falls away. I gaze down as we climb, climb, climb farther off the ground. The lift makes a soft whirring noise, otherwise it's silent. I take a deep breath – *made it* – and settle back into the seat.

"This is one of my favorite parts," Everett's deep voice breaks through the hush. "It takes me back to when I was a nobody in Colorado. Riding was the only thing that mattered. It wasn't about winning, or how big the next check would be, or how many sponsors I had. It was just me and my friends, and the mountain – chasing dreams." His stark eyes meet mine and I let his words melt into me.

"You were never a nobody."

"I didn't think you'd come." He says softer now, nudging me.

I like the way he's opened himself up to me. He's not all stony faces and little words. He's a man with a hidden world inside. I'm caught breathless.

I clear my throat, "Why wouldn't I? Someone has to show you why skiing is better." I kick my ski into his board, it sways on his foot.

A smile works its way across his face. He looks away, watching the snow and trees pass beneath our feet. I watch him.

"About last night. What I," he tilts his head to look at me. "What I said."

My heart thunders. I gulp in cold air and it's a welcome reprisal to the heat his eyes cast on me. A part of me wants to shrug it off, make a joke, let it go, but I want to know more. I want to define this *something* between us.

"I never let anyone close enough to hurt me. I'm very good at pushing people away before it can get far."

"Was that what that was last night? Am I getting too close?" *Is this as close to you as I'll ever get?*

"Not that I'm incapable of intimacy. I mean, I've been intimate with plenty of women." I blink. "Shit. Not what I mean. Fuck." He huffs a laugh and readjusts his helmet, staring at the ground.

I want to know what he means to say. Talking about anything serious and relationship-related is scary, but I want to have this conversation.

I reach over and grab his forearm with my gloved hand, "You're really cute when you're out of your element." He looks up, his mouth falling open. "And you're really cute when you're in it, too."

He laughs and shivers run down my spine. The sound is so much better coming out of him than anyone else.

"December. I like you. Really like you. But I meant what I said last night. This can't be casual for me. You're special to me and if we start something I...need to know you'll be here."

I touch his gloved hand with mine, "I'm here right now, and I don't have any plans not to be. I just...want to be close to you in a way I can't explain."

Everett nods and shifts closer, "You should wear this." He unbuckles, and removes his helmet and hat. Then tugs my hat off and replaces it with his gear. The straps dangle around my chin. His fingers brush my skin as he adjusts and buckles it securely.

I feel like Kate Hudson in *How to Lose a Guy in 10 Days* when Matthew McConaughey hands her the ugly helmet. Everett makes this helmet sexy. I bet I don't. He moves the helmet around with his hand to check the fit. It moves around a bit. Not as good of a fit as it is on him, but he seems to accept it.

"I know you've been working on your skill, Vonn prodigy, but I'd like you to reach the bottom with all your bits and pieces. I like my eggs scrambled, but not your pretty head. Unless," his eyes drop to my mouth and back to me. His mouth curves up wickedly, "I'm the one doing the scrambling."

I lean into him and nip his bottom lip. I want him to touch me. There's a heavy, warm fist of need between my legs, and I want him to satisfy it as much as I want a million dollars and my father's approval.

"What about my other bits and pieces?"

"I'll see to them all."

His gloved hand moves up my thigh. He brushes places I've been wanting him to touch again. Even through layers of clothes the sensation makes me moan. I grip the metal bar in front of me for support as my legs slip open wider. His hand dips between my thighs. He opens his hand and fans his mittened fingers over me.

"Everett," I breathe and open my eyes. "Why the fuck are we on a ski lift?"

He does it again, this time fanning his fingers open and closed where I want him most. My hips move into his hand, "I can't wait to get you out of these clothes, December."

I look across the mountain, trying to latch onto something I recognize, "Can we ski straight to your house?"

Everett laughs, sliding his hand to my knee and I almost demand he put it back, but we're at the drop off. I lift up my ski tips, touch down, and let the chair push me forward. We move away from the crowd so Everett can secure his other boot. He bends down and tightens the bindings. The puff ball on top of my white and blue hat dangling and jerking with him. I like the look of him wearing my things. Once he's ready, he hops in my direction.

"We're not going to rush this." I say once he's standing next to me. Suddenly, I'm very afraid. More of Everett and this thing fizzling between us than the mountain. It all seems very real now – and I want it, I do, but it scares me.

I lean my weight into my poles, my legs shaky. How am I going to make it down this mountain?

"We can take our time." I meet Everett's gaze and the way his eyes read; I can tell he understands me.

"Owh, owh. December and Everett sitting in a tree k-i-s-s-i-n-g."

Hendrik laughs, sliding so he's in front of us. Everett's hand presses into my hip. Claiming me. The thought makes me rush with glee.

"Ev, I never would have guessed you dug skiers, dude. Especially considering what happened earlier." He turns his attention to me, throwing his hands up. "December, you should have told me you loved the mountain air. I would've taken you out ages ago."

Everett makes a noise from deep within his throat. Hendrik hears it too, "Hey man, I'm not trying to encroach on your territory. She's a cool cat and cute as hell in a snow–"

"Why don't you move along." Everett's voice drawls, deep as a growl.

Hendrik holds his hands up, "Alright, alright. December, I just wanted to give you a heads up. There's some dude from your old agency or something, talking shit about you. He cornered me just an hour ago. Said you're unreliable and didn't produce and were fired from some agency. Then offered to represent me for ten percent less. So, obviously I told him to shove it. I don't do desperate."

He throws up a hand and then drops down the slope. I'm frozen. My face is burning. I know Everett already knows about DKS but it's still embarrassing to have my former co-worker bad mouth me. Especially when I'm trying to put new roots down. And that's exactly why he's here. He can't let me have anything. Ryan Dawson is a parasite.

"Are you okay?"

My stomach is a tsunami. I'm regretting the four buttermilk pancakes and bacon I devoured this morning.

He dips his head down to see me, "Was he talking about that Ryan Dawson guy? Is he stalking you?"

I nod then shake my head, focusing on Everett's steady eyes.

His frown deepens, "What's wrong? We'll fix this. I'll talk to that piece of shit myself. He won't fuck with you."

I take a few deep breaths and shake out the energy through my hands. In a moment I'm feeling better.

Everett is watching me, concern written across his face. My chest tugs. I love the newfound protectiveness he has for me.

"I don't want to think about him today. I just want to ski with you."

A smile curls across his mouth, "Me too."

"First one to fall is a rotten egg!" I push myself forward with the poles and begin to slide down, weaving back and forth across the mountain.

For a minute Everett lines up next to me, following my lead, turning as I turn. We smile at each other, laughing. Then he diverges onto his own trek, riding just in front of me. He squats low, zigzagging in a tightline as if he's weaving between invisible obstacles. Just before he bottoms out, he leans heavily on his heel edge, and stands up. He looks for me over his shoulder and waves, my heart zinging.

He plays like this, doing tricks, riding backwards down the mountain on his toe side so he can watch me; letting me get far ahead of him and chasing me down, and mimicking my movements again like a shadow.

"Again?" Everett says, pulling his mask down so I can see his face. "I want to show you Blue Moose."

I nod, but my mind is caught on his red lips.

Chapter 39

DECEMBER FOWL

It's dark by the time Everett and I make it back to his house.

My body is sore and cold but happy from a whole day of skiing. I haven't skied more than two hours in years, but leave it to me to jump right back in. Especially with Everett involved.

I jump down from his truck and my legs crumble underneath me.

"Are you okay?" Everett steadies me, helping lift me to my feet but I'm laughing.

"Oh my god my legs are noodles. I can't believe it," I take deep a breath and start laughing again.

He makes sure I'm steady on my feet before he grabs the gear bag out of the back. Inside, I plop down on the entryway bench and untie my boots, toeing them off, then shake off my jacket. I press my hands into my cheeks. They're warm and cold at the same time. By the time Everett gets all of our things, I've taken off everything but my long underwear.

"Ah," he pauses for a moment in the doorway. "You're – ah, not all dressed."

I hug the bottom stair post, watching as he sheds his outer gear, "I was wet."

He reaches down and pulls the joggers from my snowpants, feeling them. He lifts his brows at me, "Really? Cause they don't feel so wet."

Nipping my bottom lip, "I was thinking I should shower. Want to show me how yours works?"

"Yeah," He drops my joggers and pushes his snowpants down his thighs. He meets me at the bottom of the stairs, eyes flashing to my mouth, "It can be a bit tricky."

I nod, not taking my eyes off his. He takes my hand and leads me upstairs. My heart is racing, body tingling. Riding with him, playfully flirting with snow, and weaving down mountain trails together makes me feel so connected to him. A concept I want to experience more with our bodies.

His bathroom is the second on the right, just past his bedroom. It connects to his room through a walk-in closet. The room has double sinks, and a large tub separate from the shower. As I stare at it, I picture myself there, soaking in bubbles. Everett soaking on the other side.

I turn my attention back to the real Everett just as he's lifting his shirt over his head. Fuck. I am so dead. His obliques ripple as he shifts, pulling open the glass door. He turns the nozzle all the way to the right. The water hisses on and I get a beautiful view of his back. Wide, muscular shoulders to the hollow of his spine and dimples in his lower back.

Everett turns and catches me staring. A sly grin spreads across his face. He knows. He knows I like what I see.

Without a word I step toward him, wrap my hand around the nape of his neck, and pull him down to me. Our mouths meet in a clash. Hungry and hot. His hands settle on my hips, fingers sliding just beneath my top. I moan at the delicate pressure and heat of their presence. He wraps his arms around my waist and drags me against him. I feel his engorged cock press into me. The sensation has us both tugging and pulling at each other's clothes. Everett tugs my top over my head. I have his pants around his ankles. And his hands are on my breasts. Cupping them. Bringing them to his mouth.

"Oh fuck," I groan as his wet tongue and warm mouth send a flash of lightning from my nipple straight to my clit.

Everett backs me into the shower, stepping out of his boxers and long underwear. The hot water cascades against my back as he sucks and licks and gently scrapes his teeth on one breast and then the other.

He lifts his head, my nipple popping from his lips and grins at me. For a second, he steps out of the shower. I take the moment to admire his bare ass. He turns back to the shower, fresh loofahs in each hand. My eyes drop from the loofahs directly to his lower region. There's a trail of dark hair from his belly button leading down and then a smattering of it across his groin. My vagina clenches. His cock is long and thick, jutting slightly upwards.

I swallow, my mouth feeling suddenly wet and wanting.

I reach for him as he steps into the shower again, wanting to touch and taste. But he shifts his hips just so, shaking his head.

"Shower first and then I'm all yours," Everett gestures for me to turn around.

I do and his hand reaches around me and pumps body wash into the loofah. He steps closer. The front of his body presses against my back. His dick is against the top of my ass. I lean back and he runs the loofah along my hip, up my stomach, over my breasts. His other hand wraps around my waist. I lean my head back against his shoulder and his hot mouth kisses along my neck. Goosebumps erupt across my skin.

Everett nudges my leg with his hand, and I step wider. Gently, he runs the loofah around my inner thighs, over my vulva. It's sweet and sensual and oh, so hot. I whine when he steps away and lets the water rinse me as he washes my back. He loofahs one butt cheek and squeezes the other. I look over my shoulder at him, but he's staring down at my ass, bottom lip between his teeth.

Spinning me around, he smacks my ass. I lean in and kiss him, my tongue teasing his.

"Dry off and get in my bed," he says, shifting his mouth from mine.

"But I haven't washed my hair."

He pushes a strand of wet hair behind my ear, mouth curving, "I'll have you worked up so badly you'll need a second shower anyways."

My eyes widen and he laughs, helping me around him. I grab a towel from the bin, plus an extra, and look back at him one last time before I cross into the bedroom. He's running a loofah over his body. A giddiness swirls in my gut. I run into his room, squealing to myself, running the towel over me.

Just as I'm dry the shower shuts off. I spring into his bed unsure how to place myself. A mixture of excitement and anxiety mingle inside me.

A moment later Everett's drifts into the room. Still completely naked. I suck in a breath, watching as his dark eyes take me in. He ruffles the towel through his hair, across his chest, and then throws it to the ground. I lean back as he climbs into bed with me.

"I suppose this is a little late, but I was tested a year ago. Negative, and haven't slept with anyone since. And I'm on birth control, but always use a condom anyways."

"Guess that means I'll really have to warm you up," Everett grins, eyes glinting.

He grabs me by the hips and yanks me down, so I'm lying flat on my back. I yelp out in surprise.

"Sorry. Little excited," he laughs, moving so his shoulders are under my legs, hands on my thighs. "I was tested eight months ago. Also negative, no sex since, and I also use condoms."

"Oh," I nod, clamping my thighs shut so his face isn't right in my vagina.

"December," he gently pushes them apart. "Can I go down on you?"

My face heats. My bits and pieces are screaming *yesss! Thank you very much!* but there's an inner hesitance. It usually takes me forever to orgasm. Even like this.

"Um...I take a while."

"That's okay. I'm not in a rush."

I look at him skeptically.

He tilts his head and laughs, "Believe it or not, I love eating pussy. But," he starts to sit up, "if you don't I can do something else. Whatever you want."

"No," I practically shout and shove him back down. He grins and I pretend to be cool, "You can do that."

"Licky, licky it is."

I lay my head back, feeling a tension in my legs. Everett starts pressing kisses into my inner thighs, my stomach. His mouth is warm and soft. I take a breath and let it out, focusing on the sensations he's creating. Then he takes a long, slow lick over my lips and clit, and I practically rocket off the bed. Reaching up, he grabs my hips, fingers pressing into my skin.

He takes another long, slow lick and another. Gently increasing the pressure and speed of his tongue. I writhe, moaning. He then takes one labium into his mouth, sucking.

My hands fall to his head, gripping and gnarling into his wet hair, "Everett, fuck."

His mouth moves to my other labium and takes it in his mouth before he presses his lips around my clit. Licking one way and then another. Over, around, side-to-side, on and around the sensitive area of my clit. It feels so fucking good. The sensation builds as he plays with varying pressure and speed.

My eyes roll shut, hips rising from the bed, "More, more. Oh, fuck."

His hold on my hips tightens. He swirls his tongue tight and fast, tight and fast. Side to side, side to side around my clit.

My mouth opens. I don't mean to speak, "Oh yea. Oh fuck. Ohmygod."

The sound of his tongue and my wetness only drives me crazier. I never thought it was hot before, but with Everett it is. He changes pace, licking and stroking up and up. I'm racing fast through time and space. All I feel, all I sense is the weight of Everett's tongue and the building pressure in my core.

I moan wildly, hips moving, "Everett. Oh fuck. Everett. Ohmygod. Ohmygod."

In my mind, in the feeling, my clit is simply glowing. Brighter and brighter at the pace of his tongue strokes. And then, like a string wound tight, I break. My mouth opens but nothing comes out. Everett moves with my hips, trying to hold me steady as hot pleasure breaks in waves through me over and over.

I'm panting. My hips are back on the bed. And Everett's tongue is taking me in long, slow strokes again. I wonder if this is what a volcano feels like after it's erupted. Swollen and satiated and throbbing – but still in need.

I pat Everett on the shoulder to signal him to come up. He lifts his head and the cutest grin spreads across his face.

"Did you like that?"

I run a hand through my hair, closing my eyes as he pulls himself up to me, "Oh yeah."

His hand presses into my stomach. My clit still tingles with sensation, but my vagina is urging me for more. I want to be filled and felt and fucked.

I roll over, kicking my leg over his waist and straddling him.

He grunts, eyes flashing shut for a second, "You better be careful, or I'll slip in."

I meet his eyes, slightly lift my hips and roll myself over his cock.

He sucks in a breath, eyes shutting again as he grabs my hips.

"Condom please."

He points to the bedside table. I lower myself down to him and kiss him. His lips part with mine and I get a taste of myself on his tongue. Rolling off him, I reach for the drawer and pull out a condom. I've never been very good knowing which way is the right way to roll it on, so I hand it to him. Everett tears it with his teeth, spitting out the ripped end and strokes it on, holding the tip.

"Lube please."

"Lube?"

He gives me a look, "You haven't had sex in a year, December. And while you're wet, we'll need more to be comfortable."

My eyes drop down to his cock filling out the condom and nod, reaching for the lube.

"On your back?" He says, smearing lube over the length of him.

"Well, aren't you the bossy one, but I want to be on top."

"You sure?"

I push him down by the shoulders, kissing him, "Positively."

Straddling him, I wrap my hand around his head and slowly press his dick into the heat of my entrance. I bite down on my lower lip, as I press deeper.

"Oh fuck," I murmur, pausing at the pressure. My eyes closing.

"Are you okay?"

I gaze down at him, nodding, "Yeah. You're just so thick."

Everett lays his head back, hands still gripping my hips, "God I can't wait to fuck you." The muscles in his neck are taut, holding himself back from rocking into me.

My walls clench and I ease lower, "I like it when you talk to me like that."

He breathes out slowly, his eyes hooded, "Yeah? You're so fucking tight I can hardly breathe."

"Ahh," I moan, bottoming out hard, taking the full length of him.

His hands squeeze me. Taking it slow, I roll my hips back and forth. I moan, pressing deeper into his cock.

"Fuck," he murmurs. Guiding the movement of my hips farther back and forward again. His hips lift to join me. I tilt my hips forward and place my hands behind me, giving myself greater leverage to ride him.

He cups my breasts, rolling and pulling my nipples between two fingers. Our eyes are latched, watching each other, and I move my hips faster even as my thighs begin to burn.

"Is this how you imagined fucking me, December?"

I shake my head, riding his cock harder.

"How then? Show me. Tell me how."

I sit forward so my clit rubs against his pelvis. I ride him faster, harder.

"This? God, you ride my cock so fucking well." He slaps my ass and thrusts up into me.

I nod, "And you fucking me," I gasp, letting out a moan. "From behind."

"Let me do that. Let me fuck you."

I nod and shift off of him. He twists so he's behind me, grabs a pillow and places it, folded, between my thighs.

"For your clit."

I adjust it underneath me as Everett applies more lube. Then his hands are on my hips again.

"Ready?"

I look behind me and nod. With that, he pulls my hips towards him. Backing me over his cock. He grunts and I moan, pressing my cheek into the bed as he bottoms out. He pushes my hips forward along the length of him, nearly all the way out, and pulls me back again.

"Everett," I cry out as he thrusts.

"You like that?"

"Mhmm...Ev-ah."

He drops my hips and presses his body over mine. He thrusts, cock pumping into me. The calm, sweet strokes gone.

"Oh. Oh. Oh fuuck. Ev-Everrett," I call out, my legs shaking. He pumps into me again and again. My legs give out. I'm lying on my stomach, a moaning, writhing hot mess.

Everett doesn't miss a beat and presses harder against me as he thrusts in and out. The movement rubs my clit over the pillow. Sweet dual friction.

"Oh my. Oh my god. Ohmygod. Don't. Don't fucking stop. Ohmygod."

"Fuck. So good. You're gonna make me come so hard."

His thrusts become wild and frantic; shorter and deeper. My clit rubbing, rubbing, rubbing against the pillow. And suddenly my orgasm comes rushing towards me. I cry out, my vagina squeezing and rippling around his cock as Everett continues to pound me. My orgasm ends but he's still fucking me so good, I hurtle into another one.

"Jesus fucking—" He pushes inside me once more and stills.

I tremble around him and slowly he leans in and kisses my neck, down my back as he pulls out. Climbing off the bed, he disposes of the condom. I roll onto my back, too hot and noodly to cover myself. Everett plops into bed next to me. Even though we're both hotter than hell, he pulls me into him.

Chapter 40

EVERETT ABRAMS

O ver the next two weeks, I spend my afternoons shredding with Luc. And mornings with Haylee while Luc is home recovering from the wild nights before.

She lands her double back 1080s like she's been doing them for years. I'm pumped for her. The girl is going to kill it at the LAAX Open.

Then there's December. My favorite part of the day.

It's strange snowboarding is not the only thing I look forward to anymore. I'm not gonna lie, it's fucking awesome. I give her a few more cooking lessons, which she manages to tragically bomb. I tease her about it, but I like her so much more because of it. I have something I can do for her.

She busts her ass helping me with my social accounts, scheduling events in Switzerland for LAAX, and giving my knee its much needed daily massage. The least I can do is make sure she's well feed and fucked.

Her fingers press into my skin now. I'm stretched out across the couch, one leg jigging on the floor. She's on her knees across from me, her shoulder pressed into the back of the couch as she kneads my scar. She sucks her bottom lip in her mouth, concentrating hard. She looks like a fish. The most adorable fish. I laugh and she looks up at me, her lip popping loose.

"What?" She grins. Her eyes glisten. Her brows hitch up, challenging me to spill when I shake my head. "I bet this is what you were thinking: *December, you're so amazing. You're the most perfect, wonderful person in the whole wide world. You're like a gooey chocolate chip cookie, or the cheesiest slice of pizza.* Yeah?"

She gets it about right. She's a fresh falling of snow. The win. The highest score. My chest clenches tight. I swallow, glancing at the TV. I shouldn't be feeling this way. Not after only a few weeks. But here I am, feeling it.

"Are you sure you can't make it to Switzerland with me?"

She tilts her head at me like I've just said the most adorable thing. One of my many favorite looks from her. It's almost as though she adores me. She hops closer and stretches out. Her head rests on my peck. Her arms wrap around me.

I laugh as she mumbles into my chest. Her garbled words and breath tickle. I drape my arm around her and shift her so she's on her side.

"What was that? I think I heard you say you would?"

She shakes her head, pouting her lips. I want to kiss her more than ever.

"No," she says. "I have big things coming for a few of my newest clients. I can't leave now."

I lift her chin up with my thumb and press my lips into hers. Gently at first, then grow greedier, asking her lips to part with my tongue. Her hand finds my cheek and slowly travels down my neck to curl into my shirt over my chest. Soon the sounds of our kisses drown out the noise of the TV. My hand roams down her back. I palm her ass. An eager hum sounds from the back of her throat. I'm hard against her hip.

"Get a fucking room!" Luc hollers. A throw pillow smashes into the back of my head and December jumps.

Fucking, seriously? I could strangle Luc right now. I glower at the back of his head as he opens the fridge to fish out some food. He's been around so much more since he knows December and I are seeing each other. He's never been a cockblock until now. I'll remember this for sure. Payback is a motherfucker, asshole.

When he turns around holding a container of leftover quinoa and garlic lime chicken, I chuck the pillow at him. It smacks his hand, bouncing the container out of his grip and onto the floor.

"Ooh! *Swish*. Four-point play, baby."

"In what fucking universe? That was a three at best." He gapes at the mess, turns and digs through the fridge again.

"You're cleaning that up."

"You're cleaning that up." He mimics me, but he grabs the broom and sweeps it into the dustpan. "I'll be upstairs. Commence couch fucking, or not couch fucking. Just keep it down. And put a sock on the staircase next time." He lifts a middle finger as he walks away and dashes up the stairs.

"Asshole," I grumble.

"I like him." December declares, standing up.

I grab her around the waist and bring her down into my lap, "No you don't. You better not go liking him better than me."

"As if!"

I squeeze her tighter. Press my lips into the back of her neck, "Please go to LAAX with me."

She laughs and squirms, but I hold her tighter.

"Everett! Okay, but on one condition."

I release her and she shifts. Half standing, half sitting in front of me with her knee on the couch between my thighs.

She nips her bottom lip and tilts her head. Her hand runs up my thigh and up the length of my cock. I'm all the way hard in 0.13 seconds. Some kind of Olympic record. I groan, rolling my head back as she strolls her hand back down.

Leaning forward she whispers into my ear, "I want some of this."

I grin devilishly, "Only the tip."

December narrows her eyes.

"You said *some*. So, I'll give you *some,* like you asked."

Her plotting face appears. Her fingertips circle my head dangerously. I suck in a breath. Oh god. I'm in trouble. I needled the temptress and now she's come back with a vengeance.

"Oohkay," I grab her wrist and pull her hand away before things go too far. She smirks toothlessly. Oh yeah, she's proud of herself.

She leans in again. Her breath tickles my neck, "I want all of you. All the time."

"I got that," I nod. My heart thunders in my chest. My dick twitches. "Whatever you want."

"Don't act like you don't want that too."

"*Oh,* I do." I gesture towards my painfully throbbing erection. "No one's faking it here."

Her lips pinch together as she tries not to smile. Quietly, December climbs off my lap and makes her way towards the door. I follow her, maneuvering my erection into a less obvious position.

Dressed for the cold, she pulls the door open and moves her head so I can give her a kiss goodbye. I pull her face to mine.

"Tomorrow," she says breathlessly when we pull apart. "I'll see you tomorrow."

Luc thunders down the stairs as the door clicks shut, swings around the railing and laughs, "Dude, you have a raging boner."

"Yeah. I'm going upstairs for the longest cold shower of my life."

"You do you."

The Cove, Blue Sky's best kept secret, is tucked behind the shelves of the ski rentals. Only the locals know about it, and would rather die than share its location. Nevertheless, it's still packed when I turn up. I make my way through the sea of jackets and goggles to the bar.

"Yo, Everett!" Kade, the owner and bartender, hollers as I approach. "That dude over there is looking for you."

I follow his finger to the wall. I recognize him as the guy I met at the lift before December and I met to ride together. He lifts his hand and waves me over. I order my regular shit spinach protein drink and head in the guy's direction. Not sure who he is but he seemed all right.

"Hey," I reach out my hand, "Everett. I don't think we were ever actually introduced."

He takes my hand. His blue eyes laser focused, "Ryan Dawson."

Today he's not dressed in snow gear. I should have known something was off. He's in a stitch-patterned business jacket and dark jeans. His hair is styled like it's never seen the underside of a hat and helmet.

"Ryan Dawson?" I repeat and my mind clicks.

Fuck. What the fuck.

"You know who I am."

No bullshitting. I can do that.

"Yeah, you're the sleaze ball who got December fired and nabbed all her clients. I don't have any interest in talking to you." I flip my glove in his face and turn to leave.

"I thought you might say that. So, I brought these." He pulls some papers out of the satchel sitting on the table.

I run a hand along my jaw. "Listen, I don't want to cause any trouble, but you need to leave. Leave December alone. Leave Blue Sky. You already have all her other clients. Her job, which, you and I both know, she's better for."

"No," He sniffles in that way arrogant people do and shrugs. "I have *all* her clients. Including you."

I huff a laugh. This guy has some balls. I guess he's used to pushing people around. Getting what he wants. He has that kind of face.

I step towards him, "No. You. Don't."

He taps a finger on his papers, "It's all right here. You have a contract with me. Isn't that your signature?"

I glance at the paperwork and do a doubletake. What the fuck? My electronic signature is stamped onto the bottom of the document. My stomach sinks, thinking back to the email I received from DKS. Contracts. I signed them and sent it back. I squeeze my eyes shut. Oh fuck.

"Now you remember, don't you? Trying to be all smart guy with me. But I got you."

"You got these illegally. You sent them through December's email even though she didn't work there anymore."

"But you didn't know that, did you? Business 101: read the thing before you sign it."

I thump my fist into the table, run my hands through my hair. I fucked up.

"It's fine," I shrug even though it's not. "I'll just tell December what happened. She'll understand. You can be my publicist for a year but good luck getting me to do anything."

"No, you won't." He shakes his head. "You won't talk to December. You won't tell her about this. No contact. No mention of her ever at your events. I know what she did. She pretended to be a DKS publicist when she wasn't. That's misrepresentation. Fraud. She would go away. Would you like that? Do you want your girlfriend to never be respected or hireable again?"

I can't breathe. What the fuck is he saying right now? My mind spins. No contact with December. Fraud. Misrepresentation. Sounds a lot like what he's doing right now.

He steps closer, bows his head like he's about to share some secrets. "I know about you, too. I paid a visit to your hometown. Turns out, there's a whole lot of people who love to talk about who you *really* are. I have a piece ready. I could publish like that." He snaps his fingers, licking his lips hungrily. He's really enjoying this.

"Okay." I nod. "What do you want me to do?"

Chapter 41

Decemer Fowl

I'm walking out of Blue Saloon, feeling high when my ringtone for Suz goes off.

"Well, hello there, bestie best, best, best."

"Fuck. You're so happy and I'm going to ruin the mood."

"What's going on? Are you okay?" I shiver standing just before the gondola lift.

She sighs, "Apparently that disgusting investor you met in New York really didn't like you. I guess he doesn't appreciate having to be honest or women calling him out on his bullshit. He said it was either you leave, or he pulls his funding."

For a moment I can't think. I shake my head, "Wow. That's why I was fired. But how did you find this out?"

"Lionel, the fuck, was having issues with his computer after hours. They asked me to connect remotely and when I did, a new email came in from the slug. There was a whole thread about it. Puke. So, naturally, I forwarded it to my personal email. Just in case."

"Just in case? What do you mean?" Dazed, I walk to the gondola pad and take a seat in the next available pod.

"I think you need to contact Junie and your dad. The more recent emails said they had you on misrepresentation? I'm not sure if they really do or if it's just smoke, but I sent it to your sister."

"They what?" I sit up. Fuck.

"I know you haven't told them about being forced out of DKS but it sounds serious. And then. AND THEN. Dawson landed your guy. I'm tired of this morally empty fucking company, I'm so done."

I make a face. My guy? Dawson snatched up all my clients as soon as I was gone.

"What do you mean my guy? He has all my clients."

"Not Everett."

My chest swells at the mention of his name. With my toe I draw a heart into the floor of the pod, "He's lying. Everett didn't sign with him."

There's a strained pause and then, "Are you sure?"

"Yes, I'm sure."

"Weird. He must have been bluffing in the emails. Which would be really no surprise. The man is ninety-nine percent hot air. Anyway, Frankie and I will be there in...approximately two days."

"You're coming to Blue Sky?" I grin breaks across my face. If she is, I can't wait to show her around. Introduce her to the girls and *Everett*.

"Yeahh," she draws out, distracted then she snaps back into it. "Come Monday I won't have a job. Frankie misses his mom. I miss my best friend and it looks like you're having so much fun up there. Will I have a place to stay? I checked the hotels and they're all booked."

Suz is smarter than me, I laugh to myself remembering how I showed up here with no reservations and no plans in the heat of high season.

"Of course. You can sleep with me in Torrance's loft. I...sort of applied for a place up here." I break it to her, wincing. We've been roommates for the past four years. The best roommates ever, but my life is starting to take shape here.

She laughs, "You bitch. What the fuck. How dare you 'sort of' apply for a place without telling me? But seriously. Hate you."

I stare out at the passing snow and scenery. The view is breathtaking. Frosted trees spike from the snow-covered ground, naturally directing the riding trails. A fog has settled over the valley, hiding Blue Sky from view. As soon as the gondola dips down the next ridge the village will come into view. It will be nothing but tiny little buildings, one indistinguishable from the next, slowly growing as the pod descends the mountain. I can't wait for Suz to experience it. I think as soon as she's here she'll understand why going back to Atlanta isn't really an option.

"Just get here safe, okay? I can't wait to introduce you to everyone. You're going to love it here."

She hums, unconvinced, "I'll see you in a few long, dragging days. Hopefully Frankie won't howl the whole time."

I laugh because, poor Suz, he absolutely will. He'll howl until his meower gives out. And then he'll squawk. "I love you."

"You too, Boo."

"Suz, you're sure he said he has Everett's contract?"

"Yeah, I'm pretty sure that's what I read in the email, but now you're making me doubt myself."

"I'm sure it was something else," I say softly, my brows furrowing. Then with more certainty, "Drive safe."

There's an uneasy feeling in the pit of my stomach.

I crunch down the pavement to Everett's house. His truck is parked in front of the garage door. I couldn't wait. I walked straight here from Blue Mountain.

The door is unlocked, like it has been since our ski adventure. I see it as a sign he trusts me. He's opened up his house for me just like he's opened his heart. I'm welcome anytime. I try to remind myself of this as I step through the door.

"Everett?" I call. I kick off my boots and march towards the kitchen, not bothering to take off my jacket and hat.

He's in the kitchen, digging through the refrigerator. He thinks snowboarding is the only calming thing in his life, but I know cooking is, too. Cooking for him does what my pacing does for me. It quiets my mind. It allows me to organize my thoughts so I can see through the clutter of my brain.

Everett cooking isn't unusual. The man cooks every meal. But cooking at four-thirty when he eats at eight, is weird. My heart lurches into my throat – *is it true?*

"Hey," I say softly.

"Hey," he returns equally as soft. There's a head of broccoli in one hand; peppers in the other. He places them slowly on the counter. His face is drawn in forced neutrality.

I find it hard to keep my breath. I don't like this. My heart is racing. He just rolls the pepper around the counter instead of looking at me.

"Tell me it isn't true," I say in a rush, squeezing the mittens in my hand. "Suz called me and said Dawson was gloating you were his client."

He's silent. And it's answer enough.

I stand there. Like an idiot. Trying to work this out. I'm so lost I can't even think myself to move. There's pressure building behind my eyes, in my chest. I'm ready to implode. I'm ready to break into a million little pieces. I don't understand.

"Why?"

"I can't work with you any longer."

"*Why*?" The anger is building in my chest. He just stares at me, his face all stoically neutral and blank. I take a half-step forward, "After all I told you about him and that agency, you're going to work with them? What about all we've done? We're thirty thousand from your goal. What about us? What about all the things we've said to each other? Do I mean nothing?"

"No. You mean everything." He looks away as an array of emotion flashes across his face. He swallows like he's forcing it down.

"Everett," I take another step closer. I just want him to hold me. I want to hold him. I want to be here and figure this out. "If you mean that, talk to me. Please."

He sucks in a breath, "I fucked up. We can't work together. You can't be involved. It's all so complicated."

"I am involved. I'm invested in this, Everett. You. Me. Your career. It seems pretty fucking simple to me. Either you want me, or you don't."

His jaw works. Stone-face sets in. It's like everything I'm saying to him has the reverse-effect of what I want.

"December, I'm sorry I can't talk to you about it now. You'll understand later." His eyes spark, "You said your sister is an attorney, right?"

I blink. What the fuck. What the fuck. Something is wrong. Very, very wrong. I shake my head trying to shake things in to order. Suz's call. Now this. I take a step back. Everett takes a step forward.

He curls both hands through his hair. "Christ, if I could tell you, I would. It's bad. It's so bad, but I promise I'm just trying to protect you. You have to trust me."

"Suz called me. She said DKS has me on misrepresentation – which is true if they knew. I didn't tell you I no longer worked with DKS. But then she said you were Ryan's client now. Is it...is it true?"

Everett looks away. Hurt slices through me like a papercut to my heart. I jerk towards the whiteboard on his refrigerator and scribble down Junie's number. The last thing I do for him.

"December." He reaches for me as I walk by. I maneuver out of his reach. "I just need some help."

I lob a mitten at his head. It hits him square in his big, muscly chest. The same chest I've used as pillow almost every night.

"You want everyone's help, but mine. Am I not good enough for you, Everett?"

I know my words are biting and unfair but so is this whole situation. I wish I could be the bigger person and rise above but turns out I'm more solid than gas.

I huff to the entryway and yank on my boots. They're not even all the way on as I start marching out the door. I know he's following me. He's like a balloon tied around my wrist.

"Your mitten." He jogs in front of me, turning to face me so he has to walk backwards.

He's in his socks. Walking through the snow and slushy ice.

"It's freezing." I stop.

"More reason you need your mitten."

Everett hands it to me and I pull it on. He squints up at the sky like it will strike him with the right words to say. I'm on the verge of crying and I don't want to do it in front of him.

"You should probably get inside," my voice the gentlest it's been. "Frostbite and hypothermia are real things around here."

His mouth quirks up sadly. Stuffing his hands in his pockets, "I signed a contract with Ryan. I thought it was you. It came through your email. I didn't read it, just signed it. I'm such a fucking idiot."

I gape at him. I'm not sure I heard him correctly. Did he just say that, or did my brain make it up?

Chapter 42

EVERETT ABRAMS

D ecember paces back and forth in my bedroom like a mad woman. I sit on the edge of my bed and watch her. I'm so numb right now I can't think of anything better to do than stare. Her fingers keep moving. Brushing and pinching her bottom lip until that's all I want to do. With my lips and my teeth and my fingertips.

"This is all my fault. This is all my fault." She continues to repeat over and over and over again. For the first five minutes I would fire back, '*no, it's my fault.*' Every time she uttered it, but I figured out she's talking to herself instead of me.

"December, stop." I fall back onto the mattress and pat the spot next to me. "Come here."

The bed jolts as she throws herself down. I laugh because I thought she was too far into her head to hear a word I said, but she tosses herself down with fury. Nothing is half with her. It's full throttle.

We lay there a second. Our elbows and shoulders touching. For the first time since I told her, it's calm. I close my eyes and hold on to it. I know the next few weeks are going to be nothing but a shit storm. A never-ending avalanche.

I roll onto my side, propping myself up on an elbow. December's hair is sprawled out across the bed. I smirk, picking up a few strands. She reminds me of a frilled-neck lizard. It spreads its frill and charges when threatened. I crossed one a few years ago in the Australian Outback. Little creature, but Luc and I ran like hell when it charged.

I swallow and brush a finger along her forearm, *I hope I'm not the one she's angry with.*

Her green eyes flick to mine. She opens her mouth to speak, but before she does, I lean down and press my lips into hers. I want to remind her I do some things right. I'm not all wrong.

December deepens the kiss and pulls me down on top of her. Everything melts away. It's just the press of her lips, her warm, soft body underneath mine; the things we're saying with no words.

I cup the back of her knee and draw her leg up around my hips. I press into her, so she can feel what she does to me. She moans, biting my lip. I press deeper. She circles her hips, drawing them around and around and around my erection. My hips jerk forward. God, I want her so bad.

"Everett." December murmurs, her voice thick, as she pushes a hand into my shoulder.

"Hmm," is all I can manage.

"We have to figure this out."

My head droops, "Can't we keep doing this?"

She laughs and pushes me down so she's straddling me. My hands run up her thighs. She reaches down and picks up my phone.

"Show me the email," she orders like this is the most casual thing ever – her straddling my hips, my erection between her thighs.

"Do I have to? We could do something else." I hitch a brow.

She pushes down a smile, "No. I said I was joining you at LAAX. We're not letting Dawson get in the fucking way. Show me the email, please."

I squeeze my eyes shut but unlock the screen and pass her the phone. My groin is so heavy with desire it hurts. I like her bossy. And the way she says *we*. Like we're a team. We're in this together.

"That little sleazeball!" December erupts. She grounds herself down on my hips and bounces.

"Whoa, whoa." I stop her. "Take it easy."

"Oh, sorry." She climbs off and my dick sighs with relief. She pushes wild strands of hair behind her ear, focused. "This contract lists *my* name as your representative."

She passes me the phone then hops off the bed, hurries to the dresser where the contract Dawson gave me rests. She moves through the pages and jabs her finger into the signature line. Her voice is high, "He swapped our names. He swapped our names!"

The bed shakes as she jumps on and hops around on her knees. Her face lights up, hopeful. When I don't react with joyous shouts her face falls.

"What's wrong? Why aren't you excited? Do you...want to work with him?"

"No, no." I brush her shoulder. "It's not going to be that easy. I don't just want to declare this contract void. With all the things he's done, I want to destroy him. This shit he's doing. Who will he fuck with next?"

She slumps down beside me, "You're right. You're right. We should call my sister."

My stomach tightens. I don't want to call her sister. Her family will know what I've done. What if they think December can do better? She *can* do better.

I glance at her. She's folding her bottom lip between her fingers again, studying the written contract and then comparing it to the one in the email. My chest swells with heavy feelings. In the middle of this mess, I don't want to dissect them. I look away, stare at the floor.

"I have someone at DKS who can help us. She's a whiz with computers and...about to quit on Monday."

I shake my head, giving her a cutting look, "I only told you so you wouldn't hate me. You can't be involved."

"Everett, I told you, I *am* involved."

"Well, your part ends now."

She runs her hand up my spine, squeezes the back of my neck, "That's not how I meant involved."

"What do you mean?"

There's a pulse vibrating through me. *Say it. Say what we both feel.*

Her green eyes go wide. She squeezes my neck harder, "I..." *Yess.*

Her eyes drop. Her hands release my neck. *No, no.*

"If I had told you I wasn't with DKS this never would have happened." She meets my gaze. Her eyes are a forest fire. "It's my fault. I want to help fix it."

I clamp my jaw shut, forcing myself not to explode, but I do anyways, "He threatened you."

December jerks back, her forehead crinkles, "What?"

"He said if I don't dump you. If we don't stop talking or working together, you'll go to jail. I'm not going to let that happen, December. No matter how much you want to help."

"Everett." Her eyes soften. Her hand strokes the back of my head.

I jump up. There's that patronizing voice I've heard all my life: *Everett, sweetie, you're better than this. Kid, are you sure you want to take that class? Everett, why don't you retire?* It's the tone that tells me I don't know what I want; like I'm not capable of making my own decisions.

My voice is final, "You're not helping." My eyes dare her to disagree.

"Everett," She squeezes her eyes shut like it's the only way to keep herself from exploding, "this isn't negotiable."

"You're not listening!"

"I am!" She springs off the bed. "This is a product of both of our decisions. Mine more than yours. If I would have just told you the truth, this wouldn't be happening. And I'm going to help fix it."

We stare at each other for a moment. Glowering eyes meet glowering eyes.

I reach out and pull her closer. Any excuse to touch her. "We'll call your sister, ask your friend for help, but no one else can know. Not even Suz or Luc." She hesitates. I push her back to meet her gaze. "December, for this to work, everyone but us has to believe we're through."

"But we're not."

I shake my head. Lift her chin, "I'm not. Are you?"

Her head moves quickly back and forth. A smile peeks across her face and she runs her hand up my thigh, "I haven't had you enough of you yet."

I smile at her and trace her bottom lip with my thumb, "Is that all you want?"

She leans in. Presses her hand over my heart, "I want all of you."

I cup her breast over her heart, "Ditto."

"Seriously, groping at a time like this?"

"You started it way back when. My dick and the whole internet remember?"

"Shut up and call Junie. I don't want the whole internet thinking you're single for long."

"You're right. Better make us worldly official before I meet someone at LAAX."

She gasps and pushes me down on the bed.

Chapter 43

DECEMBER FOWL

The sun splits through the clouds and pours through the windows of Torrance's A-frame. I pace along one bright light beam until it fades. I keep pacing after it does. My fingers are at my mouth, teeth clicking against my nails. My mind is a mess.

I can't shake Everett from my mind. I've been analyzing this all night. Breaking down our conversation over and over. How long will it take Junie and her team to figure this out? How fast can Suz provide us with more evidence from DKS?

"Fish are meant to be caught and released," my best friend says from the bed. She's been watching me walk back and forth in this little bedroom since she arrived hours ago. Frankie is curled on the edge of the bed.

Suz has been a cynic since Sonya, her college girlfriend, broke it off with her. I assumed it was a phase. Casually dating. A new temporary boyfriend or girlfriend every month. But the way she's talking makes me think she believes it.

"You don't mean that."

Suz nods with her whole body, making the bed thump against the wall. Her long black hair falls over her shoulders, "I do. Love isn't meant to be kept. And that's okay. We just enjoy it while it's here and let it go when it's time."

My heart squeezes. I fight with myself. I want to tell her this is pretend. Everett hasn't dumped me, but I know why I can't. It has to appear – to everyone – that we're through.

I dive for Suz. She rears back as I grip her hand, "You don't mean that."

She *mm*'s and runs her free hand over my hair, "Baby, that's just me. Everybody and every story is different. I only mention it because I don't like seeing you so broken up and hurt over someone."

"But that just means it's real. It matters."

Suz pushes me back, her hands hold my chin, "I imagine if true, long-lasting love is real, it wouldn't hurt. It wouldn't be like this."

"Suz, everything worth having hurts a little." Her face hardens. "I mean college was hard and we cried a lot but look where we are."

She casts her arms around the room, "You mean jobless and living in a stranger's spare room?"

We both laugh.

"Can you believe where we are right now? I was fired. *Fired*." I shake my head and admit something deeper, "And I may very well be in love with my only client. Who," I squeeze my eyes shut and hate myself for lying to Suz, but even Junie agreed it was important we sell our breakup, "is now avoiding me. And my best friend doesn't believe in love."

My phone pings. I dive back onto the bed to see what it is, praying it's from Everett.

It's not a notification from Everett. It's a notification *about* Everett.

I set up my accounts to notify me when any content has been created about him. I unlock my screen and begin to read. It's an article from *The Daily Dish*, a gossip magazine centering around celebrities. But not the (mostly) good, journalistic kind like *People* or *Us Weekly*.

Everett Abrams, A Failure? There are photos of him from years ago. Even posted report cards. My chest tightens. Oh god. Someone's written about his learning disorder. Once I finish reading, I'm fuming.

"What?" Suz demands. She's been sitting beside me anxiously this whole time, rubbing my back.

I hesitate. I have an itch to call him and make sure he's okay; find out what's happening, but I can't. It rips me in half to do nothing. Instead, I hand Suz the phone. She gasps as she begins to read.

I do the only thing I know. I grab my laptop and begin to work.

.

Chapter 44

EVERETT ABRAMS

"What the fuck." I slam a handful of celebrity gossip magazines in front of Ryan.

He glances up at me with his steel blue eyes, cool and emotionless. December said I was stone-faced. I hope I never looked like this. Soulless. He picks up one of the magazines and reads the title, then browses through all the others.

I clamp my jaw shut. My pounding heart wants to jump right out of my chest. I squeeze the table leg between my hands instead of around his fucking neck.

"Looks like your girlfriend wanted revenge," his voice is dry, matter-of-fact.

I huff, shaking my head. She would never do that. Especially since she knows about this whole fucked up situation. But Ryan doesn't know she does. This is one of his games. A test.

"She wouldn't do that."

Ryan laughs, "You don't know December like I do."

The way he says it makes me want to jump across this table at him. Like he *knows* her. Is he suggesting they were once more than rivaled co-workers? Another tactic to make me mistrust her. He's good at this. He's done it before. I grit my teeth; my hands roll into fists. *Play along.*

"You don't. You know nothing about her."

"We worked together for five years. You've known her, eight months? She's angry you've come to your senses; angry with me for rescuing you."

Rescuing me. I bite my tongue. This guy in unbelievable. He doesn't twitch, he doesn't rub his nose; easy tells I've come to recognize as lying. It's like he believes what he's preaching.

"December did this. She's exposing your vulnerabilities. Trying to tear you down. Tell me, is there anything else she could get at? Anything I don't know?" His eyes are intense.

I shake my head. It's the truth, but there is one golden nugget neither of them knows about. I regret not telling her about Elevate but I'm relieved dick bag here can't get his greedy hands on it.

"Good. Now I know this is hard," he pats the magazines, "but we have to move forward. Let's discuss LAAX."

I sit and listen as he draws out his laptop and breaks down exactly what he wants from me. On the outside, I'm neutral. I just listen and nod, but on the inside, I'm tearing him to shreds. He piggybacks on December's arrangements, adding more to it. Parties, exclusive meet-and-greets. December wanted to make me a partying, bad boy, but Ryan's actually going to do it.

I'm zoned out when Ryan pulls a contract onto the table.

"I'd like you to sign this."

I glance at the paperwork, "What is it?"

He shrugs, "Something that will make you a lot of money." I stare at him until he continues, "Razor, it's a new over-the-counter drug for energy. It's about to come out and it needs a face. That face should be you."

I ease the contract into my hands, "I'll have to read it."

He smirks, "You don't need to read it."

Why, don't think I can? "You said yourself, Business 101: read the contract."

Irritation flashes across his face, "You can trust me. So, trust me, sign the contract."

"Not before I read it." Not before my attorney and Olivia read it and figure out what you're up to. Fucker doesn't think I'm smart enough to lawyer up behind his back.

"Fine," Ryan growls, "but get it back to me as soon as you can. They want you but there are plenty of other athletes lined up to get their hands on this deal."

I shove the contract into my backpack as his phone lights up. *Mike Gibler calling* flashes across the screen. Ryan snatches it up.

"We're done here." He says to me, his eyes dangerous as he gets up and marches out.

Mike Gibler. I'll give them his name, too.

Seven p.m., after a grueling day on the mountain and in the gym, is the best part of my day. I come home to a quiet house, my body exhausted but buzzing from a day on the slopes, prepare some chow, and then relax in front of the TV.

At least it used to be my favorite part of the day.

Now, this house is haunted with memories of December. As I stand before the stove, the crackle of searing chicken breasts brings me back to one of her lessons in the kitchen. All I can think about is her tight yoga pants, swinging her ass to Taylor Swift as she burned the first round of eggs. Then the feel of her soft, warm body pressed against mine as I demonstrated how it's properly done. My dick hardens, and I brace against the counter as the rest of me goes soft.

She has a weird way of doing that, even when she's not around; making me hard and soft at the same time. I adjust the erection and wish it was her touch at the front of my shorts. A hard fist coils in the pit of my stomach as blood and desire surge lower.

I turn the grill off and spoon the stir-fry into a bowl. As if on cue, Luc walks in. He's always here for the food but never the making-of or clean up. His face brightens when he sees my meal.

"Help yourself," I say dryly and wander to the couch. "You always do."

"Hey, what's with the attitude?" He says as he dumps a pile in a bowl for himself.

I slouch back against the couch and string my legs out in front of me. I lay there boneless, my food forgotten in my lap.

I feel empty. I'm not hungry. I'm not motivated. Snowboarding is the only thing that makes me feel normal, and even then, it's not the snowboarding I need to do. It's just riding up and down the slopes. I've been carving up the snow instead of breaking down and perfecting new tricks like I should be. I'm worried before this is over, December will realize what a mess I am.

I run my hands up and down my face, "This has gotten so fucked up."

"Tell me about it," Luc says, his voice muffled with a mouth full of food. "I think you need to dump that lackey Ryan or whatever-the-fuck-his-name-is and go back to December. *She* was good for you and she's still looking out for you."

"How do you mean?" I look up at him.

He shovels another mouthful of stir-fry into his mouth and when he speaks a few pieces of rice spew out, "I talked to her. She wanted me to give you this."

He tosses a magazine on the couch next to me. It's an edition of *Our World*. Unlike the standard gossip magazines, *Our World* focuses on sharing authentic stories; stories to build each other up. On the cover is a group of athletes and people dressed in black suits and skirts.

The glossy cover is littered with subtitles from 'Managing Mental Health' and 'How I Overcame my Anxiety,' but my eyes focus on one – 'Misread, stories from the neurodivergent.'

I flip through the pages until I find the interview. From CEOs, aerospace engineers, Olympic athletes, authors, and a librarian from my hometown of Fort Collins, countless stories from real people and their struggles and successes ranging from learning disorders like me to ADHD and Asperger's.

My chest clenches as my eyes roam across the paragraphs, gleaning pieces of the interview here and there. But my mind is racing so fast I can't focus on the words.

"Oh, I almost forgot this," Luc reaches into his back pocket and pulls out a note written on yellow lined paper.

I recognize the handwriting immediately as hers. I suck in a deep breath – *Everett, I'm so sorry Ryan sold your story. I can't help but feel like it's my fault. If I had just been honest with you right away this wouldn't have happened. This article is the only way I knew how to be there for you. And I hope you know your disorder and past traumas do not define you – this is my way of showing you how incredible you are & you have nothing to be ashamed of. I hope you see yourself here because I do. XOXO - December*

Her handwriting begins to blur as tears press at my eyes.

"December," I choke out, my throat tight. I've never felt so seen before.

Luc wraps his arm around my shoulder, "I've got mad respect for her for pulling this together."

I wipe my eyes and sling my arm over Luc's and squeeze. I want to see December, but Luc is the next best thing.

"You know I love you, man."

And it hits me in the chest right then – the people who matter already knew this part of me. And they've never treated me any differently. Okay, maybe a little differently. I think about Dad trying to help me read my mom's sloppy grocery list and laugh, but in the best way. I don't know why I was so afraid of sharing it in the first place.

People are going to judge me, yes. People are going to look at me differently, probably. But if I knew when I was thirteen that my heroes had similar learning and cognitive disorders as I did, I wouldn't have been so scared and ashamed of it. I wouldn't have felt like I needed to hide it like a big bad secret. I may not have been as hard on myself as I was – or let the other bullies push me around.

I take a breath and my chest loosens, shoulders falling – the sky hasn't fallen. My phone hasn't been blowing up with sponsors releasing me.

Nothing has happened.

Except, I realize, I've been released. I no longer have to carry around my past or my differences like it makes me bad or unworthy or *dumb*. Ryan tried to fuck with me; keep me small and ashamed and controllable, but now that everyone knows, I've been forced to accept this part of me. My heart sings like opening the shutters and letting the sun in after a storm.

"Luc?"

"Yo."

"What do you think about bringing December on as Elevate's PR professional?"

He takes a moment to consider then turns to me, grinning, "I think...the investors will really like our initiative and confidence. Let's do it!"

"One condition, at least while I'm still working with Ryan, we have to pretend like this is your project only."

Chapter 45

December Fowl

I blink at Luc, shaking my head.

He sits across from me at Torrance's table. A laptop, gloves, and a binder of future projects cast between us. She takes my hand and squeezes, sensing the tension in my body.

"How long have you guys been planning this?"

Luc shrugs, like this news of a secret company he and Everett are organizing is no big deal. I guess to him it isn't. What the fuck Everett?

"We've always talked and dreamed about starting our own thing. It's sort of our retirement plan if that makes sense."

I shake my head, "I don't understand why he didn't tell me?"

"Look," Luc puts his hands up in surrender, "it's clear Everett didn't tell you shit. That sucks but you'll have to take that up with him."

I sigh, "Sorry. I know. Just, can you tell me more about...everything?"

"Like I said, this has always been a dream. We worked on it here and there, but it's never been a priority. Then, after Everett's injury last year, he really jumped into it. I think it showed him he can't do this forever."

I rub my chest, just over my heart, feeling for him. Snowboarding is everything to Everett. His injury must have been a jolt awake – and I bet it hurt. In more than just a physical way. No wonder he's so venomous to Hendrik.

"Anyway, this guy we used to ride with now works with an investment firm. He got us in to meet with them. Over the years, Everett and I—mostly Everett," he laughs, "have put away about three hundred thousand. They liked the plan, the products, but wanted us to have more skin in the game."

I suck in a breath, jerking back into the chair, "That's why Everett needed two hundred thousand by January."

"Yeah. It was kind of perfect timing, you showing up here." He grins at me.

I look away, twisting out of my chair. What the fuck, Everett. I pick up their proposal packet and flip through the pages. Not really reading it but pacing around the table, trying to get my mind right.

"She does this. Paces. She'll come down in a moment," Torrance explains.

Their conversation goes on in the background. Hurt and anger swirl inside me. Why didn't he tell me about Elevate? It's a beautiful project. And he was so pissed about me neglecting to tell him about DKS when he had his own secret. Asshole.

In the beginning we didn't see eye to eye so I can understand why he kept it to himself. Kind of. But now? The last two weeks have been...my mind flashes back to lying in his bed. He's telling me a story. Holding my hand, and I'm laughing. Then we're in the kitchen. Everett making fun of me for how truly horrendous my cooking skills are, and then him softly teaching me. My mind jumps back to his bed again. The room is dark. He's on his forearms above me, kissing me with a ferocious sincerity as we...

Sucking in a breath, it felt like love. But was it? Is it?

I realize, flutters in my stomach, it is for me.

And right now it doesn't matter why he didn't tell me about Elevate. Right now, he's asking for my help. I'm going to give it to him.

"You look like you could use a snack," Torrance slides a plate of carrots, cheese, crackers, grapes, and celery with peanut butter across the booth. "Something to keep your brain juiced."

I bite into a carrot and flash Torrance the image of Elevate's logo, "Did you know about this?"

She takes the piece of paper, scrutinizing in, shaking her head, "I knew it was an idea. But I found out they were really trying at the same time you did."

"Everett. Asshole. I can't believe he didn't tell me about it."

"If they would have told me even a month ago that were starting a company, I would have laughed. Luc and whatever he's involved in is always a hot mess. But, now it seems like he may be growing up. He did come by the house later and apologize, which was weird."

My mouth drops open, "He did? After all this time?"

"I know right? I guess he's in therapy or something, which is so good. He needs it, but I should have asked him to pay for mine too," she laughs with little humor. "I know Luc pleaded his case, but if you're not working with Everett anymore, why are you working on this?"

I shrug, not yet able to admit Everett and I are faking this professional breakup, "It would be so amazing for Everett."

"You are getting paid, right?"

"As if I'd do anything without a paycheck."

She cocks a brow, "You're not actually...through with Everett, are you?"

I blanch. How did she know?

Torrance smiles, "You can't fool me. Holler if you need anything."

By the time the evening rolls around, I have a pretty solid PR plan for Elevate. Luc insisted he be the face of it, for now, but I include tentative plans for Everett. Whenever we can solve this Dawson problem. With that thought, I check my phone. My heart sinks. No email or texts from Junie or Everett.

"Excuse me?" A young woman comes along beside me.

I know her from somewhere. She has long curly brunette hair, icicles clinging to the strands around her face. Stark hazel eyes beneath fierce eyebrows. Her teeth are so white they nearly outshine the snow outside. I run my tongue along mine, suddenly feeling dirty. The young woman slides into the other side of the booth. She pulls open the first few buttons of her coat and takes off her gloves.

"I want to work with you," she says directly, her gaze serious.

A memory washes over me. She was venturing out of Everett's house the first day I arrived.

"You're Haylee, right?"

"That's me." She swings her frozen hair behind her shoulders and smiles. When she does, her whole face lights up.

"You're Everett's friend."

"Friend. Protégé. Will that be a problem?" Her eyes dare me to say it is.

"Only if it is for you."

She shrugs, "Nope."

I consider for a moment if Everett sent her here to tell me something, but she looks at me expectantly and I push the thought away. I know why she's here. I'm a damn good publicist. When someone wants to get their personal brand out there, they come to me. I'm pleased the athletes here are taking notice.

We sit and discuss her goals, me typing away like a mad woman. Haylee gazes out the window on occasion, lost in her thoughts before she answers. I can't stop staring at her. She's a snow queen – her eyes vibrant green and blue, an easy, infectious smile on her face. Not even the snow and dreary weather can dull her glow. As soon she starts discussing her goals and snowboarding, she blooms.

"What?" Her nose wrinkles.

I didn't realize I was staring open-mouthed at her. I shake my head and laugh, "We have to get you on TV."

She gives me a funny look, "Why?"

"When you talk about snowboarding it's like the world explodes with color. You're so passionate and alive when you discuss it. The world needs more of that."

Her nose scrunches, smile peeking through, "Really?"

"Seriously, aspirations: loving what you do and expressing that passion." I shake my head, "You're going to be bigger than…Vonn."

Haylee slaps a hand across her chest, "I love Lindsey Vonn. She's a skier," she shrugs, "but she's a badass and a boss-babe."

I lift my hand and give her a high-five, feeling oh-so giddy again.

Chapter 46

EVERETT ABRAMS

The set at the headquarters of LAAX is bustling. Sound and camera guys run around like the place is about to catch fire. The two producers I met for just a moment stand in the shadows both talking and gesturing loudly.

I have my earbuds in, but I can hear everything.

The host Angela whispers to her makeup artist as she dabs on a third layer of foundation. Gossiping about the weekend, clubs, and the stories to come this week. The makeup artist glances in my direction.

"He's hot," she says to Angela, none the wiser.

Angela glances over her shoulder at me, "Should I find out if he's single?"

The woman brushes on a few strokes of mascara and giggles. Her eyes dart to me again and she nods.

Single but not available.

"Thirty seconds until we're live!" Someone shouts from beyond the bright lights.

The makeup artist scurries off as Angela poses herself at her desk. She practices her smile a few times, makes a few weird noises and faces to prepare herself. Weird but not unlike how I get myself ready for a run; stretching my body, tapping my bindings for good luck, and psyching myself up for a good run.

"Fifteen seconds!"

Angela reaches across the desk and taps me on the shoulder. I jerk my head in her direction and she gives me her best smile and pulls at her ears, signaling I should take my headphones out.

I do as she asks and stuff them in my pocket.

"Are you ready?"

I shrug.

"Five...four...three..." A producer counts down with her fingers and then throws a finger at Angela. Right on cue she begins.

"Good morning, America, this is Angela Hurst. I'm sitting here today with Olympic gold medalist, and *seven-time* X-Games gold medalist, Everett Abrams. The winningest snowboarder in superpipe history. Everett," she turns to me and so does the camera, "how does it feel to carry that title around?"

I let an easy grin spread across my face, "I guess I hadn't thought about it. Probably about as good as it feels to be one of the highest ranked sports journalists in the country."

Angela beams.

"Now Everett, you're vying for a top spot at the LAAX Open – at twenty-seven you'll be one of the oldest snowboarders here. What's it like competing with such a younger crowd?"

Oh yes, the old age question.

"You're only as old as you feel, I guess. I haven't noticed much of a difference between competing when I was twenty-three and where I am now. Honestly, I think I've probably gotten better. When I was younger, I didn't care as much about eating healthy or working out. Now, I keep a rigid schedule and it's really paid off. I've only been injured once, and I was back on a snowboard in only four months. In this industry, that's nearly unheard of."

"How do you keep your routines so fresh? In previous years, the younger generation begins to surpass the older with newer, better tricks, but you've managed to stay on top."

Generation? *Really?* It's not like I'm thirty years older than the competition.

"I ride every day. I've never been the type of person to sit back. If you do, you're right, the industry takes off without you."

"You've been spotted with rising star Haylee Graudin on the slopes as well as afterparties, are you off the dating market?"

I laugh and shake my head, "No. Haylee's a great snowboarder. We train together, throw ideas off each other. We're just very good friends."

Angela cracks up, "Hear that ladies, Everett Abrams is still single! I read an article about you recently, discussing the difficulties you faced in school. Specifically, your learning disabilities. Do you think that's impacted your riding at all?"

An impish grins spreads across my face and I speak the truest words all interview, "No. Yes. I mean, I work hard to be as good as I am. Maybe I work harder because I'm not good at the regular things most people are – like reading or math. But it hasn't affected how I learn to ride or create tricks. It's all about finding your strengths. I was lucky enough to find mine when I was thirteen."

Angela nods and *hmm*s approvingly, "In all your years as a professional winning athlete, you've rarely taken any interviews. Lately you have been. What's the change?"

My chest pinches as December flashes in my mind, "Someone convinced me I was doing a disservice by not being active in the industry. She was right."

"Does this include revealing your neurodivergence?"

I swallow, knotting my hands together as I meet Angela's gaze, "Yes and no. I've been hiding that part of myself forever. A part I had no intention of revealing. It was leaked, but it was probably the best thing that could have happened." I pause, taking a drink of water to collect my thoughts–just like December showed me.

"I convinced myself I must be the best. I must have the best team, the best record, the best gear to prove I'm worth something. I've been afraid if I don't have snowboarding, I have nothing. Being the way I am, I was always afraid to do interviews and meet-and-greets, but I wanted to change the industry. It's hard to be influential when I don't engage.

"Snowboarding is more than me. It's about the community we have, building new riders, and advancing the sport. I want to win. Obviously," I chuckle, "I'm a competitor, but winning isn't my sole purpose, and meeting fans, doing interviews has really made me realize that."

"You've certainly been an influence in the sport since you entered seven years ago. From creating new combos and tricks, do you not consider those advancements?"

I nod, "I do. But...um," I tilt my head thoughtfully, "but I'd like to see more diversity in the sport. And snowboarders have a such a bad rep for being lazy, or wild, destructive. I thought I was showing the other side of that by not being involved outside of contests, but I think it backfired. Instead, I've been the successful but jerky image of snowboarding. Spreading further that snowboarders are selfish and disinterested."

"*Wow*," Angela nods her head, surprise etched all over her face. "Your friend Luc Orseno just announced his intent to start his own outerwear company. I have to say, due to your long-standing friendship on and off the slopes, I'm surprised to hear you are not involved in the project. Care to comment?"

I shrug, hoping December wasn't mistaken when she said I have a stoneface, "I am happy for him, but really want to focus on competing."

"We only have a few moments left. Everett, I want to thank you for being here today and providing such a stimulating conversation. Best of luck."

"Thank you for having me."

Angela turns to the camera and beams, "We'll be right back after these messages."

The red light flickers off and the host lets herself sag slightly in her chair. She swivels around, eyes roaming over me, "I don't think I've had such an open interview before. Your authenticity was palpable."

"You asked great questions."

She nods, and her eyes narrow a fraction, "So, you're not with the other snowboarder. What about this other woman you mentioned?"

Ryan appears on stage as though he can sense a discussion of December brewing.

"We should get going," Ryan looks down his nose at me like I'm his dog to order around. I shove my hands in my pockets to retrieve my phone, so I won't lose my cool and deck him.

The urge to do so has been building every day since he cornered me. Whenever he's around my arms feel like loaded cannons. I step down from the stool, away from the bright lights, and into the stage hall.

Dawson grabs my arm and attempts to pull me around. It's like a suckerfish attempting to direct a shark. I jerk my arm back and glower at him.

"You mentioned December. We had an agreement. You don't mention her and if asked about publicity, you sing my name."

My blood goes from cold to boiling in less than a second. This idiot thinks it's a good idea to poke me.

I step closer, "I didn't mention her name. And I won't praise cockroaches like you."

We stare at each other a moment.

"And what is this potential business your best bud is trying to get off the ground? Maybe he could use my help."

I bristle further, "Don't even think about trying to fuck with him."

Ryan squares up to me. Then, finally, he takes a step back, turns on his heel, stalking away.

"Don't mention her again. And give your friend my number," he calls back.

I grit my teeth and squeeze my hands into fists. I've never been an aggressive person, but Ryan Dawson makes me want to go *Street Fighter* on his face. I make it to my dressing room and pull out my phone. Junie answers on the second ring. Her voice is so similar to December's it makes my chest sting.

"I can't be around this guy a moment longer. I'm not a violent person but whenever he's around I have the urge to smash his face in. December understated how fucking horrible he is."

I find myself pacing the length of the dressing room, and I freeze, again reminded of December. The woman never stops moving. Especially when she's angry, or anxious, or feeling any range of human emotion. It used to drive me crazy but here I am, mimicking her behavior.

"We're working on it." Junie hurries on, "Just stay cool for a few days longer."

I'm so angry it's almost like I feel nothing. Like touching something so hot it instantly fries the nerve endings.

"Junie. I need out of this contract before I hurt someone."

I hang up and fling my phone across the room. I rake both hands through my hair, pressing my palms into my skull.

Chapter 47

DECEMBER FOWL

It's only 10 a.m. on Saturday but the girls are piled into the living room.

Jemina, Torrance, Suz, and me. Torrance had declared this Girl's Day just so we could watch the LAAX Open.

Before I left Atlanta, I never would have imagined myself waking up early on a Saturday to watch snowboarding. But it's a way of life here. I don't want to miss Haylee's interview or her run. Plus, big known secret, Everett will be riding today. And today will mark the first day I've seen him in over a week.

Torrance gives me a soft kick, "Nervous?"

"Seriously, how do you and Everett do that? It's like you have a sixth sense."

Tor shrugs, keeping her features perfectly trained as she says, "Well, we both love you, so."

"Right, Everett Abrams. The man who hasn't talked to me in a week, loves me." I study her, my heart races, hoping she'll look my way and say he called and told her so. Because I love him and I don't know if he feels the same way.

I worked out days ago that Everett and Junie had blocked me out. I was supposed to be part of the plan. I was supposed to be *involved*. I wonder, for the millionth time, if he's changed his mind. Did he realize this is all my fault and wants nothing to do with me?

I swallow down a gulp of wine and try to tell myself it's not true. It's not. I know it's not, but...why isn't he calling me? My reasonable brain tells me he can't, but I want him to. I shouldn't be so worried. I know the big picture. I have

Frankie and my amazing friends here for me. But I want to see Everett. Touch him and kiss him and tell him...

As if hearing my thoughts, the camera flashes to Everett.

I scream and clutch my wineglass, so I don't spill it. Jemina's screaming too, pointing at the screen. She flashes her finger between me and digital Everett. A second later the feed cuts into a commercial.

I glance down at Torrance. She's laughing. So is Jemina, and I'm breaking into the giggles, too.

"What did you put in this wine?" Suz demands, staring at us like we've lost it.

Everett is having an awful day.

I nibble on my bottom lip as the competitors take their turns down the superpipe. Everett placed eighth in the preliminaries this morning. His worst placing ever. It's not Everett. It hurts to see him like this.

The living room is quiet. The mood has drastically changed from the morning of bubbly optimism and conversation as we watched Haylee place in the Top 5 of the preliminaries and just off the podium in the finals. She did her double back 1080s and it made me hurt so bad, thinking about Everett teaching her that move.

On the TV, another rider drops into the pipe. I'm barely aware of his run, my mind spinning. Everett is next. I fold my hands together and hope, *pray*, he's pulled himself together.

The camera fans up to the starting gate where Everett stands. He's dressed in all black – black snow pants, jacket, bindings. Even his goggle lenses are so dark I can't catch a glimpse of his eyes. His facemask is pulled up over his nose, his features completely hidden. He leans down, taps his bindings, and slowly slips down the slope.

I hold my breath as he drops in. He doesn't perform his signature Frontside 360 as he usually does. He simply pops his board up and drops in. I watch with wide eyes as the camera follows him weaving between the walls, executing each trick and combo like he should.

"Good job, Everett," I murmur, clapping my hands together.

"It's a clean run," Jemina speaks up. She's hunched forward. "But it's missing his flair."

"No," Torrance, wriggles in her seat and directs her gaze to me, "it's missing his heart."

I swallow hard. She's right. It was a decent run, but it wasn't an Everett Abrams run. It's like he's lost himself somewhere. Guilt washes over me. If only I could help him. If I hadn't come here, none of this would be happening. Everett would be world-class, perfect Everett.

"This is all my fault. If I hadn't been fired, if I hadn't lied, if I hadn't shown up here, neither of us would be hurting. Everett wouldn't be failing at the one thing he loves."

"Snowboarding is not the one and only thing he loves." Torrance barks. She turns her attention back to the TV, "Besides, he's not *failing*. It's one contest. He's having a terrible day, but he'll bounce back. He's resilient."

"Yeah, but what if he holds this against me?"

Everyone jerks their heads in my direction.

"He's not going to."

"He wouldn't."

"Stop that, December." Suz adds.

"He's held his injury against Hendrik for nearly a year," I reason.

"Because the guy's a careless, selfish jackass." Torrance says.

"Everett could say the same thing about me."

Torrance sighs and pushes herself up from her chair to refill her wine glass, "You're smart, December, but sometimes I think you're clueless."

Hurt floods through me. To them I may be unreasonably worried, but they didn't lie to him. I broke his trust after we'd grown so close. After he had confidence that he *knew* me. After he shared vulnerable, nonrefundable pieces of himself with me. I mean, I thought he'd forgiven me, but maybe he hasn't.

The second round comes and goes in silence. Everett performs the same way: execution met but without passion. He remains in eighth place. While Luc sits on top with wild, passion-infused runs. Even Hendrik is doing better than Everett and I imagine that fact is grating against him, too.

The final round begins.

Everyone, even the riders at the bottom, are throwing down their best combos. Go big, or go home, I guess. I tuck my legs up to my chest, my arms wrapped around them.

Everett is next.

He stands stony and strong at the top of the slope, his heel edge dug into the snow. He rolls his shoulders, stretches out his chest. When he leans down to tap his bindings, Luc smacks him on the rear and vigorously claps his hands together. My heart swells. I'm grateful Luc is there for him. He needs someone to support him. Already, the commentators are speculating if this is the fall of Everett Abrams. Is his reign finally over?

Torrance growls and mutes the TV. I watch, heart racing as Everett moves down the slope to the pipe. He jumps up, graps the front, toe edge, of his board, and lands his signature Frontside 360 as he drops in. We all let out a hopeful gasp. He moves to the opposite wall and executes a massive Backside Grab.

"Yes, yes, yes!" I jump off the couch, clapping my hands together. *This* is looking more like him.

Off the next wall he does a combo trick, gathering himself tightly and somersaults through the air. He lands and zooms towards the next vert. I move behind the couch, my hands cupped around my mouth, willing Everett to get through the last two tricks smoothly.

He's lowered himself over the board and as soon as he's in the air he's spinning. Holy shit, how does he not get dizzy? I'm dizzy just watching him.

Everett untucks himself as he prepares for the landing. His board touches down. There's a spray of snow. It happens so fast. His board flips over his head, somersaulting, until he faceplants at the bottom. The momentum from the drop pushes him forward, digging his face in the snow.

"Oh my god." I gasp. My body goes still, "Is he okay?"

Everett pushes himself off his face and rests back on his knees. He sits there idly for a moment. His gloved hands rest on his thighs. The camera zooms in as two medics rush up the slope. Even with the zoom I can't see much.

"He's bleeding!" I catch a red smear across his face, some mixed into the snow, a sharp contrast to the glaring white everywhere.

I have the urge to run to him. To cradle his head in my hands and determine for myself if he's okay. But I can't. He's halfway around the world without me. Everett lets the medics examine him for a second. I growl as their bodies hide him from the cameras.

"What are they saying? Is he okay!" I rattle.

"December," Torrance places her hand on my shoulder, and I jump. I forgot they were here with me. "He's going to be okay. This isn't his first fall. See, he's already getting up."

"But should he be?" I murmur as the medic's saunter away and Everett jumps up, landing with the board beneath him. He slides towards the gate.

Jemina grabs the remote and flicks the mute off. An announcer hurries to get in front of the exit. Angry heat flows through me. How dare they get in his face right after his crash for a five second sound bite! If I were there, I would shove him out of the way and hurry Everett to the nearest hospital.

But I'm not there! My heart screams.

"Everett, Everett," the video journalist calls.

Everett slows and bends to undo his bindings. When he rises, he shifts his goggles up. I let out a gasp. A sharp line cuts across his nose and left cheek, following the path of his goggles. The snow and plastic edge must have cut into his skin when he faceplanted. Half his face is burning red from dragging in the snow. His left cheek is speckled with bloody freckles as the snow ripped and punctured his skin. He yanks off a glove and wipes at the blood line. The second he wipes it away red begins to seep through again.

"What happened up there?"

He lets out a laugh, "I was having my best run of the day and then I messed up. It doesn't feel good."

"Will this prevent you from competing in two weeks at the X-Games?"

Everett glances down at himself, patting himself down, "I'm all in one piece."

"Tell us, what went wrong?"

"Ahh...I've been off my game all week." My stomach twists. "You know when shit hits the fan and you can't rein in anything, and the more you try, the worse it gets? That's what went wrong."

Everett's dark eyes connect with the camera and electricity zips through me. I should be feeling guilty, but the way he said it with his tone and his face relaxed instead of angry, I don't. His glance sinks into my chest. It's like he's telling me his life the last week has sucked without me.

Mine, too.

His eyes flick off the camera. The warmth I just felt evaporates. None other than Ryan Dawson muscles his way through the gate. Everett's jaw tightens. Dawson waves his hand, beckoning Everett to follow him.

"Thank you," Everett says to the announcer. His eyes momentarily move to the camera. There's a look there – flashing across his face, through his soft, dark eyes.

My nails bite into my palms. My heart races and all I see is red. I hate Ryan for taking this away from me. No – I hate that I was not brave enough to be upfront and honest with Everett right away. I can't be there for Everett because of *me*.

"December," Suz's voice penetrates my brooding mind. She holds my phone up to my face. Junie's name brightens the screen. Suz hands it to me. "You need to talk to her."

I tuck my hair behind my ear and head towards my bedroom upstairs. It's about time they fill me in on the situation.

Once shut away in my room, I explode with questions, "What the hell is going on?! It's been a week, Junie. A fucking week and neither of you are keeping me in the loop!"

"I know. It got a little more complicated. Everett and I decided to leave you out of it for a bit in case it got worse, but we're almost done."

"I don't care what you and Everett decided! I'm an adult. I want to help. You can't just cut me out."

"I'm not sorry. There's a lot of moving pieces here and I don't want you to get caught up in it further."

"What is that supposed to mean?"

"It means you purposely posed as a publicist from DKS, December," Junie cuts to the bone of it. "And you really pissed of this guy Mike Gibler."

My mouth drops open, "What? Mike Gibler is involved?"

She sighs, "Yes. He kind of forced the whole: fire December thing. But that's all I'll say about that."

"What a spiteful little man-child!"

"Oh, he'll get his just desserts. I wasn't voted Most Likely to Make You Cry for nothing!"

282

Chapter 48

Everett Abrams

M y cheek stings as I step out of the med tent.

The wind bites at my fresh wounds. I raise my arm to shield most of the force and hurry to the hotel. I have a meet-and-greet in forty-five minutes. Dawson made it clear I am still expected to attend. Not like I could bail anyway, fucking dick. But now I want to.

I take the stairs instead of the elevator. Taking them two at a time. My legs need a good stretch. More and more I need to keep myself active. Quiet time alone breeds angry thoughts of Dawson. I'm already on edge with him the way it is. It's best to keep myself busy, push the resentment out.

My room is on the fourth floor. I chuck my coat onto a chair. Strip out of my snow gear and ready my things for a shower. As soon as I'm done with the meet-and-greet, I'm coming straight back, passing out, and taking the first flight home.

On the bed, my phone vibrates. I snatch it up as soon as December's face lights up my screen.

"Hey," I say, knotting a hand in my hair.

"Everett, what the hell!" I flinch. "Where are you? You better be at a hospital."

I let out a breath, relieved she isn't calling to corner me about Fuck Face, "I'm in my room. Just got back from the medic tent."

"What did they say? Are you okay?"

I grin, twisting around, "Worried about me, were you?"

"So, because *you* stopped communicating with me means I'm supposed to stop caring about you?"

"No. I–"

"I didn't call to yell at you. Junie told me she didn't want us talking, but that's not up to her. I just...want to hear your voice. Know you're okay."

"I'm okay. Nothing but cuts and bruises."

She lets out sharp breath, "You really scared me. Don't do that again. I don't want to see you hurt."

"You were worried about me." I grin despite myself. My chest swells. There's something about her fretting over me that makes me happy.

"*Yes*. Of course, I'm not as cold-hearted as you think I am."

I laugh, "I know. I just like to hear you say it."

"I know you love this, and I don't ever want you to stop. One of the things I love most about you is you love what you do. I just worry. I don't want to lose you."

"I don't want to lose you either." My chest pinches. I take a second, building up the courage to go on. "You've been saying love a lot. What is that about?"

She forces out a laugh, "Have I? I hadn't even noticed."

"You're hiding something. What is it?" I prod. Does she love me? My heart thrills at the thought.

"*Okay* Patrick Jane, enough with the mind reading. How's LAAX? Besides today, obviously."

"Without you? Miserable. I miss you. Tell me how things are at Blue."

"Aww, you're making me blush." I smile and drop to the bed. "Blue is miserable without you, too, but I have my girls."

"Yeah, Torrance is vicious. She cornered me and I thought she was going to cut my dick off for ending things with you. I've known her longer, but she is definitely more loyal to you. Tell me, what have you been doing?"

"That's my Tor," her voice sings. "I have a few new clients, which is exciting. Haylee, even. Elevate, which by the way, why the fuck did you not tell me about that?"

I should be wincing, but I grin instead, "I love that you're working on Elevate. First, I didn't want to tell you because I thought you were just a soulless, money-grabbing publicist. Then, I don't know, I think it might be an ego thing, or a fear thing? Like I wanted to do it all myself. Prove to myself I could. And also, if it didn't work out, at least you never would have known it was a possibility."

"That's bullshit. Especially since you sent Luc to break the news instead of telling me yourself."

I grin, "So, I guess one good thing did come out of Dawson."

"You're the worst."

"You love me."

"I–" She hesitates. I sit up. Is she going to admit it? "I would've rather told you in person, but Suz and I are moving here."

"You are?" The second-best thing she could have said.

"Yeah. What do you think?"

"I think..." I swallow, wiping my hands on my pants. "It's the best news I've heard in a while."

"Yeah?" There's smile in her voice.

"When? When are you moving?" *Make it this second so you won't leave.*

"Any chance this being over in the next few days? Junie said soon, but in her world that could mean next year."

I drop back onto the bed, "I don't know. I don't think so. I wish I could be there. Be your strong, muscly man and supervise you and Suz while you carry the heavy furniture."

She laughs, "Men, what are they good for?"

We're both silent a moment. Being absent sucks. We both feel it. I want to be there for her when she moves in. I want to hug her and tell her how proud I am as her client list grows. She wants to be here with me. Caring for me when I'm hurt; watching me with her own eyes instead of through a TV screen as I compete. Instead, we're starved to phone calls. Not even that.

"What are you doing?" she asks.

"Lying in bed. I have to get up soon. Shower. I have that stupid meet-and-greet."

"It's not stupid, Everett."

"It is when Ryan's behind it instead of you. He's stealing all the work you did."

"I don't care. He can have it all. I just want to see you safe and successful and...mine."

I rub my eyes, "December, you are...I–" I can't say this over the phone. Not without being able to touch her and hold her and see that I mean it.

"Yes?"

"I just...I wanna let you know, if I could, I would totally take you to the ESPY Awards with me next week. But–"

"I know. Just don't fall in love with whoever you do take."

I clear my throat, "I should go."

Her voice drops. "Good luck. You'll do great."

The call ends. I lie down a moment longer. I don't want to get up and face things without her. At least I know there's an end in sight. Hopefully.

My couch feels like a million dollar bed. A cloud compared to the cramped seats of the airline. I stretch myself out and let my brain unwind by gazing at the TV.

My phone vibrates and I eagerly pick it up to view the notification, hoping it's Junie or one of her associates. It's not. Just some airline notification thanking me for flying with them. I sigh, throwing my head back. My mind is running circles. It's been five days since I last spoke with December and I can't stop thinking about her.

I want to know everything – what she's doing. How she's been holding up without me. If she misses me even half as much as I do.

Luc is god-knows-where so the house is eerily quiet. I don't know how I used to relish being home alone with no one to talk to. Now, I just want to talk about everything and nothing with December.

My chest pinches. I have the urge to hear her voice. As soon as I told Junie about Mike Gibler, she locked December out of the conversation. Apparently, he's a high-powered investor and December's already pissed him off. I don't want him to go after her more than he already has.

I glare at the suit dangling over the back of the chair. I'm headed to LA for an award show tomorrow. Dawson's giant ego believes he convinced me to go, but December put me on the guest list a while ago. I don't want to go, but...doing the things she set up lets me pretend she's still around and pulling the strings instead of Dawson.

I lean my head back and imagine what she'd wear if she were my date. She'd be in a dark purple dress, the fabric hugging her curves. Her shoulders would be bare, and, on the way, I'd trace the lines of her collar bone with my mouth. I'd beg her not to make us go. We could stay in the limo, drive all night, doing nothing but this. She'd consider it for a moment and with each kiss be a little more sold, but she'd sigh and tell me it's important.

We'd walk down the red carpet together. My hand would be on the small of her back. At the swoosh in her figure where her body goes from back to ass. We'd stop for a few pictures, and I wouldn't have to pretend to smile. Through the entire award ceremony, I'll be waiting for it to end, but her hand would be in mine, and that would make it worth it.

December would insist we go to the afterparty. Just for a few hours, she'd say. We'd go. We'd talk, we'd barely keep our hands off each other. Then, when she's finally had enough, she'd give me a look like I've seen Olivia and Kelly share. *Let's get out of here* and we'd go back to our hotel room. I'd do the things to her I've been thinking about doing all day. We wouldn't stop until we were both weak with exhaustion. Then she'd use me as her human pillow and we'd pass out. Wake up in the dead of night and have each other all over again.

I just wish it was real.

Chapter 49

DECEMBER FOWL

"Pivot. Piivvotttt!" Suz yells as we adjust the couch in the living room.

I can't stop myself from bursting out in laughter, "Stop saying that!"

We both plop down on the couch, our bodies shaking with laughter. On the TV in front of us a Spotify playlist plays on. I squeeze Suz's arm, and I gaze around the room.

It's not much. Certainly not Torrance's cute A-frame cabin but it feels like home. Photos hang from the wall on either side of the TV. One side is dedicated to Suz's moments – shots with her and her family. Glimpses of their trip to Denmark when she met her birth mother and snapshots of Norway when they visited her twin brothers, Oscar and Noah's, birthplace. Photos of me and her, her and Frankie; Suz standing in front of monuments half a world away when she went on a break-up backpacking trip through Europe.

I always ask her why she keeps them. Her frequent reminder of Sonya Thatcher. The love and heartache of her life. She always shrugs like there's no significance to it at all. But I think she keeps them around to remind her not to get close to anyone.

The other side – closest to the floor-to-ceiling windows – is dedicated to my photo life. Images of me and Junie when we kids and close – before our parents went through their first divorce. And then separate photos with my parents: when I went to Hawaii with my dad and France with my mother. Me and Frankie squeezed together in one frame. Candid photos of Suz and I in college. And then the last photo, our first day at DKS.

"You should get rid of that one," Suz says as if she knows exactly where my eyes are lingering.

I take a breath and turn to her. She rubs my arm, "I think I'll keep it. It's a reminder of where I've been. I learned a lot from that company. I loved DKS, but now it's time to move on."

Suz smiles and rises, "I'm glad to hear it. They don't deserve us anyways."

In the kitchen, Suz rustles with boxes and packing paper. We've already moved most everything in – down to Suz's great-grandmother's silverware and dinner plates. Everything is here. All my things, and yet something is still missing.

Someone is missing.

I can't deny, as we moved mattresses and couches and boxes, I wished Everett was here. I still have the fantasy in my mind that he's my boyfriend. But I want it to be more than a fantasy.

I sigh and check the time on my phone.

3:30 p.m. Mountain Time. Or 6:30 New York time. Mom will just be getting home.

"I'll be back," I call to Suz, waving my phone at her as I walk into my room.

"I'll make you comfort food!" She calls back, knowing exactly what I'm about to do.

Mom picks up on the second ring. Her voice is frazzled, "December, where have you been?"

The next thing that flows out of me feels as natural as telling someone I graduated from NYU with honors.

"I was fired, Mom. I've been in Blue Sky ever since. I'm so, so sorry I didn't tell you before. I was...embarrassed. I didn't want to disappoint you. You'd already told so many people I landed the officer position. I couldn't face telling you."

"So, this is my fault?" Her voice pitches. I can picture her pressing her manicured nails into her chest.

"No, it's not. It's all mine. I just couldn't handle it. I wanted that job so badly. I wanted to make you so proud, so, I did the last thing I thought I could. I chased after the client who hadn't abandoned me at DKS. Turns out, he didn't know I was fired–"

"December don't tell me you *lied*."

I take a breath, "I did."

"*December*."

"Trust me, *I know*. I've been serving the punishment. Dawson is up to his snaky ways. Everett's not speaking to me which...is probably the worst thing ever. I think I'd rather be fired ten times over. But I have a couple clients. Not making nearly as much as I did at DKS, but they're great people. I'm genuinely excited to get up and work with them in the morning."

My chest swells. It's the truth. I thought I loved the people I worked with at DKS, but they abandoned me as soon as they could. My new clients know all about me and still want me to represent them, dirty laundry, and all.

The other line is silent. For the first time since admitting my mistakes, I don't feel scared. I feel stronger. No matter what my mother says, or anyone says, I know what I've done. It was wrong and I hurt people, but I also owned up to my mistakes. Obviously not when I should have, but I still did it. I made mistakes and I survived. No one can take that away from me. No one can use it against me now.

"Everett you said? Is it the Everett Abrams I've been seeing sprinkled on the news? Something about the gold medals and learning issues?"

"The one and the only."

"I've never heard of him before, save for the last few weeks. You did that?"

Pride surges through me and I hold back a smile, "Well, we worked together."

"Great work. *Phenomenal* work being on your own." I burst out in a smile. Okay, so I totally do still care what my mother thinks. "Coming home for Christmas?"

I hesitate, my eyes meet the mountain spearing the sky outside my window. My heartstrings tug, "No, I don't think so."

She clicks her tongue disapprovingly but doesn't harass me further. Instead, she rolls on with a story regarding one of her own clients. I sit down at my desk and sort through emails, happy somethings never change. She's mid-story when my phone vibrates. I pull it away from ear and look down at it. An incoming call from Junie flashes across the screen.

Ohmygod.

"I have to go Mom. I love you. Kisses." I hang up before she has any time to respond. "Junie, what's up?"

I swivel in my chair to face the window. The snow comes down in fat flakes.

"Do you want to go to an award show?" She laughs.

"Oh my god! Can I...Is everything okay now?"

"We're serving DKS, Mike, King, and Dawson their cease and desist orders tomorrow. I haven't told Everett yet though. He's in L.A. and I thought it might be kind of fun if–"

I jump out of my chair, leaving it spinning, "I surprise him! Ohmygod. Yes, yes, yes!"

Junie laughs, "I thought would you say so. I'll have my assistant book a direct flight. Do you have anything to wear?"

"I'll figure it out," My mind zips to Morgan. She's in LA now. "Thank you, thank you, thank you so much Junie."

"You're welcome. I don't want to disclose the details until it's finalized. Just get yourself to LA"

I step onto the pedestal in front of the grand mirror. The entire gown is made of a dark blue satin fabric. The skirt is overlaid with the same color of tulle.

I twist my shoulders around, making the delicate silver stitching threaded throughout the layers of the tulle skirt sparkle. Thin straps drape over my shoulders, holding the heart-shaped bodice in place. My breasts are lifted and separated to create the perfect cleavage. They're cupped in a glittery fabric that trickles down into lines of soft but intricate floral patterns, parts of it translucent to reveal my skin. Refined but sultry.

"You are stunning!" Morgan claps her hands over her cheeks. "The absolute perfect model for this gown."

I grin over my shoulder at her, before focusing on the dress again, "I'm so happy we're the same size! It is absolutely stunning. You're a talented designer."

"Now for the heels," Morgan steps away and returns with a pair of matching dark blue, velvet four inch block heels with a single strap around the toe and buckle ankle.

I squeal. These heels always made me feel so sexy in college and are my go-to when I need some extra confidence. But since leaving Atlanta, I haven't had a pair of heels – or the weather to wear them in. Morgan helps me put them on. I stand, lifting the dress to reveal the heels and my freshly pedicured toes, nails painted a glittery silver.

"You are going to turn heads."

Chapter 50

EVERETT ABRAMS

My tie is suffocating.

I jerk the knot loose from around my neck and assess myself in the full-length mirror. The suit and shirt are okay – all black and tailored to my body perfectly. I had the brilliant idea of picking out a dark purple tie, but the rental place gave me dark blue instead.

Now I can't stop thinking about who I'm missing back in Blue Sky.

I run my hand through my hair. I've fixed it with mousse, the long strands flicking up over my forehead. It looks more like the winds configured it than product, which I like. I just don't like being here without December. I don't like anything without December.

I rub a hand along my jaw. The bristles grate against my fingers. With a breath, I move to the door, but I catch myself as my phone rings.

"Tell me something good," I say to Junie.

"The judge approved the injunction! We served them papers this morning. A cease and desist order to Mike Gibler, Ryan Dawson, and Lionel King. And if they don't comply, I'm going to hit them with wrongful termination, fraud and intentional falsification of records."

I squeeze my eyes shut and lean back against the wall, "You just made me the happiest man alive. But I still don't quite understand. How did all of this happen?"

She laughs, "My firm will follow up with you and December next week to formally debrief you, but the rundown is Gibler, Dawson, and King all conspired to fire December. And that contract you sent me from Dawson, *thank you*. It was a huge piece of evidence."

"Holy shit. How so?"

"The contract Dawson tried to convince you to sign, it's for Razor, an energy pill and one of Mike's investments. They needed a face to sell it. Since it wasn't FDA approved, no attorney or agent would allow their client to represent it unless it was clearly marked and advertised as such. My team uncovered he'd falsified and misrepresented financial and other data in an attempt to make the product appear better than it was. December had called him out for doing exactly that at DKS' board meeting last year. Documentation suggests since she embarrassed, and to Gibler, disrespected and questioned him openly, he had her fired. Once she was out of their firm, they thought you were their perfect mark."

"All this for me?" I huff a laugh "Sounds like a lot of work."

"From our research, they were especially interested in you due to the upcoming Olympics. They had every intention of you making them rich."

"Wow. I'm so fucking glad the judge agreed. You've been...unbelievable."

"No one threatens my sister but me," she laughs.

"Have you told her yet?"

"She was my first call."

"Thank you so much. For everything."

"Oh, I'm still going to bill you."

I laugh, "I know you will. Well earned."

The call ends. I take a moment, lulling my head against the wall and take a breath. Fuck. I'll never sign a contract without reading it again. My body feels relieved and exhausted at the same time, as if I've been carrying around a train and just set it down. A notification on my watch dings. The car is here to take me to the ESPY Awards. I struggle for a moment, taking a step towards the bed and my things; then twisting around and taking a step towards the door.

"Fuck," I murmur, finally deciding I'll go and yank open the door.

"What is this?" As soon as I'm out the door Ryan Dawson is storming towards me from the elevator.

I step into his face, "That's a cease and desist order, fucker. My attorney got your ass. Be sure to read *real* careful so you don't miss the warning of what's coming for you and your little friends."

His face blooms red. He glances down at the order as I step around him. There's a spring in my step from no longer having to carry the weight of a two hundred pound python, or worry how tightly he may squeeze.

"You can't do this!" He stomps after me. "We had a deal. We have a contract. I'll sue you and that stupid bitch, too!"

My fists clench, blood roars through me, but I tell myself to keep walking. I've backed a snake into a corner. He's going to rattle his tail, but I'm not going to let him bite. The elevator is only a few steps away. I focus my attention there.

Behind me, Ryan lets out a sneering laugh, "I'm going to destroy that bitch's life."

He jerks my arm. My hand forms a fist. My arm draws back as he pulls me around and I let it fly.

Thwack!

A sharp pain erupts from my knuckles, lighting up all my nerve endings. Ryan falls back. From the floor, his hand flies to his face. My hands are still clenched. My chest rises and falls rapidly.

I glower down at him, "If you get anywhere near her, I'll ruin you."

Ryan pulls his hand away from his face. Ripe, red blood leaks from his nose. There's already a pink spot under his eye and growing darker. He stares wide-eyed at the blood like he can't believe someone made him bleed. His eyes glare up at me.

"I'll sue! Assault," his voice is muffled as he pinches his nose to slow the bleeding.

I point to the camera above us, "You grabbed me. Self-defense."

The elevator dings, the doors rushing open. I step inside and flip him off until they slide shut. At the first floor, I fill an ice bucket and shove my hand in, wincing. Not even the doorman says anything as I walk by.

My ride is parked out front. The driver spots me and meets me at the door, pulling it open for me.

"Thanks," I say, ducking inside. My body slides across the cool leather seat and–

I stare at the dark blue frill of a dress, almost like a ballerina skirt, not wanting to look up in case I'm wrong. But slowly, my eyes draw up. I swallow as the skirt shifts into a lacy floral mesh at her upper waist, teasing strips of her soft skin. Her breasts are perky and divine, covered in blue glitter. A strap has fallen down her shoulder. I put the bucket on the floor and push it up with my fingertips, running my hand along her skin.

Her hair is down, softly curled, and resting behind her shoulders. I reach out and tug a few strands. She's beautiful and grins at me when I meet her gaze. There's a shimmery glitter over her eyelids and around her eyes; cheekbones more defined, and lashes dark and long framing her green eyes. Lips stark red.

I lean in, cupping her jaw in my hand and kiss her long and hard.

"Please tell me we're not actually going to this award thing."

"Why? Don't you want to show me off?"

I suck in a breath, shifting away from her for a better view of her full body, "All I wanna do is look at you."

Chapter 51

December Fowl

Everett presses gentle kisses along my neck as we're driven to the Dolby Theatre. The bristles of his facial hair prickle my neck.

I push him away, "Your beard is going to make it obvious we've been all over each other."

"So," he says, trying to kiss me below my ear but I press my hand into his chest.

"I don't want the first image your mother sees of me to include hickeys and beard burn."

"Alright," Everett interlocks our fingers and brings my hand put to his lips, placing a string of kisses.

I laugh. Encouraged, Everett grabs my other hand and does the same thing. Over and over again until the car rolls to a stop.

When the driver opens the door for us, Everett slips out and reaches his hand in to take mine. I carefully step out of the car and into the flashing lights of the paparazzi and press. Everett's hand releases mine and finds a place in the hollow of my lower back. I relish the soft pressure of his hand. Like he's feral and claiming me as his own. I'll gladly be his.

We walk down the red carpet. Members of the press and media shout things at Everett. We pose and cameras flash. His hand shifts so he's holding my hip. Heat races through me and I feel it in my clit.

I take a breath through my nose and try to control my wanting of him. This is going to be a long night.

At the ceremony, my hand hardly leaves Everett's upper thigh. His arm drapes around my back, running lines and circles along my arm. He's driving me crazy. I squeeze my legs together in an effort to stop myself from exploding in desire. It hardly helps.

We're sitting around the table at the three-course dinner. Everett leans over and whispers, his breath tickling my ear, "I can't decide if I want you out of that dress or if I want to fuck you in it. Dress, heels, and all."

Not a second after he's uttered those words, he turns to the golfer next to him and starts talking about the best courses in the country. I excuse myself to the bathroom.

A few hours later, we're walking back to the car, everyone heading to the afterparty. Everett's laughing with the guys until the driver opens the door and helps me inside. As soon as he slides in after me, I grab him by the lapels and pull him towards me. My hand runs along his upper thigh and over his groin. I can feel his erection growing against my palm.

"The afterparty," he manages between frantic kisses.

"Fuck that."

He grins, hands in my hair, "I was hoping you'd say that."

Everett shifts out from under me and scuttles to the dark glass window separating us from the driver. He knocks and the glass slides down.

"Take us back to our hotel instead, please."

"Yes, sir." The driver rolls the window up as Everett slinks back towards me.

He slides in right next to me, drapes his hand over my shoulders again, and begins to draw lines along my upper arm like he did at the award ceremony. I press my fingertips into his upper thigh. We ride in silence. And the silence continues as we walk into the hotel lobby, take the elevator up; silence as we walk down the hall to his suite.

We reach his door and then the door clicks behind me as we enter. Only then does Everett presses me against the wall. We kiss hard and fast. His hand finds the nook of my knee and raises my thigh over his hip. His erection rubs against me, and I moan, tearing at his clothes.

Everett lifts me up, grabbing me by the ass and thighs, carrying me to the bed. He drops me there and falls on top of me. Our mouths clash together. *I want this more than I can say.* It's not a neat kiss, filled with desperate want. He pulls me against his erection.

"This is how much I missed you." Through his pants, he's hard and long, throbbing.

"Show me exactly how much."

He grunts, undoing his pants. I get busy unbuttoning his shirt, but the buttons are too small for shaky hands. I rip it open instead. Buttons fly everywhere. We both laugh and then his mouth is over mine again. He pushes my skirt up and his hand slides over the thin fabric of my thong. I suck in a hard breath. The teasing press of fingers leaving me breathless.

Running his hand up and down, in slow circles over the fabric of my thong, leaving me throbbing. Finally, his fingers slip beneath the fabric and touch me. My head drops back, and I arch into his touch.

My cheeks grow red and my hips buck as he continues to stroke me. Two fingers circling and strumming my clit like I'm his masterpiece.

"I want you so bad. Please," I beg.

Everett jumps off the bed, pushing his pants and boxers the rest of the way off as he retrieves a condom and lube. A moment later he's back. My legs shake in anticipation.

I lay my head back as he leans over me, his arms on either side of my head. My dress blooms out around me. Rustles as he leans in and kisses me. Softly, reassuring. I push back more feverishly, rolling my hips against his cock.

"You want me?" His breath brushes along my neck and the feeling rushes straight to my clit.

I nod.

Everett reaches between us and pulls my thong down my legs. It catches on my heels. Everett turns, carefully detangling them, and throws them aside. I grab at the bottom of my dress and pull it over my hips.

"I'm going to fuck you so good."

I bite my bottom lip and nod, curling my hands into the sheets. Gazing down at me, he presses his thick cock against me my clit, circling and stroking me, swirling over my entrance.

"Oh god." I grip his shoulders, not able to control myself and he's not even inside me yet.

Slowly, his eyes connecting with mine, watching my reaction, he pushes inside me and lets out a groan. I grip his shoulders, ready for him to drive in but he pulls back out and continues to play. I whimper, wanting him so badly I could die. As he positions himself at my entrance again, I rock my hips up.

He slips in deeper than I expect. I take in a breath, the swell of him familiar but shocking. Everett curses but holds himself steady as my body accommodates to fit him. There's pinching but mostly just an ache to have more of him.

"You feel so..." I murmur, losing my words.

I rock up against him at the same time he tilts his pelvis forward and I take all of him. For a moment, I can't think. My body zings at the intrusion, clit throbbing. He stays still but I can sense him shaking to give me all he has.

"Holy," I whimper. He fills me completely. He's everywhere.

"December?" He doesn't want to move. I know he feels good too, "Talk to me."

"Everett," I roll my hips. "It's really hard to when you feel this good."

I hear his smile, "You missed this, huh?" He pushes in deeper.

I don't even know how there is a *deeper*. He's everywhere and yet he finds areas that have never been touched.

After catching my breath, I say, "Very much. More, please."

"Slowly."

I shake my head and pout, "Not so slowly."

Everett presses his forehead into mine and pulls nearly completely out with the draw of his hips. I gasp and he presses his mouth into mine. He thrusts back in, pausing to let my body accommodate him. I hold on to his biceps. He thrusts again. Again.

Our bodies slap together as he fucks deeper, harder. I let out a string of moans, not able to control myself. My legs wrap around his waist, I feel him with each and every thrust of his hips against my clit; driving into me.

Still deep inside me, he pulls away. His eyes caught on mine as pulls at my bodice, yanking it down. My breasts spring out. Displayed up and out over the top of my dress. He leans forward and takes one breast and then the other in his mouth, licking and sucking. He then pulls away and thrusts into me. My breasts bounce and jiggle from the rhythm of our bodies joining. There's a crease in his forehead as he concentrates, watching my face and captivated by my breasts.

It drives me wild – the view and feel of my breasts out like this; the way his eyes devour me. I move my hips against his and he closes his eyes, breathing a string of curses. A tension builds in my core.

"Talk to me," he pants. His eyes opening to gaze at me.

"Everett. You feel soo good...how are–"

He thrusts deeper and my body rocks. I lose my words. He runs a hand up my body. He takes my breast in his hand and squeezes, fingers rolling my nipple. The tension building in my core snaps. My body squeezes around him. Everett doesn't stop. I arch off the bed into him. As soon as my orgasm ends, I feel another one building, this one slower and greater than the last.

"December," Everett pants as he thrusts. There's a sheen of sweat on his brow, rolling down his chest. "So good."

He adjusts his position. Lowers himself down onto his forearms and pushes my skirt higher up my waist. From here, his pelvis brushes more directly against my clit.

"Oh god," lightning flashes through me.

My legs fall open, no longer having the strength to hold on to him. His hand catches the back of my thigh. Hand sliding down to my ankle and my heel strap there, he pushes my knee towards my head. There's something about his hand holding my ankle, heels still on while he fucks me that makes my pussy ache.

He rolls his hips deeper, pushing past yet another barrier inside me. My eyes roll closed, and I moan. All I can do his feel him. His pace, his girth, his length;

the movement and heat of our bodies as I swirl into a universe of boundless pleasure.

His thrusts become less even. More chaotic and wild, as he loses himself. He leans further into me, driving faster, harder.

"Oh my god. Ohmygodohmygod," I say in an incoherent stream as waves of my orgasm wash over me.

He hisses my name as he comes. Pumping hard until I feel him jerk and swell inside me. A moment later he collapses on my chest.

We lay there a moment.

I run the tips of my fingers along the muscled plain of his spine and shoulders, relishing the way he feels. One hand still grips his bicep. I tilt my head and nip his ear. "I love you."

Even in the dark light I can see his grin, "You do?"

I nod, nipping my bottom lip. I love the way strands of his hair fall into his face. The dusting of freckles across his skin. I love his voice and his hands and mostly, his heart.

Everett rolls off and extends his hand to me, the tulle of my skirt rustling. He sits me up and unbuckles my heals. Helps me out of my dress.

I let him lead me to the bathroom. He starts the shower and I step in as he removes the condom, tossing it in the trash. He follows me in and massages shampoo into my scalp. I close my eyes and let the hot water beat down against my chest. Everett wraps his arms around my waist, pulling my back against his chest. He rests his jaw on my shoulder and holds me.

"I love you, too, December."

I turn my head and kiss his nose. My heart is so full.

Chapter 52

Epilogue - December

"Okay, we're here."

"But I don't know where *here* is," I growl. My hands twisting in my lap.

Everett begged me to come with him this morning. All he said was he had a surprise. Ridiculous as it is, my heart is racing with a vision of him kneeling in front of me with a giant ring.

After my parents' double divorces, from each other, I didn't think I wanted to be married. But with Everett...it sounds exciting. Everyone will know he's mine forever.

Everett helps me out of the truck. My stomach flutters as he holds my hand, his other finding the small of my back, leading me.

"You better not be leading me off a cliff."

"How did you know?" He gushes, "So intuitive."

I hear the squeak of a door open, and Everett lets me go. There's another voice. An oddly familiar voice as Everett whispers back and forth. A moment later, he returns and leads me forward.

His fingers fumble with the fabric at the back of my head, "I'm going to take your blindfold off in three...two...one."

I blink in my surroundings. We're in an office building. Somewhere in downtown Blue Sky. Giant, plated glass windows look out across the Blue Mountain range. I twirl around. There's a reception area at the front with a giant, circular desk. There's a meeting room and two closed off offices to the right. Open desks are scattered around the space behind reception. Etched into the wall is a logo:

A giant E about to be swallowed by an even bigger, inverted V. *Elevate* is scribbled at the bottom.

"Elevate," I read out loud. I turn to Everett, Luc, standing behind him. "You changed the logo. Does this mean...Elevate is actually happening?"

Luc drops his hands onto Everett's shoulders and winks at me, "I'll leave you two alone. Good to see you around again."

Everett's dark eyes watch me steadily as his friend retreats. I move closer and run my hand along the stiff scruff of his jaw. His eyes are liquid. I brush his dark hair from his eyes, relishing the intimacies we now share.

"I like being able to touch you whenever I want." My hand presses into his firm, familiar chest.

He quirks a brow, a grin lifts the corners of his mouth. His hand meets mine on his chest and raises it to his lips, "I like being able to do this whenever I want."

Everett spins me around, so he's standing behind me. He wraps his arms around my waist and presses me into his warm body. I get a trill of excitement. I love being wrapped up in his arms. I love being the center of his attention more than I would like to admit.

He takes a breath, "You helped me do this, December."

I twist my head to look at him, my stomach both excited and nervous, "Are you happy?"

"Very. This place is Elevate's now." He squeezes me and presses a kiss to my cheek.

I look around, "This is amazing. I'm so happy for you and Luc."

Everett spins me around and takes my hands, gazing down at me with a fondness I pray never gets old.

When he doesn't say anything, I say, "So, tell me about it! I heard the ideas from Luc's mouth but now I want to hear them from you."

His dark eyes shift to the name and logo on the wall, "We're going to make outerwear starting with mittens and socks. And then eventually boards. Luc has some pretty wild ideas."

I can't stop myself from grinning. My chest swells for him. His own company!

"What?" His eyes shift away and back again.

I swing my arms out, "I'm so proud of you."

"Thank you," he smiles. A moment later he turns and jogs towards the front door, "I'll be right back."

I mosey deeper into one of the offices, running my hand along the corner of the empty oak desk in the corner of the room. I wander to the window and wrap myself in my arms. I shiver. The view is breathtaking. The sun inches behind the mountain – a deep yellow glow surrounded by encroaching darkness. The glow from Blue Sky bounces off the trees, off the snow.

I rub a hand over my chest. My eyes blinking rapidly. Even the tallest window office in Atlanta never would have looked this good. Meant this much.

"Hey." His voice is soft.

I turn, "Hey."

Everett walks through the door with blankets in one hand and a paper bag in the other. He tosses the blankets down on the couch and dips into the bag eagerly.

"I brought snacks." He gives me a sneak peek of the goods. Grapes. Granola. "And for you," He teases out a corner of the wrapper. A giant Hershey's bar. "With almonds. For protein."

I laugh even though I want to cry, walking towards him, "You're unbelievable."

He puts the bag down and wraps his arms around me, pulling me towards him. He presses a kiss to my forehead, "I knew you'd like the nuts. You took such a forceful interest in mine before you even liked me."

"Shut up," I grin, but there's a tightness in my throat. I battle back tears. They keep forging ahead.

I grip his flannel shirt. His hands drift up my back. Softly. Like I'm something he doesn't want to shatter. I force my eyes open wide as the tears rush towards the surface, hoping the air will dry them out, scare them away.

His hands draw along my sides, across my ribs. His thumbs push up against the underside of breasts. My heart skitters, goosebumps shiver through me as my nipples harden.

"I can feel you shivering," he says, his breath hot and tickling near my ear.

He lowers his head and his facial hair scruffs along my neck. Another stampede of goosebumps cascades down my body. He presses his forehead into my shoulder, ruts his nose around in the space between my shoulder and collarbone, and pulls me closer.

"I want to hold you," he turns his head and presses a soft kiss at the base of my neck. "I'm so fucking lucky I didn't send that email so many months ago. None of this would have happened."

He climbs kisses up my neck. His mouth lingers at the extra tender spot just beneath my ear, "I wouldn't have you."

I arch into him, his warm breath tantalizing. His lips nip along my ear until I shiver against him, holding on to his flannel tightly as he cradles the back of my neck.

"You're so sweet, December."

I pull back to look at him, "You're the best thing that's ever happened to me. If you weren't bossy, you wouldn't push me. Your stubbornness levels my bullheadedness. Even though it's annoying when you tell me things I don't want to hear. You know what's good for me and you don't hold back."

He shakes his head, "I want to share this with you. Everything. I want you to squeeze yourself into every nook and cranny of my life. If you want, you don't have to, but this could be your office. Elevate could be your new home."

My chest squeezes. I blink several times, my mouth dropping open as I try to think of something to say, but how can I follow him up? After he just said everything so perfect.

"You want me to work at Elevate?"

"I don't care where you work. You're great at what you do. I mean, look at what you helped create. This... didn't even feel like it could happen until it did. It was just a fantasy until I had the keys. I'd love to have you here to help this grow. And I...want to take care of you. If you'll let me."

My heart squeezes. I don't think I could love him any more than in this moment. I never thought those words would fit together: *love* and *him*. When I first met him, I never would have thought I'd be having these feelings towards him.

I grin, running my hand along his jaw. "You don't need to take care of me. I love that you want to though. It's the sweetest thing anyone has ever said to me, but I love working for myself. I have a few clients and I'll get more. You and I can always continue to work together."

He nods though his face has fallen, "I thought you'd say as much."

I kiss him gently, "Maybe we could make ourselves familiar with this office, though?"

I feel his mouth turn up, "You're wicked."

"That's what they tell me."

I grab hold of his shirt and spin us around, so I'm pressed against the desk. My leg slowly draws up the side of his thigh until he grabs the back of my knee and hoists me up onto the desk. My leg is around his waist. His mouth is on mine, and he grinds himself against me.

My hands are under his shirt, coasting over his warm, sculpted muscles. I reach his pecks and drag my hands down. His hips spring forward, pushing my thighs open for him and I sigh.

I run my hand along the serpent hidden in the front of his jeans. He sucks in a breath, jerking his hips forward. I want him in me. I fumble with his jeans, but he steps out of my reach. I growl at him.

"Slow down."

"I want you so bad it hurts."

"Christ, December." He runs a hand down his face, looking at me like he's torn. "We've fucked desperate since you showed up in LA."

I nip at my bottom lip, "I remember. I never want you to stop doing that."

"But," Everett drops to his knees and runs his hands up my thighs, "I want to take this slow. Will you let me?"

I nod. The earnestness in his eyes makes my chest squeeze.

"This place has a great view. Let's watch the sunset and then go to your place." He stands up and I watch as he spreads the blanket over the couch.

"Let's go to your house. I miss your couch, but we have to go and pick up Frankie. He'll never forgive me if I ditch him for another man."

"I never thought I'd have to share my woman with a cat."

"Your woman, huh?" I nestle into his shoulder, melting.

Everett tears open the snacks, and we share, gazing out the window, watching the sun sink lower.

"I'm glad I showed up unannounced at your doorstep."

"Me too." He leans into me, pressing his lips against my temple.

We sit silently, wrapped in each other's arms after the sun sets. I don't want to ever get up, but Everett does and pulls me to my feet.

We walk through the main office, heading towards the exit. My fingers brush the raised symbols of their logo. *Elevate.* My eyes hook on the words. It's perfect. The logo, the name.

I hug Everett tightly around the waist, "Thank you for sharing this with me."

"I wanted you to be the first to know," he squeezes me back. "You helped make it happen."

Everett locks the door, and we walk hand in hand to his truck. I like the way his fingers press between mine, locked together. We ride in silence down dark, snow-covered roads, his hand still in mine.

I never want to stop touching him.

"Let's get some pizza."

Everett huffs, taking his dark eyes off the road, "I am still *trying* to win, you know. The Olympics are coming up. Besides, you could use another cooking lesson."

"But that will take hours and I'm hungry." I grumble.

"We had snacks!"

"Keyword: *snacks*. I need dinner."

"I love you," He laughs, and it feels like I've just won the world's greatest prize.

Did you love December & Everett's story?

L eave a review & help get *Faking It* into other readers' hands. Scan the QR code below or click HERE (for ebook) to leave a review wherever you find or buy books.

Don't forget to tell your friends & share your favorite moments in the Harstoppers Facebook group! I'd love to hear from you.

https://linktr.ee/ lydiahartautho r_reviewlinks?u tm_source=qr_c ode

Want a behind-the-scenes look? Follow me on TikTok, Instagram & join the Hartstoppers Facebook group HERE:

https://linktr.ee/l ydiahartauthor

Want a bonus epilogue?

Who will fall next?

Sign up for my newsletter & find out! Use the QR code below or click HERE (for ebook) to get your epilogue. If you're already a subscriber – no need to sign up again. You'll get an email with the sneak peek soon (if you haven't already).

https://mailchi.mp/ade 3f5686349/faking-it-r eaders

To my sister Chelle. For showing me books can be written by mere mortals.

XOXO,

www.ingramcontent.com/pod-product-compliance
Lightning Source LLC
Chambersburg PA
CBHW030642020726
47493CB00006B/1837